Alternative Ghosts

A GameLit/LitRPG Novel
of Time Travel and Alternate Realities

Head Hoppers, Book 4

MK Eidson
Emila H Thicke

EPOSIC

*This volume of Head Hoppers is dedicated
to everyone who's ever had a day where
they just didn't feel like themselves.*

When you have two alternatives, the first thing you have to do is to look for the third that you didn't think about, that doesn't exist.

SHIMON PERES

TABLE OF CONTENTS

CHAPTER ONE
Fauna: Baby   1

CHAPTER TWO
Greelia: Baby   5

CHAPTER THREE
Lady Ghost: Shattered   10

CHAPTER FOUR
Ronnie: Mother Jean   14

CHAPTER FIVE
Susie: The Future Past   25

CHAPTER SIX
Megan: Out of the Picture   28

CHAPTER SEVEN
Yuni: Special Quest   33

CHAPTER EIGHT
Nick: Bellow   41

CHAPTER NINE
Charli: Awakened   44

CHAPTER TEN
Greelia: Losing Britta   48

CHAPTER ELEVEN
Lady Ghost: Wanting Him   52

CHAPTER TWELVE
Charli: Brief Visit   55

CHAPTER THIRTEEN
Kylie: Under the Rubble   57

CHAPTER FOURTEEN
    Fauna: The Author   66

CHAPTER FIFTEEN
    Ronnie: Motorcycles   73

CHAPTER SIXTEEN
    Susie: Timeline Duel   82

CHAPTER SEVENTEEN
    Susie: No Longer Illegal   85

CHAPTER EIGHTEEN
    Mithabel: Siamese Cat   100

CHAPTER NINETEEN
    Yuni: Army of Behemoths   107

CHAPTER TWENTY
    Morrow: Ghostly   119

CHAPTER TWENTY-ONE
    Greelia: Family Bond   130

CHAPTER TWENTY-TWO
    Lady Ghost: Drawn to Nick   134

CHAPTER TWENTY-THREE
    Fauna: Gondra   137

CHAPTER TWENTY-FOUR
    Fauna: Scottsdale, AZ   148

CHAPTER TWENTY-FIVE
    Charli: Mental Dominator   153

CHAPTER TWENTY-SIX
    Ronnie: The Queen   173

CHAPTER TWENTY-SEVEN
    Susie: The Succubus   181

CHAPTER TWENTY-EIGHT
Debra: Reverie   192

CHAPTER TWENTY-NINE
Yuni: Overpowered   197

CHAPTER THIRTY
Lady Ghost: Exploration   207

CHAPTER THIRTY-ONE
Fauna: Spooky Characterization   213

CHAPTER THIRTY-TWO
Charli: Ghoul Battle   219

CHAPTER THIRTY-THREE
Ronnie: Blue-Haired Girl   232

CHAPTER THIRTY-FOUR
Erica: Home   236

CHAPTER THIRTY-FIVE
Susie: Hera Ford   242

CHAPTER THIRTY-SIX
Slithy: Back in the Game   248

CHAPTER THIRTY-SEVEN
Mithabel: Apology Delayed   251

CHAPTER THIRTY-EIGHT
Fauna: City in the Mists   257

CHAPTER THIRTY-NINE
Charli: Taking a Break   262

CHAPTER FORTY
Ronnie: Juggling Bikes   275

CHAPTER FORTY-ONE
Erica: Traveler of the Cosmos   284

CHAPTER FORTY-TWO
Kylie: Coin   289

CHAPTER FORTY-THREE
Fauna: Kevin and Dr. Splat   297

CHAPTER FORTY-FOUR
Megan: Obsidian Guards   314

CHAPTER FORTY-FIVE
Charli: Forgiveness   332

CHAPTER FORTY-SIX
Megan: Finding Ned   337

CHAPTER FORTY-SEVEN
Yuni: Delivery   345

CHAPTER FORTY-EIGHT
Ronnie: State Park   349

CHAPTER FORTY-NINE
Erica: Cloaks   359

CHAPTER FIFTY
Kylie: New Quest   372

CHAPTER FIFTY-ONE
Fauna: Equipped   378

CHAPTER FIFTY-TWO
Charli: Shadow Magic   388

CHAPTER FIFTY-THREE
Yuni: Emergency Update   391

The Head Hoppers Series

The Longest Survivor

Undone

Illegal Avatars

Alternative Ghosts

Dread Naughts

CHAPTER ONE

Fauna: Baby

I can't remember my childhood. My father was a faun and my mother human. A faun is half-goat, half-human. That makes me three-quarters human, as Ronnie calculated for me. Hence the name he gave me, Fauna.75. My parents never named me. From the thighs up, I'm a human woman. From the knees down, I'm a goat, with hooves and furry calves.

Why can't I remember my mother or father? How can I know I have parents, yet remember nothing about them? Indeed, I can remember nothing about my life before my encounter with Ronnie. I'd laid a trap because I was hungry, and I'd thought I might catch Ronnie, but he spotted the trap before it could snare him. I'd fled, but Ronnie called out to me. His voice held no hint of anger, only kindness, and I'd apologized for trying to snare him. He told me mushrooms were good to eat, and we had foraged for them together. Since then, we've been inseparable.

To be honest, I wasn't actually hungry. I don't get hungry and don't need to eat. Anything I do eat is merely for the pleasure of it.

After we defeated the giant metal spider, the world changed. More gravel covered the road, and on either side of it, the forest grew more densely. There was a house, with chipped paint, and people dressed in strange garb: The boy, Ulric. The girl, Charli. And the man, Nick, who had taken my hand and the hand of Emma the Elf. My fingers tingled at his touch.

Then came the lightning. It hadn't struck from the sky, but shot out of the tattoo on the back of Nick's hand, the hand I held. Electricity coursed through me.

The world changed again, and here we are.

Rain falls around me but not on me. Glowing, wavering magical symbols float within the downpour. Ronnie the Rogue, Emma the Mystical, and Greelia the Goblin Warrior stand with me inside the cylinder of rain, illuminated by a dim ambient light. Outside the curtain of rain is darkness… except for a tiny spark.

The spark expands abruptly into a ten-foot-diameter dome of light centered on Nick, sprawled face down and motionless on a cold tile floor.

With staff in hand, her straight blond hair swaying beneath the brim of her cowboy hat, Charli stands just inside the ball of light. Her form wavers, as though the universe has some doubt as to whether she exists. As though oblivious to his condition, she smiles at Nick over a bare shoulder but says nothing.

Also under the dome, the boy, Ulric, sits up, squinting against the light. He looks around until his gaze falls on Nick. "What happened? Where are we? Where's everyone?" It doesn't seem to have registered with him that Nick is unconscious and can't reply.

"We're here." I try to step through the curtain of rain, but the magical symbols have substance and block me. My three companions within the rain join my efforts to leave our prison, but we all fail.

That's not true. Where is Greelia?

Lightning erupts from Nick's tattoo, and at the same time lightning blasts inside my head, a brilliant whiteness replacing everything I see. As the whiteness dims, I find the rain has stopped. Emma the Mystical stands next to me still, but Ronnie the Rogue and Greelia the Goblin Warrior are gone. Nick and Ulric are gone. Legs spread apart, Charli kneels on the floor, screaming as she gives birth. Blood pools beneath Charli. The baby is covered in the viscous red fluid. It slides out of the young woman onto the floor.

"Oh, my." I run to Charli's side, Emma beside me. I grab up the baby girl. There's no umbilical cord. Shouldn't there be? How do I know about umbilical cords?

The baby is quiet. I hold her up by her ankles and smack her bottom. Blood spills from her mouth and she cries. Her skin looks darker than I'd expect, even when cloaked in blood.

Emma kneels before Charli. "You're going to be all right. The baby is fine." She gestures at me. "Find a washcloth and clean her off." Then she grabs Charli's chin and lifts the girl's head. "You've had a baby girl. What will you name her?"

Charli's chin slips from Emma's grasp and her head droops forward. Then she slumps to the floor, collapsing onto her side and rolling onto her back, her eyes staring up at nothing in particular.

"Is she all right?" I haven't gone to find a washcloth yet.

"I'll deal with her." Emma leans over Charli and feels for a pulse. "Go clean off that child."

There are no washcloths in this room. I go into another, and find cloths, but no water. There's a contraption mounted on a counter over a basin before a mirror. The contraption has two short levers and a bent metal tube. I grab the tube, and it swivels on its base. It produces no water, so I move one of the levers.

Water flows from the tube. It's warm. I soak the washcloth and then commence wiping the blood off the baby.

Her skin is *green*. How is this possible?

On the backs of the baby's hands are birthmarks, one on each hand. On her right hand is a mark in the shape of a lightning bolt, colored yellow as though it were painted. On her left hand is a crescent moon, but rather than it being white as one might expect, it's raven black. Perhaps the marks are more than just birthmarks.

The baby cries as I take her back to the room where Charli lies, still as death. Emma gives her mouth-to-mouth resuscitation, but the young mother doesn't stir. Emma looks to me, her sorrow and frustration so heavy as to weigh upon me as well.

I open Charli's arms, lay the baby across her chest, and wrap her arms around the baby girl. "You have a baby, Charli. She needs you. Please wake up."

The baby twists, turning onto her stomach. She seeks her mother's tit. I unbutton Charli's blouse and pull it back, exposing her left breast. The baby suckles for a moment and then bursts out crying.

Emma puts her mouth on Charli's again and blows, holding the young woman's nose shut. The tiniest glimmer of hope resides in Emma's eyes as she lifts her head. The glimmer dies as Charli remains motionless.

I kick Charli in the rump with my right hoof. "*Wake up, Charli. You have a baby girl.*"

Charli turns into colored sparks. The baby falls through the fading bits onto the floor, banging her head. She wails.

"I'm sorry, baby." I grab up the naked infant and cradle her, rocking her. "I guess I'm your mother now. I can't let you grow up without one. What shall I name you?"

With a wailing scream, the baby flails her limbs. Lightning blasts from her yellow birthmark, and then she vanishes, her weight leaving my arms.

But she leaves a shadow of herself behind, an insubstantial raven black infant body still cradled in my arms.

CHAPTER TWO

Greelia: Baby

Where am I and how did I get here? For that matter, *who* am I?
My name is Greelia. I'm a female Goblin Warrior.
No. I'm not a Warrior or a Goblin, and my name isn't Greelia.
I'm Charli. I'm a Shadow Wizard and a Guide.
No. That's not right. I'm so confused.
I was holding Charli's hand when the lightning struck.
My sword. I left it in the eye of the giant spider… the Arachnid Behemoth.
The map of safe routes… I had it. Where is it now?
Rain falls not on me but all around me, streaming over an array of magical symbols. Ronnie, Emma, and Fauna.75 stand with me in the glowing rain. Beyond the rain is darkness.
I step out of the rain into a sudden ball of light, my straight, blond hair swaying. I hold my staff… but I want my sword. Why do I hold a staff?
I'm Charli, the Shadow Wizard and Guide.
No. *No.* I'm Greelia… green-haired, not blond.
I *am* blond, and my name is Yvette.

No. I'm Erica. Blue hair, not green or blond.

My jaws won't budge. I can't scream. *What is happening to me?*

Nick lies on his back on the floor nearby. He's aged, looking twice as old as he should be. He glances at me, and I throw him a smile. My blouse rides down on my shoulder. A strand of blond hair swings in front of my eyes.

That's not right. I'm *not* blond.

Lightning floods the room, centered on Nick. It passes right through me, doing no harm. Nick convulses. I want to go to him, but my legs won't comply with my wishes.

"Dad?" A thirty-something man, his facial features bearing a striking similarity to Nick's, kneels beside the old man. Behind him stands a ghostly figure. Ulric.

"Mel." Nick reaches a hand towards the thirty-something fellow.

The man identified as Mel takes Nick's hand. "You're going to be fine, Dad. Can you get up?"

Lightning rolls through the room again. When it subsides, Mel and the ghostly Ulric are gone. A woman in a red leather miniskirt stands near Nick. She speaks his name. "You need to come back to Khertaan."

"Renee?"

"Yes, it's me. *Respawn now,* Nick, before the timeline shifts again."

"Nick?" I blurt his name. "Don't leave me behind. Remember me... *Charli.*"

But my name isn't Charli.

I'm Yvette.

No. I'm Erica.

"Dad?" Mel reappears. He's standing next to Renee, reaching for Nick. "Please don't leave me."

No, I'm still wrong. My green hair sways in my peripheral vision. "Remember me, Nick. I'm *Greelia.*"

"Nick, *please.*" Renee kicks the old man. "You need to respawn as Morrow *now.*"

Germinal stage commencing.

My hair is blond. My cheek itches. I scratch it. There's a scar beneath my fingertips. "Nick?"

"*Macy?* How are you here? You died." Nick chokes on the words. "You know I loved you." He wipes away some tears. "I didn't ask your father if I could marry you. He asked me if I planned to. I didn't say anything, I swear. He took that as a *yes* and then told you that he and I discussed it. You believed him and left me without even a goodbye." He wipes away more tears. "I could have married you."

Germinal stage completed. Embryonic stage beginning.

My blond hair shortens. My already lean frame shrinks until I'm back to my fourteen-year-old build. No, I'm thirteen. "Nick?"

"Yvette? Of course, you're here. I'm haunted by all my pasts. Refusing you was the biggest mistake of my life."

I keep changing, and Nick refers to each new persona by another name. I'm his siblings—Raymond, Gerard, Laura, Sammy, and Dolly. I'm his mother and father. His cousins—Sadie, Harley, Carmen, Ellen, and Randall.

I'm his Aunt Jennifer, and he's no longer an old fart, but a baby.

Embryonic stage completed. Fetal stage beginning.

I'm so bloated. My knees are weak. I need to sit, but an unseen force has me in its grip. It's like I'm possessed by an evil spirit making me repeat Nick's name in the form of a question.

Fur covers me. I'm a nameless raccoon. Nick is a four-year-old.

No longer furry, and back in human form, I'm Cara Johnson, Nick's first official girlfriend in sixth grade.

Now I'm Faith, a high school crush.

My hair is auburn. I'm a woman whose name Nick can't speak. Tears pour from his eyes. He reaches for me, his lips trembling. He shakes his head. "No."

My hair is blond. "Nick." It's not a question this time. I'm not someone else. "Remember. Where am I?"

"You're in my head."

7

"I'm not. Where am I?"

"You're in Khertaan."

"Am I?"

Now my hair is blue. "Please, Nick, don't let me die."

"Erica. Oh, God, Erica. You're alive. I thought you were dead."

"Not if you keep me alive, Nick. Please."

I drop to my knees, my legs spread apart.

A pair of woman's sandals appear before me. A woman occupies them. I don't look up to see her face, but I know her name. Jean. She drenches me in perfume. *Embrace by Vintage Works*.

Her right arm swings back and forth by her side, her right hand gripping the end of an axe handle. She hefts up the weapon. "You little blue-haired bitch."

"Nick." I whisper his name. "*Please....*"

Nick coughs up blood. "I...." He crawls towards me on his elbows, his body trembling. "Jean, don't...." He points at her, a symbol on the back of his hand pulsing yellow. Then he crumples onto his face, as the yellow glow dies.

I'm the only one who can save me. Nick couldn't even decide who he wanted me to be, and now it's left for me to decide. I don't have to think about it....

My blue hair turns green. As Greelia the Goblin Warrior, I jerk back my head, avoiding having an axe planted in my skull. I strike with my arm like a snake, snatch the axe from Jean's hands, and swing it around my head, planting it in the woman's midriff. She bursts into a spray of glowing flecks that fly away on a sudden gust of wind.

Fetal stage completed. Birth commencing.

A role in addition to Goblin Warrior is forced upon me. Am I not meant to be Greelia? Circumstances gave me no choice. Now something is happening to me that should be happening to Charli. But I have no choice in this matter, either.

I'm not one to leave everything to chance or fate.

I spring from my kneeling position onto my feet, a war cry erupting from between my lips. Then I reach inside with my left hand and yank the infant out of me. The child is covered in blood, but not so much I can't see that her skin is green like mine. I hold her up by her head. There is no umbilical cord. "You're a girl. I name you Britta."

A chorus of dancing women in green uniforms appears. In their midst stands a hooded figure.

The light in the room goes out.

CHAPTER THREE

Lady Ghost: Shattered

A young woman lies on the floor, blood pooling around her. An older woman swinging a bloody axe stands over the corpse. Swaths of dark red streak the corpse's blue hair.

Nick crawls towards the corpse. He stops when he's close enough to identify the body. "Erica... no...." He looks up at the woman with the axe. He doesn't ask her what she's done. It's bloody obvious what she's done. He knows her. She's his wife. Jean. She's murderously jealous, and the corpse at her feet belongs to Erica, the young woman who aided and abetted Nick in cheating on his wife.

Jean hefts the axe as she approaches Nick. The murder hasn't left her gaze. He rocks back onto his butt, raising a hand between his face and hers, as though that's sufficient to hide him from her. Neither of them speak, though there's a low gurgle in his throat.

She raises the axe over her head. She'll take his hand off and more besides. The axe blade descends.

The world blurs as time slows but everything is in motion, including myself. I grab the haft of the axe, halt its descent, and yank the weapon from Jean's hands. "I won't let you hurt him."

Jean searches the air for something she believes to be right in front of her but isn't. Then she dissolves like sugar in water, melting like witches in stories I've read.

The axe bursts into flames and is gone. I'm unharmed.

Nick lowers his hand. "Who are you?" He's not looking directly at me.

I kneel beside him and stroke his left ear. "It's best you don't identify me, my love. If you know who I am, your mind will reject me, and I'll be gone."

That might go for me, too. If I come to the realization of who I am, I could very well reject myself.

White light shines in the distance. A faraway voice shouts a name, though I refuse to hear it. I'm supposed to go to the light, where the afterlife awaits me, but I won't leave Nick. He needs me.

The light dims and the voice loses volume. I can still go, if I go now.

I don't go.

The room turns dark and silence overwhelms me.

But I'm not alone. Nick is here.

Lightning strikes him, and he vanishes.

I'm still not alone. The young blue-haired woman's corpse is here, floating in blood. I knew her name once. It's not Charli or Yvette or Greelia, though all of those names seem almost right.

Time passes. I stay with the corpse until the police come and carry her away. They don't ask me questions, behaving like I'm not even here. They leave. Someone comes to clean up the blood, and then they leave.

I'm truly alone.

The room divides as though I'm looking at it in a mirror and the mirror breaks into thousands of shards.

"You can't stay here." The voice is young and feminine, but not mine. "This timeline and those surrounding it have shattered. You must leave, quickly, while you still can. Come with me, if you like."

"Who are you?" The question is out of my mouth before I consider the speaker might wish to remain as anonymous as I do.

A blond woman with black-spotted red skin, wearing fringed tan loincloth and blouse, leaps through the air and lands before me. "I'm Slithy. I'm a Frogkin." An army of frogs leap from nowhere to land around the two of us, their numbers stretching into the distance in all directions. "These are my friends. You're welcome to join us. We're going to clean up a mess." She assesses the three-dimensional array of shards and then points at a slender, thin fragment as tall as she is. "There's the one we want. You coming?" She holds out a hand to me as the frog army leaps thirty by thirty at the designated shard, vanishing when they touch it. Slithy beckons. "Come, come. The shards will all fade soon, and you'll be stuck here in limbo. If you don't want to come with us, then choose some other shard, but choose one, quickly."

Her last frogs disappear into the fragment she chose. "Please. You mean a lot to Dad. It would tear him up inside to think you were lost forever in the void between timelines."

"Who's your Dad?"

"Nick, who else?"

"Which shard is he in?"

"All of them. Look, I have to go. You do too. *Pick one.*" Slithy touches the shard of her choice and vanishes.

The array of shards shimmers and then dims. I want to move, to choose one of the thousands, but I can't. If Nick is in all of them, how can I choose just one?

The pointy, jagged shards turn in the air to aim at a focal point in their midst, pointing their tips at the center of their collective mass. They move towards the focal point—slowly at first, but increasingly faster by the second. I need to choose *now*. I reach for the one Slithy touched, but it's too far from me and I'm out of time. The nearest one will have to do.

CHAPTER FOUR

Ronnie: Mother Jean

Rain falls around me and my three female friends—Fauna, Greelia, and Emma—but not directly on us. It's like we're surrounded by a curtain of water. Caught within the watery shell is a smattering of inch-high metallic symbols with a faint orange glow, locked in their position in space and time, though the flowing water continually distorts their appearance. The metal and the water are elemental forces at odds with each other… reflecting the confrontational nature of reality.

I push against the curtain of water, and it pushes back. I'm not meant to leave this space… this prison.

What lies beyond is blurred by the falling water, but I can make out the general situation. An old man lies face down on the floor. A younger man kneels beside him. The old man rolls onto his back, pulling his knees up to his chest.

The younger man strokes the older one's hair. "Dad?"

"Mel? I love you, Mel." With help, the older man sits up.

Beyond the two men, a dozen women in green uniforms dance in a circle. At the center of the circle stands a woman in a black cloak, her shoulders drawn back, her chin up and protruding from the shadow of her hood. She hurls an axe....

I can't let a curtain of water stop me. I grab hold of a metallic symbol, the entire thing enclosed inside my fist. As I had surmised, it's immovable, providing me an anchor to pull against. I grab a second one, and with one in each hand, I pull myself forward and through the watery curtain.

The thrown axe still flies end over end through the air in slow motion. I casually step in the path of the flying weapon and take hold of it as the handle turns towards me. "That wasn't nice."

The hooded woman swirls her cloak as the circle of dancers cease dancing. She walks out of their ring towards me. "Do I know you, boy?"

Mel rises to stand beside me. "Leave us alone, Mother. You can't even see your own evil."

"Stay out of this, Karen." The woman gestures, and the axe flies from my hand to hers. She closes the distance, stepping around me. Lifting the axe over her head, she aims it at the old man, who looks a lot like Nick, but older. Maybe he's Nick's father.

The axe descends, but it's still in slow motion, and I catch the handle again, halting the strike. "I said, that's not nice." I offer her a mushroom with my free hand. "You must be hungry. Please stop being a monster."

"Give me back my axe."

"I don't think so." I wrench it from her grip.

"How...?" The hooded woman trembles. "You're just a figment of *his* imagination. You aren't even real."

"I'm real enough to take your head if you don't leave this old man alone."

"You're a demon." The woman takes a faltering step back. "It doesn't matter. I'm coming for you, Nick. I'll find a way. Once I destroy you and your minions, no one can stand against me." She walks backwards until she enters the circle of uniformed women, who resume their dance.

Mel—whom the cloaked woman had addressed as Karen—runs after her. "*You're* the demon, Mother. Why do you have to be this way?" He breaks through the circle of dancers. The cloaked woman fades away. Mel fades from existence too an instant later.

I can't let him face the cloaked woman alone. Axe in hand, I break through the circle. The entire room, including the old man, fades out around me, replaced by nothing.

The cloaked woman had addressed the old man as Nick. Such an old man can't be the same Nick I met.

❧☙☙☙❧☙

Darkness surrounds me. The axe is in my hand and the floor is under my feet, but I'm unaware of anything else. I stash the axe in my inventory.

A footstep sounds in front of me, accompanied by Mel's voice. "Mother? *Mother.* Where are you?"

I strain to listen, but all is silent except the in and out of Mel's breath.

He takes two more steps. "Mother? *Please.* I don't hate you. Let me help you."

Fingers like metal close over my forearms. I can't tear free of their grip. Mel struggles noisily against his unseen captors as well. I'm lifted off my feet. A slight wind on my face tells me I'm moving. I'm forced into a seat and strapped in. I try to break my bonds, but I'm not strong enough.

"*Let me go.*" Mel yells from my left, struggling as much as I am, if not more. "Mother? Why are you doing this?"

"You will sit, and you will watch. Both of you." Her voice is cold, factual, coming from behind me. She lays a hand on my shoulder. "You shouldn't be here, but since you are, I ought to introduce myself. My name is Jean. I'm Karen's mother. Who are you?"

"I'm Ronnie. Who is Karen?"

Mel continues struggling and shouting. "You're possessed, Mother. Don't let the demon control you. You're stronger than it is, Mother. *Fight it.*"

Some distance ahead of me, a window opens to a starry night sky, admitting minuscule light. My eyes adjust enough for me to see something of my surroundings.

I'm seated in a large chair reminiscent of a throne, with arms and a high back. Metal bands clamp my neck, forearms, thighs, and calves in place, with a larger band across my chest. Mel is in a similar situation, sitting to my left.

Slipping her hand off my shoulder, Jean steps forward between me and Mel. She taps a wooden staff on the floor, twice. The stars streak by like comets, their tails blurred. When the motion stops, a planet comes into view, close enough to fill the entire height of the window. The geography of the continents isn't one I know. Come to think of it, I don't know the geography of the continents on any planet, mine, or Earth, or otherwise. But something tells me this isn't my home planet or Earth.

"Destroy it." Jean's monotone voice could pass for male or female.

Originating from out of frame below the window, a beam of light shoots at the planet. Dark green liquid washes over the surface of the world, flooding it in its entirety. No land-dwelling creature could survive such a deluge.

The planet has become a ball of green liquid. As though squeezed by an unseen giant fist, it spurts back at us, flooding the view. When the gushing stops, no liquid remains, and no planet, either.

That world is simply gone.

Mel ceases fighting for the moment. "Nice special effects, Mother. Now let us go."

"It wasn't a special effect, Karen."

"My name is *Mel*. Don't call me by my dead name."

"Your name is *Karen* while you're in my house."

Mel grunts, straining against his restraints. "*This* isn't your house, and *I'm* not here of my own free will. *Let us go.*"

"In *this* timeline, this is *my* spaceship. *My* home. Your father is not a stupid gamer named Nick, but a long-dead nameless consort of mine. *You* weren't born of your own free will or named of your own free will. You are *my* daughter, and *mine* to name. *Karen* is not your dead name, but your *birth* name, given to you by the one with the right to name you—me. By attempting to change your name—your identity—you disrespect *my* rights to name the daughter *I* bore in *my* womb for nine painful months, to whom *I* gave a part of *my* life to create.

"*You* belong to *me*, Karen. I owned you from the day you were conceived and will own you until the day I die. You think you are your own person, that you can choose for yourself who and what you are. But you are mistaken. You are the product of generations of ancestors who came before you. Without *any one* of them, you would not be. *You* may desire to change your name and identity, but *others* must choose to acknowledge your desired changes, or they mean nothing. *Nothing.*

"Trillions of creatures live, each individual with its own ancestry, and every single one of them ignorant of the history of its ancestors except possibly through hearsay, only concerned with its own troubles and turmoils, believing it knows what is best for itself, oblivious to the long bloodline stretching behind it of all those whose decisions led to its birth. And do you think, because you exist in the moment and have achieved the singular act of surviving for a few dozen years, that you are the only one with any rights concerning you and your name?

"In the timeline you remember, 'society' and its 'laws' allowed you to change your name and identity, but society itself consists of other feeble minds living only in the moment. In that timeline, the man named Nick McKenzie long ago succumbed to the siren call of the *now*, voluntarily blinding himself so he could taste its temptation, only to struggle against the very bonds society placed upon him. He called you by your imagined name and referred to you by your imagined gender. But *I* refuse. It is not for *you* to force *me* to change *my* mind. Upon your birth, I had the right to name you, and I have not given up that right. I will never relinquish it. You are *Karen*, my *daughter*, and you always will be, no matter how much you pretend otherwise or convinced Nick and the rest of society in his timeline to play along.

"Society, consisting of ignorant, spineless individuals, cannot help but be corrupt. It is, by its very nature, evil. Indeed, where there is life, there is evil. Life cannot exist without consuming other life, be it plant or animal, resulting in an endless cycle of birth, death, more births, and more deaths. Every single individual cares only about itself and what it must do to have the 'best' existence during the time it exists. Individuals care about other individuals only to the extent that it makes existence 'better' for the self. Well, *I'm* an individual, and what makes *my* life 'better' for *me* is for the *daughter* I birthed to respect *my* choice of name for her."

"You're insane, Mother." Mel clenches his teeth, grinding them.

"Ah, *sanity*." Jean paces before us. "What is sanity, exactly? Might it be better referred to as *conformity*? If my thoughts don't align with the ideas that serve those in power in society, they label me insane. Well, I'm the one with the power here, and I place the labels on whomever I want. *Society* is insane. Corrupt. Evil. *Unnecessary*. Constantly at war.

"*I* have unmatched, ultimate power in this universe, and to this universe I will bring peace. No more struggle. No more disagreements. No more names or labels or individuals laying claim to rights they never earned. All will cease to exist, and in destruction all will know conformity.

"You think only of me as your mother. Others may perceive me as a weak, old, scorned woman. Indeed, the man named Nick McKenzie scorned me in his timeline, trading me for a young woman named Erica. In that timeline, I took Erica's life. In this timeline, there is no husband to scorn me, but everyone else does, including my own daughter. I forgive you, but not *them*. Everyone else with a sentient thought will die. *All* of them, human or otherwise.

"But *you*, my daughter, will be with me until the end, to see the destruction of every thinking thing—except you... and perhaps Ronnie here. Before I speak the Final Word to destroy myself and my nurses, you *will* believe what I am telling you. No one will remain but you and some young man—perhaps this one. You will see. It will be upon the two of you to repopulate the universe, if it is to be repopulated. And for that, my dear Karen, you will need to be the *woman* you are, not the *man* you imagine yourself to be. You will accept your femininity, becoming the All-Mother, or you will be the Ultimate Destroyer, as it will be by your decision whether to establish a new Garden of Eden in which you are Eve or to stubbornly stand by your ideals, embracing masculinity at the cost of all else."

Mel ceases struggling against his restraints, finally realizing the futility of it. "My father worshiped you. You called him a Satanist. I guess you would know, because you *are* Satan. You talk of destruction because others don't agree with your world view. That's the height of arrogance and evil. And you claim to have ultimate power? What... like God? You are deluded beyond belief. I don't know how it's possible I came from you, even in part. You make me wish I'd never been born."

Jean stops pacing, halting before Mel. "In some other timelines, you *weren't* born, Karen. But I can't concern myself with them. It's incumbent upon me to bring peace in this timeline. And that's exactly what I plan to do."

Mel scoffs. "Let me go, Mother. Turn yourself in to the cops and get the help you need. Lord knows I can't give you that kind of help."

A hoarse laugh sounds from Jean's throat. "I don't need help. I have all the power I need to do what needs doing. I've already demonstrated it to you, yet you don't believe. So I will prove my power to you with a more convincing demonstration."

She taps her staff on the metal floor. Stars blur outside the window for a few seconds, moving in the opposite direction of their previous blurry motion. When the motion stops, another planet appears outside the window. I don't know why, but the geography of the continents of this world have an inexplicable familiarity.

Mel's mother drags the end of her staff across the floor as she approaches the window, her silhouette partially obstructing the view. "There's Earth, Karen. I'm going to show you what is happening there now, but not on screen, given that you think what you see on the screen is a movie. Instead, I'll create a protective bubble for you on the planet's surface. If you stay inside the bubble, you'll be safe. If you go outside the bubble, one of my minions may very well kill you. After one hour, whether you're in the bubble or not, if you're still alive, you'll be automatically transported back here. You'll then understand this is the safest place to be until the end."

"*Fine.*" Mel tugs at his bonds. "Anything to get free of this chair."

Jean waves a hand in a sweeping arc. "Illuminate."

Light floods my surroundings, and I close my eyes against it. When I can peek between my eyelids without feeling blinded, I open my eyes.

The throne in which I sit is constructed of green metal, as are the bands that bind me to it. The window—what Jean referred to as a *screen*—stands twenty-five feet away, forty feet wide and twenty feet high, spanning from floor to ceiling. Walls stretch into the distance to either side of the screen. The room is entirely constructed of green metal with a glossy finish.

Standing at attention before silvery metal pedestals arranged in a grid, spaced about six feet apart, are dozens of women in lacy green outfits with flared skirts... Jean's nurses. As my eyes adjust to the light, they pirouette. Then they dance around the pedestals, some traversing in clockwise circles and others counter-clockwise. Some of the dancing nurses stop, while others continue. If there's a method to their movements, I fail to see it. More dancers stop, and then more, until all of them are standing in place.

As if on cue, a quarter of the dancers do handstands on their pedestals, with no apparent pattern to which ones do the handstands and which ones don't. Their skirts fall about their waists, exposing the entirety of their legs. They wear lacy green panties and glassy green slippers.

Hissing surrounds me, and green mists rise from upturned slipper soles. The mists slither through the air like wispy serpents and waft to the ceiling. They flow beneath the flat surface to converge on a six-foot diameter dome of clear glass protruding from the ceiling. The mists pass through the surface of the dome, entering a spherical space, swirling within until they fill it. Then they vanish, and the glass ball becomes clear inside again.

Displayed on the screen, a ball of green liquid flies down at the planet. Burning a hole through any intervening clouds, it impacts the ground, leaving a green speck where it strikes in an otherwise predominantly gray area. The 'speck' could be miles across. There's no way for me to reliably gauge its size from here.

Other nurses do handstands on their pedestals, generating more wisps of green mists that flow across the ceiling to the screen, where they collect on its surface, obstructing the view of what's outside.

Two dancers approach me, gyrating as they draw near. Two others approach Mel. All four wear gloves sparkling with green glitter. Reaching me, the pair grab me by my wrists, one nurse on either side of me. The bands fall free of my body, and the nurses pull me from my chair. They haul me towards the screen. Their strength is beyond my ability to resist, as my first impulsive attempt proves. But I sense an interesting adventure lies ahead of me, so why not plunge into it head on? With any luck, maybe I'll run into Fauna, Emma, and Greelia. There's not much chance of that if I stay where I am.

Mel and I reach the mist-covered screen at the same time. The nurses push us forward. Instinctively, I brace myself for impact, but it doesn't come. We pass through the screen and emerge in a room with padded blue walls. The mists evaporate, and no trace of the green metal room, Jean, or the nurses stands in evidence around us.

Blinking red, a metal eye looks down on us from over a padded blue door. The entire ceiling glows white, illuminating the room.

I get my first good look at Mel. We're about the same height. We both have brown eyes. His brown hair is cut about like mine, short, above the ears.

There are differences, of course. The shape of his face is more oval while mine is more oblong. His Adam's apple is missing. His chest is more busty than mine—one could imagine him having slight breasts under his loose-fitting shirt. His legs are longer than mine, while I'm longer than he above the waist.

"Hi, Mel. I'm Ronnie." I extend my hand. "I'm sorry about your mother."

Mel shakes my hand. "Nice to meet you, Ronnie, though one could wish for better circumstances. I'm sorry you got dragged into this."

"Hey, life's an adventure, and I'm happy to have someone to adventure with."

Examination of our surroundings proves there's but a single exit to the room. The metal door is unlocked, and Mel opens it. Beyond is a ten-foot wide hallway with painted blue walls. Not padded. The ceiling out here glows, too.

We pick a direction and follow the hall that way. We round one bend, then another. We round one more and stop in our tracks.

A wall of translucent green energy spans the hallway ahead. Just beyond the see-through wall, the hallway opens into a large room, the floor covered with rubble. Exterior walls have crumbled, and the ceiling lies in pieces on the floor. Bloody corpses lie strewn among the ruins.

A man in a light-colored robe, his head bowed and his face buried in his hands, stands over one of the dead, trembling.

"Sir," Mel calls. "What has happened here?"

He lifts his head and turns to face us. "Oh, my God, someone else is alive."

A shadow falls over him, and he looks up. His expression turns from hopeful to horrified. A long, pointed metal shaft lances the man's chest. Dark blood spurts across the front of his robe. He gurgles and the light leaves his eyes.

From over our heads walks an Arachnid Behemoth. It shakes the skewered man off its pointed leg. The fresh corpse sprawls on the floor before us, just on the other side of the green see-through wall. The Behemoth strides over a ruined exterior brick wall into a field of empty, wrecked horseless carriages. In the distance, other Behemoths stalk other ruined buildings, searching for other survivors.

Mel gags like he's about to vomit.

CHAPTER FIVE

Susie: The Future Past

For how long does Seth continue destroying civilized planets? Why is there nothing I can do to stop him? I have the ability to travel back in time. Why have I not done what was necessary to end this slaughter?

Back when Timmy and I were thinking of getting married, I'd spent some time in Spring Green Mental Health Facility. Dad had been there, too, and he'd claimed the year was 1991. But he was wrong. It was 2008. I was seventeen. With my freakish ability, I could have traveled back to 1991, but instead, I skipped from Monday night one week to Thursday morning later that same week, not in 1991, but 2008. Dad believed what he wanted to believe, and I believed what I wanted. To this day we still maintain what we each believed about that time. Neither of us will ever believe the other is right. He'll always believe it was 1991, and I'll always believe it was 2008. Is it possible we were both right? That doesn't seem bloody likely. But which of us was right also seems impossible to know.

On that particular Thursday in 2008, everyone was telling me that Timmy was dead. I hadn't experienced the immediately preceding Wednesday yet, the day he'd supposedly died, so I couldn't believe them. I thought the hospital staff were joining Timmy in pranking me, that I was on a reality TV game show where the objective was for an unknowing contestant not to break while being gaslighted by the other participants. It was something, I'm sad to say, I'd imagined was possible of Timmy and that he'd set me up, trusting that I wouldn't break, so we could win a million dollars and have the kind of wedding, honeymoon, and lifestyle we wanted.

Although that hadn't been a reality TV game show, what if something like that is happening to me *right now*? I mean, I do believe I'm on a spaceship, because I flew up to it and teleported aboard. But all this destruction of planets? I'm seeing it on a screen. I've seen movies with special effects just as grand as what I'm seeing here. Okay, I admittedly saw an energy beam shoot down at Earth when the ship's eye opened and I was right there next to the raised eyelid. That was when I first came aboard, before Seth's alien minions caught me and brought me to him. But that first beam hadn't destroyed the planet. It had been aimed at a specific spot on the ground and did next to no damage, certainly nothing on the scale of a Planet Buster.

Every time Seth has claimed he was destroying a planet, he might have been showing Timmy and me a movie with animated graphics and special effects.

But, no, I don't buy that. I don't believe Seth is human, but he has human traits and I'm able to read him. I think. His body language tells me he hasn't been pranking us. When he said all those planets were being destroyed, he meant it.

Even so, I refuse to break.

Time passes. I don't know how much, because my internal clock is alarmingly out of whack. Gray-skinned aliens meander about the ship for some unknowable purpose. Some of them bring tablets to Seth for him to peruse, and then walk away with them once he's finished reading. Seth's body language usually indicates his satisfaction with what he's reading, but occasionally there's a shuffling of his feet or a clenching of his fists that betray a degree of dissatisfaction.

I've been sitting on this stool for what must be hours. "Would you mind if I stand for a while? My legs are numb from all the sitting."

Seth faces me, his features hidden by his shadowed hood. "I still have thirty-five planets to go before I've finished destroying all the sentient beings in this universe not on this ship. It will be less than an Earth hour until we're finished. You can wait that long."

I laugh. "What's an Earth hour, now that Earth is destroyed?"

He ignores me. A tall gray alien hands him a tablet. He looks it over, nods, and hands it back. He straightens, drawing in a breath, his chin up and his hands clasped in front of him. He chuckles. "I've underestimated you, Susie McKenzie." His chuckle takes on a sinister tone. "I don't need Nick. I only need you. He passed some of his nanobots to you. Once I've finished destroying this universe, I can use your nanobot technology to move my Planet Buster to an adjacent universe. The multiverse is truly now entirely at my mercy, all thanks to you."

It will do me no good to deny his claim. But I will hold onto hope. Glynda—future-me—told me I'd eventually get this collar off and get my powers back. From the burn marks I'd seen encircling her throat, heating the collar will likely be involved in its removal. When it comes off, I'm to teleport to the spot where I met her and time-jump back twenty-four hours. She said I'd know what to do then.

If there's anyone I trust, it's myself from the future.

CHAPTER SIX

Megan: Out of the Picture

The bed frame is in pieces and the mattress shredded. Mithabel did that hours ago. Debra stashed the remnants in inventory, for practice in stashing items, but also to clear the debris from the room. She and Dylan share the same unlimited inventory space. I share inventory space with Mithabel, but our shared space is limited... not that we've had any great need for more.

Using our specialized skills and traits, both Mithabel and I have examined every cubic centimeter of the room's interior for anomalies. We've found nothing.

Despite the despair we're all feeling, we don't give up. Continually reviewing our abilities, we try every scheme, no matter how wild, to find a way out of the pocket dimension we're trapped in.

Mithabel and I transform to Siamese Cats and scratch at the walls, floor, and ceiling of our bedroom prison, hoping our claws will catch on the slightest crack, where a secret trapdoor might lie. We even compress our bodies in cat form, making our claws as small as possible, hoping they'll better catch on fine hairline cracks, if any exist. It's to no avail.

Dylan brings out two ceramic jugs of water. Mithabel takes one and I take the other. We each work half the room. We pour out the water and look for it to seep through the polished wooden floor. It doesn't. We use our Control Water skills to push the water around, up the walls and across the ceiling, using the liquid to test for any porous spots. We find none, but we do get some practice with the Control Water skill. I can sense exactly where the water lies, the contours of the pool it makes. If any of it had seeped even partially into the wood constructing the room, I'd have known. The room may look to be made of wood, but it's not wood like any from Earth.

With a thought, I direct the water I'm controlling to flow back into the ceramic jug from which I poured it. "These walls look like wood, but don't act like wood. They're magical in some way. Do we have a way to remove enchantments? Or maybe the walls are illusions, and we need to disbelieve them." I focus on a portion of wall, striving to see through it, but the wall doesn't fade away, and when I touch it, it's still solid.

Dylan stands beneath the framed photo. "I don't have a way to remove enchantments. All my attempts to disbelieve have failed. I still think this picture must be the key to our escape. It was our way in, and there is no other way out."

I equip Ghost Maker, the enchanted battle axe I received in exchange for the Severed Orc Ear in Maron. "Maybe destroying the photo will unlock the portal."

"No." Dylan raises a hand to stop me. "If it's vital to our return and must be intact to work, then destroying it ruins any chance we have at escape. Let's exhaust all options involving it in an unharmed state before irrevocably removing all such options."

"Fine." I stash the axe. "Can it come off the wall?"

"No." My Elf Tank avatar lays her hand on my shoulder. "It wasn't even possible to force water behind the frame."

"Is there glass over the picture?" I touch it. There's no glass in the frame. Another thought strikes me. "How is it that Kaleisha and Magnum can manifest here so that all of us can see them? How is it that Debra is here, apparently in the game, though she was never given an in-game body like I have? Mithabel… Kaleisha…, do you remember? There's one place we've been before where we could all interact with each other."

Mithabel forms a silent *ah* with her mouth. "I remember. When we fought that tentacled creature, the Dominator."

Dylan whistles. "You think we're in the spiritual realm?"

A metaphysical longsword, its blade engulfed in blue flames, appears, its hilt snug in my upraised hand. "I do. How else could I summon a Sword of Faith? Just like the one Mithabel, Kaleisha, and I used to defeat the Dominator that attacked us."

Mithabel grimaces. "But when we fought the Dominator, our physical bodies were still in the physical realm, berserk and fighting each other. If these are our spiritual bodies, then where are our physical bodies? If they're still in the physical realm, then Dylan and I are still standing in the hallway with the city guards."

We all exchange knowing glances. That has to be it.

My avatar continues. "Time flowed faster for us in the spiritual realm. If this theory is correct, then your physical body is still in the desert, Megan, about to die from the triple explosion you witnessed before your spirit was whisked here. If that's the case, then all we really need to do is wait until you die. That should release you and me and I assume Kaleisha, too." She turns to Dylan. "To get you, Debra, and Magnum out of here, we can ask the city guard to kill you."

"No, something still isn't right." Dylan turns her attention to the Sword of Faith. "We've seemingly spent hours in this place. The time differential between the spiritual and physical realms wasn't that great during our Dominator battles. By now, Megan should have already died, if her physical body is still in the desert. The death explosions she witnessed would have killed her already."

I'm not ready to quit on the idea yet. "My guess is we're in a pocket dimension in the spiritual realm. The flow of time in the pocket dimension could be different than typical for the spiritual realm in general. It feels like hours have passed here, but maybe only a fraction of a second has passed in the physical realm."

Debra scuffs a bare foot on the floor. "That makes as much sense to me as anything else said so far. But here's a chilling thought. What if time in this place is *frozen*, just like how it's frozen on Earth? We might experience eternity here, while no time actually passes. Our spirit bodies might be trapped in a single moment of time. And if we never get out of here, then our physical bodies will effectively forever be in comas."

"That explains why we're in a pocket dimension." Dylan exhales slowly. "Someone has gone to great lengths to take us out of the picture."

"Out of the picture." Mithabel laughs. Everyone glares at her. "Does no one else get the pun?"

"Oh, Goddess, you're right." Dylan stares at the photo. "In the hallway, we were *in* the picture, all of us except our AIs. Here, we're *out* of the picture. If this is a metaphysical place, as the presence of Megan's flaming Sword of Faith implies, then being *out of the picture* might be what's holding us here."

Mithabel purses her lips. "Then how do we get ourselves back *into* the picture?"

A quill appears in Debra's grasp, cold blue flames playing over it. "The pen is mightier than the sword." Standing below the picture, she reaches up. "Someone give me a boost."

"I can help you with that." Dismissing my Sword of Faith, I sit with my back to the wall. Closing my eyes, I transfer my awareness to Debra, passing my Flight Speed skill to her as well. She flies up until she's eye level with the photo. Laying the metaphysical quill to the picture, she begins to draw. I transfer my Alertness trait to aid with the finer details. My knowledge of graphics design assists with shading, fine-tuning color choices, and other areas Debra has difficulty with.

Debra draws all six of us on the photo. "I realize Kaleisha and Magnum weren't in the picture hanging in the hallway, but I'm putting them into the picture here, so as not to take any chances they'll be stuck here when the rest of us leave."

She finishes and floats down to the floor to admire her work, dismissing her quill. I reclaim my awareness.

Standing beside her, I take her hand and squeeze. "We work well together." The images she's added to the photo look just like our little group of six—all with wide smiles. I can't help but smile back.

The Dylan in the photo is holding her cudgel aloft. We all take hands, Kaleisha completing the circle with a hand on Dylan's shoulder while the Polynesian Priestess holds up one arm. A metaphysical cudgel appears in her hand, aglow with blue flame. "Let's reverse the process by which we came here. Is everyone ready?"

We're all beyond ready.

She touches her metaphysical cudgel to the illustrated one.

A bright light envelopes us.

CHAPTER SEVEN

Yuni: Special Quest

My fat cat AI—a furry ball a foot in diameter, with four paws, a feline head, and a springy tail—bounces on his stub of a tail and grins. "I have great news for you, musume." His whiskers shake with excitement. "You have gained 7,480,000 XP. You've attained level *19* Priestess of War and level *10* Anjai...."

"What...?"

"That's right, musume. And... you've got new Anjai skills. Flight Speed. Hide. Shapeshift Crow. And Wind Control. They're at levels 9, 8, 6, and 4, respectively. And... you've earned two attribute points and two trait points. Is that cool or what?"

"Oh, Inuki, I could just hug you. How did I get so many XP?"

"They came from the defeat of... four Arachnid Behemoths, six Pteranodons, and... one Giant Pteranodon Boss. The Behemoth that captured you was one of them. The three Behemoths holding your other party members have also been killed, which means... the rest of XStorm are free! They'll rejoin you as soon as they respawn, which could be any moment."

I'm blown away. I'd imagined having trouble finding my party again, somewhere out there in the vast desert, captives of an army of giant spiders, making it impossible for me to respawn at their location. We hadn't expected such tough opponents at this stage of the game, and when none of our attacks had any effect on them, we found ourselves surrounded and quickly webbed, unable to escape. We called out for help, but of course no one replied.

But then the spiders had been attacked by Pteranodons. The dinosaur birds killed the spider that carried me. The spider exploded, killing me... but in the process setting me free. My death had caused my player, Saiko Aimi, to awaken. I respawned once she went back to sleep. After I returned, the rest of my party was involved in the deaths of the three other Behemoths and the Boss monster for the Desert of Doom. They're worth so many XP!

It's now obvious we aren't powerful enough to take on the Desert of Doom. Was there something we missed in Maron, something that would have bumped us up enough levels and given us the skills needed to be effective against the Behemoths?

As soon as I respawned in Maron, I ran into party Quantized. They took on some quest in the city, but what did it do for them? They aren't as high level as we in XStorm are. So I don't get it.

Party MAD is here, too, and they've somehow reached level 23 already. The disparity is crazy. But they're wanting to travel across the Dunes with Quantized, and they all agreed to let me travel with them. That was before the rest of my party died. They were going to help me rescue the rest of XStorm.

But an issue concerning Mithabel delayed our travel plans. The city guard took her into custody. I don't understand why. Dylan went with her. I can't believe how gorgeous that woman is. She's the Sun to my Darkness, the Serenity to my War. I can't believe I'll be traveling with her. She'll drive me to distraction. Now we're waiting for her and Mithabel to return. They've only been inside for a minute, but it feels like hours.

I tap Amarynth on the wrist. "My party has been freed. They should be respawning soon. We don't need to rescue them after all."

The Viking woman takes my announcement in stride. "That's good news, Yuni. Will you still be traveling with us across the Dunes?"

"I hope so. It's not my decision any longer. ChrisCross is our leader. We've all agreed to do what he decides. Although, if party MAD has an open slot...." It would be so nice if they did and invited me to join them. I'd switch parties in a heartbeat, even though it would mean not being in the same party as my brother, Bradford. Before the competition started, his player and mine agreed that we avatars would stick together in the same party, but I'm not bound by any agreement made between our players. I may be Aimi's subconsciousness on Earth, but here in Khertaan I'm the one with free will.

Amarynth gives me a sad frown. "Your switching parties could cause friction we don't want if our parties are to travel together. I think it best if you stay in XStorm."

"It's okay." But if ChrisCross doesn't want XStorm to travel with party MAD, I might just go with them anyway, if they'll let me.

I know. I'm letting my crush on Dylan influence my decisions. "Have you been in the Dunes yet, Amarynth?"

She shakes her head. "Why do you ask?"

"I was wondering if you've encountered the Arachnid Behemoths. I'm thinking you must have killed some to get to level 23."

Amarynth glances at the little dragon by her side.

His name is Rolag. I've heard he's tough, but I've yet to see him in action, though some of my party have tangled with him, and he left an impression. He's small, but then, at five-foot-two-inches, I'm relatively short for an adult human woman, and I'd like to believe I pack a punch in my small package, so I won't sell him short. His fangs are wicked. He snorts a wisp of smoke.

The Viking Archer turns back to me. "We aren't sure how we earned all our XP. One of our party is traveling separately from us, and we assume she's earning the XP that keeps dumping on us. We've tried to contact her, but can't reach her on any chat channel, not even party or private chat. But she's still on our party roster. My guess is, she decided to block us. It would be nice if we could hook up with her again and find out just what she's been doing. I don't suppose you saw a teenage girl with brown pigtails and a cowboy hat while you were in the desert...? Answers to the name *Charli*."

Inuki waves a stubby paw in my face. "I have info on that name. Charli is the NPC who killed the Longest Survivor before the update... and earned the million XP bounty. She's also currently the avatar with the highest total XP in the entire game."

Thanking Amarynth for sharing, I walk away to continue my private conversation with my feline AI. The yellow-and-white-striped cat has a head that's half again the diameter of his body. He's got stubby legs and tail, white whiskers a foot long, and two fangs more prominent than the others—I call the two prominent ones his vampire fangs. He's been with me since I entered the game. He looks so cuddly, I wish I could hold him, but when I tried, my arms passed right through him, just as he said they would.

"Inuki, what other info can you get on Charli?"

Planting the tip of his tail on the ground and supporting his body on it, he spins around three times. When he stops, his eyes continue spinning in his eye sockets for a few seconds. "There appears to be a disconnect between Charli and the System. I've reported the issue. Wait.... The System has granted you a bonus of two million XP for the report. Congratulations, musume, you are now level 20 Priestess of War, level 11 Anjai. You have also been granted a special quest, if you choose to take it. The quest is worth two-hundred-million XP, enough to put you to level 26 Priestess, should you complete it. Are you interested?"

My knees buckle. I reach out, trying to catch my balance with a hand on Inuki's head, which results in my crashing on the ground, because my AI is insubstantial and can't bear my weight.

Amarynth is immediately by my side. "Yuni?" She holds out a hand to help me up. "Are you okay? What happened?"

Inuki wags his head. "You can't tell her about the special quest, or you forfeit the opportunity. You can't tell anyone about it, not even your fellow XStorm members. If you complete it... only you will receive the XP for it."

I gladly accept the help to stand. "Thanks. I'm too anxious. About everything, I guess." I give her a smile. Not too weak but not too forced. "I'm fine."

She watches me with concern. I bow my head and continue to smile, unwilling to say anything for fear it might be the wrong thing. Finally she takes her leave, going over to talk with Rolag.

"Inuki." I resume my private conversation with my AI. "Tell me about this special quest."

The striped cat bobs his over-sized head from side to side. "I can't... not until you accept or reject it. If you reject it, you may not know what it is. You have ten minutes to decide."

"I don't need ten minutes. I'm accepting the special quest. Can I know what it is now?"

"I'm sorry." Inuki meowed. "I don't know what it is yet myself. I'll let you know about it as soon as I can. In the meantime, let's do some point assignments. Your Constitution has been increased to nine as you requested. Your character traits are: Pain Tolerant, at level 1; Metal Resistance, level 1; and Wakeful, level 2. Traits max out at level 4. If you put both points on Wakeful, you'll recover lost hit points and expended Auni at the fastest rate the trait allows."

That sounds good, but I'm intrigued by the other two traits as well. "At what character level will I earn another trait point?"

"Level 24. Then one more after that at level 30, and that will be it."

"Hmm." I'm acting on a whim here, though I like to think of it as Insight, since that's my second highest attribute. "Put the two points on Metal Resistance."

"Yes, musume. That raises the trait to level 3. And I've just been granted more info about it. With your trait at level 3, all attacks against you with metal weapons can only harm you if they are enchanted with level 4 magic, and only then if wielded by someone of a level higher than 20. If you gain another level in the trait, you'll be immune to all damage from metal weapons, no matter who wields them against you. Nice."

I like what I'm hearing. I feel I made the right choice.

Inuki looks thoughtful. "Those Arachnid Behemoths are level 20. Their webs are light metal chains, not silk. Their legs are metal, too. Your having level 3 Metal Resistance makes you immune to the attacks of the Arachnid Behemoths. They won't be able to web you or skewer you."

My knees are weak again, but this time I don't fall. "I'd rather not need to put it to the test, but that's a good thing to know."

"Yuni!" The voice of my twin brother, Bradford, emanates from down Main Street. His player, Saiko Haru, and my player, Saiko Aimi, are twins on Earth, and the System officially made us twins in-game. Picking him out from the pedestrians dressed in Victorian style is easy, since he's in full-body brown leather armor. He's running towards me. Ruby easily keeps up with him, even with her Faithful Companion Penelope on her back.

ChrisCross, our leader, follows them, walking casually and confidently in his white quilted armor and bare feet. He's a lot nicer guy than I'd expected after discovering his kindred to be Elitist. Yes, CC can be an arrogant bastard at times, but only to people outside our party. He's always courteous to everyone in XStorm. He's of the Martial Artist class and has a thing for Asian culture. He talks about anime and manga with Bradford when we're traveling. He has a thing for Asian women, too. I've made sure he knows I'm not looking for a guy.

As is often the case while traveling, CC's Magical Companion, the Electric Serpent, Lance, is wrapped around his waist. The snake is smaller than Rolag, but Lance saved CC, Ruby, and Penelope from death early in the game when we faced our first Boss monster. His electric blade attack was surprisingly effective against the Ferro Serpent.

I catch Bradford in my arms. "You made it."

He briefly squeezes me. "Did you get the seven million XP?"

"I sure did. I'm level 20 Priestess of War and level 11 Anjai. You?"

His brow crinkles. "Um… I'm only level 19 Wizard and level 10 Life-Stealer. The others are all level 19, too. How did you gain a level on us?"

I need to tread carefully here. "My AI discovered some issue with the game and reported it. The System awarded me bonus XP for it. Don't ask me what the issue was."

"It must have been quite an issue to be worth that much bonus XP." CC is still approaching, but interjects into our conversation, since we're holding it on party chat. "If my AI is right, you must have earned nearly two million XP for that bug report."

"What can I say?" I'm not going to tell anyone that I got the bonus XP for asking questions about Charli. That would only lead to other questions I've been instructed not to answer.

Inuki waves a paw to get my attention. "I have news, musume… the nature of your special quest…."

"Let's have it then."

"There's a shopkeeper approaching from your left. Go meet him. He has something for you. Take and stash it."

"And then I'll get two-hundred-million XP? Wow. I could use a lot more special quests like this."

Inuki sticks out his tongue. "No… that's only the first part. I'm not privy to the rest of the quest."

"Excuse me." I slip between CC and Bradford, both of whom watch me with curious gazes. A man dressed in a white shirt and black pants, jacket, hat, and bow tie makes his way through the throng of pedestrians, headed in my direction. Stretching my arms over my head, I pretend to be yawning and looking at the sky. As the shopkeeper nears me, I turn my back to him and place my hands behind me, open with palms up, ready to accept any item placed in their grasp.

He bumps into me. "Oh, so sorry, miss." He places a cold, stone ball in my hands before he stumbles away. "My head is in the clouds today, I'm afraid."

I stash the ball in inventory. It's a black sphere just under an inch in diameter, called a Shadow Marble. "What is this Shadow Marble for, Inuki?"

"No idea, musume. We'll eventually find out, I'm sure."

"The sooner the better." Where are Dylan and Mithabel? I'm eager to travel.

CHAPTER EIGHT

Nick: Bellow

Which timeline do I occupy?

I kneel beside Erica's corpse, blood pooling beneath her and matting her still-vibrant blue hair. The hooded Seth stands ten feet away, swinging an axe in one hand and leaning on his staff with the other. He hefts the axe handle higher in his grip and twirls the weapon. Around him stand his circle of nurses in green. Everyone else in the room fades from existence. Or perhaps I have fleeting memories of timelines that could have been.

I lay a hand on Erica's cheek. It's so cold. Her death drains the warmth from my fingers. Can I find her alive in some other timeline? I must.

Seth clears his throat.

I know what he wants. He wants ODYSSEY, even if he doesn't realize it.

He shakes the axe, as though assessing its weight. "I'd initially thought I needed to kill you. I have the capability now. I may not be with you in the nexus you've created, but this axe *is*, and it's under my command. I could strike off your head if I liked, and no one to stop me. But you have me curious. How *did* you create this nexus? That might be the last bit of essential knowledge I'm missing. Tell me, and buy yourself a little more time."

Not even a clock ticks in my presence. A clock hangs on the wall in the kitchen, but there are a thousand different kitchens, any one of which I could choose to walk into from here, though the very act of choosing a kitchen would also choose its corresponding timeline. I've no doubt I can access the Fanciful Pegasus timeline from here, if I but choose the right kitchen to enter. Once there, I could respawn Morrow in Khertaan. ODYSSEY got me close to the FP timeline, but with the timelines shattered, it was impossible for him to land me exactly where I wanted.

Everything I've done based on my own knowledge ended up badly—because I have so little empathy for anyone and anything, so little faith in myself or anyone else. I'm barely hanging onto hope, the single thread holding the multiverse together. And that's where we are. That's the state of the world, of the universe, of all existence. A single choice remains to be made, out of an infinity of possibilities, and it's on me to choose. Of all the people Destiny could pick as a champion, I'm the worst possible fuck-up ever to have the fate of the world placed on their shoulders.

If there's one good thing about me, it's that I don't quit on those I love. Even when I was ready to kill myself, I chose to live for the sake of lady ghost. And while I may not have the empathy to know when a loved one is in trouble, once I become aware of it, I do whatever is possible to get them out.

Which brings me full circle back to my dilemma. I'm willing to do what must be done. I just don't know what to do. Who would? I need inspiration.

Seth taps his staff on the floor. "I asked you a question. Answer me. How did you create this nexus?"

The weight of all life pushes into the crook of my neck. The next sound from my mouth will shape Destiny. I'm a very logical person, and when have I ever been in a position when I needed logic to serve me more?

Yet logic fails me now. I must give over to my primitive side, the way Susie did when confronted with a reality she couldn't comprehend. I vividly recall the primal look upon her face when she threw back her head and screamed at the heavens.

Susie is my inspiration.

Instinctively knowing what will happen to me, I reach into the primordial soup that is my soul, yank out its essence, and cast it from me through my throat. The sound of it does not echo, but permeates the very fabric of the multiverse, pulling together every broken timeline into a compact bundle with the power to punch through whatever metaphysical obstacle had blocked and broken them.

In the Beginning is the Bellow, and the Bellow is with Me, and the Bellow is Me. Lightning erupts from my tattoo, fusing sundered timelines.

Nick McKenzie is no more, and neither are his nanobots. Creating a new reality consumes its Creators.

CHAPTER NINE

Charli: Awakened

XP tracks merged. You are level 24 Guide, level 15 Wizard, and 25% of the way to level 25. You have gained the Hide Party skill, currently at level 3, and the Desert Teleport skill, now at level 1. You have earned 2 attribute points and 1 trait point. You currently reside in the territory named Spire of Desire.

Ugh. I ache all over. Am I back in Khertaan? It seems so.

Thud.

What was that?

I'm jostled about, my body slung in a chain net on the side of a large metal sphere. A boulder groans as one is removed from a pile of many. The removed one is tossed aside, causing another thud as it lands on the floor of a dimly lit cavern.

Crash.

"Keep going, Spyder." The voice belongs to Kylie the Angel, speaking over party chat. "There can't be an infinite number of boulders. I'm so far negative on my HP, it might take me forever to heal, but spending time healing will be better than spending eternity crushed between these rocks."

"Kylie?" I can't believe I'm hearing her voice again. I'm truly back in Khertaan.

"*Charli?* Oh, Goddess, is that you?" Kylie's voice quavers. "I thought you'd never wake up. Do you know where Morrow and Slithy are? I would have thought they'd have respawned by now."

"I thought Morrow would be back when I came back." The chains press into my flesh. "Why am I hanging in a metal net?"

"Morrow?" Kylie's voice is eager, hopeful. "Are you there?"

There's no reply.

I squirm in my chains. "Kylie, can you free me from this net? It's really uncomfortable here. Who's Spyder?"

"I invited her." There's a hint of pride in Kylie's voice. "She's been a great help to me in the absence of everyone else. Without her, you and I would have died. Your body, that is."

"Glad to make your acquaintance, Charli." Reminiscent of metal sliding on metal, Spyder's voice comes from nearby. "I'm glad to finally put a voice to the body I've been carrying. I can free you from your sling, but please promise not to be afraid when you discover what I am."

"I promise." Anything to get myself out of this net.

The chain sling lowers. One side of it comes lose and unrolls, dumping me onto hard ground. With more bruises to my ego than my flesh, I sit up.

I'm in a domed cavern, its ceiling nearly as high as the sky. The far side is open to the outside, admitting full sunlight. A road comes up to the opening, as though carriages were meant to be driven inside. From the cavern, the road leads to a city. Many high structures—some of white stone and others of red—tower over a multitude of one-story buildings, some made of brick and some of wood.

Something twice the height of those one-story buildings stands tall inside the cavern on my periphery. Cranking my neck, I see it, and despite my having an extraordinary Temperance score, I nearly faint. Invoking my Hide skill, I roll away, anticipating an attack.

But no attack is forthcoming from the Arachnid Behemoth. It draws up its webbing—the chain net I rolled out of. "I mean you no harm, Charli. I am Spyder, an Arachnid Behemoth, as you can see. Kylie invited me to party TimeTrippers, and I've been traveling with her since, carrying your unconscious body and protecting it from Pteranodons and Harpies. I hope we will be friends. I've already become quite attached to you, to the extent of my ability to feel emotion, which admittedly is sub-human level."

I can scarcely believe it. How is it possible for a Behemoth to have accepted an invite to our party, much less receive it? There's only one possible answer. "You reprogrammed a Behemoth, Kylie? That's incredible."

"I've got ODYSSEY nanobots in me." Kylie sounds happy for the recognition. "They did all the work, of course. But, yeah, it was my idea. I'd hoped they could reprogram this cavern, too, but no such luck. I'm buried in the cave-in, under a ton of rock. You'll never guess what my HP score is."

"One?"

"Try negative seven thousand."

"How are you even alive, Kylie? That's insane."

"It's my level 4 Pain Tolerant trait at work. I apparently can't die from physical wounds." Kylie doesn't sound so proud, but exasperated. "I don't know how I'm getting out of here. I don't suppose you have any ideas."

"I might. But I'm really concerned why Morrow isn't here."

"I'm sure you know better than I why my love hasn't returned to me, Charli."

Kylie's words cut me deep. In this timeline and this world, Kylie and Morrow are husband and wife. Their players, Nick and Kendra, are also married. Susie—Slithy's player—is Nick and Kendra's daughter. This isn't the same timeline where Nick and I were married and I became pregnant with his child.

I gave birth before I returned to Khertaan. What became of my baby? Does she not exist in this timeline? That's a heartrending thought.

Britta. That's her name. It comes unbidden to my mind, uttered by a voice belonging and yet not belonging to me.

The cavern trembles as a scream of yearning and desire pierces me to the core. "What was that?"

"It must have come from outside," Spyder says. "Or perhaps it came from the Boss for this territory. It was a cry befitting a resident of the Spire of Desire."

"I need to get out of here," says Kylie. "If the Boss is coming, I need to be up there with you two...."

Her last words fade out as darkness swallows me.

CHAPTER TEN

Greelia: Losing Britta

Thunder roars and lightning flashes, accenting the movements of a circle of women writhing to a disco instrumental. At the center of the circle stands a hooded figure. Outside the circle, Nick lies sprawled on the floor, and I stand with legs spread over his head, grasping Britta by the scalp in one hand and my stolen axe in the other. My baby girl wails like a banshee, letting me know she's alive.

Lightning flashes again, and Nick kneels before me, facing the enemy. Except, he's different now. His hair—green as my skin— stands straight and tall. A yellow sigil glows on the back of his right hand. Bolts of lightning spring from the sigil, striking the ceiling.

The man-who-is-Nick-but-isn't holds a staff in his left hand, pointing it at the hooded man and the dancing ladies. "Begone, vile one." Lightning erupts from the tip of his staff, streaking between two dancers to crash on the hooded one. With a wail, he's gone. Their screams cut short, the dancers erupt into sprays of pixels fluttering to the floor.

As yet unwashed after being born, my baby goes quiet, a sign she hungers, and I press her bloody face against my exposed right breast. She bites my nipple, to flavor the milk not only with her blood but mine too.

The Lightning Wizard rises to his feet and turns to face me, the sigil on his hand pulsing yellow but no longer shooting bolts. He stares at me in confusion. "Greelia?"

"That's me. Meet our baby girl… Britta." It sounds wrong somehow to refer to Britta as *our* baby girl, but this man is the father and I am the mother, even if the sex resulting in the conception was between two other versions of us, Nick and Charli. I don't confess to understand the logic of it, but the knowledge resides with my spirit. "Should I call you *Nick* or *Lightning Wizard*?"

He blows out a breath. "I'm Morrow, Punk Lightning Wizard, at your service." He glances around. "I'm not where I expected to be. This doesn't look like Khertaan."

"I never knew the name of my homeland." I glance at the bloody, suckling baby in my arms.

"Is this the correct timeline?" Morrow surveys the room. "It most assuredly is not the correct place. I should be in Khertaan." His gaze settles on me. "You're an avatar, too… not from Khertaan, but from a nameless Tunnels and Troglodytes campaign world." He's clearly thinking aloud. "Neither of us are in the world to which we belong. Is this Earth? Then why isn't Nick here instead of me?" He pauses. "I'm unable to sense him inside me. It's like he doesn't even exist." He looks me up and down. "This child of yours… she's some kind of Earth/Khertaan/T&T hybrid?" He glances around again. "*Where the hell are Nick and Charli?*"

I chuckle at that. "The better question for me is *what do we do now?*"

He puts a finger to his chin. "Maybe both our questions are related. Let's focus on our players and see if we can look through their eyes to see where they are. Try it with me."

"I can do that." I don't like this feeling of disconnection from my player either. Closing my eyes, I turn my thoughts inward, searching my inner being for the connection I know I have with Charli.

An unfamiliar, artificial voice speaks. "We have a visitor. Identify yourself, green-skinned woman." In my head, the name *Spyder* appears, identifying the speaker.

"Charli, *where did you go?*" Another unfamiliar voice speaks—a female to whom my avatar brain assigns the name *Kylie*. Her voice trembles. "Who is *Greelia*?"

I open my eyes. One of those metallic Arachnid Behemoths looms over me, the sharp tip of a raised leg pointing at me. If it meant to kill me, I'd already have been skewered. A domed cavern ceiling arcs above the Behemoth. Light filters in through a cavern opening. A pile of rocks lie in shadow at the rear of the cavern, where a tunnel has collapsed.

I have no idea where I am, but Morrow isn't here. My bloody baby Goblin girl is still cradled in my left arm, sucking on my exposed green right teat. I bow my head over her, my green hair brushing her cheek. "Drink your fill, Britta." I raise my head to glare at the Behemoth. "*I* am Greelia, Goblin Warrior." With my right hand, I brandish my axe. "Be you friend or foe, I am not afraid of you, Spyder. I've killed one of your kind once and can do so again."

The Behemoth moves closer, keeping the one leg pointed at my head. "What have you done with Charli?"

I stand my ground. I'm not afraid. Britta continues to suckle. "I…." A tear runs down my cheek.

Impossible. Goblin Warriors do not cry. I clench my eyes shut.

The weight of Britta lifts from my left arm. Opening my eyes, I find her gone, my breasts clothed as though she was never at my teat. "*Britta, my little Goblin girl*….." I spin around, looking high and low for the baby thief, ready to accuse Spyder, but the Behemoth isn't there. It's only me and Morrow the Punk

Lightning Wizard. I'm back in the contemporary world, missing one baby girl.

In this moment, I am not a Goblin Warrior, but a Goblin Mother who has lost her child. I cry my rage at the world, shaking my axe at the ceiling. With no one else here for me to vent my rage upon, it's all I can do to stay my hand and not strike down the Punk Wizard.

CHAPTER ELEVEN

Lady Ghost: Wanting Him

A light flashes, emanating instantaneously from the shard I've touched. A primal roar thrills me, its origin none other than my Nick. I go to him.

He stands facing a young green-skinned woman who suckles a bloody baby and wields an axe. He wears skin-tight black leather armor and a green mohawk, and wields a wooden staff. A lightning bolt symbol on the back of his right hand pulses with magical yellow light. He appears confused as he stares at the green lady. "Greelia?"

The green lady nods. "That's me. Meet our baby girl… Britta."

A pang of jealousy jars my ghostly presence. If anyone is to have a baby with Nick, it should be me. I'm his true love, the one he summons when he's alone. Even though he's in the company of Greelia and Britta, he's suffering from loneliness now. Why else would all my thousands of presences have been drawn together—*here*?

Greelia points her chin at my love. "Should I call you *Nick* or *Lightning Wizard*?"

He blows out a breath. "I'm Morrow, Punk Lightning Wizard, at your service." He glances around, and I flit upward so he won't see me.

How can this man not be Nick? I'd recognize him anywhere, not through sight alone, but by the spiritual bond between us. Admittedly, the connection between me and this man who calls himself Morrow isn't as strong as I expect it to be with Nick. I understand there are multiple versions of Nick in the multiverse, but I've always been drawn to the *real one*—the one with true awareness, not some sad loser running through life on autopilot.

This Morrow fellow doesn't seem to be on autopilot. He's clearly a thinking person. So he's got to be my Nick. Doesn't he? If he's right about not being Nick, does that mean I can no longer detect my love? That kills me.

The two of them focus on their connections to Charli and Nick in an effort to locate them. Yes, Morrow, please find Nick, because all I can find is you. I don't want you—I want my Nick.

What just happened?

Where Greelia stood an instant before now stands a young woman with softer features, pink flesh, and blond hair instead of green. The axe Greelia had held is gone, replaced by a wooden staff not unlike the one Morrow holds. She wears a wide-brimmed hat, giving her the look of a Cowgirl. The child has vanished. The Cowgirl opens her eyes. "My baby…."

"Charli?" Morrow chokes on the word.

"Morrow?" The Cowgirl chokes on her reply.

If Greelia could trade places with Charli, perhaps Morrow can trade places with Nick. He needs to try harder.

I want to be with Nick so badly, it's driving me out of my mind.

And then Charli is gone and Greelia is back, wielding her axe instead of the wooden staff. Green hair hangs in her eyes. Her blouse is closed over her breasts. Her green arms, in a cradling pose, are empty. *"Britta, my little Goblin girl….."* She spins around, looking high and low for her baby. It's all I can do to prevent her from seeing me and to stay out of Morrow's sight, too.

Greelia lifts her axe, brandishing it as though ready to attack Morrow. She doesn't, but shouts her rage, her eyes darting about as though looking for someone to attack. I can't let her spot me.

Where is my Nick? I want to scream at Morrow to try harder.

CHAPTER TWELVE

Charli: Brief Visit

Shadows and dim light replace the darkness, granting me sight of my new surroundings. I'm no longer in a cavern, but a contemporary room with couch, table, and chairs. A familiar face looms over me.

"Charli?" Morrow chokes on the word.

"Morrow?" I likewise choke on my reply.

He laughs. "It worked. Greelia did it. I didn't expect her to draw you here, only to contact you, but it's great to have you here. Did she trade places with you?" He strokes my cheek where a tear might have been.

I draw away, longing for Nick's touch, not Morrow's. "I'm so confused. I was just with Kylie and Spyder. I don't know what happened to my baby. I gave birth, was dragged into Khertaan without her, and now I'm here, wherever here is." I struggle not to cry.

He cocks a brow. "You've gone back to Khertaan?"

"I was just there."

"How is Kylie?"

"Trapped in a cave-in, at negative seven thousand percent HP. She can't die because of a maxed-out trait. We were discussing how to free her when I was whisked away to here. Was that Greelia's doing?"

"I believe so." He briefly claps a hand over his forehead. "I asked her to focus on her connection to you. She and Britta disappeared, and you appeared in their place."

"Goddess, this is so messed up." I ache for my child, to hold her in my arms. I can scarcely hold back the tears. "Does this mean Nick is in Khertaan? Did you switch places with him?"

Morrow sighs. "I wish I knew where Nick is."

A tear wells in my eye and I blink it away as I drop my head, my blond locks swaying on either side of my face under a wide-brimmed hat, reminding me of who I am. I'm Charli, not Greelia.

But for a second, I felt like someone else. I'm truly confused.

My blouse lies open in front, exposing the pink flesh of my breast. I cradle my baby in my left arm as she sucks a pained nipple. But the pain is nothing compared to the maternal joy swelling inside me. Tears stream onto Britta's naked, bloody green body. I don't know why her skin is *green*, but it doesn't matter. I *know* she's my daughter.

Kylie speaks instead of Morrow. "What's going on out there?"

I'm back in the cavern in Khertaan, but now I'm holding my baby girl. Whatever you did, Greelia, thank you.

CHAPTER THIRTEEN

Kylie: Under the Rubble

My HP has fallen to -8460% but is now holding steady. I can't feel anything. My whole body is numb, with my nervous system completely shut down.

The rocks are no longer falling. From the sound of it, Spyder is no longer moving rocks away. Damn, I wish I was out of this mess. How am I getting out of here? It seems every time Spyder removes a rock, a ton more fall on top of those already stacked on me. There's got to be a limit on the number of rocks in this place, doesn't there?

Who am I kidding? This isn't Earth. It's a game world my player helped program. Numbers can keep ticking upward to the extent of the machine's precision, and the machine can always start a second counter after that. There's no way Spyder will ever clear out the rock pile above me.

But as worrisome as my predicament is, I've got another issue needing attention. Someone named Greelia is on the party roster for TimeTrippers, and Charli isn't. "What's going on out there?"

But no sooner have I asked the question than Charli's name replaces Greelia's, restoring the party roster to normal.

"I do not understand this," Spyder says. "Charli, what happened to you? A green-skinned woman was here in your place for a moment. Now she's gone and you have a green-skinned baby in your arms. Please explain."

"Her name is Britta." The Cowgirl sobs. "I thought I'd lost her."

"That is not an explanation."

"I didn't know you had a baby, Charli." But how am I not surprised? "Perhaps if you could get me out of here, I could take a look at her."

Suppressed laughter bursts from Charli's lungs. "I'm sorry, Kylie, I'm not laughing at you. I'm just so happy to have my baby girl back. I don't know why her skin is green, though it must have to do with Greelia, my Goblin avatar in T&T. She's not a threat. If she shows up here again, please don't kill her. I think she's like an alternate version of me. If she were to die here, I'm not sure what that would mean for me."

"She threatened me and claimed she's killed one of my kind before," Spyder says. "If she attacks me, I will defend myself."

"Yes, well," says Charli, "Greelia can be a bit of a braggart, though she did in fact kill an Arachnid Behemoth in her world... with help. Just make sure she realizes you're a friend, and she won't attack you, I'm sure. I think right now she's with Morrow... on Earth or some place like it."

"*With Morrow?*" That's got my interest. "Did you see him? What do you mean, *on Earth?* How is that possible?" Could he have shown up in the computer lab in Nick and Kendra's house like Charli did before? "Is he coming here?"

"I don't know, Kylie. He wants to, but there's a question as to where he really is and where Nick is. Greelia traded places with me temporarily, and Morrow tried to do the same thing with Nick, but it didn't work. Morrow has no idea where Nick is, and sadly neither do I."

"Is there a way we can help my husband get back here?" I'm desperate for Morrow's return. He'd have an idea for getting me free of this rubble.

"I don't know how Greelia made the swap happen for me and her, and Morrow didn't know, either. I'm sorry, Kylie. I'm sure you miss him. I wish I could bring him here for you, but I can't."

"Damn." My Temperance score is 14, but it's stretching thin with everything that's happening. "I wish you could, too, Charli. I do miss him, and I hope he finds a way to join us. But he's not here, and you are. I really need your help. I don't know what all you can do, but if you have any way to extract me from beneath these rocks, could you please? I'm a pulverized mass of flesh, blood, and broken bones down here, unable to die and unable to heal. I can't switch to Spirit Form without going berserk, which would only make my situation magnitudes worse."

"Let me think." Charli pauses, and no one else speaks until she does again. "Tell me why you'd go berserk if you switched to Spirit Form."

I'm happy to explain if it will help get me out of here. "I'm straddling a barrier that exists in the spiritual realm but not the physical. If I take Spirit Form, the barrier will split me in halves, rendering my SP to zero. That would expel me from the spirit realm back to the physical realm, where my physical form would go berserk due to lack of spiritual control.

"And that's not the worst of it. Because I can't die from physical damage due to my maxed-out Pain Tolerant trait, if I go berserk, I'll be mindlessly flailing useless limbs for eternity.

"But I can't *go* anywhere because of these damned boulders. They're too tight together to allow me to fly out, even though my body is more jelly than solid.

"So, do you think you can help me? Please say *yes*."

"There are things we can try."

Charli's words give me hope, and if my heart were whole, it would be racing. "Then let's try one."

"Let me find a good sitting position. Spyder, please keep an eye on me and Britta. I'm going to transfer my awareness to Kylie, so I won't be aware of what's happening here." Charli falls silent for a moment. "Okay, Kylie, let me into your head."

"Whatever it takes." I've yet to do an awareness transfer and don't know what to expect, but bring it on.

"Oh, my, how horrid." The words belong to Charli, but form as though integral to my personal thought stream. "How long have you been like this?"

"It seems forever. Can you help me?"

Her mind is not fully exposed to me, nor mine to her, but the metaphysical membrane separating us is sheer and translucent. If we both allowed it, we could read each other's minds, delve deep into each other's secrets. I'd love to know hers, but not this way and not now. Getting free of these boulders is the pressing concern.

"I'm transferring all my traits and skills to you, Kylie. Accept them all, and we'll see if any of them can get you out."

My eyeballs are squashed to bits between boulders, so I've only been viewing the world with my Third Person POV, and even then, all I've been seeing is my support AI, Georgie, surrounded by impenetrable darkness. Now a wall of text appears, a list of skills and traits belonging to Charli. I accept all of them.

"I've never tried it in this type of circumstance." The thought originates from Charli. "So I can't guarantee it will work to extract you. But I'm thinking my Shadow Passage skill might allow you to maneuver between the boulders. It's worth a try."

"What exactly does the Shadow Passage skill do?"

"It transforms you into a shadowy figure that can move quickly among the shadows. Since you're in total darkness, that qualifies. I'm hoping once you invoke the skill, it will enable you to move in the air spaces between the boulders and find your way out."

I'm not given to spontaneity, and need to know more. "When I'm transformed to this shadowy figure, will I still be in the physical realm, or does the transformation place me in some other realm?" If I stay in the physical realm, it might just work. If I'm moved into another realm, I could easily find myself severed into halves by a barrier in that realm.

"I'm not sure." Charli shrugs in my mind's eye. "I don't have full information on it, but I'm guessing there's a shadow realm lying next to the other realms, and that's where you'll be."

I call for Georgie. "Can you confirm any of Charli's hunches as being true?"

The support AI squeezes his red ball of a nose, honking it. "I've just received new info on the skill, since you now have access to it. I'll put it up as text, so both you and Charli can see it, in case she's missing anything."

Skill: Shadow Passage, **Level:** 10
Description: May only be used while in the physical realm. May be used to transport up to three connected characters per skill level. Transforms the bodies of affected characters into Shadow Form. The volume and shape of transformed bodies don't change from what they were before the transformation, and no special attack modes are granted to the transformed characters.

Non-Shadow objects or areas that present as obstacles to one's original body still behave as obstacles to one's transformed body. Shadow objects or areas do not present as obstacles to the transformed body, provided the objects or areas are non-magical or are of a level of magic not greater than the level of the skill.

When transformed, the character is able to travel on, in, and through passable areas of Shadow at a speed of X feet per second, where X is the level of the skill. Speed is increased by a factor of ten in areas through which the character has previously traveled. The Shadow Passage skill stacks with the Flight Speed skill when traveling through passable areas of Shadow.

If the character also has the Increased Movement trait, the character can teleport from one place to another, provided a continuous path through passable areas of Shadow connects the origin and destination, and provided also that the character has previously been to the destination and can form a mental picture of it. The entirety of the chosen path must lie within Z miles of the origin, where Z equals Y squared times X, with Y being the level of the Increased Movement trait and X being the level of the Shadow Passage skill.

"Interesting," says Charli. "There's no mention in this readout of a shadow realm. I could have sworn I was leaving the physical realm when I used the skill, but I see I was wrong. I thought I was safe from physical attacks when I used the skill, but it sounds like that was wrong thinking too. Yikes. I'll have to stow that tidbit of info away for safekeeping. So, after reading that, I'm not sure how it will help your situation. The boulders will still represent the same obstacles to you in Shadow Form as they do currently."

"I agree." I try to sense my feet, but they're numb beyond feeling. "I wouldn't be able to free my feet from the boulder they're infused with even if I were in Shadow Form. I am, however, interested in this bit about teleporting."

Charli perks up at the idea. "Do you have the Increased Movement trait?"

"I do." I bring up my own character sheet as much to verify it for myself as to show her. "I have the trait at level one. So, if I'm understanding correctly, your skill and my trait are enough to allow me to teleport up to ten miles away to a place of shadow I've visited before and can remember."

"As long as the destination is connected to you by a path through shadow," Charli adds. "Sounds like we can maybe get you out of your mess after all, as long as we can find the right destination spot. Did you spend any time in this cavern, where

Spyder and I are now? The whole back portion of the cavern is in shadow."

I can't reliably call to mind a mental picture of the cavern area. "Spyder, can you move into the shadows, please? I can clearly picture your back, so I'll teleport onto you. Let me know when you're ready."

Metal scratches rock as the Behemoth repositions herself. "Ready."

"Here goes nothing." I focus on my Increased Movement trait and the borrowed Shadow Passage skill. I've spent plenty of time recently on Spyder's back, so my mental picture of it is a strong one.

An unfamiliar sensation comes over me, like I'm enveloped by a fine, dry mist.

Third Person POV shows me Spyder at the rear of the cavern. Boulders are strewn across the floor and piled in the mouth of the entry tunnel. An intensely black blob lies atop Spyder's back, and that black blob is me. I'm still in Shadow Form. I'm afraid to switch back. My body is pulp, and I don't want to see it in this condition.

Charli's limp body reclines against the cavern wall to Spyder's left. A green-skinned baby snuggles against the Cowgirl's exposed breast. It appears to be sleeping, not suckling.

"Aw, my little Britta," says Charli in my head.

I want to ask how she came to have a child, but I know I won't like the answer. I also don't like having Charli in my head like this. Chatting in a way that feels like telepathy is one thing. This transferal of her awareness into my head is too intrusive. "Do you want to return to your body, Charli, so you can better bond with your little green girl?"

"Only if you're ready for me to go, Kylie. You'll lose Shadow Form, but if that's all right with you...."

Her mind leaves mine, taking her skills and traits with her. My body returns to the physical realm. And, yes, like Charli mentioned earlier, I'm horrid. A bloody mass of ripped flesh and splintered bones, with my feet intact but nothing else recognizable.

I switch to Spirit Form. Oh, this is better. Here in the spiritual realm, I look like my Angel self. "Georgie, what are my hit point percentages?"

My clown friend frowns hugely. "Other than HP, they're all at 100%. Your HP is at -8460%. If you sleep, you'll heal at 4% per day, which means it will take no less than 2140 days, or just under six years, for you to fully heal without assistance, and that's assuming you sleep the entire time. I don't know how much healing must take place for your physical body to pull itself together enough for you to walk or fly or wield a weapon.

"If you had the Wakeful trait at level four, that would divide your healing time by a factor of sixteen, reducing the required sleeping time to less than four and a half months."

This is not sounding good for me. I'd sooner just die and then respawn at full HP.

Georgie isn't finished. "If you had the Accelerated Healing trait at level four, you could heal your lost HP at a rate of 24% per hour, or 576% per day. That's in addition to any other healing. So the trait alone would heal your HP to full in just under fifteen days. If you combined the Wakeful trait level four with the Accelerated Healing trait level four, you could heal at a total rate of 640% per day, which would bring you to full HP in just over thirteen days.

"You can travel in Spirit Form, but such activity could decrease your healing rate…. It could help if you could avail yourself of healing magic. Magic from a healer of about your character level would heal you at roughly one percent per point of Auni expended, but since you have Auni Resistance at level 20, that reduces the effectiveness on you of magical healing. Someone would have to spend twenty Auni just to get past your resistance, and then spend more Auni beyond that to have any effect on you."

I'm basically screwed when it comes to doing anything physical in the near future. "Well, ladies," I say over party chat, "it appears I'll be traveling with you in Spirit Form for the foreseeable future. You won't see me, but I'll see you. I'll keep you informed of my whereabouts and activities over party chat as necessary. Our first order of business is to find a way out of this cavern, which I believe requires us to defeat the Boss monster for the Spire of Desire. Any suggestions on how we force it to come to us?"

Charli climbs to her feet, cradling her sleeping kid. "Before we get to that, I need a safe place to stash my baby."

Across the domed cavern ceiling, a dozen holes open. Tentacles drop through the holes, each long enough to reach anywhere in the cavern.

Georgie grimaces. "Head's up, pumpkin. Those tentacles belong to a Mental Dominator, the Boss monster for the Spire."

CHAPTER FOURTEEN

Fauna: The Author

Tears roll down Emma's cheeks as the echoes of the baby's scream fade. "I couldn't save her. What happened with her baby? Where did that lightning come from?"

I stretch my arms before me. Across them lies a shadowy three-dimensional figure, insubstantial as mist. "The lightning came from her birthmark, I swear it. I don't know what became of her, but she left her shadow behind. I don't know what to make of it."

Emma touches the shadowy form, but it gives no resistance to her finger. "How are you able to hold it? My hand passes right through it."

"I don't know, but I'm afraid to let it go. I don't think the baby is dead, and I don't think it's complete. We have to find the baby and reunite her with her shadow."

"What about Charli? Is she dead?"

"I don't think so." I blink back a tear, hoping beyond hope I'm right. "The baby and Charli are together, I can feel it. Find one, we find the other."

Renewed energy lights Emma's eyes. "Oh, I hope you're right. Assuming you are, how do we find them?"

A door opens in another room. Footsteps grow near.

Emma and I freeze.

Ulric enters the room and stops, his expression one of surprise. "I must be dreaming."

I shake my head.

Crossing the room, Ulric squints at us. "Did Nick put you up to this? Your outfits are awesome." He points at my hooves. "Nice touch. Where's Nick? What happened with Charli?"

"Um...." Emma wipes a tear. "We don't know where either of them are. We really need to find them. Especially Charli."

"I'd like to know where Ronnie is, too." I'm lost without him.

"What are you holding?" Ulric peers at the shadowy figure in my arms. The young man reminds me of Ronnie, but he smells cleaner than the Rogue. He tries to touch the shadow, and his hand passes through it like Emma's did. "It looks like dirty smoke, but shaped like a baby. How do you do that?"

There's nothing to be gained by lying. "She's shaped like a baby because she *is* a baby. Charli's baby girl, though not exactly. Charli disappeared and her baby right after, but they left this shadow baby girl behind. I know it sounds crazy, but I swear it's the truth."

"It is." Emma wipes away more tears. "You have to believe us. Now we don't know what to do. But we both feel this shadow needs to rejoin its body."

"You're both serious." Ulric sets his jaw, gives us each a prolonged look, and then nods. "Okay. Let's search the house for clues."

With no other plan, Emma and I do as Ulric suggests. We find no one else home. We do find Nick's Tunnels & Troglodytes rulebook with some pencils, dice, and sheets of paper.

Ulric picks up one of the sheets, peruses it, and hands it to Emma. "This is your character sheet." She takes it. He picks up another one and offers it to me. "This one is yours."

"Can you hold it up for me to read? I don't want to risk dropping Spooky."

Emma looks up from her sheet. "Spooky?"

"That's what I'm calling this shadow baby until she's back with her body."

"I like it."

Ulric grasps the top of my character sheet with one hand and suspends it before my face.

Name: Fauna.75 (Fauna)
Player Name: Nick
Basic Info:
Level 10 Rogue
Female Faun (Faun father, Human mother)
Age: 18
Height: 5'1", Weight: 120 lbs
Stats:
Strength: 17
Intelligence: 26
Luck: 61
Constitution: 23
Dexterity: 24
Charisma: 19
Speed: 37
Auni: 44
Adds: 66, Missile Adds: 78
Languages: Common, Caprine
Gold: 0
Weapons: Hooves, 2d6+2
Armor: Fur, 4 Hits Taken
Spells:
  Sense Magical Vibes
  Lock
  Unlock

Light
See Hidden
Treasure: Shadow Baby Girl (Spooky)
Specials:
Unaffected by fire-based effects, but afraid of fire
Able to see in the dark

When I'm finished, Ulric looks it over, too. He nods, the corners of his mouth turned down. "You're an experienced adventurer with a mix of melee and magical capabilities. Your stats are all decent for your level and class, though your Speed and Auni are higher than I'd have guessed for a level 10 Rogue. You can talk the Common language and a language called Caprine, which I don't know anything about. You can attack with your hooves, and the fur on your legs acts like armor, even if it's not much. This is interesting… Spooky is listed as treasure. And… this is funny… you're unaffected by fire, but you're afraid of it." He chuckles. "You can also see in the dark."

"What idiot isn't afraid of fire?" I seriously didn't know I was supposedly unaffected by it. "Can we see your sheet, Emma?" I crane my neck.

She holds her character sheet up for me to see.

Name: Emma the Mystical
Player Name: Nick
Basic Info:
Level 10 Warrior-Wizard
Female Elf
Age: 19
Height: 6'0", Weight: 160 lbs
Stats:
Strength: 20
Intelligence: 42

Luck: 87
Constitution: 22
Dexterity: 31
Charisma: 48
Speed: 15
Auni: 35
Adds: 102, Missile Adds: 121
Languages: Common, Elven, Trollish, Caprine
Gold: 0
Weapons: Wizard's Staff, 2d6
Armor: Leather, 6+1 Hits Taken
Spells:
  All first level
  Dark Sight
  Heal
Treasure: None
Specials:
  Unaffected by flesh-to-stone effects

"That's interesting," I say in the Caprine language, sounding like a bleating goat.

Ulric looks at me like I'm off my rocker. "Huh?"

"Wow, I understood you." Emma replies in Caprine. "That's funny. We have a secret language."

Ulric looks at Emma. "Let me see your character sheet." He tugs on it until she lets it go. "You two are speaking *Caprine*? What's that, goat language?"

"Yaa." I laugh.

"Well, if you're not speaking my language, I'm not hanging around." Ulric hands the sheet back to Emma and heads for the door.

"We'll be good." With a lunge, Emma catches his wrist. "Please. We need your help."

He turns back to her. "Where is Nick? The truth."

I have a bad feeling about all this. "When did you last see him, Ulric?"

His eyes briefly gloss over. "I can't remember…."

Emma lifts her chin, like she has figured something out. "What's the last thing you remember before you saw us?"

Ulric picks up the T&T rulebook. "Charli was running a game for me and Nick…."

The Mystical Elf slides three dice in front of the teen. "What's your Intelligence score, Ulric?"

"I wouldn't know."

Emma points at the three dice. "Let's find out. The dice know. Roll them."

As though in a trance, he takes the three dice in hand and shakes them. He rolls, and the pips come up six, six, one, for a total of thirteen.

"Okay, then." Emma slides one of the dice aside and points at the remaining two. "Roll a level two saving roll on your Intelligence. You need twelve or better. Doubles add and roll over."

He rolls the two remaining dice, and the pips show five and six.

Eleven… one point shy.

"I can't remember exactly." Ulric's gaze moves to something far away. "I met Ronnie. I shook his hand. You two were there. Lightning flashed…. I can't remember anything after that until I saw you two…. No, wait…. There was a woman with an axe…. No, a man in a hooded cloak. Nick was on the floor…. Ronnie was there. The woman threw the axe. Or did the hooded man throw it? I can't remember. I caught the axe… no, Ronnie caught it. There were symbols floating in the air… letters and numbers… and rain coming down, but not on me." He lays down the T&T rulebook and points at something on the cover. "I saw this name in the falling text."

Emma and I lean in to see where Ulric is pointing. His finger rests on the author's name.

"Are you sure?" My voice shakes. My insides turn to jelly. The author's name has power over me.

Emma the Mystical meets my gaze. "We have to find this Ken St. Andre. He'll know how to help us."

We both turn to Ulric.

He holds up his hands, palms out. "I wouldn't know where to begin."

We both keep looking at him, saying nothing.

The teenager's shoulders slump. "Okay. I'll help you. We'll find him."

Ulric has a heart of gold. I love him to death. Same as I love Ronnie.

CHAPTER FIFTEEN

Ronnie: Motorcycles

The wall of green energy, I deduce, marks the boundary of our protected space. As long as Mel and I don't pass through it, we won't be harmed. Without weapons with which to fight or mushrooms with which to charm, we're vulnerable if we enter the ruined portion of the building.

I kneel by the wall. On the other side lies the corpse of the man we'd talked to just a moment ago, before the Arachnid Behemoth ran him through. Unsure what to do, I lay a palm against the wall. It's solid though translucent to the point of being transparent, except for the green hue it lends to everything on the other side, like green glass.

Is there anything I can do here? I call up my character sheet.

Name: Ronnie
Player Name: Ulric
Basic Info:
Level 10 Rogue

Male Human
Age: 16
Height: 5'10", Weight: 170 lbs.
Stats:
Strength: 20
Intelligence: 21
Luck: 147
Constitution: 33
Dexterity: 23
Charisma: 15
Speed: 21
Auni: 15
Adds: 154, Missile Adds: 165
Languages: Common
Gold: 0
Weapons: None
Armor: None
Spells: None
Treasure: None
Specials: None

Wow. I'm already level 10. Defeating that Arachnid Behemoth on my home world earned me a ton of XP. My attributes have increased too. My Luck of 147 is way higher than I'd ever have expected. A bit of quick math… I'll always make any Luck saving roll at level twenty-seven or lower, provided I don't get an automatic failure… a roll of one and two or of one and three.

Could my Luck allow me to move through the barrier? I press with all my Strength as I call for a Luck saving roll.

Two red dice measuring somewhere around a foot-and-a-half per side tumble out of the air onto the floor beside me. When they stop spinning, one die shows a three and the other shows a five, enough for a level twenty-eight saving roll.

The dice disappear as the barrier transforms from solid to gelatin under my hand. I reach my arm through past the elbow, to lay my hand on the corpse's face. The flesh is already chill. The blood has drained out of him. I withdraw my hand and stand up with a shake of my head.

Mel looks almost as pale as the corpse's cold cheeks. "I can't believe my mother is behind all this cruelty. This is evil."

I test the barrier again, pushing against it with an open palm. It's solid. I don't call for a saving roll, but push with all my Strength. The barrier doesn't budge or give, and I step back. "If we stay on this side of this green wall, I don't think anything else will get through to us. But if we want to go through, I think we can. As the saying goes where I'm from, it's better to be lucky than good, and my Luck score is really high."

"My mother has made her point." Mel steps close to the barrier, testing it with a poke of his finger and failing to push through. "Let's stay here until she brings us back to her. Then I'll see if I can talk some sense into her, though I don't have high hopes."

"We still have the better part of an hour to wait."

In the distance beyond the ruined walls strides a Behemoth, occasionally stabbing straggler humans.

Mel and I watch in silence as the Behemoth continues its killing mission, soon joined by another Behemoth. Minutes drag by....

A deafening scream rends the air. The floor trembles beneath my feet, and the walls vibrate. The corpses beyond the barrier fade from sight, as though they were never there. The building rubble vanishes, too.

Where the rubble had been, a large room takes shape, throughout which are scattered couches and chairs occupied by seated, living people, the majority in tunics and breeches but some in skirts. Other living people walk by in light-colored robes. No one enters our protected space or looks our way. Judging by their movements, some of the people are speaking, but neither their words or their footfalls reach my ears. None of them seem real. There's an ethereal quality to the whole scene, like everything and everyone would vanish if I blink.

Mel takes a step back. "What the hell? Are you seeing this, Ronnie?"

"I *am* seeing it. It's like they're ghosts."

"I meant… *me*."

Oh. I can almost see through him. He's as ghostly as the figures beyond the wall. I look down at myself. I'm still substantial, as is the hallway here inside our protected area. "I don't understand, Mel. Why are all of you ghosts, but I'm not?"

"It was that scream." Mel effortlessly reaches a hand through the translucent green barrier and then draws it back. "It's like I don't belong in this world anymore. I should have disappeared, just like that corpse, but something is keeping me here." He points at the people in the room beyond the barrier. "Whatever is keeping me in this world is keeping them here, too. They should all be dead. That room should be in ruins. But that scream… it's like it reshaped history, and in this new version of history, I was never born, and the giant metal spiders never attacked. That's good about the spiders, but it's not so good about me." His eyes take on a faraway look. "That would be a tough choice, wouldn't it? *Would you rather never have been born, or have the world overrun by giant metal spiders? Is that my choice to make now?"*

I don't understand what he's on about, and say nothing.

A ball of fire blasts a hole in the far wall of the large room. The green barrier blocks any sound made by the explosion. Through a billowing cloud of smoke comes a wheeled metal ox. Holding onto its horns, an Orc Wizard sits astride it, his cape flowing in the wind behind him. He and his mount are no more ghosts than I am. His gaze locks with mine as his mount comes to a halt. He sneers as he draws back his hand, a fiery sphere growing in his palm to the size of a melon. He throws the fireball… at me.

I leap to avoid the flaming missile, and attempt to tackle Mel, to keep him from getting hit as well. My body passes through that of my companion, and I slam against the wall.

The fireball hits the green barrier and splatters across it before dissipating. All the ghostly people flee the area, their eyes wild and their mouths gaping as though screaming. I still hear no sound from that side of the barrier.

His face contorted with frustration, the Orc Wizard urges his wheeled metal ox forward. Smoke gushes from his mount's rear. The front wheel bumps against the barrier and stops abruptly. With pinched face, the Orc dismounts and approaches the protective wall. Laying his palm against it, he verifies the nature of the barrier between us. It doesn't allow him through. He doesn't appear to strain, so he's not putting all his Strength into it. Chances are he doesn't often rely on his Strength or Luck. Wizards are more into spells and Intelligence.

The Wizard gnashes his fangs and, holding up his right hand, equips a staff. He begins a chant I can't hear.

Mel backs further away. "What's he doing?"

It's obvious to me. "He's trying to dispel the barrier."

"Can he do that?"

"We're about to find out." But maybe I can influence the outcome of the Orc's attempt to reach us. I call for a saving roll on my Luck. If I can use Luck to get through the wall of green energy, maybe I can use Luck to reinforce it, too.

The two red dice tumble out of the air onto the floor. One of them stops rolling, showing a one. Ooh, that's not good. If the other die stops on a two or a three, that's an automatic failure. The die spins and spins… and falls over to show a four. Whew, I've made my saving roll at level twenty-seven. That ought to be good enough. If it's not—if the Orc can operate at level twenty-seven ability—there's no way I'm surviving for long.

The two dice fade from sight.

The Orc Wizard's mouth works, but when he finishes his casting, the barrier still stands. He can't reach us.

Behind him, more fireballs blast through the building wall from outside. In come six more wheeled metal oxen and their Orc Wizard riders. They approach the barrier, stopping their mounts beside the first Orc. I'm facing seven enemies in total, all of them eager for my blood. In unison, they hurl fireballs, but the barrier holds. Lucky me.

I'm wearing tunic, breeches, and sandals… not carrying any weapons or mushrooms. I've not much to go with. If I need to fight, it will be with my bare hands, relying almost solely on my high Luck. Against the combined magical firepower of the Orcs, I don't stand a chance. Once this barrier is no longer separating them from me, I'm a goner.

All seven Orcs are chanting and pointing their wizardly staffs at the barrier. They're trying to dispel it again, working together. I don't know whether their efforts stack, but I'm guessing seven together can do better than one alone.

Mel waves to get my attention. He points back the way we came from. "We should run."

I shake my head. "We need this barrier to stay up. If it comes down and they come through, there's nowhere for us to hide. If they can get through this barrier, they can get through anything in this building. I *have* to pit my Luck against their skill." I call for another saving roll.

The two red dice tumble onto the floor before me. The first one stops rolling on a four, and I exhale in relief, knowing it doesn't matter what the second die rolls. As before, once both dice come to a stop, they both disappear. They're only present for as long as needed to determine saving roll results.

The Orcs finish their attempts to dispel, and the barrier remains intact. I laugh at them. They pound on the barrier with their fists.

They hold a brief discussion amongst themselves.

Nodding eagerly, they try a new tactic, throwing fireballs at the concrete wall to either side of the hallway. Their scowls tell me all I need to know. Dismounting from their metal mounts, they spread out to either side, throwing more and more fireballs in an attempt to find a way through. They work their way further and further away from me, throwing fireball after fireball, adding more and more rubble to the room, but not finding a way to get to me and Mel.

Their wheeled metal oxen sit unattended. Placing my hands against the barrier, I call on my Luck again. The dice roll a total of seven, and the barrier allows me passage. I slide forward on my belly. Hiding behind rubble the best I can, I crawl on my stomach to the metal oxen.

I touch the front wheels of two oxen and stash the metallic beasts to my inventory. I stash two more before the Orcs notice what I'm doing. They run my way, but I stash two more before they're halfway back. Ducking low behind the rubble, I quickly stash the last one. A fireball flies overhead and slams into the barrier.

Without my calling for them, the red dice tumble where the oxen had been and turn up double fives, then double fives again, and then a two and a three. Excellent roll. I assume it was my saving roll for getting back behind the barrier without getting flamed. I tumble through the barrier, clearing it right before another four fireballs splatter behind me.

Mel stares at me, arms akimbo. "What the hell were you thinking?"

The label for the stolen items in my inventory is *motorcycle*, rather than *wheeled metal ox*. "I just stole all their motorcycles." I laugh as seven snarling Orcs converge on the barrier, flattening their faces and bodies against it and pounding it with their fists.

My ghostly companion looks at me askance. "Do you know how to ride a motorcycle?"

"I'm assuming you sit on its back and hold onto the horns."

"I think there's more to it than that."

"If an Orc Wizard can ride one, I'm sure I can." I draw one out of my inventory. "Here, see if you can stash it."

Mel shakes his head. "I'm not sure what you mean."

"Just touch it and will it into your inventory."

Still wearing a look of skepticism, he lays a hand on the seat and squints. His hand sinks into the motorcycle, but nothing else happens. "Sorry, I can't do it, Ronnie."

"Try again." I call for another Luck roll. The dice appear long enough to roll a result of seven.

But his hand once again passes through the motorcycle like it wasn't there, and yet it still is. He can't stash it the way I can. I frown. "If you can't even touch it, you can't ride it. I was hoping we could ride one of these things out of here."

"My mother said we wouldn't be harmed if we stayed in the protected area. Let's just wait out the hour and she'll whisk us back the same way she put us here."

I'm not so sure. "I think maybe your mother isn't in control now. After that scream and the world changed, I think someone else took control of the timeline, or shifted us into another one. Maybe your mother doesn't even have a spaceship now. I don't think these Orc Wizards belong to her. I suspect she won't be snatching us out of here after all, and those Orc Wizards will eventually find a way through the barrier. If that happens, we're toast. Literally." I climb onto the motorcycle, positioning myself on the seat the way the Orc Wizards did, and grab the horns protruding from either side of the neck. "If they get through, I'll try to make a run for it on this thing. Maybe you can sink into the floor and hide from them there."

Sadness dims Mel's eyes. "I don't want to be alone, Ronnie."

"Can you fly?"

He raises an eyebrow. His feet lift off the floor. "I guess I can."

More fireballs splash against the barrier. I call for another Luck save, and the dice roll a total of nine. The barrier holds. If the dice had rolled a total of three or four, could the Orcs come through? I'm guessing so. "How do I turn this thing on?" No sooner do I ask the question than smoke gushes from the rear of the motorcycle and the metal beast growls. "If I take off, Mel, maybe you can fly up and track me from above. I'll do what I can to lose these Orcs and we can meet up somewhere out there."

He purses his lips. "If I'm a ghost and they aren't, maybe their fireballs can't harm me. Maybe their fire will pass through me like the bike does."

"Bike?"

"The motorcycle. It's another name for it."

"I see. It's not worth the risk. Stay high and out of their range." I call on my Luck once more as the Orc Wizards blast the barrier again. The dice appear and roll on the floor. The first die stops on a one. I grit my teeth. The second die stops on two. Uh oh.

In other words, automatic failure.

The barrier comes down. Fiddlesticks. It's time to go.

The motorcycle farts smoke and growls louder than before. At my mental command, it zooms forward. The Orcs scatter to get out of my way. Instinctively, I lean to the right and then to the left and then back to the right to skirt piles of rubble. Then I drive through one of the holes created earlier by the Orcs. I'm outside the building and clear of its rubble.

A glance over my shoulder reveals a mass of fireballs heading my way, and I lean into a sharper turn. Surprisingly, riding the motorcycle comes naturally to me. The fireballs tear up pavement to my left, where I would have been if I hadn't swerved.

"Ouch." Mel is flying beside me on my left. "I got singed. Guess their magic can affect me after all."

"I thought you were going to fly high, Mel."

"I tried, but I couldn't. I'm drawn to you. It's like you anchor me in this timeline, and I can't stray from you. Swerve left—here comes another bunch of fireballs."

I do as directed, and chunks of asphalt hurl by me on my right. "We make a good team."

He laughs. "Yeah, but I'd rather be solid flesh and riding my own bike. I believe we're out of their range now. But they're running after us, so you can't stop yet. Keep going until we lose them. I'll let you know when."

CHAPTER SIXTEEN

Susie: Timeline Duel

A masculine bellow of rage rocks the ship, catching the attention of every gray-skinned alien in sight, as they all stop in their tracks. Seth jerks his head up to listen, too.

Why does the sound remind me of Dad? Is he here?

I glance at Timmy, who looks just as confused as the rest of us.

Dancing ghostly women appear in the room, dressed in green uniforms one might associate with nurses. Their movements slow to a halt, their raised eyebrows and gaping mouths betraying their perplexity. Metal pedestals take shape, one pedestal next to each dancer.

Another ghostly woman appears, standing before Seth, facing him. Except for her womanly figure giving shape to her dark cloak, the newcomer could pass for Seth, dressed identically to him, with a hood shadowing her face. She wields an axe in one hand and a staff in the other. The two stare at each other in silence, their expressions hidden in shadow. Do they each regard the other as friend or enemy?

Thousands more insubstantial cloaked beings appear, their bodies overlapping each other and those of Seth and the woman. They speak, not quite in unison, their voices a mix of masculine and feminine. "I am Seth." They each assert their dominance over the others, with none sounding more convincing than the next.

Ghostly Seth bodies merge with other ghostly Seth bodies. Some of them merge with the original Seth, while others merge with the ghostly woman, who steadily gains more substance, becoming less and less translucent by the second. The woman and the original Seth don't move, staring at each other from under their hoods until the woman loses her last vestige of transparency, when the final ghostly body merges with her.

The woman brandishes her axe. "There's only room on this ship for one of us, and that's me."

Seth's hand strikes like a snake and grasps the axe handle. "We both know this is my universe."

She shakes her head. "*I* am its Queen."

"No," he says, "you're *Jean*, a nobody. You have the ego to be ruler, but not the power or the authority. You're not even of this universe, so begone."

"Our universes have merged, and now so shall we." Jean taps her staff on the floor.

Seth and his gray-skinned aliens lose substance, becoming shadowy versions of their original selves. The dancers in green become more substantial.

The weight at my neck lessens. The collar at my neck doesn't feel like metal to my touch, but gelatin. Timmy's collar has lost substance, but so has Timmy… and my own limbs. A battle for the timeline is underway, and if Seth loses to Jean, Timmy and I might cease to be. This is not good.

Enveloped in smoke and flames, a motorcycle charges across the floor two feet in front of me. A young woman drives the bike, with a younger man seated behind her. Spinning around so that the driver faces me, the bike squeals to a halt before it crashes into a pedestal and dancer. Smoke billows around the bike and its riders as the flames die.

The female rider locks eyes with me. There's something in her gaze, something pulling at me, as though my soul wants to leave my body and occupy hers. Without vocalizing, we hear each other, as though communicating through telepathy.

"I'm Susie, Nick and Kendra's daughter."

"I'm Mel, Nick and Jean's son."

She's not female, after all, but male. Her appearance doesn't jive with her assertion, but to each their own. The important thing is that we're not siblings, but incarnations of the same being, and only one of us can continue to exist. If the timelines merge into one, can only one incarnation of each being survive?

Mel's presence fills my senses. I'm losing the battle against him. Timmy is losing substance at a rapid rate. He'll be completely gone in seconds. Is the other rider on the bike his alternate incarnation?

Seth and his gray-skinned aliens are almost gone, too. The version of this timeline that he occupies, which is the same one both Timmy and I occupy, is about to lose to the version where Jean is Queen and where Mel and the other motorcycle rider are real.

In seconds, I'll cease to exist, along with Timmy, Seth, and the gray aliens. I need to fight back harder, and so does Timmy and Seth. How is it possible that Seth could lose out to this impostor? What could drive her harder than Seth's psychosis drives him? An even more severe psychosis? Does she also have help from Mel and his friend?

The collar at my neck fades from existence. But *I'm* not entirely faded out. I teleport. I know exactly where I'm going. Glynda drilled it into my mind.

CHAPTER SEVENTEEN

Susie: No Longer Illegal

I'm in the shaded hallway where I met Glynda. Through the passing of time, I've become her. The hallway is as empty now of aliens as it was when I first entered the ship. My body is ghostly but still visible. As she instructed, I don't hesitate, but time-jump back twenty-four hours, though with a jump this long, I've got next to no control over it.

Whenever I time-jump—especially if I move forward or backward in time by more than a few minutes—I never know exactly *where* I'll end up. I often don't occupy the same physical location I occupied before the jump. I inadvertantly time-jumped one night from my bed at home to a bed in a mental health facility, a place I had never visited before. This time, I expect to still be on the Planet Buster ship, joining two of my past selves, because that's what Glynda did, or so I assume.

But when I last saw Glynda, her neck bore scorch marks. And since I'm now her… I think… my neck should bear the same markings too. I'd assumed her scorch marks were due to her collar being removed by heating or burning. But that's not how my collar was removed, and my neck doesn't feel hot. Something is off here....

This is not the spaceship.... Where have I time-jumped to?

Ghostly humans in business attire occupy a busy, well-lit office divided into cubicles by short walls, seated in wheeled office chairs at desks with computers. I'm seated in a chair, too. Not bound, thank goodness. Everyone and everything here is as insubstantial as I am, flickering on the edge of non-existence. How can this be? I had hoped time-jumping back twenty-four hours would put me into a time frame where I'd be my normal, solid self, with twenty-four hours to do what was needed to prevent my demise. But the disease contaminating this timeline has spread backward along it. This is bad. Just how long do I have to save myself? Or am I already too late?

And why am I *here*?

None of the other people present pay me any heed. With distant, muted voices, they're shouting at each other, mostly to ask what's happening, and typing away at their keyboards. For what? Can they find the solution to this problem on the internet? Do they expect an announcement in their inbox? This is crazy.

Just where the hell am I? Glynda never told me about this. I'm not experiencing events the way she'd led me to believe I would. When I time-*jump*, I move forward or backward in time within the same timestream. But now, I think I've not only time-jumped but time-*shifted*, too, out of the timeline I occupied when I met Glynda and into some other one. It must be because of the dueling timelines. They've messed up all Glynda's plans. Now it's up to me to roll with the changes and recover. No pressure....

"ODYSSEY? If you have any energy at all, you need to talk to me."

"I'm here. We've shifted timelines, but not in the way you think. Fanciful Pegasus existed here, and it's providing me a remote source of energy to tap into. I'm recharging as we speak."

"I don't like how you used the word, *existed*."

"None of what you see here, including yourself, can be said to exist at the moment except as memories of what might have been. A number of timelines have melded along their entire lengths, and the Fanciful Pegasus one is not dominant. Jean is winning the battle of wills against Seth in this merged timeline. Initially she had a goal similar to Seth's, it seems, to destroy everyone and everything... except her daughter and a potential mate, so they could repopulate the multiverse. But for some reason she changed her mind and is no longer hell-bent on destruction. Now she's asserting a timeline in which she never married Nick but had a daughter, Karen, by another man. She has squeezed Nick out of existence, along with Erica, the young woman he cheated with. It seems there truly is no fury like that of a woman scorned."

I suck in a breath. "If this Jean wins, which you say she's about to, then you're saying my dad won't exist in any timeline, he will have never married my mom, I will never have been born, we will never have visited Khertaan, and.... what else?"

"On the bright side, Seth will never have destroyed any planets." ODYSSEY pauses as though accessing more data. "However, it's fifty percent likely that Jean won't only co-opt Seth's role in this merged timeline but his Planet Buster, too. Given her state of mind, I'm unable to calculate any percentage chance that she'll eventually revert to her idea of destroying everything. We need to proceed under the hypothesis that she will."

"Can we stop her?"

Footsteps sound behind me. I twirl around in my wheeled chair, expecting to be accused of trespassing, but come face-to-face with... another ghostly version of me. "Glynda?"

"Hey, Suze."

"Am I glad to see you. How do we save ourselves?"

She grabs a chair from another cubicle and wheels it over to my cubicle. "Scoot over, please."

"By all means." I wheel aside as Glynda positions herself before the computer keyboard.

Glynda presses a power button, and the screen comes to life, portraying a logo of a winged horse and a clock, accompanied by the words Fanciful Pegasus. Below the logo is displayed a user name of Raphael and a prompt for a password. Her first attempt at supplying the correct password works.

I saw but didn't catch what she typed. "How did you know the right password?"

"ODYSSEY told me."

Oh, I see. Since she's future-me, she's got ODYSSEY in her head the same as I do, but hers is a future-ODYSSEY. My ODYSSEY just observed the password she typed and will remember it for when he becomes her ODYSSEY.

She nods at me. "Go ahead and time-jump back thirty-three seconds."

If I only jump in time a few minutes or less, I gain a high degree of control over how far I jump, in both time and space. It's not that I need to jump back exactly thirty-three seconds, I'm sure. But the number gives me something to focus on, which always helps.

Performing the time-jump, I'm still in the office, standing three steps behind my past self. Suze is seated in a wheeled chair in one of the cubicles. I walk up close, my footsteps louder than one might expect from a ghost.

She whirls around in her chair. "Glynda?"

"Hey, Suze." I grab a chair from another cubicle and wheel it over. "Scoot over, please."

"By all means." She wheels aside.

I position myself before the computer keyboard and press the power button. I know what I'm doing because I saw my future-self do it less than a minute ago. I've become that future-self.

The screen comes to life, portraying a winged horse and a clock, accompanied by the words Fanciful Pegasus. Below the logo is displayed the user name, Raphael, and a prompt for a password.

"The password is capital X, 8, p, capital Q, 3, %, 7, c, capital H, r, 9, $, m," says ODYSSEY in my head.

Suze cranes her neck for a better view as the password is accepted and the Fanciful Pegasus logo pops up. "How did you know the right password?"

"ODYSSEY told me." I nod at her. "Go ahead and time-jump back thirty-three seconds." I don't know why that number, but it's what my Glynda told me, and I'm not switching it up for my Suze.

She doesn't question me, but immediately vanishes, having jumped back in time the half-minute or so we spent together.

Talk about déjà vu.

"So, ODYSSEY, How did you know that password was the *right* password?"

"Past-us observed whether it worked or not. If it hadn't worked, there'd have been no need for us to jump back in time to deliver the password to our past selves. Because we'd only choose to jump back in time if we had the right password, that eliminated all possible paths where we jumped back with the wrong one. The only two paths that remained were either jumping back with the correct password, or not bothering to jump back at all."

"Interesting." I learn more about time travel all the time. Ha.

A snowy mountain scene serves as the computer background image. Several icons dot the desktop and line the task bar at the bottom of the screen. ODYSSEY instructs me to click the email icon. I'm not one to violate someone's privacy, but this is a business account, not a personal account, and the fate of the multiverse weighs in the balance. I click the icon.

The subject line of the first unread email is *Late Arrival*. The message appears to have been sent from Raphael's mobile device to his supervisor at 6:28 AM, Thursday, with a cc to Raphael's inbox here. The body of the email indicates Raphael would be late arriving to work "today," hoping to arrive within the hour.

A glance at the bottom right of the screen tells me it's 3:00 PM on Thursday. It appears either Raphael's traffic problems were worse than he'd originally thought. Or maybe he's simply somewhere else in the building.

Another unread email bears the subject line, *New Messages in Khertaan*. The body of the email is simply a link. "Should I click it?" I say it aloud, as much to myself as to ODYSSEY.

"Allow me, Suze."

I nearly jump out of my skin at the words uttered from behind me in my voice. This time I don't spin around to face future-me, but wheel my chair aside as she takes the vacant one next to me.

Glynda clicks the link. A browser window opens, displaying the Fanciful Pegasus logo at the top of the page. A header declares **KHERTAAN** in bold letters and all caps. Below the header is a sub-header, *Developer Access*, and below that is the user name, Raphael. A password field awaits an entry. Glynda types in a string of characters and clicks the Login button.

A new page loads. Below the logo and the **KHERTAAN** header, a line reads, "Welcome, Raphael." An icon in the top right corner is marked with a red numeral two.

Glynda glances at me with a smile. "The password worked. Go ahead and time-jump back."

"Of course." I jump back a few seconds, materializing directly behind my past-self.

She asks, "Should I click it?"

"Allow me, Suze."

She's obviously startled by the sound of my voice, as I knew she would be, but she rolls out of my way and I take the other chair.

I click the link, and a browser window opens, displaying the Fanciful Pegasus logo; the **KHERTAAN** header; the *Developer Access* sub-header; the user name, Raphael; and an empty password field.

ODYSSEY tells me the password. I enter it and click the Login button.

A new page loads, with the Fanciful Pegasus logo, the **KHERTAAN** header, and the line reading, "Welcome, Raphael."

I glance at Suze. "The password worked. Go ahead and time-jump back."

"Of course." She vanishes.

Though I don't fully understand ODYSSEY's methods, he and I together could hack into *any* account on *any* computer network, apparently.

I click the icon marked with a red numeral two. The page reloads, showing a long list of subject lines. The most recent one reads, *AL5936 - Warning: Possible Intrusion Program Detected.*

Could this message be about ODYSSEY? I shiver at the thought and click the subject line. The body of the message loads....

Unexplained events and potentially illegal avatars have been detected. Refer to the alert log for details.

The phrase *alert log* is underlined, so I click it. A new tab opens in the browser and displays a long list of additional subject lines. A readout at the top of the page informs that the subject lines presented are filtered on the alert number, *AL5936*.

The most recent subject line reads, *Suspected illegal avatars confined - Kylie and Spyder*. I click to open the full alert message....

Suspected illegal avatars Kylie, Spyder, Morrow, and Slithy have been confined or refused respawn. NPC Charli may be responsible for their creation and is also confined.

At the bottom of the log message are two links:
1) Purge suspected illegals and errant NPC
2) Additional options

Wow. I could eradicate avatars from the game with a click of a link. I'm nauseous just thinking about it. That's the horrifyingly obviously wrong thing to do here. I click for additional options. The message area expands and offers more information.

Avatars Kylie, Spyder, Morrow, and Slithy, and the party to which they belong, TimeTrippers, cannot be verified in the System and are suspected as illegal. Avatars Kylie and Spyder have been confined to their present location, SD (0, 0, 9000), Spire of Desire, Top Exit Cavern. Morrow and Slithy are not present in the game, having been slain. Morrow attempted respawn, but his reentry into the game was successfully blocked. Slithy has not attempted respawn. NPC Charli appears to be connected to the creation of these illegal avatars, though the nature of the connection is unclear. Pending further investigation, Charli has been confined with Kylie and Spyder.

The list of links below the message has expanded.
1) Purge suspected illegals and errant NPC
2) Purge suspected illegals but release NPC
3) Force-legalize and release all
4) Continue To Restrict
5) Add notes
6) See attached notes
I click to see the attached notes, which expand below the links.

Added notes by user Ivanhoe: DO NOT PURGE OR FORCE-LEGALIZE THESE AVATARS. Further investigation is underway.

"What do I do, ODYSSEY?"
"Unfortunately, the System detected party TimeTrippers in Khertaan. It will be difficult for you or any of your family to take action in the game at this point unless we force legalization of your avatars. I recommend you click the force-legalization link, and then hope this Ivanhoe doesn't notice anytime soon or take the matter to a higher up, like Franklin. Let's hope this whole 'being-ghostly' thing has everyone's attention more than the game right now."

Moving the cursor over the desired link, I hesitate to click it. "Who's Spyder?"

"I wish I knew. If we were in Khertaan, I could ask the ODYSSEY nanobots in Kylie's mind. But don't let that bit of uncertainty stop you from clicking the link."

My heart races as I click to force-legalize my avatar Slithy and her family in the game. A dialog pops up with an empty text field and the prompt, *User Raphael, please enter the notes for this action.* Below the text field is a disabled OK button and an enabled Cancel button.

"Tell me what to type, ODYSSEY."

My nanobot collective doesn't pause to think. "Enter the following: *Specified avatars were created for special task. Lifting restraints on them now.* And then, in all caps, type, *DO NOT RESTRICT THESE AVATARS AGAIN.*"

I type his words. The OK button becomes enabled, so I click it. The dialog vanishes and another one takes its place, with the prompt, *Please confirm Force-Legalization action.* Below the prompt are two enabled buttons, Confirm and Cancel. I click on Confirm.

The dialog disappears. A new alert shows at the top of the alert log, *AL5955 - Warning: Force-legalized avatars - party TimeTrippers.* I click it. The body of the alert reads...

Suspected illegal avatars Kylie, Spyder, Morrow, and Slithy have been force-legalized by user Raphael. NPC Charli has been verified as not responsible for their creation. All restrictions on Kylie, Spyder, Morrow, Slithy, and Charli have been removed.

Below the message are two links.
1) Reinstate restrictions
2) Additional options
I click the latter link, and the list expands.
1) Reinstate restrictions

2) Lock legalization
3) Add notes
"Lock it," ODYSSEY urges.

I click the second link. A dialog pops up with the prompt, *Enter security phrase for lock*. Below the prompt are two empty text fields and two buttons, a disabled OK and an enabled Cancel. "What do I enter now?"

"You're creating a special password for the lock, so enter anything you want," ODYSSEY replies, "but use the same phrase in both fields. I'll remember what you enter. If anyone else wants to unlock your lock, they'll need to know this password you're creating now, or have elevated privileges."

I type *Slithy waSn't HeRe 42* as my security phrase in both password fields. I click OK and then Confirm. The dialog goes away, and another dialog asks for action notes. I type notes similar to those I entered earlier...

These avatars were created for a special task. Restraints have been lifted accordingly. DO NOT RESTRICT THESE AVATARS AGAIN.

A laugh rolls out of my throat. "I think this means I can respawn Slithy now if I want." I glance at the clock in the bottom right corner of the desktop. The time is 3:00 PM. That can't be right. That's what it read earlier, minutes ago. It's like time is stuck.

"That's because it *is* stuck," ODYSSEY says. "Which may be why we haven't vanished completely from existence. We aren't in the dominant thread in the merged timeline, but the dominant thread can't completely dominate the merge, because doing so takes time, and time is stuck. I suspect Jean is trying her best to make it *unstuck*, but until she does, we have a reprieve. So let's keep digging and see if we can find something helpful to our situation."

The top alert is the one created in response to the force-legalization of party TimeTrippers. The next subject line reads, *AL5954 - Assignment: Special quest.* I open the message.

Special quest accepted by: PC Yuni
Requirement for completion: Locked by user Ivanhoe
Reward for completion: 200,000,000 XP.

I drill down to the complete list of links.
1) Cancel special quest
2) View quest completion requirements
3) Purge special quest item
4) View special quest item details
5) See attached notes
I click to see the attached notes.

Added notes by user Ivanhoe: DO NOT DELETE OR ALTER THIS QUEST. DO NOT PURGE OR MODIFY SPECIAL QUEST ITEM OR REMOVE IT FROM PC'S INVENTORY.

"Oh, I got to see what this is." Anything this secret has my interest. I click the second link, to view the quest completion requirements.

A dialog prompts me for the secret phrase. This is the phrase created by Ivanhoe when he locked the item. Of course, I don't know it and can't guess it, but ODYSSEY and I have our tried and true hacking process. After a short time-jump, we have the secret phrase. We're in and have new info.

Special quest accepted by: PC Yuni

Requirement for completion: Deliver special quest item to NPC Charli
Reward for completion: 200,000,000 XP.

I click the fourth link, to view the special quest item details. I'm not asked to enter a new secret phrase, but am allowed to view more new info…

Special quest item: Shadow Marble
Special item abilities: Shadow Summons IV
Item location: PC Yuni - stashed in inventory.

I've no idea whether this is a good or bad thing. "What do we do, ODYSSEY?"

"This Ivanhoe fellow strikes me as up to no good, but Charli having such a powerful item seems on the surface to be a good thing. Let's leave this alone for now and take a look at another log message."

"Sure." The next subject line reads, *AL5953 - Warning: Suspected illegal avatar confined - Mithabel.* Hmm. I open it up.

Suspected illegal avatar Mithabel has been confined. Associated avatars, some of which may also be illegal, have been confined with Mithabel.

At the bottom of the log message are two links:
1) Purge suspected illegals and associated avatars
2) Additional options
I click for additional options. The message area expands and offers more information.

PC Mithabel appears to have an alternate avatar acting simultaneously with her original avatar. If true, this serves as disqualification of PC Mithabel. Alternate avatar was approved by user Raphael, but only for purposes of comparison to original. PC Mithabel was instructed to choose one of the two avatars as the permanent one going forward. This has not been done. PC Mithabel has been confined along with the alternate avatar in a pocket dimension pending further investigation. Access to the pocket dimension is restricted.

In confining PC Mithabel, PC Dylan was also confined.

The pocket dimension in which PC Mithabel and PC Dylan are confined was constructed with properties of both the physical and the spiritual realms to make escape difficult while retaining the possibility for the avatars to be released. The pocket dimension itself does not, however, occupy any of the four realms.

Confinement in the pocket dimension has resulted in unanticipated side effects. PC Dylan has independently formed an alternate avatar, which has become active. This would disqualify PC Dylan from winning the game if both her original and alternate avatars are released from the pocket dimension and become active.

Another unexpected side effect of the pocket dimension confinement is the materialization of Kaleisha and Magnum, the support AIs for PC Mithabel and PC Dylan, respectively. While their release and subsequent ability to take actions within the game would be unconventional, such are not grounds for disqualification of their PCs.

Below the additional info is the expanded list of links.
1) Purge Mithabel and associated confined avatars
2) Purge Mithabel but release Dylan
3) Purge 2nd alternate avatars and release originals
4) Force-legalize 2nd alternate avatars - release all
5) Force-legalize 2nd alternate avatars - no release
6) Add notes
7) See attached notes
I open the attached notes.

Added notes by user Ivanhoe: DO NOT PURGE OR FORCE-LEGALIZE THESE AVATARS. Escalation to Franklin.

Added notes by user Franklin: FORCE-LEGALIZATION APPROVED FOR ALTERNATE AVATARS. DO NOT PURGE ORIGINALS OR ALTERNATES. DO NOT RELEASE, BUT ESCAPE IS ALLOWED IF THEY FIND A WAY OUT.

I'm interested in seeing how the observed side effects play out. If escape is achieved, both PCs Mithabel and Dylan are to remain qualified to win.

I wonder if we should help out this Mithabel avatar and her companions. "What do you think, ODYSSEY?"

"It doesn't appear that anyone has carried through on the force-legalization that Franklin approved. What with everyone here in an uproar at being ghosts, I doubt any of them will be worried about what's happening in Khertaan. If we can help anyone in the game to advance quickly, I think we should. I still think Khertaan holds the key to giving us the power to fight the inter-dimensional invaders, whether they be led by Seth or Jean. If we could find a way to infuse all the avatars in Khertaan with enough XP to push them to level thirty, that would be the best thing to do. Failing that, the next best thing we can do is make it as easy as possible for them to earn XP. I say never mind what Franklin wants. I say force-legalize the avatars and release them all."

I click the fourth link, *Force-legalize 2nd alternate avatars - release all.* Good luck, Mithabel and Dylan.

A dialog pops up and prompts for action notes. I type in, *Force-legalization performed on Franklin's go-ahead.* I don't say anything about releasing the avatars. It's not like anyone will be looking at these notes, what with everything else that's happening. I click OK and then Confirm.

Another dialog pops up with a message and a single Dismiss button. The message reads, *Force-legalization action succeeded, but release action failed. All avatars in question have already escaped from the pocket dimension.*

Well, good for them.

Enough of these log messages. I go back to the main Developer Access page for Khertaan and peruse the available links. Maybe I can make some major modifications in this game, something to help *all* the avatars hit level thirty quickly.

CHAPTER EIGHTEEN

Mithabel: Siamese Cat

Before the brightness could fade, the tip of a metal blade pressed into the back of Mithabel's neck. She raised her hands. "Someone has a blade at my back," she said over party chat.

"Lower your weapon, guardsman." Dylan spoke from beside Mithabel. "There'll be no need for violence here."

The weapon's cold touch retreated. "I trust you, Priestess. But we weren't expecting six of you."

Mithabel blinked to clear her vision of the light's lingering afterimage. The familiar walls of the prison hallway rose to either side of her, framed photos hanging on the walls, the floor sloping down before her. The Tank and five others stood in a circle in the hallway—Dylan, Megan Wright, Debra Jones, Kaleisha, and Magnum. The guardsmen could see the two support AIs, which up to now they wouldn't have. Could the support AIs interact with the game world like NPCs now, and if so, could they be killed?

"Move on down the hall, please." The guard behind Mithabel pointed his sword past her. "We still need to assess you, Mithabel."

Kaleisha waved for attention. "I have a message that may have some bearing on this situation."

Magnum nodded. "As do I."

The guard stashed his sword. Perhaps as an NPC he'd also received whatever information Kaleisha and Magnum had received. He stepped to one side of the hall and nodded up the incline. "My apologies, Mithabel. You're free to go. I trust this incident has not been too much of an inconvenience for you. All of you... you can go."

The group filed past him up the ramp towards the exit that would take them outside to join Amarynth.

"What's the message you received, Kaleisha?"

The Jamaican AI came abreast of Mithabel. "Your secondary avatar, the one Megan Wright inhabits, has been legalized. In fact, Debra Jones has been recognized by the System as a secondary avatar for Dylan, and has also been legalized. Moreover, both Magnum and I have gained material forms in the physical realm, and may take actions to aid you in the game. Having no skills, traits, or stats, our aid is limited, but we won't take damage and can't be killed. We can be trapped, unfortunately. We're also able to talk over your party chat. Lastly, in addition to all these things to your benefit, you and Dylan remain qualified to win the game, should either of you be the first to reach level thirty."

Mithabel laughed. "Holy sweet mother. Dylan, did you hear this?"

Dylan chuckled, too. "I can't believe it. Our developer friend, Raphael, must have come through for us."

"It sounds like both Debra Jones and I are allowed to help you win this game. And your AIs, too." Megan Wright followed close on Mithabel's heels. "This is amazing. What's the catch?"

Kaleisha frowned, gliding along a few inches above the floor. "The System has deducted two points from your Constitution score, chief, and from Dylan's as well. Your Constitution score is now 1, and Dylan's is 8."

"*What?*" Mithabel kept her reply between her, Megan, and Kaleisha. "That's bogus. File a complaint, please, Kaleisha."

"I don't think it's as big an issue as it sounds," said Megan. "Remember what I told you about the guards having a negative Constitution and effectively being immortal? That could be us. Since we always lose two Constitution at a time, as long as our attribute is an odd number, we won't hit the magic number zero. Let's just keep it to ourselves that we're down to one life. We don't want anyone treating us special."

"The complaint has been rejected," said Kaleisha. "Between you and Megan, you have one life remaining."

"Are you shitting me? Well, I hope you're right, Megan." Mithabel reached the door at the top of the incline and switched back to party chat. "Amarynth, are you there?"

"I am," the Viking Archer replied. "Are you finally coming out here? Quantized went on without us. But someone else is here, and you won't like who."

"Tell me."

"XStorm. Not just Yuni, but the whole party. They showed up a minute ago."

Mithabel gritted her teeth. "You're right, my mood just soured. Can you get rid of them before we come out? Tell them we've informed you we aren't coming out for a while and they shouldn't wait for us."

"It's okay, Mithabel." Dylan laid a hand on the Tank's forearm. "Let's give XStorm a real chance to work with us."

Megan Wright turned to Debra Jones. "Are *you* all right to travel with XStorm? You do understand that their leader, ChrisCross, looks almost exactly like Christopher Warden, and is as much an aspect of him as Dylan is of you."

Mithabel clucked her tongue. "And his kindred is Elitist. That should tell you all you need to know."

Dylan huffed. "It's just a label."

Mithabel mimicked her friend's huffing. "A label *he chose*."

"Not necessarily." Kaleisha cringed as though fearing the brunette Elf Tank's wrath. "As you may recall, Mithabel, you didn't exactly choose to be a Tank. You inquired about the Tank class, and it was locked in without your confirmation. Something similar could have happened with ChrisCross. He might have asked about the Elitist class without actually saying he wanted it, and the System locked it in anyway."

"I'll be okay." Debra Jones rubbed her face. "If he says or does anything untoward, then we ditch them."

Magnum cleared his throat. "Madam, if you will…." He addressed Dylan. "When XStorm asks about Kaleisha and me, as I assume they will, what will you tell them? They'll also likely have questions about why both you and Mithabel have secondary avatars and how they might acquire their own."

Dylan shook her head. "We can tell them you and Kaleisha are NPCs traveling to Minook and have asked to tag along with us for the company. Megan, you can use your Hide skill to avoid being seen. Then we only need to figure out what to say about you, Debra."

Megan clapped her hands. "I have an idea. Instead of my using the Hide skill, I'll Shapeshift into a Siamese Cat that Kaleisha can carry. Then I'll transfer my awareness to Debra and lend her my Hide skill. That will keep XStorm from knowing about either me or Debra." She giggled. "It could work."

Everyone looked at each other, nodding with Optimism.

Mithabel punched her secondary avatar on the shoulder. "No one can say you're a dumb blond. Let's do it."

Raising an eyebrow at her primary avatar, Megan dropped to all fours, taking feline form as she fell, and landed on her paws. She rubbed against Kaleisha's legs. "Will you do me the honor of this dance?"

"Of course." The Jamaican AI took the Megan cat into her arms and stroked her fur. "Nice kitty."

"Okay, I'm going to sleep now." Megan lay her head against Kaleisha's breast. "Don't drop me."

"Never." The Jamaican AI continued stroking her new pet as the cat went still.

A moment later, Debra disappeared. "Can you see me?"

Mithabel concentrated on the spot where she'd last seen Dylan's secondary avatar. Because she knew where to look, she caught sight of fluctuations in the air, and seconds later she made out Debra's ghostly form. "I can, but it won't be easy for anyone to spot you unless they already know you're there. Just don't bump into anyone. In fact, Megan why don't you lend her your Flight Speed skill too, for better maneuverability. Hell, you might as well lend her all your abilities."

"Sounds good to me," Debra said.

Megan agreed, but made the point that she couldn't transfer her Siamese Cat Shapeshift ability, since she was using it herself.

Once all the transferring was complete, the group was ready to exit.

"May the Goddess shine her blessings upon us." Dylan thrust the door open and strode out.

಄ೞೞೞ೯ೞ಄ೞೞ

Mithabel clenched her fists, diverted her gaze to the ground, and focused on the sounds of the city—the whinnying of horses, the rush of wheels, the indistinct mutterings of pedestrians traversing sidewalks on autopilot. She stayed close to Dylan with the intent to protect her friend, but her Temperance filter strained to contain her anger, the anger that would explode if she heard one word pass the lips of the XStorm party leader.

How was Dylan so calm and collected? The Priestess only had an average Temperance, whereas Mithabel's was in the extraordinary category, two categories above Dylan's. It had to be the Presence skill that gave the Priestess the appearance of calm.

The Tank couldn't imagine how Debra Jones and Megan Wright must feel about coming face-to-face again with the avatar of the person who back on Earth had verbally assaulted Debra, while Megan, who heard it all, hid in her cubicle, so shocked by the words coming from the man's mouth, she couldn't even stand up to make her presence known. Debra had forgiven Megan for her inaction, but Megan had never forgiven herself.

"You're here." Yuni approached at a run, stopping short of throwing her arms around Dylan. A smile flickered on the short Asian woman's face as she glanced from Dylan to Mithabel and back. "Are you both okay?"

"We're fine." The Polynesian Priestess of Light took Yuni's hand in hers, covering it with her other hand. "I'm glad the rest of your party has been freed and that you'll be traveling with us across the Dunes of Doom. I think it behooves us all to work together rather than against each other. Don't you agree, Mithabel." She turned to face the brunette Tank.

Mithabel met Dylan's gaze. "If we're going, then let's go. Who has the map of safe routes?"

The Angel Zyekt held up a parchment. "Quantized took off with the one they had, so I procured another. The proprietor gave it to me freely after I mentioned I was in party MAD. He seemed rather distracted, and closed the shop after I left, so we need to share this one with XStorm if they are to follow the safe path too."

"Good job, Angel." Mithabel beckoned to him. "I'll take it, if you don't mind."

"You're the one with the Danger Sense trait." The Angel Psyon fluttered his white wings and half-flew, half-hopped to Mithabel. He handed her the map.

She snatched it from him and flew towards the city gate. "Then come on, everyone." On the MAD party chat, she said, "Debra, stay beside me. Kaleisha, follow a step behind Debra to block the accidental view of her by those behind us."

To their credit, no one in party XStorm aside from Yuni spoke a word to anyone in party MAD. XStorm followed at a distance behind MAD, the exception again being Yuni, who walked abreast of Dylan. Judging by their impromptu smiles and knowing glances, the two Priestesses had a private chat going, exchanging jokes and innuendos.

If anyone in XStorm noticed Debra Jones, they said nothing about it. None of them commented on the presence of Magnum or the cat-carrying Kaleisha, or begged for introductions.

"When we're traveling through the Dunes of Doom," Megan said, "everyone needs to stay in contact with the ground or form a chain with someone who is. Otherwise, we'll attract wandering mooks."

No one made a reply, and Mithabel didn't slow down.

CHAPTER NINETEEN

Yuni: Army of Behemoths

Dylan is the most beautiful woman I've ever seen of any race. Her brown eyes hide so many secrets, both tragic and tranquil. Her dark purple braids beguile me with their motion, their rhythm, back and forth to match her stride. And her skin—I want to feel its smoothness under my fingers. Let me search for a single blemish, and I'll be searching forever, but that would be fine with me.

My heart will be broken too soon. I know this, but I don't care. Until that time, I'll appreciate every moment I spend in her company, my short legs struggling to match her graceful pace across the sand.

No one is talking on local chat for inter-party communications. Any conversations happening right now are either on party chat or private chat. Our parties don't want to talk to each other. "Dylan." I invite her to a private conversation.

Towering half a foot over me, Dylan looks down with a smile and raised eyebrows. "Yes?" The glimmer in her eyes is solely for me.

"Have you seen any undead in this game? The Command Undead skill seems like a waste of a slot."

Confusion clouds her face. "You have Command Undead? I don't have that. Is that a Priestess skill?"

Now I'm confused. "It is. I just figured, I mean, we're both Priestesses…."

Dylan scrunches her face. "Hmm. I bet you don't have the Light skill either. What's your highest level skill?"

I double check my character sheet. "I have the War skill at level 32. No Light skill." I'm thinking what she's thinking. "Just because we're both Priestesses doesn't mean we have the same skill set. I'm a Priestess of War in particular, just as you're a Priestess of Light."

She nods. "That must be it. So let's compare our Priestess abilities. I have Light, Attraction, Healing, Morale, Turn, Presence, Blinding, and Followers. What's yours?"

I read down my list. "War, Attraction, Enervation, Morale, Command Undead, and Presence. You've got two more than I do. What level are you? I'm level 20."

The Polynesian Priestess holds up three fingers. "Twenty-three. You should pick up another skill at your next level, and then another one at level 23. I wonder how many skills we get all together. What do your War and Enervation skills do?"

I chuckle. "I figured them out fast. The War *skill* enhances my War *spell*, which can be used to enchant a weapon or give my entire party dark sight. At the moment, if I combine my Morale and War skills, I can effectively enchant a weapon at +56. As for my *Enervation* skill, it enhances my *Enervate* spell, which allows me to deal damage in any domain—physical, mental, emotional, or spiritual—to any target I touch. It's Auni-based, so the more Auni I put into the spell, the more damage it does.

"At its current level, my Enervation skill adds 27 per casting on top of the Auni-based damage. So for one point of Auni, I can do a minimum of 28 points of damage to a target, and I can choose whether I do physical, mental, spiritual, or emotional damage. For some mooks, it's a lot easier to defeat them in a domain other than the physical. The Shadow Amoebae in the Mystic Cornfield, for instance… we could only harm them with enchanted weapons and mental-domain damage. My Enervate spell worked wonders on them.

"I noticed you didn't have any skill for damage dealing. How did you fare in combat encounters?"

The sun hangs in the western sky despite it still being morning according to the System clock. Its rays accentuate Dylan's cheeks, favoring her over all others present, even when she grimaces. "I didn't fare well for the longest time. It took me a while to figure out that my Light spell could be used to enchant weapons. But Mithabel, Amarynth, and Rolag were the best… great at protecting me. If not for them, I'd never have earned the Longest Survivor title.

"I noticed *you* don't have a Healing skill."

I force a grin. "Yeah, initially, I didn't have any means of healing. I'd found that strange too, what with me being a Priestess. I finally picked up the Heal spell, but I have no Healing skill to go with it like you do. Imagine that, a Priestess of War being better at dealing damage and a Priestess of Light being better at healing it. Who would ever have thought it?"

Our simultaneous chuckles at my facetious remark draw attention, especially from Mithabel, who glares over her shoulder at me as she continues to lead the way along the safe route. She says nothing verbally, but her eyes say everything. I'm not the only one here with a crush on Dylan. Jealousy rides the Tank's shoulders like an imp whispering in her ear, maligning me.

A dark-skinned woman with long, brown braids and a skimpy electric outfit glides over the sand beside Mithabel. I've not seen her traveling with party MAD before. Abreast of Dylan on the other side from me is another person I've not seen before, a man in black and white formal attire, someone I'd taken to be just another citizen of the Victorian-style city of Maron. But why is he accompanying us? I point my chin in his direction, but keep my question on the private chat with Dylan. "Is that man with you? He's not with XStorm."

"Oh, where are my manners?" Dylan sends her reply over local chat. "I believe you all know me, Dylan, Polynesian Priestess of Light and Shuriken Specialist. You also know Mithabel, Elf Tank and Anjai. Behind me is Amarynth, Viking Archer and Crossbow Specialist. Her Magical Companion is the Pseudo Code Dragon Rolag, a Winged Fighter and Were-Giant.

"Also with us are some NPCs you've not met before. The Angel, Zyekt, a Psyon and Life-Stealer. His Faithful Companion is the Mouse Niav, a Guide and Mentalist. They're officially members of party MAD."

"Hi, everybody," squeaks Niav from her perch on Zyekt's shoulder. The Angel bows his head in greeting. He's even shorter than I am, but size isn't a reliable indicator of power in this game. Given that he's been adventuring with MAD, he could easily be a higher level than those of us in XStorm.

Dylan continues the introductions. "Here beside me is Magnum, a British butler, not technically in our party but in my employ. And up there we have Kaleisha, a Jamaican dancer employed by Mithabel. Magnum and Kaleisha's abilities are not fully known at this point, but we hope to help them discover them on the journey ahead of us. Just to be clear, Magnum answers only to me, and Kaleisha only to Mithabel. If you have a problem with either of them, bring it to Mithabel or me, please."

Magnum doesn't avert his gaze from the dunes lying before him in the distance. Kaleisha faces the rest of us, flying backwards, her body writhing in rhythm to some song only she hears. Smiling, she waves at us. "Hello, everyone." Cradled in one arm is a sleeping Siamese cat.

I wave back. "I'm Yuni, Asian War Priestess of party XStorm. My subclass is Anjai." Pointing over my shoulder, I single out each of my fellow party members. "May I introduce you to my brother, Bradford the Fire Wizard and Life-Stealer. Next to him is Ruby the Centaur Fighter/Barbarian and Penelope the Goth

Fighter/Guide, riding on Ruby's back. Then there's our fearless leader, ChrisCross, affectionately known as CC, an Elitist Martial Artist and Psyon. And wound around his waist is his Magical Companion, Lance the Serpent, an Electric Warrior and Rogue."

My Empathy is low average, but my Sensing and Insight are both high average. It's not my imagination... both Dylan and Mithabel flinch as I introduce CC. Are they biased against his kindred label, *Elitist*? I confess I don't care for it, either. But I promised myself not to hold the label itself against him. He's been nothing but nice to me the whole game, and taken every measure possible to protect me when I've been in trouble.

Amarynth had mentioned friction between our parties, and I'm beginning to see it for myself, sadly.

We continue our march across the Dunes of Doom towards Minook. If anyone speaks, it's not on any chat channel I have access to. I want to continue my private chat with Dylan, but my mind won't settle on anything appropriate to say, and apparently neither will hers.

Fifteen minutes or so into our trek, Mithabel halts. "There's movement on the horizon." She shades her eyes with a hand. "Arachnid Behemoths. I have it on good authority they don't respect the safe route. Party MAD can fly over them. We'll keep our time in the air to a minimum so as not to attract wandering mooks. How about you in XStorm? Can you fly?"

"Just me," I say.

Mithabel turns her gaze on me. "Any ideas on how the rest of your party gets past these things?"

I wait for CC or Ruby to say something. They're the ones who hash out all our strategies. Maybe they're discussing the matter on private chat.

Ruby rides up, Penelope on her back. CC, Lance, and Bradford keep their distance. The Centaur stops beside Amarynth, a few steps behind me and Dylan. She tosses her long, red curls. "We have a plan to get past the Arachnids, but ask that Yuni be allowed to go with you in the air. We also ask that if our plan fails and we're captured, you do what you can to free us. Failing that, please kill us. Yuni, we're counting on you. If we die, we'll respawn at your location."

"I won't let you down." A lump forms in my throat. I don't know how high or fast I can fly. But in addition to Flight Speed, I have the Hide skill, which can help me stay out of sight of any random mooks that might show up once we leave the safe route and take to the air.

Bradford clears his throat. "How do we know the Arachnid Behemoths don't respect the safe path?"

Mithabel waves the map. "We have information from someone with previous experience in the matter."

"Oh, yeah? And who might that be?" Leave it to my brother to press on the matter.

The Tank bristles. "XStorm is welcome to go it alone to Minook. Traveling with us doesn't give you the right to know all our secrets."

"Bradford, please." I turn puppy dog eyes on him. "They aren't beholden to us. Ruby has a plan, and I trust her. We're so much more capable now than when we encountered these things before. We can do this."

My brother's shoulders relax. "You're right, sis. Let's go."

"All right, then." Mithabel refers to her map and leads on.

Dylan touches my wrist, reassuring me. "Stick close to me, Yuni. I'll make sure you get past the Behemoths."

Why do I have the sudden urge to cry?

ഇൽ൫ൽൽ൫ഇൽ൫

We're still well outside the range of the Behemoth web attacks when party MAD agrees it's time to take to the sky.

"One moment." Facing XStorm, I raise my fist high and focus on my Morale skill. "May the blessing of Athlea be upon us all.

See you on the other side, my friends." All their actions will be at +24 against the giant metallic spider army. It's the least I can do.

Taking her cue from me, Dylan calls for the blessing of Scintilla on party MAD.

Mithabel, Kaleisha, and Magnum fly without the aid of wings. With Niav clinging to the Angel's shoulder, Zyekt takes hands with Dylan and Amarynth, flaps his wings, and rises into the sky with his charges. I lift off the ground beside Dylan. Rolag follows in our wake.

I immediately fall behind. My Flight Speed skill isn't on par with the capabilities of party MAD.

Rolag passes over my head. "Grab onto my legs, Priestess."

I do as instructed, but it only serves to slow him down. "It's no use." I let go.

Dylan glances back. "Slow down, Zyekt. I don't want to leave Yuni behind."

"Let me try something." I haven't tried all of my most recently acquired skills. I invoke Shapeshift Crow.

My body shrinks, turning black and covered with feathers. My vision sharpens. My arms have become wings. I spread them, catching the wind. Oh, this is crazy in the extreme.

Another skill I have yet to try is Wind Control. Sounds like that could help. I focus, picturing the wind flowing in the direction I want to fly. It picks up, giving me lift and increasing my forward momentum. I caw with glee as I easily catch up to the others. I'm going faster than Mithabel now. I slow to match the speed of my traveling companions.

Dylan laughs. "Wow, you Anjai and your shapeshifting abilities."

Oh, yeah, that's right, I'm not the only Anjai here. "What can you Shapeshift into, Mithabel?"

The Tank/Anjai ignores my question.

"Don't mind her," Dylan says. "She likes keeping secrets."

"I can understand that. It's her prerogative."

We're halfway over the spider army when I notice a change in their behavior. They're no longer heading towards my XStorm friends. The Behemoths are amassing beneath me and party MAD, tracking us. Or trying. They can't move as fast as we can fly. But they're doing their best to keep up with us while ignoring the XStorm members still on the ground.

"Um, hey, MAD." It's my brother on local chat. "The Behemoths are turning around. They're not coming at us anymore. They're after you." He switches to party chat. "Sis, let us know when you've landed and are back on the safe path. Stir up as much sand as you can to leave us a trail."

"I will. We need more flying capability in our party."

"Don't I know it. Good luck, sis. Stay alive."

"Look sharp, folks." Mithabel points up.

Screeches sound from overhead. Six dark, winged shapes drop towards us… prehistoric birds… Pteranodons.

Amarynth keeps hold of the Angel's hand while equipping her crossbow in her free hand. A bolt loads of its own accord. She takes aim and fires.

The bolt divides into two bolts, streaking towards two different targets. Each bolt strikes and obliterates a mook. That's bad ass.

Dylan holds up her free hand, and a metal star forms between her finger and thumb. She flings it upward. It doesn't divide into two stars like the Archer's crossbow bolt, but it finds its target, killing it instantly. Three down, three to go.

I don't have a range attack. My Enervate spell causes damage by touch. My War spell enchants a weapon, but I have no missile weapon to apply it to. All the range attack capability of XStorm is with the other XStorm members.

As I reflect on my shortcomings, another shuriken from Dylan and a double bolt from Amarynth put an end to the last three remaining Pteranodons. The mooks were still fifty feet away, and they're already dealt with. Two party members of MAD just took out six Pteranodons in roughly six seconds. The mooks never stood a chance.

"Congrats, musume. Because you are accompanying party MAD as an ally, you have received 480,000 XP. You are 8% of the way to level 21." Easily flying along beside me, Inuki looks pleased to deliver the good news.

"Hey, *nice*, sis." Bradford chuckles over XStorm party chat. "Keep getting us free XP." Everyone in my party earned the same XP I did.

"Dylan." I flap my beak out of habit, though it has never been necessary to move one's mouth when speaking in the game. The motion helps me form coherent sentences.

The Polynesian Priestess turns her brilliant smile on me. She enjoyed killing those Pteranodons. "Yes, Crow Yuni?"

Inwardly, I giggle at her use of the *Crow* appellation. "Why don't you and Amarynth take a moment and kill those giant spiders below us? You've got the range attacks to do it. They're sitting ducks, and their webs can't reach as high as you can shoot. Take them out and let's be rid of them once and for all. Think of all the XP they must be worth."

"I'm all for it." Amarynth's broad grin says better than words how eager she is to execute my plan. She aims at the ground.

"*Amarynth, no.*"

But Mithabel's admonishment is too late. A bolt streaks from the Archer's crossbow, becoming two bolts on the way down. They strike the abdomens of two Behemoths.

"That's depressing." Inuki frowns. "The two Behemoths are each now at 97% HP. It will take all day to defeat this army at that rate. There are hundreds of spiders down there."

Mithabel glares at Amarynth. "We're lucky you didn't have the power to kill them. We need to be as far away from them as possible when they die. Their death explosion can reach at least fifty yards, probably a lot more, maybe even double that."

Dylan grimaces. "I don't have anywhere near a hundred-yard range."

"I do." Amarynth holds up her crossbow. "Normally it wouldn't be recommended to shoot a crossbow from that far away, but I'm so stacked up on crossbow skills, I'm betting I can hit my targets every time even from that distance. But I'll need a boatload of enchantment on my crossbow if we're to kill even a few of these things before a Boss shows up. Do we have that kind of enchantment power available to us?"

The Polynesian Priestess glances at me.

I try to shrug, but I doubt it comes across as one, me being in Crow form and all. "Only one way to find out."

We fly higher, think about stopping, and then fly higher still. "Move far away from the spiders," I tell my XStorm companions over party chat. "Maybe a couple hundred yards."

"This is about 120 yards, I'd say." Amarynth signals for us to stop, and we do. "Which of you Priestesses want to give me an enchantment or two?"

I wing my way to Amarynth. "Allow me." She holds her crossbow out, and I grasp it in my talons.

My Goddess, Athlea, speaks across a private channel to me. "Amarynth is a Daughter of mine. Enchant her crossbow using all the Auni you can spare, and allow no other deity's enchantment upon it. Heed my words, and I will double your spell effect."

I put 90 of my 124 Auni into the spell. "May this weapon show your foes the true meaning of War, in the name of Athlea." The crossbow turns black. I look to Dylan. "Amarynth serves the War Goddess, and the War Goddess will grant her all the assistance she needs. Save your Auni this time."

Dylan inclines her head. "As you wish."

The spiders amass beneath us. Some climb on top of others, trying to get closer to us. We fly up a bit further.

"This is good." Amarynth aims and fires. The bolt splits and flies at two different targets, both hitting bulbous abdomens.

Both Arachnids explode. *Bam.* Dead. Wow. My enchantment and Athlea's blessing did this.

Fire and smoke billow out and up. We all instinctively fly further upward as fast as we can go. My body warms beneath my feathers.

The fire and heat subside and the smoke dissipates, leaving the air clear. "Damage report, Inuki."

"No one in party XStorm or MAD took damage from the explosion, musume. Two Arachnid Behemoths have been destroyed. None of the other Behemoths were harmed."

"*What the hell*, sis?"

I chuckle at Bradford's outburst. "Glad you're okay. Stay back. We're taking out the whole Behemoth army."

"Cool. You go, girl."

Amarynth fires again, and then again and again, each missile fired dividing into two. Six more Arachnid Behemoths go bye bye in the span of a few seconds.

"Damn," Bradford mutters. The others in party XStorm make similar utterances. Pride swells my chest and quickens my blood. Because of me, my party will likely be gaining another level or two soon.

The Viking Archer waits out a cool down period and then fires three more times, killing six more spiders. They're dropping like flies.

"You and I work well together, Archer." I feel so at home with this group. Granted, Mithabel isn't likely to express any respect for me and what I'm helping to accomplish here, but her silence will be no worse than what I'm used to from my XStorm companion Penelope the Goth. There's a silent type in every crowd.

Another minute passes, and Amarynth has already killed a total of fifty Behemoths. She's beginning to make a dent in the Arachnid army. How much time do we have before more Pteranodons show up?

Ten minutes later, no Pteranodons have appeared, and the Arachnid Behemoth army is destroyed, not a one of them remaining. Four hundred and four giant metal spiders destroyed in total by Amarynth, my enchantment, and the blessing of our Goddess.

"You have gained four-hundred-and-four million XP, musume. Congratulations, you are level 27 Priestess, level 18 Anjai. Your War skill is now level 49. You gained two new Priestess skills, Demoralize at level 7 and Followers at level 5."

I'm light-headed. This was my doing. Well, mine and Amarynth's. If either of us had acted alone, that army would still be down there, and I'd still be level 20. I jumped seven whole levels from this encounter, and can almost taste level 30.

"I feel faint," squeaks Niav. "Only *three more levels* to go."

"*Sis*, you are *the* best." Bradford speaks for all of XStorm over our party chat. "*Level 27? We are freaking out of our minds down here.*"

"Good job, Amarynth." Mithabel gives the Archer a thumbs up. "You, too, Yuni." She actually smiles at me.

I check my character sheet. Ah. Maybe my level 45 Attraction and level 30 Presence are serving to sway Mithabel's opinion of me.

I'm still not as attractive as Dylan and never will be.

CHAPTER TWENTY

Morrow: Ghostly

The seething, short green woman is poised nearby, gripping her axe handle like she's ready to chop something in half. Greelia isn't from Khertaan or Earth, but some other game world.

She swings, burying the blade in the table top, throwing up splinters. Reminds me of how Jean took a similar action not so long ago, but she'd actually been aiming for Nick. Greelia is taking out her rage on the table so she won't be using her weapon on me instead. The female Goblin Warrior easily yanks the axe free of the table, something Jean had struggled with.

As for Jean, she's not here, and neither is Seth, for which I'm truly thankful. As far as I'm concerned, they can both go to hell. Let them go together. They deserve each other.

Above Greelia floats Nick's lady ghost. I don't look at her, not wanting her to leave, because Nick wouldn't want it. She's constantly on the periphery, flitting about to stay out of sight the best she can. Her presence can mean only one thing. She senses me as Nick. I have no reason to tell her she's wrong… from one way of looking at it, she's right. I'm all that remains in the multiverse of Nick's awareness, being his subconsciousness manifested as a game avatar. Is she aware of what I am and that I'm not the person she's looking for? She must be.

"Britta. Britta. Britta." Screaming the name repeatedly, the Goblin Warrior chops and chops until she splits the tabletop into halves. "Aaaagh." She turns her wild gaze on me. "This is *your* fault, *Morrow*. I shouldn't have listened to you. Now my baby is gone." She drops the axe, and it clatters on the floor. Her chin drops to her chest, green strands of hair hanging to hide her face. We're both silent for a minute or maybe ten. Then her fists clench and shoulders tense. "Come back to me, Britta." Her whispers are soft growls forced through clenched teeth. "Come back to me. Come back to me."

My avatar heart races. Tears dampen my cheeks. Everything wrong in the multiverse is Nick's fault, and I need to fix it. But how? Nick would have asked ODYSSEY, but I don't sense any of the collective with me.

Greelia straightens her knees, her chin still down, her fists raised before her breasts. Veins pop out on her green arms. She continues her murmured growling. "Come back to me."

The walls fade around us, but not completely. They're as ethereal as lady ghost. Other ghosts appear. Renee, dressed in her usual red leather miniskirt, stands before me, her opacity wavering by degrees. I reach for her. "Renee. Where are you? Do you have any nanobots with you?" If I recall correctly, she has some of the ODYSSEY nanobots integrated with her programming. I hope to hell I'm right.

Her body trembles, her eyes wide. "I'm scared, Morrow."

"Of what?" She's not programmed to have emotions. How can she be scared of anything?

"I'm vanishing. You're vanishing. We're all vanishing. You started this, and you need to stop it."

"It wasn't me. It was Nick."

Renee's sexy figure flickers like a dying light bulb, but her shoulders aren't shaking as much. "You're all that remains of him.

He merged the timelines. But the Fanciful Pegasus timeline isn't dominating. It's a matter of time before we're pushed out of existence. We're already ghosts. Look at us."

I hold up my hands. Fuck, I can see right through them. "Do you have *any* of the ODYSSEY nanobots, Renee?"

"Yes, but I don't dare talk to them. They're engaged in keeping Khertaan running. If they stop, if they're even distracted for a moment, I'm afraid of what will happen."

"Come back to me." Greelia's exhortation to her lost child persists. The Goblin Warrior stands bold and solid in a sea of mists, the hue of her green skin stark and bright. She's a game avatar, but she's the only thing in this room not losing substance.

"Greelia." Her name flutters off my tongue like the last gasp of a dying man. It's not enough to get her attention. I go to her, but my hand on her shoulder falls through her body. I wave my hand before her eyes, but she has them clenched shut.

She doesn't relent. "Come back to me, Britta. Come back to me." The Goblin Warrior presses her fists together. A dark, hooded cloak appears, covering her body and shading her face.

Did I cause that?

I couldn't have. I'm drained of willpower and emotion, with nothing left to give. "I'm sorry, Renee, but I's so fucking tired... fully spent. Our fate is up to ODYSSEY and Greelia now."

Renee shakes her head with vigor. "We can't give up. What do you want to know from ODYSSEY? I'll take the risk to ask one question." Her gaze loses focus. "Wait. He just pushed a bunch of data at me. Give me a second to assimilate it."

I dare to hope.

My support AI purses her lips. "Nick attempted to merge the timelines. He wanted the Fanciful Pegasus timeline to dominate, but others resisted, and he failed to override them all. Jean and Seth are each championing their own, neither of which grants access to Khertaan. They're locked in a battle of wills over which one of their timelines will dominate. Hell hath no fury like a woman scorned, and Jean is pushing Seth out. If Jean wins, the dominating timeline will be one in which Seth doesn't exist and Nick was never born, where Jean was impregnated by someone other than Nick and gave birth to a daughter named Karen, who never came out as trans. If Seth wins, the dominating timeline will be one in which he has already destroyed Earth and countless other worlds occupied by sentient beings.

"Greelia has also entered the battle of wills. She's pushing for a timeline with her own private world where she has her baby with her. That timeline doesn't include access to Khertaan and doesn't include you, Morrow, but it does include Nick as the father of her child. While we want a timeline with access to Khertaan to become dominant, it's good Greelia joined the battle of wills. If not for her intervention, Jean would have already won against Seth. But Greelia can't overpower them both. The three of them are at a stalemate. For now."

I'm missing some key piece of info. "How can Greelia participate in a battle of wills? *She's a game avatar.* She's basically a figment of Charli's imagination, *and Charli isn't even real.*"

"Just as *you and I* aren't real, Morrow?" Renee raises her hands to her forehead and sweeps them down her body. "This is what no one understood before ODYSSEY went timeline hopping with Nick. *Everything is real.* Everything you read in books or on the internet. Everything you see on TV or in the movies. Everything you hear over the radio, in a podcast, or spoken by an influencer or politician. *It's all the truth.* Humans don't have the creative capacity to imagine new things. As the saying goes, there is nothing new under the sun. Every so-called figment of imagination corresponds to a real existence in some timeline. Charli is real, Greelia is real, and so is Britta.

"Every time a writer writes a piece of fiction, whether or not they intend to share it with the public in some form, they're opening their minds to an alternate universe where what they think they're imagining isn't imaginary, but real. But more than that, every piece of fiction created weakens the membranes between the universes. The fiction doesn't even need to be recorded on a physical medium. *Imagining* is all it takes to tap another world.

"The growing number of creative people on Earth has stressed the metaphysical membranes separating the timelines like never before, which made it possible for Nick to merge so many of them with his willpower. They were already bleeding into each other, overlapping to the extent that people were doubting their own realities, and with good reason. But the merge took everything from Nick—and by association, nearly everything from you—so that now the fate of the merged timelines rests with three entities who don't have our best interests at heart. Our ability to access Khertaan is fading away.

"You're real and I'm real, too, as long as our timeline continues to exist. If our timeline goes, then so do we. We'll be wiped from history and memory."

The spark of hope resting inside me has yet to flare into flame, but I'm not dismissing its chances yet. "Thank you, Renee, for not giving up. We're not done, and until we are, we fight. So... we understand the problem. Did ODYSSEY tell you the solution?"

Forcing air between her teeth, Greelia continues her refrain. "Come back to me. Come back to me." The Goblin Warrior's back straightens and her chin lifts, but her eyes are still shut. The green skin of her fists darkens, while her knuckles whiten.

My AI lady in red huffs. "ODYSSEY can't say with 100% surety that any attempted solution will succeed. But if no one bends their will towards making the Fanciful Pegasus timeline the dominant one in the merge, it will vanish, as will everything that has happened in it. Not only will access to Khertaan be gone, but Nick won't marry Kendra, and Susie won't be born. Nick will never meet Charli... and you'll never manifest as his Khertaan avatar.

"I realize your willpower is all tapped out, Morrow. I'm focusing on sustaining Fanciful Pegasus and access to Khertaan as much as I can, but I'm no match for Jean, Seth, or Greelia. We need help, because we need to overpower *all three* of them."

123

The Goblin Warrior raises her voice above a normal conversational level. "Come back to me."

I go to a window. White mists lazily swirl beyond the pane, blocking my view of anything else. I go to the front door and open it. A wall of fog fills the doorway. Probing with my right foot finds no solid ground beyond the threshold. It's as though the house is afloat in a fog bank. There's no mobile phone in the place. I pick up the receiver for the land line. There's no signal. "Fuck. How can we find help? We can't even leave the house or call out."

Renee hovers by my side. "You might not ought to leave here. It's like Seth said earlier. Nick created a nexus, a bubble trapped inside the attempted merge, and that's where we are now. It's not in any timeline, but it borders on them all. Once a timeline dominates the merge, it will obliterate even this nexus. On the other hand, if you leave this nexus before a timeline becomes dominant, the nexus will fail, and all the timelines in the merge will unravel and be lost, undoing everything Nick tried to accomplish by sacrificing himself."

"Great." This conversation is testing my patience and sanity. "So I'm right back where I started, unable to do anything to help... other than quietly sitting here in this fucking dimensional bubble."

The AI nods. "I can affirm that even with my help, you're in no shape mentally or emotionally to make any difference in the battle of wills waging between Seth, Jean, and Greelia. The two of us together can't overpower all three. We need allies, but neither of us have the means to recruit them, and my nanobots can't do it, either."

There must be options neither Renee nor I have thought about. "Does it have to be me who stays in the nexus? Greelia isn't going anywhere. Would her presence keep the nexus intact?"

"I don't know the answer to that, my love."

Her term of endearment strikes me to the core. She's only an AI with no human understanding of love, but I do care about her, just as I care about Greelia, a character from a tabletop role-playing game universe with a manifestation in this place. If the Fanciful Pegasus timeline becomes dominant, will Greelia and Britta cease to exist? Or will Britta still exist as the child of Nick and Charli? Will Nick come back if a timeline wins where he's meant to exist?

Greelia has advanced to shouting, and her refrain has changed. *"Come back to me, both of you."*

The room spins, but I'm not ready to give up. "Renee, is it possible for me to enter Khertaan while technically still occupying this nexus?"

She shakes her head. "My nanobots are straddling the membrane between the Fanciful Pegasus timeline and this nexus. They could facilitate your passage to the FP timeline and from there to Khertaan, but you'd have to cross the membrane and thus no longer be in the nexus. As your support AI, I'd be automatically drawn in with you, so I'd be gone from here, and thus my nanobots, too. If you go to Khertaan, only Greelia will remain in the nexus. Maybe she could keep the nexus intact and still make a difference in the battle of wills, but there's a significant chance she won't. *You really should stay here.*"

I'm *not* giving up. "How did your nanobots get all that information for you just now?"

She's silent for a moment, presumably asking ODYSSEY. "Initially the nanobots needed hosts with a certain genetic makeup. They were restricted to Nick, Kendra, and Susie, and their avatars, you, Kylie, and Slithy. But the nanobots have adapted and are spreading to others like a virus, a few of them implanting themselves in each infected person, striving to multiply and establish their own collective. A few of mine have gone to you over the past few minutes, for instance, replenishing what you lost. They aren't strong enough to benefit you yet, but they'll grow… eventually. Likewise, some of my nanobots have spread to Greelia, too.

"As to your question, some of the nanobots have infected Jean, in a timeline where UTOPIA FOUR is active. My nanobots can access UTOPIA FOUR in that timeline as well. If the nanobots in Khertaan could access UTOPIA FOUR, that could create a means for us to communicate with Kylie and Slithy through the nanobots. But, sadly, neither Khertaan nor the Fanciful Pegasus timeline have UTOPIA FOUR."

"Okay, scratch that idea." I wrack my brain for another one. "Tell me the exact process by which avatars respawn in Khertaan."

Renee shrugs. "A player goes to sleep and their subconsciousness inhabits their in-game avatar. That's all I know."

I swallow a lump in my throat. "Nick is my player, and he's gone. So how do I even exist?"

"You didn't listen to me." Renee pushes her face in front of mine. "Everyone in or from Khertaan is *real*. Nick and Kendra created a program to gain access to Khertaan, *but Khertaan itself resides in its own timeline*. How the program accesses it, I don't know, and maybe neither do Nick or Kendra. But you and I are not dependent on the existence of Nick or Kendra. We are our own entities. It's just that when your body here isn't inhabited by Nick's subconsciousness, you're an automaton going through the motions of living, like a program."

I step back. "Well, I'm clearly not an automaton. So, I should still be as capable as ever, right? Can I do here what I could do in Khertaan? I mean… Charli could use her Khertaan abilities when she and Nick were on Earth. So let me try something…. *Rancor*, buddy, I summon you, my Magical Familiar."

"Ha ha ha." My Woodpecker friend pops into existence right before my eyes, flapping his wings to stay aloft. "About time you brought me back into the game."

"We're not in Khertaan, buddy."

"Whatever you say, Morrow." He perches on my right shoulder. "But then, I'll peck, where are we?"

"We're in a nexus created by my player, Nick, who doesn't exist as a player anymore, but that's beside the point. As the last vestige of him, it's too risky for me to leave the nexus. I want you to go back into Khertaan and spread the word: Everyone in Khertaan—and I mean everyone—needs to concentrate on keeping Khertaan intact. Otherwise, it could vanish, and everyone in it. Can you do that for me, buddy?"

"Ha ha, sure. Just show me the way, and off I go."

Renee raises a hand. "Might I add something?"

"Please do."

The corner of her mouth turns down. "What you're telling our little friend isn't correct."

I'm confused, and say so.

Renee huffs. "The Khertaan timeline is not in danger of vanishing. We need help in maintaining the *Fanciful Pegasus* timeline, from which Nick and Kendra accessed Khertaan. If the Fanciful Pegasus timeline isn't saved, all the PCs in Khertaan would lose their players, which could turn them all into automatons."

"Well, hold on then." I thought I understood it, but I still need clarification. "Are you saying we have *two* timelines to worry about, the one where Khertaan is real, and the one where Nick and Kendra created the program to access it? If they're distinct timelines, don't we need to save them both?"

"No. Khertaan itself isn't in the group of timelines Nick attempted to merge. Khertaan will continue whether Nick and Kendra do or not. They discovered a way to access it and connect to their alternate selves there… to you and Kylie."

I hold up a hand, palm outward, index finger touching a brow. "I don't understand any of this timeline shit. I thought I did, but I clearly don't. What can Rancor say to the others in Khertaan to get their help in saving what needs saving?"

"He could ask everyone to concentrate on Charli and her story. She's the bridge between timelines." Renee strokes my raised arm, though her ghost flesh goes right through me. "If her history remains intact, then so will the alternate universes she's visited, which includes not only Khertaan, but the Fanciful Pegasus timeline and others."

"You're talking about making *multiple* timelines dominant in the merge? Is that possible? Doesn't that undo Nick's attempt to merge them into one?"

She shakes her head. "He succeeded in preventing a multitude of timelines from disintegrating. The best way he could think of to do that was to bring all the broken timelines together in one powerful bundle that could punch a hole through a metaphysical obstacle. They didn't actually all merge into one, but they were strong enough as a partially merged group to break through. What he did sufficed and would continue to suffice if Jean and Seth weren't trying to take advantage of it. They are trying to force the bundle of timelines to fully merge into a single timeline they control. If they can be stopped, there's no reason why the timelines couldn't return to their normal, separate selves. But with Jean and Seth involved—and now Greelia—all trying to make a single timeline rule the group, the timelines we want to continue on are in jeopardy of being consumed.

"It's up to us to shape what happens next. Focusing on one timeline is an easier task than trying to save two. But if we have multiple minds working at it, why can't we save multiple timelines? And Charli is the key to that possibility."

I give it all a minute to sink in. Even Nick failed to understand everything as well as he thought he did. "Very well. Rancor, I need you to ask everyone in Khertaan to focus on Charli. They can't let her slip from their minds." I incline my head to Renee. "Now that we have all that settled, can you get our buddy Rancor here into Khertaan?"

Her eyes light up. "I believe so." She turns her gaze on the Woodpecker. "But you won't be in the game as Morrow's Familiar. You'll be like any other NPC, with autonomy."

"Ha ha, really?" Rancor flutters his wings. "That would be cool."

I wave for attention. "If he's to be an NPC, can I invite him to our party?"

Renee grimaces. "Sorry, no, dear. Within this nexus, he's still your Familiar. He won't be an NPC until he's in Khertaan." She turns back to Rancor. "You'll initially be on your own, Woodpecker. You can join another party if they'll have you, create your own party, or go solo. It's up to you. So… whenever you're ready." She beckons to him.

"What do I do?" My Woodpecker familiar launches from my shoulder and wings his way to my support AI.

She points. "Fly into my head. Concentrate on where you want to go, or who you want to be with."

"Go to Kylie," I interject. "Soon as you get there, ask her to invite you into TimeTrippers."

"Ha ha, will do, Morrow." Rancor winks at me.

"Oh, before you go, Rancor…." I bring out a small object. "Take this. It's the coin I received from Ezmerelda when we visited her hut. I don't know what it's for, but I seriously doubt it will be of use to me, whereas it might be of use to you in Khertaan." I flip the coin up in the air.

The Woodpecker zips over and grabs the coin before it begins its descent. "Thanks, Morrow." The coin vanishes as he stashes it. "Ha ha, bye." He aims for Renee's forehead and passes through her ghostly skin into her skull. He doesn't reemerge.

CHAPTER TWENTY-ONE

Greelia: Family Bond

I bury my axe blade in the table top, throwing up splinters. It's better than taking out my rage on the Punk Wizard. *"Britta."* I yank the axe free. *"Britta."* I hack at the table again. *"Britta."* I keep chopping and shouting.

The tabletop lies on the floor in halves. "Aaaagh." I turn to face the Wizard and throw the blame at him that my baby is gone.

He has nothing to say for himself. I ought to toss my axe at him—plant it in his forehead. I drop it to remove the temptation. The clattering on the floor sounds as hollow as my heart.

I drop my head, my straight green hair falling before my gaze to block my view of everything else in the room. I don't want to see any of it. Not Morrow, not my axe, not the ruined table. I block it all. Even if only in my mind's eye, all I want to see is my baby.

Britta. I repeat her name in my head, as though through my will alone I can bring her back. And why not? I lost Britta when I switched places with Charli. My baby is with the Cowgirl now. And it's not really Morrow's fault. It's *mine… I* made the switch happen. Which means, I can switch us back. Better yet, I'll bring Britta here. I don't want us to be with Spyder. I'd rather be with Morrow than the Behemoth.

Hell, if I'm going to change the world with my willpower, why not go for everything I want? Nick is Britta's father, not Morrow. Nick, Britta, and I should be together. But one thing at a time. Once I have Britta again in my arms, then I'll concentrate on the two of us being with Nick. I can do it. After all, Nick and Charli pulled me from one world to another, all through the power of the mind. Is their willpower greater than mine? I think not.

No. *Come back to me.* I force the words through clenched teeth, calling my baby girl.

Repeating my mantra, I drop to my knees, raising my fists before my chest, as though I could punch through the fabric of the multiverse and pull my baby through the breach.

The veil separating me from Britta stretches thin under my mental assault. Mists rise around me in protest. Within the mists stand two hooded, cloaked figures in silhouette, one feminine in form and the other masculine, a foot apart and facing each other, as though in a staring match. They occupy a circular cross-section of a wooden floor, wisps of mist swirling lazily beneath and around the disk on which they stand. The male's knees bend beneath the concentrated willfulness of the female.

Like the disk, I'm afloat and drifting in the mists. With my legs folded beneath me, I draw close to the competitors. This is a fight I must join, for this is the battle to win it all. The two standing before me want the same thing I want—to have their own way with the multiverse.

He is Seth the Destroyer, driven to destruction. In his desired reality, he has already destroyed countless worlds. Having partially completed his goal has given him a sense of entitlement, weakening his resolve. Too bad for him.

She is Jean the Scorned, driven by a zealous self-righteousness rivaling that of a wronged Goddess. She seeks to crush any timeline containing even a trace of Nick. She wants a child with a different mate. The child is a daughter named Karen, who will become a polite, heterosexual woman bowing to every whim of her overbearing mother. Jean hasn't succeeded in gaining *any* of what she wants, but this only serves to intensify the fighting spirit within her.

I am Greelia the Grieving, unable to accept my loss. Like Jean, I'm a mother, but my loss is greater than hers. She's ungrateful for the child she does have. My child is missing. "Come back to me, Britta. Come back to me." Fulfillment of my mantra is the only way to appease me.

Straightening my legs, I plant my feet on the edge of the wooden disk and face its center, smashing my fists together in front of my chest. A hooded cloak manifests upon my body and a cone of light centers on me from directly above.

Two other perfect cones of light split the darkness before me, one cone centered on Seth and the other on Jean. Without bending a knee, the two of them swivel and glide along the edge of the wooden disk until the three of us stand at equidistant points on the circle, each of us facing the center, where colored beams of light shoot upward through an inch-diameter hole in the disk. A red beam passing through the hole occupies more than half the available space. A blue beam fills a quarter of it. A smattering of other colored beams shoots up through the remaining space.

Each beam is a timeline. The red one is Jean's and the blue one is Seth's. Britta and I don't exist in either of their chosen timelines. This won't do. Which one is the one I want? Gritting my teeth, I exhale and concentrate.

A green beam of light wavers, and I focus on it, pouring all my willpower into strengthening it. That's my timeline, the one where Nick and I have a daughter named Britta.

No, something is missing from the timeline.

Nick.

The father of my child doesn't exist in *any* of the timelines. In the timeline represented by the green beam of light, Britta is of virgin birth, and I am her mother.

Virgin birth? No way. I'll not be the mother of a religion. There must be at least one timeline in which Nick exists.

My mantra doesn't change, but its focus does. I'm not only seeking Britta to return to me, but Nick, too. "Come back to me, *both of you.*"

Seth and Jean stop staring down each other and focus on their corresponding beams of light. Jean's beam grows in diameter. Seth's holds steady. Some of the tiny beams all but blink out. The green beam I'm focused on flickers, which is understandable, since it's not precisely the one I want. But the one I want doesn't seem to be available.

Nick existed once, even residing in multiple timelines. Where are *those* timelines? I need one containing the three of us. I *must* have it.

The disk spins, or perhaps the mists rush around it. Up from the hole in the center shoots the thinnest ray of green light. That's mine. Nick, Britta, and I live as a family in that frail timeline, one that had already been crowded out, but which has sprouted again from my hope and determination. No matter how long it takes, I *will* win this war. Seth and Jean have *nothing* on me.

CHAPTER TWENTY-TWO

Lady Ghost: Drawn to Nick

Below me, the Goblin Warrior woman hacks at the table top, all the while shouting the name of her lost child. When the table lies in halves, she drops her weapon, berating Morrow like everything bad is his fault. It's infuriating. I resist the urge to pick up her fallen axe and behead her.

She drops to her knees, chanting. Everything except her turns as ghostly as I am. This isn't good. Morrow already bore only a weak trace of Nick, and now he's nothing more than a ghost. What is happening? It must be the Goblin woman's doing.

Other ghosts appear, but one of them stands apart, a woman in a red leather miniskirt. Morrow addresses her as *Renee*. She's trembling and admits she's frightened. She confirms what I'm seeing, that both she and Morrow are vanishing.

If Morrow fades away, there is no Nick. If there's no Nick, then there's no *me*. I can't exist as a ghost unless Nick exists too... somewhere to some degree. Whenever and wherever he is, he'll always draw me to him, whether he notices me or not when I arrive. I'm not being drawn elsewhere—I'm *here* because some vestige of Nick is *here*. The only way I wouldn't be drawn to him is if he were in a timeline where I have a flesh-and-blood existence, and even then fate would bring us together. We're soul mates, Nick and I, and we both know it.

"Greelia." Morrow whispers the name of the Goblin Warrior. She ignores him. He touches her, but his hand passes through her body. He waves his hand in front of her eyes to no avail. She continues her chant, calling for Britta, her baby.

The Goblin woman rises to her feet and presses her fists together before her. A dark cloak manifests, covering her body, with a hood to hide her face. Her chanting grows increasingly louder, until she's shouting. *"Come back to me, both of you."* Hmm. She's tacked a phrase onto the end of her mantra. She's no longer calling only for her baby, but for someone else, too. Who?

The world spins around Greelia and me. The floor beneath her feet takes a solid appearance. She's on the edge of a wooden disk, facing the center. Two other cloaked figures, one feminine and one masculine, also stand on the edge of the disk. Cones of light shine upon the three of them, one cone centered on each, their positions forming an equilateral triangle.

Straight up from a one-inch hole at the center of the disk shine several beams of light—a thick red one, a blue one about half its size, and several needle thin ones. One of the needle thin ones—a green one—glows brighter than the other thin ones.

I'm looking upon a metaphysical representation of a segment of the multiverse, the bundle that Nick created to push through the metaphysical obstacle that shattered them. The light beams are timelines, and the disk is the obstacle. The needle-thin green beam calls to me, signaling that my lovely Nick might be there. Though it's a weak draw, not even as strong as the one I get from Morrow, I need to investigate.

I fold in on myself and fly into the chosen beam, its greenness engulfing me. The light dims fast and then extinguishes, leaving me in darkness.

A baby laughs. I don't know how far away it is, but I feel the pull in its direction.

What kind of world is this? Am I outside, in a building, or in a cave? I don't know, because my sight can't penetrate the darkness and my sense of touch fails me. I could be passing through walls or trees or solid rock, and I wouldn't know. I'm drawn in a certain direction, and that's where I go.

A bonfire flares in the distance. The baby's laughter comes from that direction. I fly closer.

Cavern walls reflect the light of the flames. Seated on the ground next to the fire are two adult humanoids dressed in ragged shirts and loincloths. One of the two is Greelia, holding and rocking a baby.

The other is Nick, looking like the Nick I know, *not* Morrow and *not* wearing a mohawk. He's smiling, cooing, stroking the cheeks of the baby. He turns his smile on the Goblin woman. "We made such a beautiful baby, Greelia."

The Goblin woman smiles back. "I couldn't be happier." She puts her mouth on the baby's bare stomach and blows raspberries. "Who's a little warrior? Britta, that's who. Britta is a little warrior."

The baby laughs, making fists. She punches Greelia in the mouth, and the Goblin woman joins in the laughter.

Nick looks around. "Something isn't right."

I flit aside as his glance comes my way. If he looks straight at me—sees me for who I really am—his disbelieving mind won't allow me to exist anymore.

He whips his head and locks his gaze on me.

My soul rips down the middle.

CHAPTER TWENTY-THREE

Fauna: Gondra

"As I see it," I say, "we have two problems. First, we need to know where to find this Ken St. Andre, and second, we need a means of transportation."

Ulric holds up an index finger. "We could maybe find Mr. St. Andre's address online, if we had a computer with internet access. We could go to the library."

I grimace at that. "Is this library of which you speak nearby? Can we walk there?"

He shrugs. "I don't actually know where we are."

The walls of the room turn incorporeal, not fully disappearing but becoming see-through. White mists encircle the room, swirling around it like a hurricane—and we're caught in the eye.

"Looks like we're not going anywhere." I throw a sideways glance at Emma.

She's not looking back. Her eyes are wide, her eyebrows up, her mouth gaping. I turn my head to follow her gaze.

Ulric has become a ghost of himself, as translucent as the walls. Grimacing, his head cocked to one side with one eyebrow raised, he studies his hands. "This is unexpected."

Emma's jaw drops another half-inch. "How can you be so calm, Ulric? You're *disappearing*. The *whole room* is disappearing."

He turns his attention to her. "And yet, you're not. Neither is Fauna. Neither is the T&T rulebook or the dice on the table. I don't know what's happening, but it may be that only you two can do something about it."

The cyclone of mists encroaches on the interior of the room, consuming the walls. Ethereal furniture—a couch, a rocking chair, and a standing lamp—are sucked into the swirling tempest. We're inside a cylindrical space gradually decreasing in diameter. The floor is solid beneath my hooves, but it's vaporizing at the edges.

"The rulebook is at the dead center of the storm." Emma pulls out two chairs. The table and chairs are still solid. "We have to game this to survive. Both of you, sit down."

I take one of the offered seats, still cradling Spooky.

Ulric moves his legs like he's striding towards the table, but his body doesn't come any closer. He frowns. "I can't. It's up to you two."

Emma hurries to his side. She tries to grab his wrist, but her hand passes through him. "Oh, Ulric."

His face blurs, like a smudged painting. He no longer looks human.

"*Ulric.*" I jump from my chair, careful not to drop my bundle of darkness.

The storm tugs at him. He waves Emma and me away. "Go. Save yourselves."

And then the tempest swallows him.

Emma and I stare at the spot he just vacated.

ಸಿಥಿಂತಿಖಿಸಿಥ

Taking a seat, Emma grabs up the rulebook and flips pages. I take my seat again. It's difficult to think straight, but Emma acts level-headed. She stabs an index finger at a line of text. "Scottsdale, Arizona. That's where we need to go. That's where we'll find Ken St. Andre."

I don't reply, not sharing her optimism. The image of Ulric being sucked into the storm haunts me. All I can do is sit.

"Are you with me, Fauna?"

I loose a sigh. "What if all that's left of this world is right here at this table? What if Ken St. Andre no longer exists?"

Emma grabs up the dice. "No. If the rulebook is immune to the storm and so are we… characters controlled by its rules… then where did that immunity stem from? Think about it. T&T… and, by extension, *we*… were imbued with certain qualities by its creator. How could our creator imbue us with qualities he didn't have? I'd wager he's seated at a table somewhere in Scottsdale, Arizona right now, just like we are, with a similar storm spinning around him." She points off to the side. "Look. The storm isn't closing in any further. We're safe from it for now. But if we want to do anything other than sit here, we need to leave this place. I have an idea how we can go to Ken St. Andre's location. But first, you need to run a game for me."

"I don't know how to run the game. Besides which, I have my hands full with Spooky." How can she be thinking of playing a game when we just lost a friend?

We're not from the same universe as Ulric and didn't know him that long, but his loss pains me as much as the loss of Ronnie does. Emma couldn't turn off the tears when we lost Charli. But we lose Ulric, and she's stalwart. I'm the one about to crash and burn. It's good we have each other. I can't imagine how either of us would function if we lost the other now.

She picks up two dice and shakes them. "Just tell me what level of saving roll I need to make for us to meet a benevolent, level eleven wizard."

"You think Ken St. Andre is a level eleven wizard?"

Emma shakes her head. "He's not from inside the game. The level eleven wizard I'm looking for doesn't need to be anyone in particular. They just need to know certain spells and be friendly towards me."

"Fine." I'm tempted to say she needs a level eleven saving roll, but she wants the wizard to have certain spells and be friendly, so I increase the level by two. "You need to make a level thirteen saving roll on Luck to run into an appropriate wizard."

My Elf friend does a mental calculation. "I need 80 total. My Luck is 87. That's an automatic success… unless I roll an automatic failure. Come on, five or higher." She rolls the two dice. The first die shows a four, the second one a two. She pounds a triumphant fist into a palm. "Six. Made it. Okay, so what does this level eleven wizard I've encountered look like?"

I take a moment to think. "He's six feet tall, wearing a dark cloak and a hood. He has a wooden staff in one hand."

Emma's eyes light up. "Good, good. Does he hold some scrolls in the other hand?"

"Roll another level thirteen saving roll on Luck."

She rolls, and the dice come up four and two again. She's made it, and she rubs her hands together. "Goody."

I nod. "Yeah, he's holding some scrolls, rolled up in his other hand. He asks why you've come to see him."

From the mists swirling around our gaming table strides a man wearing a hooded cloak.

Emma and I both gasp.

This guy isn't in our imaginations.

As he exits the mists, his hood draws back of its own accord to reveal a face covered with gray and green scales. He holds a wooden staff in one bony hand and some rolled-up scrolls in the other.

After glancing around to take in the situation, he taps the end of his staff on the floor. Within the perimeter of the misty cyclone, a dome of green light materializes over us. "I am Gondra. Who are you, please?" He holds the final sibilant in a prolonged hiss.

My Warrior-Wizard companion stands and bows. "I am Emma the Mystical. My friend here is Fauna.75…."

"You can just call me Fauna." I don't stand, but hold up the shadow baby. "This is Spooky."

Gondra holds up the scrolls, pointing them first at Emma and then at me. "I sense traces of Nick McKenzie from you. Explain."

Emma shrugs. "He's our player. We left our world and met him in his, but then we got separated from him. We've no idea where he is now. How do *you* know him?"

The cloaked Wizard's gaze narrows, giving him the look of an angry serpent. "So Nick managed to bring avatars from Khertaan to his world. Good. I had hoped for as much. And you've kept your form even when this world hasn't. I'd expected you would. I'm pleased you managed to summon me."

I fail to understand exactly what he's talking about. "We don't know anything about this place you mention. Khertaan? We're from an unnamed T&T world. We're trying to find a way to reach Ken St. Andre, the creator of T&T, to enlist his help with Spooky and this storm. We were working on the matter when you showed up."

Gondra's gaze narrows even more as it moves to the Tunnels and Troglodytes rulebook. "T&T, you say. You're not from Khertaan?" He picks up the rulebook and thumbs through its pages. His posture and expression relax. "Nick drew you from a table-top gaming universe. How resourceful. Works just as well, and in this instance has worked faster than bringing in avatars from Khertaan. For your edification, Khertaan is a video game universe that Nick and Kendra, his wife, found a way to access from their timeline, aka the Fanciful Pegasus Earth timeline. They may have had some nudging in the right direction from yours truly.

"Khertaan—like the anonymous world you come from—is far, far removed from this timeline, and it's that distance that allows you to keep your form in this disintegrating world. Indeed, more than just this world is falling apart. For you to help, you need to understand what's happening. So I ask your patience with my telling, and I'll try to be quick, for the sooner you begin, the easier it will be for you."

Emma makes a twirling motion with her finger. "Carry on."

Gondra obliges. "Nick had his way of traversing the timelines. The two of you have a different method. Either way, wherever one's awareness is, that's where one's actions can make a difference. Nick shuffles his awareness between different physical forms in different timelines. He doesn't take his body with him, only his mind. In contrast, your method is to take your body with you, shifting it from one timeline to another along with your awareness.

"My nemesis—he who calls himself Seth the Destroyer—is much like Nick, typically only shifting his awareness between the timelines. I'm like you, taking my body with me from timeline to timeline. There are others who have learned to shift timelines as well, some very recently. One such is the woman called Jean, who in one timeline is married to Nick. I believe her method of timeline shifting is similar to yours and mine.

"Another shifter like us is one of which I know little. Stubborn as a Cowgirl in Khertaan, she has green skin and hair and is fond of the axe—"

"Greelia." I grimace at Gondra's surprised look and give him a nod. "She was with us, too. She's a Goblin Warrior."

Gondra flicks a serpentine tongue. "Greelia. She has a strong will."

Emma chuckles. "Sounds like the Greelia we know."

Leaning on his staff, our visitor bows his head over the table. "She has inadvertently saved the multiverse... temporarily. Seth is strong of will, but Jean is stronger. If not for Greelia's sudden involvement, Jean would have overpowered Seth already. To my knowledge, no one else in the multiverse is stronger willed than Jean."

I shake my head in disbelief. "This Jean woman is really strong if she's stronger than Nick and Greelia. How can anyone hope to defeat her? What can Emma and I do?"

Gondra hisses as he sighs. "No one had Nick's will, but he has sacrificed himself to save the timelines. Not *all* of the timelines, mind you... a large number of them, yes... but there are infinitely many more he did not affect."

"What do you mean, he *sacrificed himself*?" I feel hollow.

Emma nearly comes out of her seat. "What did Nick do?"

Our visitor raises his staff. "Traces of Nick remain, as evidenced by the two of you, who wouldn't exist otherwise. His Khertaan avatar, Morrow, carries a trace of him. There are other traces of his spirit out there. But he converted the bulk of his awareness into energy to mend and strengthen several broken timelines. His spirit is now thinly spread across all those timelines, and thus, there are traces of him to be found in all of them, making him ubiquitous and yet not omnipotent, and certainly not capable of animating the body of the man who was Nick McKenzie."

Like Emma, I'd come partially out of my seat, too, and now I lower back into it. "Are you saying...?" My lips tremble.

Gondra lifts his head to meet my gaze. "You might still meet some versions of Nick in the timelines. But none of them will be *the* Nick you know. They'll all be automatons, going through the motions of their lives. None of them will recognize you. None of them will have the mental capacity to open portals to other universes. If you meet any of them, you will only be saddened by his lack of personal connection to you."

Emma speaks softly but firmly. "But we can save him. Tell us how."

The cloaked one shakes his head. "For that, there is much more you must understand."

My voice trembles. "Tell us."

Gondra taps his staff on the floor. "The timeline we now occupy is a member of a group of timelines that struck a metaphysical obstacle, something called a *metadisc*… though now it's a *metadonut*, which we'll get to in a minute.

"Metadiscs occur naturally in the multiverse, causing havoc wherever found, obstructing the normal flow of time for those timelines that strike them. Everything in a blocked timeline ceases to function normally. Time all but stops, crawling forward agonizingly slow as the timeline applies pressure against the metadisc in an effort to push through. Often the metadisc will crumble under such force, and time will again proceed at its normal rate, even if it isn't quite in sync with the rest of the multiverse.

"But the particular metadisc blocking our current timeline and its neighbors was too strong. When the timelines couldn't push through of their own power, they shattered. Nick compacted the broken timelines together into a bundle strong enough to pierce the metadisc at its center. I don't know how he accomplished such a feat, and I doubt I could do the same.

"When the timeline bundle pierced the metadisc, it created what's called a *metadonut*. The timelines once blocked by the metadisc aren't blocked now, but they're competing with each other for dominance in a smaller metaphysical space. There's not enough room inside the metadonut hole for all of them to thrive, and only a few can possibly prevail. In fact, because of how Nick bundled them, it's possible that one of the timelines will come to dominate all the others within the metadonut hole. Anyone existing in the other timelines could easily be erased, or, at best, find themselves suddenly thrust into an alternate reality.

"Jean, Seth, and Greelia are each championing their own timelines in the bundle. In Jean's timeline, she is the Supreme Ruler. In Seth's timeline, everything and everyone is destroyed, and he intends to destroy even himself. In Greelia's timeline, the world is an underground complex of caverns in which she, Nick, and their baby live, hunting creatures in the dark and cooking them over a bonfire, as is the nature of the Goblin race.

"In Greelia's timeline, a physical form of Nick exists. If her timeline were to become dominant, it's possible that Nick's awareness would return to his body. But that would present a different problem. No one but Nick, Greelia, their baby, and the creatures they hunt exist in her timeline. Billions of other lives could be wiped from existence and from history.

"What's needed is for a timeline to become dominant that not only contains a version of Nick, but also as many other people and creatures as can possibly be saved. That's where you two come in. You need to band together against Jean, Seth, and Greelia to champion a more appropriate timeline. If you can find help to do it, then all the better."

I swallow hard. "How do we find the right timeline? And once we find it, how do we *champion* it?"

"I wish I knew all the answers. You'll need to follow your instincts. That's what Greelia did. If she can do it, so can you." Gondra brandishes the scrolls. "I assume you want these. I don't know why I would have them otherwise. Before I showed up here, I had no scrolls in hand. This proves to me that you have the power to shape your own destinies. Continue to exercise that power, focusing it the best you can on what needs doing. I can offer no better advice."

Emma holds up a hand, palm out. "Don't unroll them yet, please. One should be a scroll for the T&T spell, *Teleport Self*, and one should be for the spell *Teleport Other*. I was hoping you'd be a Wizard who could teach me those spells, so I could use them to go to Ken St. Andre."

"I see." He shakes the scrolls at her. "And how will you know if they are what you need unless we unroll them?"

A weight lifts inside me. I know how. "Roll a level fifteen saving roll on Luck, Emma."

With grim determination knitting her brows, she rolls two dice. They show six and one. With her Luck score, that's enough to make the target saving roll. She holds out her hand to Gondra. "Hand me a scroll, please."

He places one in her open hand.

She unrolls it. Her eyes light up. "Teleport Self... we have one of them."

The second saving roll, by the very nature of the game, must be more difficult, so I bump it up a level. "Roll a level sixteen saving roll on Luck for the other scroll."

She nods her understanding. "I need to roll eight or better." She rolls the dice. They show two and two, for a total of four. The rule in T&T is that doubles add and roll again. On the next roll, the dice show six and one. Adding that to her running subtotal, her new total is eleven, enough for her to make the saving roll. She slams her open palm on the table. "*Yes*. Give me."

Gondra hands her the other scroll.

She unrolls it, and her grin widens. "Teleport Other... we've done it. We have the necessary scrolls." She holds one up to show me. "Okay, Game Master. Do I need a wizard to teach me these spells, or can I learn them from the scrolls? I assume even if I can't learn them from the scrolls, I can still perform a one-time casting of the spells from the scrolls, but I'd like to have them in my repertoire."

I shrug. "The rules don't go into that detail." Though I've never read the T&T rulebook, its contents are my laws of nature, inherent in my bones.

Emma mimics my shrug. "Which is why I asked you. You're the GM."

"I'll allow a warrior-wizard to learn spells from scrolls. You must have the required Intelligence and Dexterity to cast the spell, and an Auni score equal to or exceeding the base Auni cost of the spell. I'll also require a saving roll on Luck at the level of the spell being learned." That seems totally reasonable to me.

"Great. I have all the required attributes for both spells. I'll try for the Teleport Self spell first. It's level ten. I need five or better." Emma rolls, and the dice come up five and one. She's good. One of the scrolls vanishes from her grip. She grabs up her character sheet and chuckles. "Goody, goody. It's on my list of spells now.

One down and one to go. The Teleport Other spell is level eleven. Still only need a five or better." She rolls again. The dice come up six and five. She jumps in her seat as the second scroll vanishes. "*Yes.* I learned them both. *Hallelujah.*"

Gondra claps without enthusiasm. "I am glad to have made your acquaintance, Emma the Mystical, Fauna.75, and Spooky. I go now to seek out other traces of Nick. My best bet is to find other virtual characters such as yourselves with whom he's had some involvement."

My heart races. "You already know about Greelia. There's also Ronnie. They weren't his characters, but they were in the game with us. They might carry some trace of him."

"Thank you for the information." Gondra flicks a serpentine tongue. "Goodbye, and good luck."

The green dome dissipates, scattered particles drifting to the floor. Gondra walks backward into the raging mists, his scale-covered face the last thing we see of him.

CHAPTER TWENTY-FOUR

Fauna: Scottsdale, AZ

"So, Fauna, what do we do?" Emma leans across the table towards me. "If we're following our instincts, then at least one of us should go to Ken St. Andre, if possible. Thing is, I only have enough Auni to cast one of the two spells, and I'd need to recover some Auni before I could cast the other. If we're both to go, I'd need to cast Teleport Other on you first. Then I'd need to rest for… um… six hours… before I could cast the Teleport Self for me to follow you. I'm assuming that since Spooky is recognized as treasure on your character sheet that she will go with you when I teleport you."

Panic grips my chest at the possibility of losing Spooky during the teleport. The fact that she's listed as treasure on my character sheet is reassuring, but doesn't alleviate all concern.

I don't understand the concept of *stashing* items, never having done it, but the idea comes to me nonetheless. It's like Nick is in my head, inspiring me. I imagine *stashing* the shadow baby, carrying her in some invisible *inventory*, keeping her with me though not in my arms.

Her dark figure vanishes from my arms. I snatch up my character sheet. She's still listed as my treasure. "Wow. I *stashed* her." To calm my nerves, I will her to come out of inventory, back into my arms—and there she is. "This is lovely. I can send treasure to inventory and then bring it back out." I stash her again, and she's gone, but still listed as a treasure. *Hurray!* I can act freely and not lose her.

I hold up my empty arms. "Okay, Emma. Teleport me to Ken St. Andre in Scottsdale, Arizona. I'll expect to see you there in six hours. That's a *long* time.... I'll find out what I can from Mr. Ken in the interim. Unless something urgent comes up, I won't go anywhere else during those six hours until you get there."

"Maybe you should take your character sheet." Emma hands it to me.

I try to stash it in inventory, but it won't go. It's not listed as treasure, so I guess that's why. I roll it up like a scroll and grip it tightly in my right hand.

"All right, then." Emma points her wizard's staff at me. "Fauna.75, I cast the spell, Teleport Other, upon you. Do not resist. I send you to stand beside Ken St. Andre, creator of Tunnels and Troglodytes, in Scottsdale, Arizona. Be ye gone."

Emma melds with the mists. All around me is swirling, raging whiteness.

Colors come into focus, streaking the white. A table and two chairs take form, identical to those where Emma and I were just sitting. On the table rests two dice. One of the chairs is occupied. I materialize, standing behind the other chair.

A cyclone of white mists swirls around the table, reminding me of the room I left behind. A circular patch of floor, a bit more than ten feet in diameter, remains intact and solid beneath the table and chairs. The storm rages outside the boundary of that circular patch. If there's a ceiling here, it's obstructed by mists swirling overhead.

Across the table from me sits an elderly gentleman wearing a brown Fedora hat. He's leaner than Nick, and just as tall. He lifts knowing eyes to meet mine, tilting his head back so his gaze clears his hat brim. "Welcome. I've been hoping someone would show up." He motions at the empty chair. "Please, have a seat. I am Khenn Arrth. Whom do I have the pleasure of meeting?"

I take the offered chair. "My name is Fauna.75, or Fauna for short. I'm a level ten Rogue from an anonymous Tunnels and Troglodytes world. I was hoping to meet Ken St. Andre. Do you know where he is?"

"Do you know where *your* player is?"

"Um… no. Are you saying Ken St. Andre is your player?"

"I'm not saying that, but we can go with it, if it makes you comfortable. I'm the closest you'll come to speaking with Ken."

I incline my head. "Then I'm very excited to meet you, sir. Mr. Ken is like a God to me."

"He's the Trollgodfather in his realm, as am I in this one, but, please, call me Khenn." His smile is welcoming. "My apologies. I'd offer you food and drink, but I'm unable to visit the kitchen just now. If I'd known to expect a white tornado springing up to confine me thusly, I'd have conveyed refreshments here beforehand. But it's the nature of surprises to take us unawares at inconvenient times, and so here we are."

"I'm not particularly hungry or thirsty, anyway."

"That's good. So, Fauna, did you bring your T&T character sheet?"

"I've got it right here." I hand it to him.

He peruses it, hands it back, and points at my shoulder. "You're on fire."

Gasping, I push back my chair and jump to my hooves, slapping at invisible flames.

He chuckles. "I'm sorry for alarming you. It says here you're unaffected by fire-based effects but are afraid of fire, and I simply wanted to see how well you fit your role. Quite adequate, indeed. That's a good thing. Now, why don't you tell me what drove you to come visit my abode? Start from the beginning."

I tell him everything I can think of. He asks questions as we go and jots down notes.

Emma shows up. Has it really been six hours? I introduce them to each other. Khenn offers his chair to her, but she refuses it, saying she'd as soon stand anyway, besides which, she has a staff to lean on.

He nods sagely at Emma. "Very well. May I see your character sheet, please?" After a moment's perusal, he says something to her in a guttural language I don't understand, drawing out many of the letters.

Emma smiles and replies with more unfamiliar words. She glances at me with a grin. "I never thought I'd meet anyone who knows how to speak Trollish."

Khenn tips his hat to Emma. "I don't often have visitors who can carry a conversation in my preferred language. But I suppose we shouldn't use it while in Fauna's company."

"I'd appreciate it," I say in Caprine.

The Trollgodfather laughs and makes his reply in the goat language. "Where are you keeping Spooky, this shadow baby treasure of yours?"

"She's not *my* baby, per se. That is, I'm not her mother." I concentrate on bringing Spooky out of inventory. Her dark figure appears, lying across my arms. Leaning across the table, I offer the shadow baby girl to Khenn.

He tries to lift her from my arms, but his hands pass through her. He raises his eyebrows. "Seems it is not for me to take her from you. Have you successfully handed her off to Emma?" He's still speaking in Caprine.

I stick with the goat language, too. "I haven't tried." I turn to Emma. "How about it?"

The Elf Warrior-Wizard takes Spooky from me without problem. Cradling her in one arm, she tries to stroke Spooky's forehead, but her hand passes through the shadow baby girl. She chuckles and replies in Caprine. "I've never seen such a contradictory kid."

All three of us laugh at the pun, made even more hilarious for having been spoken in the goat language. I reach for Spooky, anxious to take her back. Maternal instincts drive me to protect and nurture her. My anxiety fades as Emma returns the shadow child to me.

Khenn smiles broadly. "Well, then, my newfound friends, now that introductions have been made all around and the nature of the scenario understood as best it can be, shall we game our way out of the current predicament?"

CHAPTER TWENTY-FIVE

Charli: Mental Dominator

Oh, geez, there's no time. The Spire Boss is attacking, and Britta is still in my arms, vulnerable. My heart in my throat, I try to stash her in my inventory, but it doesn't work. She doesn't qualify as equipment.

What happens if she dies in Khertaan? Would she respawn? I don't even know her attributes. What if her Constitution is a mere 1? A single death could put her out of the game and might wipe her out of existence entirely.

No, please, no.

I'm suddenly flooded with XP. My character sheet shows an additional four-hundred-four-million XP, raising my level from 23 to 27. My Auni increases from 132 to 156. I don't know where the XP came from, but it came at a great time. An exclamation from Kylie tells me she's just experienced the same XP influx.

Pumping 100 of my 156 Auni into the spell, I cast Shadow Warrior, my best bet for protecting Britta. An all-black nude figure materializes beside me, black sword in hand. Though masculine in build, he has no genitals. Poised next to me, he's ready to attack anything that comes near. I step back into the shadows, and he moves with me. He'll be tougher and harder to see here.

I focus on my level 41 Hide, level 20 Avoidance, and level 7 Hide Party skills. Hide Party stacks with Hide, so it helps me even if it helps no one else. It only helps my party members if I'm touching them or chained to them. Spyder may be too big to be effectively hidden with a level 7 skill, and I can't touch Kylie when she's in Spirit Form, even if I knew where she was. I'm touching Britta, but she's not in my party. Can I invite her? I try.

Her name pops onto the party roster. Oh, gosh. If we weren't about to be attacked by a Boss monster, I'd be giving what just happened a closer examination.

Dangling tentacles abruptly lash across the cavern, mostly aimed at Spyder, the largest target here. Three tentacles swipe in my direction.

My Shadow Warrior leaps forward to meet the first of the three attacking appendages, severing it with his blade in one swing. He spins around, continuing the swing, and slices off the second incoming tentacle as well. The third one smacks into him, dealing 4% damage. We seem off to a good start.

A glance towards Spyder reveals she's ripped off six tentacles, and they writhe on the floor. Oh, geez. With eight legs, the Behemoth can easily use six of them for physical attacks. In the span of less than ten seconds, eight of the twelve tentacles have been destroyed. Of the surviving four, three pound on Spyder's back, making some dents, bringing her down to 97% HP. I'd feared the Boss would be tougher than this. But I won't breathe easy until it's dead. Boss monsters often have secondary attacks that aren't evident from the outset. A Boss referred to as a Mental Dominator is bound to have a mind-based ability it's just waiting to unleash on us. Gosh, what if these tentacles are illusionary?

Everyone pauses for their combat heartbeats to reset. I take the time to focus on my Monster Lore trait. What can I find out about this Mental Dominator?

It's a giant octopus, but with twelve tentacles instead of eight. It's incapable of supporting its body on its tentacles, so it needs some other means of support, such as floating in a body of water or resting on the ground or a slab of stone. Each tentacle deals both physical and mental damage when it strikes. Ouch. The tentacles can be severed by dealing a sufficient amount of physical damage to them, but to defeat the monster, its bulbous body must be slain. It has both physical and mental hit points, but no spiritual or emotional hit points, so it can't be hurt by either spiritual or emotional attacks. If its mental hit points are reduced to zero, the thing doesn't die, it simply goes into a coma. The physical hit points of the thing must be reduced to zero for it to be considered defeated and to clear the way for us to leave its territory. I convey all the information I've learned to the others over party chat.

My combat heartbeat resets, and so do those of all the other combatants. The Boss strikes again, only to have three more tentacles ripped off by Spyder. My Shadow Warrior deals with the last tentacle.

"How much mental damage did you take, Spyder?"

"I don't have mental hit points, Charli. So... none."

"That's nice." My Shadow Warrior doesn't have MP either.

No more Boss appendages dangle from the ceiling. But the Boss encounter isn't over yet. "Kylie, are you okay?"

"I'm fine."

"We need to kill the body of the Dominator to finish this encounter and be allowed to leave this cavern. Can you reach it in your Spirit Form?"

"No. It's lying in an air pocket above us, outside the metaphysical barriers surrounding the cavern. The only route to its body is through the same holes the tentacles attacked through, and even that route is blocked to my Spirit Form. Spyder, can you reach the ceiling?"

"I believe so." She rears on her two back legs and reaches high with a front one, which she slides into a hole. "I can get my leg in only so far before the channel bends. My metallic limbs can't make the turn. There's no way I'll be able to damage the Boss from down here. We need something small and flexible."

Kylie chuckles. "You mean like a baby? I see Britta on our party roster."

Spyder returns the chuckle with one of her own, sounding like metal scratching metal. "She would fit."

I'm in shock. I finally manage to find my voice. "You can't be serious."

"Why not?" Still in Spirit Form, Kylie remains out of sight as she speaks over party chat. "Britta is in our party. Maybe we can head hop to her. Are you willing to try that much, Charli?"

"I'm not sending my child into one of those holes." I can't believe Kylie thinks for one second I'd be okay with this plan.

"I'm not suggesting you do, Cowgirl. Not yet. But head hopping might prove useful in protecting her in future encounters. You owe it to your little one to do everything you can to protect her."

I bristle at the implication that I'm being lax in protecting my baby. "Don't you dare think you can guilt me into something I don't want to do, *Angel*."

"I don't mean to guilt trip you into doing anything, Charli. I'm just being logical. If she were mine, I'd take every step to ensure I could protect her to the utmost of my ability. I'm sure you feel the same way. Hopping into her head is a logical step in that direction. What might come after that is beside the point at the moment."

The Spirit Warrior has a point, I admit... to a degree. But if I do this and the head hopping succeeds, I know where this is going. Kylie will continue nudging me further and further down the path towards having Britta crawl into the ceiling to kill the Boss monster. Even thinking about it makes me angry. I don't want to go there.

Britta growls and makes two fists. Her facial expression is fierce.

Maybe she's pooping.

Does a half-breed avatar/Earth person need to poop? She's been eating. Well, drinking. I hold her naked body at arm's reach. If she is pooping, I don't want the mess on me.

She opens her fists. Her fingernails are more than nails. They're claws, extended and pointed. With another growl, she swipes her hands through the air, as though attacking some invisible enemy. She's not pooping. My little Goblin girl wants to fight something. Oh, geez. Does she understand what Kylie and I are saying on the party chat? Is she agreeing with Kylie?

There's only one way to find out. "Okay. I'll try to head hop to you, sweetie. But only me." I sit with my back to the wall and lay Britta on my lap. "Spyder, keep a watch over us. I'm head hopping now. Assuming it works.... Britta, if you understand me, accept my awareness transfer request."

I mentally reach for my little girl, the same way I first reached out to Amarynth so long ago when we first started our adventures in Khertaan. I wasn't sure it would work then, and I'm not sure it will work now. We knew almost nothing of the rules back then, and I still don't know all the rules. No PC or NPC does. The PCs have support AIs that help them ferret out the rules as they apply to their skills and traits. I don't even have that. I can put in my own requests to the System for information, but such requests typically go ignored unless I'm using a skill. For the most part, the information I receive is limited to System-wide notifications.

I miss Amarynth and the others in party MAD. I didn't intend to be separated from them for this long. I only wanted to escort party Quantized to Ezmerelda's hut so they could get rings and a quest from her. Okay, I also wanted to fetch the Scarecrow ashes. I'm not sure why. It's because I'm a Wizard, right? Wizards can use spell components, supposedly. Gathering those ashes was me acting on a hunch. Had that hunch come from the System? Now *there's* a rabbit hole if I ever saw one.

Let me into your mind, little one.

A hat-wearing head droops over me, blond locks suspended over me, eyes shut. The face I see is mine. I'm inside my kid's head, looking at myself from her POV.

Britta, could you let Mommy have control in here?

She blows a raspberry. Intuitively, I know she means *no*. She's not letting me take over her mind to make decisions for her. Stubborn kid.

I'd really like to know her Constitution score, and for that I'll need to see her character sheet, assuming she has one.

As though she's reading my thoughts—which makes sense with me being inside her head—her character sheet manifests in our shared view.

Britta, Female Cave Goblin
Class: Assassin
Level: 1
HP: 100%, **MP:** 100%, **SP:** 100%, **EP:** 100%
Attributes:
Physical:
Brawn 9
Sensing 10
Dexterity 13
Constitution 15
Agility 12
Toughness 12
Mental:
Willpower 9
Understanding 9
Logic 16
Sanity 10
Intuition 9
Memory 13
Spiritual:
Faith 14

Conscience 13
Favor 16
Belief 12
Insight 9
Morals 5
Emotional:
Passion 9
Empathy 13
Charisma 13
Hope 9
Temperance 12
Optimism 10
Cave Goblin Kindred Traits:
Claws Attack
Dark Sight
Special Movement - Burrow
Character Traits:
Regeneration, level 1
Shadow Self, level 1
Iron Will, level 1
Level 1 Assassin Class Skills:
Vitals Strike, level 1
Disguise, level 1

Geez, she's got 15 Constitution. That's 5 more than I have. And she's got 16 Logic and 16 Favor. Wow. My highest stats are Temperance and Optimism, at 14 each. This kid has one sub-par stat, Morals, but everything else is in the average category or better, rated 9 or higher. I don't have any sub-par attributes, but I've got five in the low-average category, including Morals. My Conscience is also in the low-average category, whereas Britta's Conscience, at 13, is high-average. What does that combination of sub-par Morals and high-average Conscience mean for her? The low Morals score means she can't easily tell the difference between right and wrong. The high Conscience score means that if she does think she's done wrong, she'll feel guilty about it. I can only hope that her extraordinary Logic score will help her reason out the right thing to do, even with low Morals. And maybe those of us traveling with her can teach her.

I'm still processing her character class.

My baby girl is an *Assassin*.

Not only an Assassin, but an Assassin with a Conscience.

Oh, geez.

If by some stretch of the imagination she were to kill the Mental Dominator Boss monster in the ceiling, she'd need to understand that killing it is the right thing to do. It wouldn't do for her to feel guilty about killing that thing.

Kylie's disembodied voice sounds over party chat. "What's the verdict, Charli? Can your little bundle of joy deal death for us? Shall I transfer my awareness to her now?"

"You're not going to believe this, Kylie. She's an *Assassin*. Level 1. She's got traits and skills, and a bunch of attributes that are higher than mine. I'd like to find out what we can about her traits and skills before we go any further. Can you ask your support AI for info on the Special Movement - Burrow trait? Maybe it could be used to dig a straight hole through the ceiling, so Spyder can carry out the attack on the Boss instead of Britta."

"Let me check with Georgie." Kylie is silent for a few seconds before continuing. "He says he can't get info on her traits. For him to have a chance at getting the info, either I have to head hop into her mind, or she's got to come to me."

"Okay. Give me a moment."

"Like I'm going anywhere."

Britta, do you understand what we've been saying?

"Aagh." Her vocal reply is the first attempt at language I've heard from her since she was born. Does it mean *yes* or *no*, or is it simply coincidental?

Britta wouldn't need to be involved in killing the Boss monster, if I can convince her to transfer her awareness to me. If she hopped to my head and lent me her Special Movement - Burrow trait, I could expand one of those ceiling holes.

Britta blows a raspberry. She doesn't like what I'm thinking.

Baby girl, can we put our minds into Mommy's body instead of yours?

She blows another raspberry. She doesn't want to go with my plan.

Please?

Her tongue vibrates between her lips. She's not doing it.

Do you want to kill the Boss monster, Britta?

"Aagh." She doesn't blow a raspberry this time. *Aagh* means *yes* and a raspberry means *no*. Got it. Fine.

If that's what you want, let Mommy transfer her skills and traits to you. Will you allow that?

"Aagh." The transfer is made. My naked newborn Goblin girl has all the abilities of a level 27 Guide, level 18 Shadow Wizard, and level 1 Assassin. But does she know how to use them?

She blows a raspberry. That's a *no*.

How can she kill the Boss if she doesn't know how to use any of the skills she has?

She growls, knowing something that will help, but having no way to communicate it to me unless I ask the right yes-or-no questions. It's already been established that she doesn't want me in control of her actions, so what's the alternative, if she doesn't know what she's doing?

Do you want me to tell you what to do, Britta?

"Aagh."

Okay then. Seems we're doing this. Both Kylie and Britta want it. It's time for Kylie to join us, metaphysically speaking.

Britta, my dear, let the nice Angel, Kylie, transfer her awareness in here with Mommy's, okay?

"Aagh."

"Come on in, Kylie. Britta is expecting you." I can scarcely believe we're sending my baby to kill a Boss.

"Hey, girls." Metaphysically, as visualized inside Britta's brain space, Kylie looks like her normal Angel self, not a fleshy, bloody pulp. "Glad to meet you, Britta. I'm Kylie. Thank you for having me in your head. I see you have your character sheet up already. Goody. Let's see how much we can ascertain about your abilities."

She addresses her support AI, Georgie.

Since I now share a head space with Kylie, I can see her AI. He presents as a thirty-something human male in a polka-dotted outfit, with painted white face, bulbous red nose, and glasses with blue lenses shaped like five-pointed stars. A clown. Okay then.

Kylie reads off the list of Britta's traits and skills. Georgie nods and holds up a hand signaling for us to wait.

He lowers his hand. "Here's what I got. The Claws Attack trait gives Britta a natural weapon, her claws. Dark Sight allows her, when in areas of no light or very dim light, to see her surroundings in shades of gray. Special Movement - Burrow allows her to dig through earthen solids—dirt, stone, brick—at a relatively fast rate. The exact rate can depend on a variety of factors, but digging through the cave ceiling should go pretty fast.

"Her Iron Will trait is akin to the Cowgirl trait of Stubbornness. If she gets an idea or plan in her head, you won't talk her out of it without using an ability, spell, or power, and even then your success won't be guaranteed. Iron Will also gives Britta resistance to abilities of a mental or perceptive nature, such as the Beauty, Charismatic, High Social Status, Name of Rank, Nondescript, and Trackless traits, or skills like Hide, Disguise, Inspect Character, Locate Character, Feint, Negotiate, and many others. Higher levels of the Iron Will trait grant increased resistance, with level four granting full immunity."

Like mother, like daughter. I don't have the Iron Will trait, but since I'm a Cowgirl, I naturally have the Stubbornness kindred trait.

Georgie holds up his hand again. "One moment." He drops it. "I have detailed descriptions for both the Regeneration and Shadow Self traits. Let me put up the text for Regeneration first."

Eidson & Thicke

Regeneration: *Returns all lost or mangled body parts to full functionality after Y days, where Y is the number of seconds in the character's combat heartbeat. Each level of the trait scales the regeneration time to the next smaller time unit. Thus, Regeneration level 2 restores body parts after Y hours. Level 3 requires Y minutes. Level 4 requires Y seconds. No partial functionality is restored until the full regeneration time requirement has elapsed. The level of activity during the regeneration time does not accelerate or impede the regeneration process, nor does the Wakeful trait have any bearing on the time required for regeneration.*

"I'll bite," Kylie says, "how long is a combat heartbeat?"

"The default is ten seconds." Georgie shrugs. "I don't have any information on how the length of one's combat heartbeat might be changed. Yours is ten."

Kylie gasps. "I need this trait. Level 4 would be awesome, but level 3 would be great, too. Level 2 would be okay. Level 1 isn't that impressive, but one has to start at the bottom and work their way up. Oh, Britta, I hope you get a ton of experience, crank up the level on that trait, and let me borrow it. I really really hope so."

Britta giggles. "Aagh."

I cock my metaphysical head at Kylie. "You're in luck. She's on board with the idea. Given what Georgie said about her Iron Will trait, you can count on it happening."

"Oh, Goddess." Kylie's smile gives her metaphysical face a white aura. "I can't thank you enough, little Goblin Assassin girl."

Britta growls.

I make the correction on Kylie's behalf. "*Cave* Goblin Assassin girl."

The Cave Goblin girl giggles.

"This next trait is really interesting, too." Georgie waves, and a new wall of text pops up, replacing the previous.

163

Shadow Self: Once invoked, the character does not cast a shadow. The character gains a Shadow Self, a separate, autonomous entity with all the same skills, traits, and classes as the character. The two share the same XP and hit point pools; that is, any XP earned by either the character or the Shadow Self are added to the character's XP pool, and any hit points lost of any type by either the character or the Shadow Self are subtracted from the character's associated hit point pool. If either the character or the Shadow Self dies for any reason, both die. When the character respawns, the Shadow Self respawns, each with the ability to choose their own respawn point, within any limitations stipulated at the time by the System.

The Shadow Self is a three-dimensional being, with a default shape and size equal to the default shape and size of the character. Skills and traits used to change the size or shape of either the character or the Shadow Self do not cause an automatic change in the shape or size of the other. The Shadow Self is invisible when residing totally within shadow, but otherwise appears as a translucent, shadowy figure.

At will, the character may tap the senses of the Shadow Self, to see what the Shadow Self sees, hear what it hears, feel what it feels, etc. This can also work in reverse, but only if initiated by the character—the Shadow Self cannot voluntarily tap the senses of the character. The character and the Shadow Self may telepathically communicate with each other over any distance.

Higher levels of this trait create additional Shadow Selves, one per level of the trait.

I'm floored. I've paid no attention to whether my little girl casts a shadow, but then we've been enveloped in shadow most of the time. Might there be a Shadow Britta now, and if so, where is she? "Darling, do you already have a Shadow Self?"

"Aagh."

"Do you know where she is now?"

"Pbbt." That was the raspberry meaning *no*.

"Would you look through her eyes now for Mommy? We want to know where she is."

Britta giggles. "Aagh." The view in her First Person POV is replaced with a uniform grayness... not darkness, but not light, either. It's like a large piece of gray paper is held before her eyes. Wherever Shadow Britta is, she's not in this cave. It's like she's trapped in limbo. When and where did she become separated from Britta?

"Okay, Britta, you can stop now." Sadly, we have no better idea of where Shadow Britta is. We can investigate further once we deal with the Boss.

Britta's POV is filled once again with my drooping head, the cavern wall against which my unconscious body is propped, and the cavern ceiling.

Kylie grimaces, metaphysically speaking. "Not helpful. Oh well. Onward we go. Do you have anything else for us, Georgie, about Britta's skills or traits?"

Her clownish support AI nods. "I don't have detailed descriptions, sadly. But I can tell you that her Vitals Strike skill can be used to attempt an instant kill attack. Its success depends on whether she is in a position to reach at least one vital organ of her target, as well as the following attributes and abilities: Sensing, Dexterity, Agility, the level of her Vitals Strike skill, and any levels she might have in the Increased Movement or Alertness traits.

"The skill is automatically resisted by the target unless the target is Stunned or Held. If resisted, the target's character level comes into play, as do the target's Sensing, Agility, and Toughness attributes, any levels they have in the Vitals Strike skill and possibly other skills affecting awareness or perception, as well as any levels they have in the traits Increased Movement, Presence, or Alertness. If a Vitals Strike attack is attempted but the instant kill effect is resisted, the attack still deals normal damage.

"Moving on to the Disguise skill... it can be used to give the character the appearance of someone they aren't, even to the point

165

of mimicking the appearance of a specific, known person. The higher the skill level, the higher the degree of difference possible between the character's natural appearance and assumed appearance, and the more precisely the character can mimic a specific, known person.

"With the level one skill, Britta could look like a different Cave Goblin girl baby, or a girl baby of another kindred, such as a Human girl baby or an Elf girl baby, but she couldn't take on the appearance of, say, a Cave Goblin boy baby or a fourteen year old Cave Goblin girl. She'd need to have the skill at level two, at least, to look like a Cave Goblin boy baby, and level five to take on the appearance of a fourteen year old Cave Goblin girl. She'd need to have the skill at level ten or higher to attempt to mimic some specific, known person.

"A casual observer won't see through the disguise. Certain skills, traits, spells, or psionic powers can help a casual observer become aware the character is disguised, but the disguise can only be penetrated to the point of underlying character identification by someone focused on doing so. Even then, the success of the attempt depends on their Sensing, Intuition, Insight, and Empathy attributes, and any appropriate perception-based skills or traits they have, such as the Spot skill or the Alertness trait."

When Georgie finishes, silence falls on the cavern. It's a lot to take in.

Kylie is first to speak. "Well, now we know what we have to work with. Are we ready to do this? I can transfer a bunch of my traits and skills to you, Britta. My Flight trait will get you to the ceiling. I'll transfer all my resistance skills, as added protection. Increased Movement, Heightened Sense of Hearing, Scute Armor, Melee Damage, Stun, and Dominance might help. So, if you're ready to accept them, here they come."

"Aagh."

The transfer is made. Not even a full day old yet, and Britta is a super-powered killing machine. "Okay, baby girl, are you ready to kill the big, bad Boss monster so we can leave this cave?"

"Aagh."

"I want you to focus on the Flight trait that Kylie gave you. Fly a little ways up, so you're not in my arms anymore. We just want to see that it works first."

Britta floats on the air, rising off my arms and hovering a few inches above them. She giggles.

Oh, my. I'm not surprised, but I'm amazed. A part of me rebels against going any further with this, but another part of me swells with pride for my baby girl. I let my pride sway me. "Fly up to the ceiling, Britta."

She rises, leaving the close proximity of my unconscious physical body. Panic rises in me, but I crush it. I'll direct my baby girl to burrow through the ceiling and then tell her to retreat.

Britta blows a raspberry. She reaches the ceiling and commences slashing it with her claws, displacing dirt by the handfuls.

One of my feet is buried under the edge of a mound of displaced dirt by the time Britta's little tunnel in the ceiling breaks through the top, breaching the air pocket in which the Boss resides. I'd hoped the hole would come up under the Boss, but the Boss is off to the side. Spyder can't use the hole to attack the Boss. "Come back down, Britta, and dig a different hole."

"Pbbt." She rises into the air pocket housing the limbless Boss and flies toward it.

Grrr. "If you're not coming down, daughter, then at least use my Hide and Avoidance skills, please."

"Aagh."

The gaze of the Dominator locks on Britta's flying form, a sign it senses her presence. A streak of blue light lances across the space between the Dominator's octopus eyes and my baby girl. The blue beam strikes Britta in the forehead. She laughs.

Georgie groans. "Yikes. The Dominator launched a Mind Spear attack. But Britta's borrowed Mental Armor trait blocked it."

I want to scream. My Monster Lore hadn't revealed the Mental Dominator had a Mind Spear attack. What else did my level 45 Monster Lore skill miss? "Please retreat, baby girl."

"Pbbt." Britta is determined to defeat this thing, and she won't give up until either it or she is dead. Stupid Iron Will trait… and I'm so stupid for letting her go.

Kylie offers my baby some advice for success. "Try my Hypnotic Gaze trait on the Dominator, Britta."

"Aagh." Britta flies above the Dominator, looking down into the monster's eyes.

Georgie claps his hands. "The Boss has succumbed to the power of your trait, pumpkin. Hypnotic Gaze is in effect. The Boss is effectively Held for one combat heartbeat."

So as not to lose my nerve, I don't hesitate with my next instruction. "Vitals Strike, *now*, Britta—top of its head with a Claws Attack."

Baby Britta dives at the Mental Dominator's forehead and plunges her claws into the bulbous flesh.

The Mental Dominator blasts apart, flooding the air pocket with glowing pixels that fade out like dying sparks.

Oh, geez. It's done. *It's done.* My baby girl *did it*, and she didn't take a scratch. Oh, gosh. I couldn't be more proud—or relieved. I shed metaphysical tears.

Metaphysical Britta laughs. "Mommy."

My heart breaks on hearing her first actual word. "Oh, Britta, come out of there now, *please*."

"Congratulations, pumpkin." Georgie is obviously addressing Kylie. The term of endearment is cute. "You've gained four and a half million XP. You're now 72% of the way to level 28. Moreover, the metaphysical barriers around the cavern have been removed, and party TimeTrippers is now allowed to depart the Spire of Desire territory."

"Woo hoo." Kylie beams at me. "Your baby girl did it, Charli. We're finally free of this place. City of Minook, here we come."

My own character sheet shows I'm 73% of the way to level 28. I have a few million more XP than Kylie, and at this stage of our advancement, it only amounts to a 1% difference in our progression towards the next level. "Britta. Mommy said to come back now, please."

Giggling, my baby girl returns through one of the ceiling holes. She flies down and settles into the arms of my unconscious body. Satisfied with what she has accomplished, she isn't putting up a fight to retain any borrowed skills and traits. Kylie and I both retract the abilities we lent, but neither of us transfer our awarenesses back to our bodies yet. We're both too curious for that.

"Britta, show Mommy your character sheet, please."

A wall of text pops up, longer than what was there before. I scan for differences and additions. She's level 18 Assassin *and level 9 Mentalist*. She hadn't asked anyone for advice on what subclass to take. Was it automatically assigned to her? Does it matter? What's done is done.

She's added two points to her Sensing attribute, raising it from the average category to high-average. Her trait boosts raised her Regeneration from level 1 to level 3, and her Iron Will from 1 to 2. Again, I don't know if that was by her choice or if the boosts were automated by the System.

I scan down her list of skills and powers.

Level 18 Assassin Class Skills
Vitals Strike, level 28
Disguise, level 26
Hide, level 23
Ranged Vitals Strike, level 20
Poison Touch, level 16
Flight Speed, level 12
Level 9 Mentalist Subclass Skills
Mislead, level 10

Anticipate, level 9
Levitate, level 8
Displace, level 7
Inspect Character, level 5
Teleport Self, level 3
Level 9 Mentalist Psi Powers
Mind Spear
Mind Shield
Mind Read

From but one encounter, my baby girl is of a higher level than many of the first PCs to enter the game. I suspect some of the beginning parties are still grinding on Brass and Iron Goblins in the Brassy Grassy Field and have yet to make level six.

My Shadow Warrior spell has expired and the naked black man is gone, indicating the encounter is truly over. I transfer my awareness back to my own body and lift my drooping chin.

"Can I borrow your Regeneration trait now, dear Britta?" Kylie is anxious to get her body back in functioning order.

Transferring her awareness to Kylie, Britta goes limp. Her motionless body weighs heavy in my arms.

I comb my character sheet. In all the hubbub, I've not decided on some trait and attribute boosts. My last attribute boost is from level 14, and my last trait boost is from level 12. At level 27 now, I have three attribute boosts to make, and two trait boosts. I don't put much thought into the attribute boosts, adding all three to Constitution, taking my number of lives available from 10 to 13. For the trait boosts, I bump Mental Armor to level 4, maxing it out.

I don't see the benefit in raising the level of my Ambidexterity trait. I've used the trait only once so far, when I used it to trick Mithabel and kill Dylan for the Longest Survivor bounty. That seems so long ago… and it was, for me, with all my travels in alternate realities before I last respawned… but in Khertaan it was only yesterday.

So, I assign the other trait boost to Complex Personality. If it works like it did before, I can create an additional personality for myself. I haven't fully explored the trait, but I suspect if I wanted to go back to being a fourteen-year-old girl, I'd just focus on the trait and make the switch. Not that I want to go back to that age. But having boosted the trait, I can create a personality older than eighteen… maybe twenty-eight. I'll have to think about it.

I'm down a hundred Auni that needs replenishing. "Kylie, I'm gonna chance a nap while you're regenerating. Please wake me immediately if anything happens."

"Will do."

Ten minutes later, Spyder nudges me awake with the tip of a metal leg against my shoulder. I've recovered ten Auni. Britta stirs in my arms and gives me the cutest smile.

"I'm back." Kylie the Angel appears before me in physical form. She's no longer a bloody pulp. Her limbs and head and wings are all in their right places. "The borrowed Regeneration trait worked… thank you, Britta. Though my HP is at -7438%, I can function normally." She snickers. "Is everyone ready to get out of this cave? I'm ready to see what the city of Minook is about."

Giggling, Britta rises in the air. Oh, geez, she has her own ability for flying now. Then she vanishes. Ha. She's using her Hide skill. With average Understanding and Intuition scores, a high average Memory, and an extraordinary Logic, she has learned quickly how to activate her abilities.

I concentrate on seeing her, calling upon my high average Sensing attribute and my level 38 Search skill.

A naked, green-skinned woman about my age appears before me, long green hair flowing over her bare shoulders. Mischief glints in her green eyes and on her curved lips. With a giggle, she flies away from me, towards the cavern mouth.

Oh, geez, what have I unleashed? Now that Britta has the skills of a high level character and knows how to activate them, coupled with sub-par Morals that fail to impart to her a strong notion of right and wrong or consideration for decency, what kind of trouble will she get into? I point after her. "Kylie and Spyder, we need to follow that woman. She's Britta—in disguise."

Spyder looks in the direction I'm pointing. "What woman?"

CHAPTER TWENTY-SIX

Ronnie: The Queen

Reality fluctuates as though some deity can't make up their mind what they want. I'm alone on the motorcycle one moment, then with Mel riding behind me the next, and with me riding behind Mel after that. Sometimes he's ghostly and other times not so much. We ride a lonely country road with cornfields to either side one moment, and the next we're on a dirt path in a dark forest, which suddenly becomes a paved street in a crowded city.

A flaming wall erects itself before us. A ghostly Mel is driving, and there's no time to stop. We burst through, and find ourselves back on the bridge of the spaceship, as Jean had promised. Mel wills the bike to stop, and we squeal to a halt, spinning around, narrowly missing a uniformed nurse and a pedestal she's dancing on. Smoke billows around us.

Jean stands to one side, facing a man in a hooded cloak similar to hers. They stare at each other. Directly in front of us sits a young blond woman, older than me, a metal band around her neck. Not far from her sits a young man about her age, also wearing a metal collar. His eyes are scarcely open but he isn't asleep. Maybe he's drugged or drunk.

"I'm Timmy." The voice comes from the drugged guy, although he doesn't open his mouth to speak. I just know it's him, communicating with me telepathically. "I'm a Ring Ghoul. I should be dead, but I'm not."

"I'm Ronnie." I reply in the same fashion. "I'm a Tunnels and Troglodytes Rogue. I shouldn't be alive, but I am."

"I think only one of us is supposed to exist, Ronnie. Either my timeline will win out or yours. But if mine wins, the man in the cloak destroys everything."

"The same goes for the cloaked woman. She wants to destroy everyone in mine. What can we do about it?" It doesn't feel right to share that Jean would spare me and Mel in her timeline if she wins this war of wills.

"Can you kill them both?" Timmy is dead serious.

I shake my head. "The woman is Jean, Mel's mother. I won't kill her."

"Then we have to change her mind. Because changing the mind of the man—Seth—is impossible. He only exists to destroy. We *can't* let him win." He points his chin at the young woman wearing a metal collar. "That's my good friend, Susie. Even if it means she and I no longer exist, Seth has to lose. Add your will with mine against him. Focus on Jean being someone of importance other than a Destroyer, like a Queen. It might appeal to her. It's our only hope to save the multiverse."

I bend my will to the task as Timmy has requested of me. He and Susie quickly lose substance, while Mel regains it. Susie's collar fades away, and then she disappears, too. Timmy's figure flickers, as does Seth's. A bunch of gray people in the area also hover on the edge of reality. Jean and her nurses don't flicker at all, and neither do I.

A crown appears on Jean's head. The bridge of the spaceship reshapes itself into an audience chamber fit for royalty. The nurses stand at attention on either side of a red carpet leading from a main entrance to a grand throne.

Timmy is gone.

Queen Jean smirks. "Bow before me, Seth the Destroyer, and perhaps I will allow you to exist in my timeline."

"I bow to no one."

"Then die."

"Hold tight, Ronnie." Mel speeds the bike at his mother. Does he want to run her over? Does he realize what's happening? Killing Jean is the last thing we want. Being rid of Seth is what Timmy sacrificed himself for.

I try to stash the bike before we hit the Queen, but it won't stash, because it's under Mel's control at the moment. We're five feet away. A crash is inevitable.

Jean gestures, and another wall of smoke and flames appears inches ahead of the front of the bike. We can't stop or avoid it. Into it and through we go.

Emerging from the other side, I'm driving. Mel is a ghost, flying beside me. I've lost my focus on the battle for timeline dominance. We might have distracted Jean enough that Seth regained the upper hand. Not good.

I try to focus my will against Seth again. Is it working? Judging by Mel's continued ghostly appearance, I don't think so. There's too much on my mind for me to concentrate. "Why were you trying to kill your mother, Mel?"

"I'm sorry, Ronnie. I'm having difficulty remembering anything. What just happened?"

"A guy named Seth was battling for control of the timelines against your mother, who opted for power over destruction. It was what we wanted, but you tried to kill her."

"I don't remember any of it. Sorry."

"I don't know what we do now, Mel."

"I feel we should keep driving."

Accompanied by a ghostly companion, I ride a motorcycle on ghostly streets packed with ghostly traffic and ghostly

175

pedestrians. I drive right through everything and everybody. The only things not ghostly are the giant spaceship hovering over the world and the hundreds of giant metal spiders dropping from it, plummeting to the ground without parachutes. They belong to Seth. I do my best to focus on opposing him.

As I ride, the Arachnids and the spaceship fade from existence. Whoa. The streets gain substance. Tall buildings previously non-existent loom over the streets and block the horizon. The front of my motorcycle bumps into the rear of a horseless carriage.

Mel, who was still flying beside me as a ghost, falls to the ground with a thud. He doesn't fall far, fortunately, and climbs casually to his feet, brushing off his clothes. He's no longer translucent, but substantial, like me. Whatever alternate universe we're in, he's a real part of it. Jean is winning again. As long as she's not the Destroyer, that's good, I think. I still wish I knew exactly why Mel had tried to run her over.

A door opens on the horseless carriage I bumped into, and a man comes barreling out. "*Hey*. You hit my car, punk."

I back up the motorcycle. "Sorry, sir. I'm Ronnie. This is my friend, Mel. How can I make this right?"

"I'm Horace, and you can fucking pay for the damages, that's how." He's bigger than me and grips a pistol in one hand. I've never seen a gunne up close. They're powerful weapons in T&T. I suspect they're powerful in this alternate universe, too.

"I have no money, but I'm not looking for a fight, either, Horace." I summon a motorcycle from my inventory and set it next to mine. "Would you take this motorcycle as reparations?"

He does a double take, looking at me, then the unoccupied bike, and then back at me. Then he looks at Mel. "That your bike? You the one who hit me?"

Mel rubs his shoulder and shakes his head.

I point at myself. "I hit you. Both of these motorcycles are mine. You can have that one. Go on. Take it. I've got more where it came from."

"It got a title?" The disgruntled driver sidles up to the bike.

I shrug. "I don't know what that is."

"It doesn't." With a chuckle that might be forced, Mel points his chin at me. "He doesn't believe in titles, if you know what I mean."

Horace takes a closer look at the back of his horseless carriage. There's not even a dent that shows. He nods. "Okay, deal. I take the bike and let you two leave. No police reports."

"Thank you, sir." I mentally command my motorcycle to move, leaving the one for Horace where it sits, for him to do with as he will. I guide my bike around the passenger side of the carriage.

"Um, Ronnie," Mel calls after me.

I stop the bike. "Yeah?"

"I can't fly. I need a ride."

Horace pays no attention to us. He holds a rectangle of metal and glass to his mouth and talks at it.

Mel climbs on the bike I'd given Horace. "Where we headed?"

"Um...."

He drives past me. "Coming?"

Horace suddenly pays us some attention. "Hey." He raises his pistol.

I take off after Mel. A shot rings out and a bullet whizzes past me, striking a passerby. The ensuing commotion tells me that Horace has more to worry about now than the loss of a motorcycle he didn't deserve.

Mel relinquishes the lead, and we speed away, careful not to hit people or carriages this time. I don't know where we're going, or if we still need to be trying to escape Orc Wizards, but I want to put some good distance between us and Horace.

We near an intersection, cords strung above the road. The cords support a lantern containing colored sheets of glass—red, yellow, and green—the red one illuminated from inside the device.

"*Stop.*" Mel sounds panicked.

I come to a halt. "What's wrong?"

He pulls up beside me and points at the lantern. "Red light. You have to wait for it to turn green."

It's lucky we did stop. Several carriages and other motorcycles speed through the intersection in front of us, merely ten feet away. Soon the cross traffic slows and then halts, leaving the intersection vacant. It's a fine time to drive through, but the light is still red. Finally, the red pane dims, and the green one shimmers. I drive through the intersection.

Mel stays abreast of me. "I think we've gone far enough to stop somewhere and discuss things."

"Sure." I pull off the side. Mel follows and dismounts. I stash both the motorcycles in inventory and glance around for a place to sit.

Mel motions for me to follow him. "You like coffee? I may have a little cash."

We walk side-by-side along a sidewalk. Does he know where he's going?

In the distance stands a building forty or more stories tall. Halfway up the building hangs a black screen, far larger than the one Jean showed us planetary images on. This one rises ten stories tall and spans half as wide. Mel and I both stop in our tracks as an animated image appears on the screen.

The image is a moving head shot of Mel's mother, Jean. She wears golden accessories—a crown, earrings, and necklace. White lace lays over her shoulders.

Her voice booms across the city. "Citizens of Jeaniverse, I come to you with alarming news. My daughter, Princess Karen, has been kidnapped. The kidnapper is a young man by name of Ronnie, last seen in medieval attire." My image replaces Jean's. "If you see this man, you are authorized to kill on sight. The bounty on his head is set at one million dollars." An image of Mel replaces my image, but he's dressed in pink clothes with white frills and has longer hair, a silver crown, and silver jewelry. "This is my daughter. Do not harm her, or your life and the lives of your families are forfeit. That is all."

The screen turns black for three seconds, after which my image flickers to life again, with *Wanted, Dead or Alive* planted above my head, and *Reward: One Million Dollars* plastered across my lower extremities.

Mel says what I'm thinking. "Shit."

I materialize two motorcycles. "If you know somewhere safe, lead the way."

"I might, if this reality is anything like the one I'm originally from."

Someone nearby shouts, *"It's them."*

We hop on the bikes. Mel takes the lead, and I follow, keeping my head down. A bullet whines past my ear, missing me and hitting a bystander, who goes down. Another shot fires. It, too, misses me. I hope it didn't hit anyone else.

The roads are packed, forcing us to drive on the sidewalk. More bullets whine by from down the sidewalk and across the street. A blue-haired girl on a bike rides after us on the sidewalk. Pedestrians cry out and scatter, some of them hit by bullets and others running for cover. I want to stop and help those who are shot, but if I do, I'll die. From what I know of T&T, a character like myself only has one life. Magic could possibly bring one back from the dead, but it's unlikely anyone would exercise such powerful magic for a nobody like me. I also have my doubts as to there being any other T&T characters in this universe.

I want to live, and the best chance I have for that without causing more unnecessary civilian casualties is to immediately vacate the premises. Mel drives as fast as possible without hitting people, and I stay as close as possible to him. "Keep your head up so people can see your face, Mel. They won't shoot if they think you're the Princess."

"Why would they think I'm the Princess? I don't look anything like her."

"Uh, yeah, you do. Your face looks *exactly* like hers. You could be twins." I don't tell him what I really think. He doesn't just look like the Princess. In this alternate universe, he *is* the Princess. This alternate universe is called Jeaniverse, his mother is Queen of it all, and she wants Mel back by her side, fulfilling the role of Princess Karen. He must realize that.

In Jeaniverse, there's no more need for Ronnie the T&T Rogue. Queen Jean wants me taken out of the picture, because I have too much influence on her offspring.

This can't be the same Jean who sent Mel and me down to the planet to begin with. That version of Jean was bent on destroying everything, to force Mel and me to restart humanity by me getting Mel pregnant. Which alternate universe is worse, one in which its Queen wants me dead, or one in which she wants basically everyone else dead? I don't like either of these options, but the option of giving Seth full rein doesn't work for me, either. There's got to be another option.

I wish Nick were here. He'd know what to do.

CHAPTER TWENTY-SEVEN

Susie: The Succubus

With ODYSSEY's help and after much typing, clicking, and time-jumping to learn passwords, I find the page I was hoping to find — the Khertaan parties list. A quick scan proves that no party is maxed out to six members. Many of them have six or more avatars associated with the party, but some of the avatars are Companions or Familiars, and don't count against the party limit.

More digging… ah, here we go… the means for manually altering party composition with a drag-and-drop interface. I'm lightheaded just thinking about the power I have at my fingertips.

The Khertaan program was altered by ODYSSEY to allow Charli to be in both TimeTrippers and MAD. That same alteration, I'm hoping, will allow her to become a member of any and all parties. If that's possible, then she'll be the conduit to cause all parties to gain all the XP earned by any party. I won't be arbitrarily assigning XP to avatars or bending yet another rule. I'll merely leverage a rule already bent.

But I don't see how to use this interface to leverage the bent rule. It being drag-and-drop, if I drag Charli from one party and drop her in another, she'll be removed from the original party. I need a different interface, one that lets me—in code-speak—create a new pointer to an existing object. In other words, I need access to the actual running code.

There's a good three dozen parties in total, but nearly all of them are inactive, their members never having respawned after initially dying. I want to add Charli to *all* the parties anyway, even the inactive ones. If they figure out how to respawn, then I want Charli to already be in their party. I won't likely have a chance to manually add her later. For that matter, I'd like to have Charli automatically added to any new parties formed, too.

"Okay, ODYSSEY, you know what I want to do. How do I do it?"

No sooner does the question form in my head than my future self shows up. Glynda pulls a chair over as I wheel mine out of the way. I watch as she types and clicks and opens new windows, one of them filled with a constantly changing blob of text and numbers. She gives me a smile. "We got it now, Suze. See ya later."

So I time-jump back. I pull over a chair as my past-self wheels hers out of the way. She watches as I type and click and open new windows at ODYSSEY's direction. One of the windows is filled with a constantly changing blob of text and numbers, which ODYSSEY informs me is what we'll need to edit. I give my past-self a smile. "We got it now, Suze. See ya later." She time-jumps back, and I return my attention to the morphing text.

"Scroll down." ODYSSEY gives me direction, and I obey. "Stop. Put the edit cursor at line 3847, column 17. Now go to the Macro menu and let me see the shortcuts. Go ahead and select Start. Okay, hold down the Shift key and click on column 24, same line. Okay, press Control-C. Now move the cursor back to column 17 and down 6 lines. Press Alt-V. Press Alt-E. Good. Now press Alt-M. Press Alt-M again. Okay, it's working. Keep pressing Alt-M until I say *stop*."

I'm nearing the fortieth time of pressing Alt-M when ODYSSEY stops me.

Returning to the drag-and-drop interface, I reload the page. Charli now shows as a member of all the parties. She shows up twice in parties MAD and TimeTrippers. I point at the duplications on the screen. "Will that be a problem, ODYSSEY?"

"Drag one of them out of the grid for the party it's in... *don't let go*... and now drop it back on."

I do as suggested, and the extra Charli in party MAD disappears. I do the same for party TimeTrippers, and only one of Charli remains there. "Okay, she's in every party, and only once in each. Now if we could just get the members of all these inactive parties to respawn, they could all start earning tons of XP. Is there a way to force avatars to respawn?"

Glynda pops in. "Out of the way, Suze." I give her control of the keyboard and mouse. After she finds the desired documentation, I time-jump back, take control of the keyboard and mouse from my past self, and with direction from ODYSSEY navigate to the appropriate documentation.

The answer to my question of forcing avatars to respawn is *no*. According to the documentation, the player is required to sleep or otherwise be rendered unconscious, which allows the subconscious to animate an avatar in the game. "So, it's like dreamers participating in a shared dream."

ODYSSEY agrees. "But what are dreams? Some believe they are windows into alternate realities."

Is my nanobot collective suggesting what I think it is? "Is that something you believe? Are you saying Khertaan is an alternate reality rather than a virtual one?"

"I believe so."

I wait for him to say more.

He finally continues. "Unlike dreams, the Khertaan program, I believe, is not a *window* to an alternate reality, but a *portal* to one. What you've up to now considered a virtual world is as real as the world we call home, but with an entirely different set of natural laws. Khertaan is in its own timeline, one distantly removed from all the timelines Nick, Seth, you, or I have ever time-shifted to. It's so distant, it could take forever to reach it by exercising our time-shifting abilities. But it can be accessed via what I'll call a metaphysical *wormhole*, created by mathematical manipulations within the program Nick and Kendra created for Fanciful Pegasus."

I gulp at a thought. "If Khertaan is so distant a timeline from our regular stomping grounds, and we only get to it through this metaphysical wormhole of which you speak, how is it that Seth's minions are there? Did Seth find a wormhole into Khertaan too?"

"I don't know the answer to that," ODYSSEY admits.

Ghosts mill around us, all of them desperate for answers to their own questions. None of them pay me any mind, this stranger seated in their midst, staring at a computer screen just as ghostly as they are.

"Click that *Party Template* button," ODYSSEY urges.

I do as requested. A form pops up with some empty fields.

"Type *Charli* in that first empty field, select NPC from the option menu next to it, and save your change."

I do as directed and then click a link that looks like it might lead to a page with more information about respawning in Khertaan.

The header of the new page reads, *Map of Respawning Chambers*. I scroll down. What the hell? I've found a map of the building where the Khertaan players are housed. Each room is labeled with the player's name, below which is displayed their avatar name. I click on a room identified as that of the player Hera Ford, avatar name Mylynna. A new tab opens, with a character sheet for Mylynna.

INACTIVE PC
Eligible for Respawn
Mylynna, Female Mist Succubus

Skin: Green
Hair: Long, Curly, Red
Eyes: Green
Class: Houri, Level: 6
Subclass: N/A
HP 100/100, 100%
MP 150/150, 100%
SP 110/110, 100%
EP 120/120, 100%
Auni: 0/0
Psi: 36/36
Attributes
Physical
  Brawn 9
  Sensing 13
  Dexterity 12
  Constitution 13
  Agility 13
  Toughness 8
Mental
  Willpower 12
  Understanding 13
  Logic 6
  Sanity 6
  Intuition 11
  Memory 12
Spiritual
  Faith 12
  Conscience 10
  Favor 5
  Belief 11
  Insight 13
  Morals 12
Emotional
  Passion 16

Empathy 14

Charisma 9

Hope 8

Temperance 12

Optimism 7

Equipment:

Leather Armor (equipped)

Guitar (equipped)

Mist Succubus Kindred Traits:

Dark Sight

Temptation

Mist Passage

Party Mist Passage

Character Traits

Pain Tolerant, level 2

Empathy - Demon, level 1

Natural Weapon - Claws, level 1

Level 6 Houri Class Skills

Seduce, level 6

Attraction, level 6

Rejuvenate, level 5

Presence, level 4

Hide, level 2

No Subclass Skills

Level 6 Houri Psi Powers

Seduction 1

Rejuvenation 1

Below the character information is an enabled button labeled, *Crystal Ball*, and another one labeled, *Allow Premature Exit*. The first button has me curious, and I move the mouse cursor over it, but.... "Wait a minute. If Khertaan is an alternate reality and not a virtual one, how can a program be used to alter what's happening there?"

Eidson & Thicke

ODYSSEY chuckles in my mind. "That's a funny question coming from someone who can alter their own reality with nothing but the power of their mind. Because it comes easy to you, you take time-jumping for granted. In opening a wormhole between two universes, the Khertaan program alters them both. To extend that capability to altering other natural laws beyond the creation of a wormhole doesn't seem a far reach to me."

Whoa. Did my nanobot collective just imply something much stranger than he'd intended? "You make it sound like the program could alter reality in this timeline, too, not just in Khertaan."

"You are astute."

I click the Crystal Ball button.

A full-screen window opens, displaying the interior of a room, its floor cluttered with books, scrolls, and clothing. Is the room ghostly, or does it appear that way because it's displayed on a ghostly monitor?

A nightstand sits to the right of a bed at the far side of the room. The foot of the bed faces me, and there sits a lean young white woman, her shoulders slumped forward, shaking like she's sobbing. She holds her face in her hands. Quivering, curly red locks flow over her shoulders, not quite concealing her yellow tank top. Sandals—nothing fancy—and blue jean shorts with frayed hemlines complete her outfit.

A prompt across the bottom of my computer screen reads, *Video and audio channels open.* To the right of the prompt opens a small, circular window displaying the face of my avatar, Slithy. That's unexpected. I assume that's what Hera will see when she looks at the display on her side… which I'm thinking might be via a crystal ball…?

The amazing thing that almost slips by me is that the video interface I'm using recognizes me as Slithy's player. Facial recognition aside, the System knows more about me than I would have expected, since I never registered as a player.

I grab a set of headphones from the desk and put them on. They're already plugged into the computer's audio jack. An attached microphone hangs before my mouth. "Hera Ford?"

The woman jerks her head up, leaps to her feet, and rushes towards the camera. Her face all but fills my screen. Tears stream from her green eyes, down cheeks blushed pink but streaked with mascara. She grabs at the camera, one hand on either side, and her image trembles on-screen. *"Please, whoever and whatever you are, let me out of here."*

My heart breaks at the desperation in her voice. "Hera, I'll do my best to help you, but I need you to calm down and talk to me first. Can you do that?"

Her gaze locks with mine through our devices. Hope flares in her eyes and her voice drops almost to a whisper. "Please tell me you can open the door to this room. I'm going out of my mind in here."

The *Allow Premature Exit* button makes sense now. "Listen to me. I don't know what lies outside your room. It could be chaos, or everything might be fine. It could be the door is locked to keep bad things out as much as to keep you in. The world is a bit crazy right now."

Darkness erases the glint of hope in her eyes. "What do you mean?"

Knowing how insane I'm going to sound, I say it anyway. "I mean there might be aliens outside your room. I just escaped from their spaceship myself."

Her gaze narrows. "I'm still in the game. I knew it. I thought dying in the game would wake me up in the real world, but it didn't. I'm still an avatar, thinking I'm in my real body, because my virtual body looks like my real one now. Oh, God. Oh, God. Okay, so... this is like a mini-game, one you have to play to get back into the main game. But what do I have to do? I've tried everything I can think of to open that damned door. So it must not be about the door. What else can it be? Please, give me a hint. *Please.*"

On her character sheet, Hera's Understanding is above average, but her Logic is sub-par. So are her Sanity and Favor attributes, for that matter. Her Hope and Optimism are below average. If I can explain it to her properly, she'll understand what I say, but who knows where her mind will take her in attempting to extrapolate from my revelations? She's got enough Hope and Optimism to reject the notion that actual aliens might be outside her door. But how far can she stretch that positive outlook before it breaks? I should be more careful in what I say. If she comes to seriously believe aliens lurk outside her room, that could spell the end of our conversation. "Hera, I'll help you get back into the main game, but I need you to answer some questions for me first. Does your room have a misty quality to it?" I shy from using the term, *ghostly*, with her.

She nods. "Happened just a few minutes ago. Everything is still solid, but the place looks like a room for ghosts. It was freaking me out, but it's understandable now that I know I'm still in the game."

Part of me wants to correct her, but for her sake, I let her continue with her mistaken view of her situation. "Hera, are you able to communicate with anyone else in your party?"

Her curly red tresses sway side to side as she shakes her head. "Believe me, I tried. Are you saying there's a way to do it, but I just haven't found it? Is that what I need to do to win this mini-game?" She glances around her room.

That wasn't what I meant, but I don't discourage her from looking.

She picks up a mirror from the nightstand and carries it close to the camera, holding it up so I can see. "Is this it?" She looks into the mirror. "This is Hera Ford calling Benny Jackson. Answer your mirror, Benny." A grin spreads across her face, giving me a secret thrill to see her fear flee.

A masculine voice speaks up. "*Hera?* Oh, my God. Are you still in your room, too? How do we get back in the game? Are you able to leave your room?"

189

Tears well in Hera's eyes. "*Benny*. You don't know how glad I am to see you and hear your voice. Are you okay?"

"I'm fine. Better now than I was a second ago."

Hera's smile brightens. "Listen, I have a nice amphibian lady named Slithy on my crystal ball. She helped me figure out how to contact you, and she's going to help me get back into the main game. Don't open the door to your room. Aliens wait out there, and I think we're meant to engage them sometime later." She turns her attention to me. "Okay, Slithy is there something else I need to do before going back to the main game?"

"Yes. I'll tell you, but don't do it yet. Promise?"

She nods with gusto. "You have my word."

"You'll need to go to sleep. That's how you respawn and get back in the main game. Tell Benny, but ask him to contact your other party members first who might need to do it, too. Also, when you are able to check your party roster again, you'll see the name *Charli* in the list. *Don't oust her*. Tell the others in your party. She's traveling elsewhere in Khertaan, but as a member of your party, any XP she earns will be earned by all of you. It will help you gain levels fast. Tell Benny and the rest of your party about her. If you oust her, you're not likely to get her back."

Hera glances at her mirror. "Did you get all that, Benny?"

"Yep. Sweet."

I raise a finger for attention. On-screen, it appears my avatar is holding up a webbed finger. "Benny, use your mirror to contact your other party members. Hera, say goodbye to Benny. I want you to do one more thing for me before you respawn."

"Thanks, Slithy," Benny calls from the mirror. "Bye, Hera. See you soon. I can't wait to get back in the game. *Finally*."

Hera bids her farewell to Benny and looks askance at me. "Lay it on me, Slithy. Am I getting a special quest?"

"I don't know if it will work, but I want you to try something for me. Use your mirror to contact Charli."

Shaken only for a moment, Hera shrugs. "Sure, why not? Can't wait to meet my new fellow party member." She stares into the mirror. "Hello, Charli. Can you hear me? Hello? Earth to Charli."

"This is Charli. Who is this?"

My heart races at the sound of the Cowgirl's voice, and a tear wells in my eye.

Hera replies. "Hi, Charli. You don't know me, but my name is Hera Ford. I'm *Mylynna* in Khertaan. I belong to the party TwoWorldOrder. I have someone here who wants to speak to you." She turns the mirror's face to me.

Charli looks back at me. Not the fourteen-year-old girl I knew, but a woman, filled out in places that make the few extra years obvious. Her pigtails are gone, long blond strands flapping in the wind instead, and her wide-brimmed hat miraculously staying on her head. She's flying, putting an outcropping and cave opening behind her. Her mouth mimics the cavern, gaping wide. "*Slithy?* Where in blazes are you?"

CHAPTER TWENTY-EIGHT

Debra: Reverie

Party MAD backtracks to rejoin XStorm. I focus on staying hidden from them as well as I can using the abilities borrowed from Megan, while squelching the skills and traits I've inherited from Dylan as her secondary avatar. Attraction and Presence are far from what I need right now.

Yuni switches from Crow to human form and runs to meet the members of her party. She throws her arms around her brother, Bradford. The Asian Priestess has such an outgoing personality, it's surprising she chose War over Light as her religious focus. But her choice proved to be a great one, helping Amarynth wipe out an entire army of Behemoths in the space of ten minutes.

Come to think of it, my personality is so dark, it's surprising Dylan chose to serve a Goddess of Light. It's like the repressed parts of our Earthling personalities come to the forefront in our avatars. Dylan is everything I'm not. Beautiful. Confident. Brave.

If she and I share a quality, it's survival. She freaking won the title of Longest Survivor. I've done whatever was necessary back on Earth to survive. Yes, that included turning to prostitution for a while. I'm not proud of it. The money I made from it didn't help as much as I'd expected, but it got me through some rough patches.

Christopher Warden was one of my clients. His avatar, ChrisCross, is built like him with regards to height and weight and how his mass is distributed on his frame. Their faces are similar, both square-jawed… but ChrisCross has a straight, leonine nose, whereas Christopher's is noticeably bent to his right, possibly the result of a fist fight. But the biggest difference between Christopher and his avatar is the haircut. ChrisCross wears curly, shoulder-length black hair. Christopher has black hair, too, but wears it in a crew cut. The man is uncouth, full of himself, and rough in bed. I never felt more out of control of my own body than when he was on top of me. Allowing him to do what he wanted with me was simultaneously exhilarating, frightening, and demeaning. I've never despised myself more after being with someone.

But where Christopher was forward, arrogant, and threatening, his avatar, ChrisCross, is quiet and reserved, standing at the back of his party, his hands behind his back, his feet bare. Is ChrisCross what lurks within Christopher's subconsciousness? The avatar's expression isn't smug, but exudes wisdom, as though he sees and understands everything without taking any great pride in it.

It's as though our avatars have given us permission to be who we secretly wish to be. Megan Wright, my dearest friend in the world, froze with paralysis when Christopher verbally assaulted me in the office. Mithabel the Elf Tank would ram her blade without hesitation through the mouth of anyone who treated Dylan that way.

Amarynth the Viking Archer is half the age of her player, Anna Milligan. Both avatar and player are direct, courageous, and no-nonsense. So they aren't complete opposites. I suppose none of us players are the complete opposites of our avatars. But where Anna

Milligan is slow and deliberate, Amarynth is the epitome of speed and spontaneity.

Are our avatars better people than we players are? Do we all bottle up our best selves, having been trained by the world and its shit to hide them for their own protection?

Our group heads once again for Minook.

I really don't want XStorm to know I'm here, because if they find out about secondary avatars, they'll all want them. If Christopher Warden were to show up as a secondary avatar, I'm not sure how I'd react, but I'm guessing Megan would not take kindly to his presence.

"You know it."

"Damn, Megan. You're listening to my thoughts?"

"I told you that's how this awareness transfer works. We can hear each other's surface thoughts. Sorry I didn't remind you again sooner, but I didn't feel like interrupting your soliloquy. You made some very good points. And, um… sorry about eavesdropping on the really personal stuff. I never realized how tough you must have had it."

At this stage of my life, the idea that I'd had hard times in my younger days is almost laughable. "Times were tough back then because I dared to dream. Trying to get people to pay attention to my music and talent drained my funds, not to mention my soul. I sold my body to pay for professional head shots, demo tracks, and contest entry fees. I paid for studio time and musicians to create a single that I then paid to have distributed to all the streaming services.

"I was so proud of what I'd accomplished, and yet nothing came of it. Nothing. I didn't earn one cent in royalties. I thought if I created an EP of five tracks, maybe that would get more notice. So I sold my body some more to pay for it. *Still nothing*. Naturally, I wasn't considering giving up. I kept selling my body and laying down more tracks until I had enough for a full album. And you guessed it. *Still nothing. No one* cared about my music. *No one* listened.

"I might have kept going, kept doing the exact same thing, thinking if I put myself out there enough, someone would eventually listen. I'd eventually make a big splash. But I graduated from college, found a job writing technical documentation, and decided enough was enough. It just so happened that someone who'd paid for sex with me in the past also worked at the place where I landed my new job. You know what that led to.

"So now I'm unemployed, up to my neck in student debt, and lying in a bed somewhere in the Fanciful Pegasus facility, playing in a weird video game contest, hoping to take home a huge cash prize. Oh, and there's something about aliens attacking the earth, and I'm supposedly training to fight them. *Little ole me*. And you, Megan…. If we drive the bad things off the planet, do you think we'll be paid for doing it? I assume if we don't drive them away, money won't matter. Humanity will be wiped out. But once we save the world, assuming we do, what will our lives become?"

We're speeding along the safe route towards a distant spire. Someone named FepXveq from party Quantized speaks over local chat. "Party MAD, is that you?"

Some specks in the distance might be an adventuring party.

Mithabel waves a hand. "We're here. How the hell did you spot us? Even knowing you're there, I can scarcely make you out."

"Hey, Mithabel." The reply comes back on local chat from Ger-Alt, a Goblin woman. "You're catching up to us. Good deal. We were hoping you'd help us defeat the Boss for this territory."

I've never met Ger-Alt in person. But I know what Dylan knows, and she's already met everyone in Quantized. So I have a mental picture of them—a Goblin woman who rides a Cheetah; a Dark Elf woman with a big black afro; a female Faerie with leathery bat wings; an unremarkable yet adorable Squirrel; and a Falcon that can throw up a dust storm. They're only level ten or so. How the hell did they get past the Behemoth army?

Dylan has the same question, and she asks them over the local chat channel.

195

Ger-Alt laughs. "What can I say? It was a combination of things, really. Flying helped those of us capable of it. For the rest of us, the abilities to hide or move super fast—or stay on the back of someone who moves super fast—got us all through. The Meditative Focus trait helped, big time. It's super useful when you can spot the enemy coming from a long way away. It might also have helped that they didn't seem to be all that interested in us. Once we were past them, they didn't try to follow. I assumed they were after bigger fish... like you, maybe. But I don't see them behind you, so... did you vanquish them all, or what?"

It's Dylan's turn to laugh. "Yeah, we vanquished them all. To give credit where credit is due, it was Amarynth and Yuni who defeated them. The rest of us just kept out of the way and tried not to die when the Behemoths exploded."

Gasps echo across the desert sands from the Quantized members. Anyone in the Dunes of Doom listening to the local chat channel could hear them. No one from MAD or XStorm tells Quantized how many XP we earned from the victory, or that everyone in their party might have earned as much, too, if they'd only waited back in Maron and traveled with us.

The local chat channel goes quiet. We're all a bunch of introverts with little use for small talk.

Yuni walks next to Dylan. They hold hands. If Mithabel has noticed, she's biting her tongue. I could tap into Dylan's thought stream if I wanted and hear her private conversation with Yuni. But I don't.

My primary avatar—which is to say, my subconsciousness—has reacted in a positive way to the Asian Priestess. I can't help but wonder what Yuni's player is like on Earth and how she and I might get along if we ever meet.

Megan, I know you're listening to my thoughts, and I assure you, you're the one for me. So, please, don't be jealous, and don't let Mithabel get jealous, either.

"I love you, too, Debra."

CHAPTER TWENTY-NINE

Yuni: Overpowered

How does a person know when they've found something good? Even when their heart flutters in their chest and every nerve in their body is on fire with desire, how do they know if the cause of the fluttering and burning is *good* for them?

Dylan's hand in mine might as well be a grip on my soul. I never want her to let go or pull away from me. This trek across the Dunes of Doom should never end. Let's forever be walking hand-in-hand towards the horizon.

Though the sun doesn't traverse the sky, the spire looms higher and higher above us, a constant reminder that change is inevitable. I don't know how long this relationship will last, whatever this relationship is, but I cherish every moment of it, every squeeze of her hand, every squeeze I return, every sideways glance exchanged, every lick of the lips. It's like we're opposite poles of two magnets, and the stronger we get, the more we're attracted to each other. How will it feel to go our separate ways once the game is over?

It's difficult to believe our attraction to each other is entirely due to our traits and skills, but we don't know each other that well, so what other basis can there be? Yet I ache inside at the thought of parting from her. How can such feelings arise solely from numbers on character sheets?

There's only one way to know whether our feelings are based on game mechanics or run deeper. Our players need to meet on Earth. If they like each other as much as Dylan and I like each other, then what we have is greater than this game.

"Dylan?"

The smile she turns on me is priceless. "Yes?"

"How would you feel about our players contacting each other once this game is over?"

She hesitates, and my heart drops in my chest. Then she nods. "Perhaps we can exchange names and numbers. What our players do with the information will be up to them. My player is Debra Jones."

My heart soars. "Mine is Saiko Aimi. You can call her Aimi. It's Japanese tradition to place the family name first." I spell the family name for her, s-a-i-k-o. English speakers spell my family name wrong more often than not, spelling it to start with p-s-y and ending in c-h-o.

Dylan laughs. "I'm betting Debra will have fun with that."

I laugh in return.

We trade phone numbers, too.

"Inuki, please record the contact info for Debra Jones in my game log."

"Yes, musume."

Even though it's recorded in my log, I repeat Debra's phone number in my head for what feels like a thousand times. Maybe it's more. I stop when we finally reach Quantized in the shadow of the spire.

They're a motley crew... three humanoids and three animals: A slinking, yellow Cheetah on whose back rides a short, green-skinned Goblin woman with a furry gray Squirrel perched on her shoulder. A violet-skinned foot-long Faerie with leathery bat wings spanning three feet. A tall Dark Elf woman with the deepest black skin and a black afro in which nests a Falcon with blue, gray, and white feathers and dark brown eyes ringed with yellow.

"Hail." The Goblin brandishes a purple battle axe. "I see some new faces among you, so let me begin the introductions. We're Quantized, and I'm Ger-Alt, a Were-Fighter and Psyon. My mount here is Zip, a Barbarian Tank. The little fellow on my shoulder is Skeeter, a Mentalist and Psi-Thief. Don't feel bad if you have trouble remembering him, because he's got the Nondescript trait, which tends to push him into the background in everyone's minds. This tall lady is FepXveq, a Bandit and Spirit Warrior. Atop her head is her Magical Companion, Falco, a Rogue and Dust Wizard. Last but not least, if you train your eyes very close to the ground, you might spot Toxxi the Faerie, a Life-Stealer and Winged Fighter."

Toxxi flaps her wings, as though the action were necessary for us to notice her. It's *not* necessary. She's not repulsive, but her regal posture and smirk spell *danger* and *distrust*. Her gaze thrusts daggers at Mithabel, and the Elf Tank's body language sends them right back. There's bad blood between those two. But we're all friends here, right?

Dylan introduces the members of MAD in much the same way she'd introduced them to us. Over party chat, CC asks me to make the introductions for XStorm. I'm the only one of us with Presence, so I'm always the one tasked with endeavors of a social nature.

Once the introductions are all finished, Ger-Alt points her battle axe skyward. "We've seen a gigantic Pteranodon in the clouds. We figure it's the Boss for the Dunes. As I understand the rules of the game, we need to kill it before we can leave its territory. I don't know if we need to kill it alone, or if another party can help us. Do any of you know?"

I nod. "I know from experience that a person can gain full XP from an encounter just by traveling with another party as an ally. It's not quite what you're asking, but I'm guessing the answer is similar."

Inuki mimics my nod. "If someone earns XP from a Boss kill, that counts as them defeating the Boss for purposes of leaving its territory." I relay the information on local chat for everyone to hear.

The Goblin woman's eyes light up. "So, if we send Toxxi and/or Falco up there with your best flying fighters, and the Boss is killed, that should garner us full XP for the Boss and allow us to leave the territory? That's great." She glances to the Faerie, who's now seated cross-legged on the sand. "You want to go up with them, Toxxi?"

"Of course." The Faerie grins, and I sense mischief behind it.

Amarynth's crossbow appears in her right hand. She turns to the Angel. "What do you say, Zyekt? Want to take me up?"

"I'd love to." The Angel glances around. "Who else is going, and what kind of enchantments and blessings can we get before we go?"

All eyes fall on me and Dylan. If Amarynth, Daughter of True Aim and servant of the War Goddess, needs a weapon blessed, my spell will achieve more than one from Dylan, a Priestess of Light. I raise my hand. "I can bless your crossbow, Amarynth, as much as I did before, or even more if you think it necessary. The Boss Pteranodon is on par with the Behemoths, if not worse."

A woman cries over local chat. "O-a-ooh." Where is her cry coming from? It sounds again. And again. I've got distance attenuation for territorial chat turned low, so I can hear anyone in the Dunes speaking on local chat. I gradually increase the attenuation to decrease the volume, but the cries don't stop. I turn off local chat, but still hear the cries. "Inuki, what channel is that woman's cry coming across on?"

My cat-headed furry ball of a support AI yawns. "It's coming on the special effects channel, musume. You can't mute it."

"Whatever you're doing, best do it quick." Mithabel points towards the spire. "I don't know what it is or how many or even the exact direction they're coming from, which is strange, but my Danger Sense is picking up a group of mooks, not an individual. I have a sense those cries represent more than a physical threat."

Also in possession of the Danger Sense trait, Zip the Cheetah and Skeeter the Squirrel echo their agreement with Mithabel's assessment.

The feminine cries are noticeably louder… I hear overlapping cries, indicating multiple creatures. I'd wager they're flying creatures with ranged attacks. But try as I might, I can't spot any mooks approaching by land or by air.

"I don't feel so good." Talking over local chat so we all can hear him, Zip the Cheetah settles onto his belly on the sand with Ger-Alt still on his back. The Goblin woman hops off and kneels beside her mount.

"Me, either." On top of the Dark Elf's head, Falco repositions himself as though trying to get comfortable.

"I'm feeling a bit sick to my serpentine stomach, too." CC's Electric Serpent, Lance, confines his revelation to XStorm party chat. He doesn't want to show weakness to the other parties.

"The group is under spiritual attack, musume." Inuki's tail jerks from side to side. "I don't know the identity or location of the enemy, but Lance has taken a 10% hit on SP. Zip the Cheetah is down to 89%, and Falco has dropped to 86%."

"Why are we being attacked? We're on the safe path." Mithabel scans our feet. "Is someone not touching the ground?" She refers to her map and then waves the parchment. "I don't get it. It looks like we're all on the safe route. Why are we being attacked?"

"O-a-ooh." The cries clearly come in multiple voices, some high-pitched, some lower-pitched, but all feminine and in unison. They're closer than before.

Lance, Zip, and Falco moan their pain, with Falco falling out of his nest atop FepXveq's head. The Dark Elf catches her bird Companion in her arms.

Penelope and Amarynth grab their stomachs and look ready to puke.

My fat cat AI reports the group's status. "Lance is at 80% SP, Zip is 79%, Falco 73%, Penelope 92%, and Amarynth 90%."

Unfortunately, I don't have a spell for healing spiritual damage, only physical damage.

Where the hell *are* our attackers? I look high and low and all around. Dropping Dylan's hand, I raise both of mine over my head. "Athlea, Goddess of War, please lay your blessing on all present as you will." I don't know if my Morale skill can help those outside my party, but I phrase my request with the hopes it can. It might at least help Amarynth, being a follower of Athlea.

Dylan calls for the blessing of Scintilla on everyone whom the Goddess of Light is willing to assist. If her Morale skill and mine both can affect Amarynth, do they stack? That would be awesome.

"Well, now that we're all buffed up...." Mithabel stashes the safe route map. "Who of us has the ability to see into the spiritual realm? We need to know what's attacking us."

Cradling her Falcon companion with one arm, FepXveq points with her other hand. "I see Harpies flocking in the distance. There could easily be a few dozen of them. It's hard to see them in the spire's shadow, but I have the traits Far Sight and Dark Sight, a decently high Spot skill, and an extraordinary Sensing attribute.

"The Harpies aren't bearing down on us, so I doubt they know we're here. Your guess is as good as mine as to why their cries are affecting us here on the safe path. But since they are, we need to deal with them sooner than later, or they'll continue to damage our spirits, and those of us vulnerable to their cries will eventually be rendered berserk, losing control of our own faculties. I believe the Harpies can be damaged physically. They can likely deal physical damage in addition to spiritual damage if we engage them."

One hand clamped to her stomach, Amarynth waves Zyekt over. "Take me to them." Grimacing against the pain, she grasps the Angel's outstretched hand and equips her crossbow with her free hand. "FepXveq, keep us on target. Yuni, will you come with us, in case I need an enchantment?"

"Of course." I Shapeshift to my Crow form, call up a wind to help me fly faster, and launch skyward.

"I'm coming, too." Toxxi's purple Faerie figure speeds past me. "I want Quantized to earn XP for the encounter."

"I think I'll stay here, if that's all the same to you, Zyekt." Niav hops off the Angel's shoulder, landing on the sand.

Dylan lays a hand on Amarynth. "May Scintilla soothe your spirit. Should I go with you?"

"Thanks for the spiritual heal, Priestess. I'm good now. Soon as we get near enough, those things are all going down." The Archer pats Dylan's cheek and then gives Zyekt a thumbs up.

We've not gone far when another wave of spiritual damage hits. Inuki gives me the report. "Dylan had healed Amarynth to full, but now the Archer is back down to 90% SP. Falco is at 59%, Zip at 69, Lance at 71, and Penelope at 84. The Harpy attacks grow stronger with every passing moment, but so far you have taken no damage to SP, thanks to your Spiritual Armor trait."

I'd initially wondered how much my Spiritual Armor trait would come into play in the game, and it has proved to be more useful than I'd imagined.

FepXveq feeds us course corrections as we go. "They're coming toward you." Which makes sense, now that we're off the safe route, though I don't know why they bother. Amarynth, Falco, Lance, Zip, and Penelope are hit with another round of SP damage before we're even halfway to the flying mooks.

This time, even Skeeter the Squirrel is hit with 14% SP damage. The number of affected targets is steadily growing.

As we draw near to the Archer's crossbow attack range, Zyekt falters mid-air. "Keep tight hold of my hand, Amarynth. I'm being affected myself now. It won't be good if I lose my grip on you."

Inuki tells me the group status. Amarynth is down to 71% SP. Falco is the worst off at 32% SP. Not only have Lance, Zip,

Penelope, and Skeeter taken more damage, but Zyekt has dropped to 92% SP.

Amarynth's arm shakes as she aims her crossbow. Whispering the name of our Goddess, she fires. The bolt flying from her weapon splits into *six* missiles, each headed for a different target. They all strike home, and every Harpy struck evaporates, spreading trails of colored pixels behind them. The Archer fires *thrice* again in rapid succession, each shot taking out six Harpies. Just like that, she's taken out half of the bird women flock.

The Angel clears his throat. "We're about to have other company. The Boss will be appearing in twenty seconds."

No one asks him how he knows. He must have some ability granting him insight about the future.

The remaining two dozen Harpies open their mouths to scream. I steel myself for a concerted cooperative combo spiritual attack. Even with my Spiritual Armor trait, I can't imagine I'll come out of this attack unscathed.

"Be silent, Harpies." Zyekt issues the command in a calm, confident voice. The two dozen bird women keep their mouths open but no sounds issue forth. They hover in place, as though unsure what to do next. Amarynth peppers them with another four volleys of crossbow bolts, finishing them off.

Zyekt waves for my attention. "As soon as the Boss appears, enchant the Archer's crossbow."

"The Harpies encounter has ended." Inuki gives me the lowdown. "You have earned nine point six million XP from the encounter. You're now over halfway to level 28."

Toxxi gasps. "By the sacred ancestors. I've just jumped from level ten to level nineteen."

Zyekt points straight up. "Get ready for the Boss. Ten. Nine. Eight...." He continues counting down. He hits zero, and a gigantic black shape blocks our view of the sky. "*Now*, Yuni."

With my Crow's talon, I clutch Amarynth's crossbow. I call for Athlea's blessing upon it, pumping a full one hundred Auni into the spell.

"You honor me, child." The Goddess speaks in my head, her voice soft yet authoritative. Athlea's magic darkens the crossbow in the Archer's hand.

As soon as I let go of her weapon, Amarynth fires. Her bolt doesn't divide this time. The single missile strikes the giant Pteranodon. Sadly, the Boss doesn't die. Inuki reports its HP at 27%.

As Amarynth fires again, a cone of black liquid erupts from the Boss's mouth, centered on us. This is going to hurt.

Toxxi darts out in front of us, flapping her wings hard, raising winds. The acid collides with the Faerie's storm.

Seeing what she's doing, I help with my Wind Control skill, increasing the speed of the winds diverting the acid attack.

Acid falls like rain to the sands below, and despite our efforts, some of it sprays us. It burns my skin, but—ha—I only feel a tickle... my Pain Tolerant trait at work.

Amarynth's second missile strikes home, and the Boss bursts into a cloud of black pixels swept away by the wind.

"Congrats, musume." Inuki grins, bobbing his head side to side. "You've earned three million XP for yourself and everyone in XStorm. You've inched another couple of percentage points towards level 28. Your HP is at 87% due to the acid attack."

"How is everyone?" I glance at Amarynth. "I wish I had a way to heal your lost SP, Archer."

Her eyes are downcast, despite the win we just had. She might not be badly injured physically, but there are other ways we avatars can hurt, and she's experiencing one of them.

We're all down by ten to twenty-something HP percentage points, which might have been much worse if not for Toxxi's quick thinking and her Repulsion abilities. None of us are close to dying, but it will take a good amount of Auni to heal us all.

We return to Dylan and the others. Amarynth collapses onto the sand, falling onto her back and staring up at the sky in silence. Her SP loss has drained her of the motivation to continue traveling.

The Polynesian Priestess is already tending to Falco, Zip, Skeeter, and Penelope. With the Advanced Healing spell, Dylan can heal spiritual damage, something I can't do. It would be nice if I could purchase the spell at the next village we visit, but I have no idea where I'll get the money for it.

"Save your Auni, Yuni." Dylan uses a spell to heal my acid-burned skin. "How does it feel to have been one of those to defeat the Boss?"

"It hasn't sunk in yet." I don't say what I'm thinking. We found a way to exploit the System and now… *we're overpowered.* I'm guessing that Boss was designed as a level twelve to fifteen challenge, and we're way above that now. Two shots to a Boss, and it's dead—yeah, we're *way* overpowered.

In the span of two minutes, Dylan has healed everyone back to full HP and SP. She chuckles. "Hardly put a dent in my Auni. Shall we continue to yonder spire? Quantized, you can bring us all up to speed on your level advancement as we go."

"Thank you all for helping us." Zip the Cheetah stretches his legs and yawns.

"Indeed." Falco settles into his nest atop FepXveq's big, black afro again. "It was unsettling to be so… uncaring. Not a good place to be. But now—thank you, Dylan—I'm more motivated than ever to push forward. And thank you for risking your lives, Toxxi, Zyekt, Amarynth, and Yuni. Because of you, I've gone from level ten to level twenty, and cannot *wait* to try out my new skills."

"Me, either," echo the others in Quantized.

With all three of our parties traveling and working together, how can anything in Khertaan be a threat to us? We are definitely overpowered. *I hope.* Because if we're not, I can't imagine what we'll be facing.

CHAPTER THIRTY

Lady Ghost: Exploration

This is the moment I've dreaded. If this were a timeline in which I had a flesh-and-blood existence, this would be a moment of joy. But I don't belong in this timeline, and now Nick's mind will enforce my absence. He's about to recognize me for who I am, and then he'll think, *you don't belong here*, and his words will banish me, whether he speaks them aloud or only in his head.

Nick cocks his head, his gaze locked with mine. "Do I know you, ghost?"

Greelia jumps to her feet, still snuggling the baby in her arms. Bristling, she faces me across the bonfire. "Be gone, spirit. This world is not for you."

The man climbs to his feet and puts his arm around Greelia's shoulders. "You heard her, spirit. Be gone from this place."

I back away. They're right. This world isn't for me, because that isn't my Nick. There is no recognition of me or desire for me in this incarnation of him. The resemblance to Nick in this facsimile drew me here, because I'm so desperate to find him and even Morrow isn't projecting much of his spirit at the moment.

I'm so hollow, and it's not only because I'm a ghost.

Folding on myself to reverse the process of entering this timeline, I fly out of the darkness into the greenness and from there into mists. Below me are the three cloaked figures on the circular disk with the colored light beams. The red beam has grown nearly fifty percent in size. The blue beam has diminished maybe ten percent. The green beam hasn't changed in diameter and burns brighter than either the red or the blue. The other thin ones that had been present are fewer in number, crowded out by the growth of the red beam.

I focus on each beam in turn, trying to sense my Nick. There's the faintest pull from the red beam, not even as much as from the green one, indicating the presence of another loser with some resemblance to Nick but not hosting his awareness. None of the beams other than the red and green ones have a draw for me at all.

Any hope I have of reuniting with Nick rests with Morrow. The mohawk-wearing Punk must be saved. I need to get back to him.

The nexus resides in the mists. I close my ghostly eyes and reach out with my mind. Where is Morrow?

The sensation comes like a rope tugging my soul, and I give myself to it, letting it take me where it will. The mists thin. Then they're gone, and I'm inside the nexus, in a room with Morrow and Renee. A hooded and cloaked Greelia stands by the ruined table, her axe still lying at her feet. Her eyes are shut and she doesn't so much as quiver, her fists still pressed together before her chest.

The Greelia I saw on the disk was a mental projection into a metaphysical space. The Greelia I saw in the cave timeline with Nick and their baby is hosting Greelia's awareness at the moment. The Greelia here is locked in a trance until her awareness returns, if it ever does.

If anything were to happen to Greelia here in the nexus, what effect would it have on the other two versions of her? Might it distract her from the metaphysical battle for timeline dominance?

I lower myself behind Morrow, the only vestige of my Nick left to me, and whisper to him. "I'm here, my love."

If it weren't for Renee's presence, perhaps Morrow and I could be happy living in this nexus forever, just the two of us, aside from what might as well be a statue of Greelia. No matter how thin her green beam of light, she'll never let it be extinguished. As long as the green beam shines, Greelia will remain in this nexus, unmoving, while her alternate self enjoys eternity with her created versions of Nick and Britta.

"Lady ghost." Morrow doesn't turn around to look at me. "Did you find any other trace of Nick?" He instinctively knows I went searching.

My reply is still a whisper. "I found a Nick residing in a timeline where only he, Greelia, and Britta exist. They would not allow me to stay with them."

Renee sighs. "That's the timeline our Greelia here is concentrating on keeping intact."

Morrow nods. "Yes. We mustn't disturb her, or Jean triumphs. We can only hope Rancor carries my message to Kylie and the others, and they can save Charli and her timelines before Greelia exhausts herself. Do you know anything else that might be helpful to us, lady ghost?"

I describe everything I saw and experienced between my departure from the nexus and my return—the disk and its occupants, the beams of light and their sizes, the mists, the cones of light shining on the combatants, the bonfire, how I entered the green beam, and what I sensed of Nick. Everything. If I omitted anything, it wasn't on purpose.

"Can you do something for me, lady ghost?"

"I will do anything for you. Even if it ends my life, I will do your bidding."

"I wouldn't want that."

"What do you wish of me, my love?"

Morrow pauses as though pondering the risks of what he's about to ask. He cares about me, even if there's not much of my Nick left in him. "I'd like you to go into the red timeline like you did the green one. Come back and tell me what you find of Nick there. Be very careful. That's Jean's timeline of interest, and she has a vengeful spirit. If she suspects you're someone Nick cared for, she may attempt to destroy you."

"I'll be careful."

I return to the mists beyond the room's walls.

Moments later, I fold in on myself and merge my spirit with Jean's red beam of light, entering her preferred timeline. Dread seizes my soul, doing its best to crush even my ghostly existence.

I stand on a sidewalk in a busy city. Buildings loom over me. People and vehicles move all around me, sweeping me up in a flood of flesh and metal.

Oh, my. In this timeline, *I'm* in the flesh. I don't understand this at all. Does Jean want me in her timeline so she can torture or kill me? Why else would she want me to have a flesh-and-blood existence here?

A distant building stands forty or more stories tall. Halfway up the building hangs a black screen, ten stories tall and half as wide, displaying the head shot of a woman who's face I easily recognize—Jean. She wears a golden crown, earrings, and necklace. White lace adorns her shoulders.

Her voice booms across the city, notifying everyone of the kidnapping of her daughter, Princess Karen. Jean's picture is replaced by that of the supposed kidnapper, a young man named Ronnie, attired in medieval garb. I've seen him before, with Nick and Greelia.

Jean continues. "If you see this man, you are authorized to kill on sight. The bounty on his head is set at one million dollars." An image of a young woman replaces Ronnie's. She's familiar, too, and is someone close to Nick. His daughter. No, this is his transgender son. On the screen, he's dressed in pink clothes with white frills and has longer hair, a silver crown, and silver jewelry. Jean identifies the young woman as her daughter, who is not to be harmed.

Ronnie's image returns to the screen, along with the banners: *Wanted, Dead or Alive* and *Reward: One Million Dollars.*

Someone nearby shouts, *"It's them."*

Two motorcycles speed by. A bullet whines past me, missing me and the bikers, but hitting another bystander, who goes down. Another shot fires, taking down another bystander.

The roads are packed, forcing the two bikers to drive on the sidewalk. I rush after them. If only I were in ghost form instead of fleshly form, I could move faster, going through people instead of around. As it is, I run in the wake of the bikers and make decent time, since they're clearing a path. But at some point they'll get away from me if I stay on foot.

More bullets shoot down the sidewalk or across the street. Pedestrians cry out and scatter, some of them hit and others running for cover. I'd love to stop and help those who are hit, but I wouldn't know what to do, and I can't lose Ronnie and Princess Karen.

That name isn't right. Nick called his son by the name Mel, not Karen.

There's a kid with a bicycle. He's unchaining it. Sorry, kid, but I need that. If I ever meet you in another universe, I'll make it up to you.

The sidewalks are becoming less crowded, which is allowing the motorcycles to go faster. Damn. I'd nearly caught up to them. I need a faster mode of transportation. I'm close enough right now, I could call out their names, but that could be the distraction that gets them killed.

Instinctively, I know… the two I'm chasing aren't from this timeline. This Mel is the offspring of my Nick, and if this Mel exists, then my Nick must exist, too, and not only in the form of Morrow. I need this Mel to remain Mel, and not become Princess Karen. I need this Mel to stay alive and lead me to my Nick.

But, dammit, the way ahead has become too clear. Mel and Ronnie tear out of sight. How I ache to call out their names, but bullets are still flying. If I were the cause of their deaths, I couldn't bear it. I pedal until my legs wear out, but my quarry is long gone over a distant rise.

I turn around and take the bicycle back to its owner. "Thanks, kid." He's just glad to get it back, and speeds off on it.

What now? I assess myself. I'm wearing a white blouse with lacy pink frills. There's a leather collar around my throat, with a buckle. I can't see it, so don't know for sure, but I'm confident it's pink. I'm in a black miniskirt with a pink leather belt, and I'm wearing white tennis shoes with pink laces and pink soles. My straight, shoulder-length hair is blue. I'm not carrying anything, not even a purse.

"You, there." The voice is gruff and aimed at the back of my neck, making the vellus hairs stand up.

I slowly turn around.

The hulk addressing me leers. "How much?" He's twice my height, with biceps as thick as my waist. He holds an over-sized pistol in one hand, and he's covered in leather straps from the neck down.

"Nothing I have is for sale."

"Great." His grin broadens, showing his teeth, which are whiter than I'd expected. "Then I'll take what I want for free." He waves a pistol at a nearby doorway. "In there is fine. Go on."

I run, but he lunges and grabs my arm, lifting me off my feet, and carries me to the door. I struggle all the way, screaming for him to let me go. Passersby don't even give me and my predicament a glance. In this world, it's every woman for herself.

I'm not lady ghost in this timeline, but lady flesh-and-blood. And all this bastard wants from me is to bury a bit of his flesh inside a bit of mine, whether I want it or not.

CHAPTER THIRTY-ONE

Fauna: Spooky Characterization

The Trollgodfather looks from Emma to me and back. "So tell me, what actions are you attempting?" He's still speaking in Caprine. Looks like that's the language we'll be using for continued conversation. It's more than fine with me. I am part goat after all.

Emma throws up her hands. "I look around for Nick."

Khenn stands and turns in place three-hundred-and-sixty degrees before returning to his seat. "He's not here. What next?"

I stash Spooky again, tucking her away in inventory where I know she'll be safe, where I can't lose her. "I push back the storm surrounding us with the power of my mind."

"That will take…." Khenn wrinkles his brow. "A level five SR on Intelligence."

"I'll try that, too." Emma points her chin at me. "You first, Fauna."

I pick up the two dice. My Intelligence score is 26. For a fifth level saving roll, I need a total of 40 or better, so I need to roll at least a 14, only possible if I roll doubles. I toss the dice. The pips come up five and three, for a total of eight. Not enough. I only made a level three save.

Emma takes the dice. "I have an Intelligence of 42, so I just need to not roll an automatic failure." She rolls them. The first die shows a two. The second die keeps spinning. As long as it isn't a one, she's good.

The second die finally slows. It looks like it will be a three. But then it wobbles and falls onto a different side.

It's a one. Automatic failure.

"Damn." Emma turns away from the table to stare at the mists rushing by. "I try again."

Khenn bobs his head side to side. "It will be a level ten save this time. Only one of you may try. A failure this time means no one can try again."

Emma mutters to herself then turns back to the table. "So I'd need to roll 23 on the dice. Not impossible, but I'd need at least one pair of doubles and probably more. How about you, Khenn? If you tried it, would it be level ten, or might it only be level five, since you haven't tried it yet?"

The Trollgodfather holds up his empty hands. "This scenario isn't for me. You must rely on yourselves and what you have on your character sheets. I'm here as GM and nothing more. The multiverse demands it."

Something doesn't feel right here. "Emma and I were doing fine taking turns being GM for each other. We need more from you, Khenn Arrth, than just being a GM. There must be something else that needs doing that we couldn't have done without you."

He cocks an eyebrow. "That can't be true."

Frustration swells inside me. "So you're saying it was useless for us to come here."

He smirks. "I did not say that."

Emma makes a fist, but instead of pounding something, she rests her weight on it on the table top. "You know something you're not telling us, Mr. Arrth."

"That is the GM's prerogative. But it is in your power to learn it without revelation from me. Don't be afraid of failure. All the best adventures come from trying and failing and then trying something else. What is my mantra?"

I know that one. "It's better to be lucky than good."

He nods. "And how does one court Lady Luck?"

Emma slaps the table. "By continually trying to do stuff. Because eventually the dice will fall in your favor."

I can't help but add, "As long as you don't die."

"But what is death?" Khenn Arrth reaches for my character sheet. "And what is life?"

My Warrior-Wizard friend gasps and hands a rolled parchment to the Trollgodfather. "If you keep our character sheets, can you revive us?"

"Are you serious?" I thrust my character sheet into his hand.

He sets the two parchments on the table before him. "Put it this way. If I hold onto your character sheets, the two of you can travel together, and if either or both of you die, it's my prerogative as GM to determine whether and how you may be brought back to life. I've done the same for others before you, so the universe won't come apart at the seams if I do it for you. But resurrection won't be automatic or quick, so don't take any unnecessary risks. Also, if you die, there's a risk you'll lose any treasure you're carrying, so you might want to take a moment to think about that."

Emma shrugs. "I'm not carrying any treasure."

"No, but I am." I bring Spooky out of inventory once more. "I couldn't bear to lose her. How can I keep her safe?" I gaze deep into Khenn Arrth's eyes. "You can keep her with you."

He shakes his head in sorrow. "I can't stop you from leaving her here, but I can't protect her. I can't even hold her. If a wind swept through, picked her up, and carried her away, I could do nothing about it. But perhaps there's an alternative or three you've not considered."

The Warrior-Wizard snaps her fingers. "You said we could lose treasure we're carrying when we die. But what if we're not *carrying* it? What if Fauna keeps Spooky in her inventory? That's not really carrying her, is it?"

Khenn Arrth harrumphs. "The T&T characters I know don't even have this invisible container called *inventory*. You've basically got an inter-dimensional bag you're stuffing her into, and fortunately for her she doesn't need to breathe. But anything you put in that bag is considered as being carried by you. Sorry, but that's not a loophole. Good try, though. Any other ideas?"

I wrack my brain for some. "What happens to treasure we lose when we die? Is there a possibility of recovering it after we're resurrected?"

"There's always a possibility. I wouldn't recommend relying on it." Khenn Arrth drums his fingers on the table.

Emma taps her forehead. "What about treasure we're *not* carrying when we die? If we set something down somewhere and then die, can we go back for it after we come back to life?"

Khenn continues drumming his fingers. "It's the same difference. You need to realize you're not the only ones traveling the realms. If you leave something behind and are gone for long, it's highly likely someone else will find it and claim it before you can return. Or some environmental phenomenon might occur that affects your abandoned treasure and makes it difficult to recover, even to the point of destroying it."

"We don't want that." I stare at Spooky. "If only she weren't considered treasure. Why is she considered treasure anyway?"

Khenn Arrth stops drumming his fingers. "Does she have a character sheet? No. So she's considered treasure." He holds up his empty hands. A pencil appears in one and a parchment in the other. "But we can remedy that, if you want."

Three dice rest on the table where before there were only two.

Emma and I exchange glances. I pick up the dice. "So we can roll her up as a first level character?"

The Trollgodfather closes one eye and frowns. "Perhaps Spooky should do the rolling."

"Very well." I place her butt on my left forearm and sit her upright. Then I press the dice into her tiny right hand.

"Pbbt." Spooky refuses to close her fingers over the dice.

Setting down the dice, I turn Spooky to face me. She has no distinguishing features, only shadows, but I know which side of her head bears her face. I speak to her in Common. "Spooky, dear, do you understand me?"

She shakes a fist and giggles.

"Can you say, *Fauna*?"

"Fauna."

"Oh, my." My grip on her slips.

Freed, she flies straight up.

I grab her ankle, haul her back down, and hug her against my chest. "What just happened?"

Emma inhales sharply. "She's not a treasure, Fauna. She's already a character, with abilities."

The Trollgodfather leans across the table. "I believe you're correct, Emma, and all that needed to happen was for you two to realize the truth." He scans my character sheet. "She has already been erased from your treasure list, my friend, and not by my doing. As Emma has alluded, Spooky doesn't need us to create a character sheet for her. Somewhere she already has one, and it's not for a T&T world. She's from a different gaming universe. Which one, I don't know. There are many possibilities."

Tears well in my eyes. "If Spooky isn't from our world, I bet she's from Khertaan."

"I'd never heard of the place before you told me." Khenn Arrth sits back. "If she's from a video gaming world, the rules she lives by are likely much different than the T&T rules. It's interesting she can coexist with you. And I have some bad news for you. This universe no longer considers Spooky a treasure, which means you can no longer stash her in your inventory. She's recognized as a character in her own right, which means she can die. But I don't

217

have her character sheet, and have no way to bring her back to life.

"There is hope for her, however. In many video gaming universes, characters who die are allowed to respawn, returning them to their world. Perhaps such rules apply to Spooky. We can only hope. Still, it's best if you don't let her die in the first place.

"But at least now you know why you came to me. Leave your character sheets with me, and should either of you die, I'll do what I've done for others in the past to give you a chance at life again. Take care with Spooky. Now, go and do what you will. I'll be watching, and will roll the dice for you when you need it."

"Don't fly away again, Spooky. Stay with me." I rise from my seat and face the storm. "What are we doing then, Emma?"

The Elf Warrior-Wizard turns away from the table and points her staff straight ahead. "*Sense Magical Vibes.*" She claps a hand to her chest. "Okay, bad vibes. Shouldn't have been a surprise, I suppose."

"What happens if we walk into the storm?" I turn towards the Trollgodfather, but he's no longer present. Neither are the table and chairs. Emma and I stand on a wooden disk in the calm eye of a raging cyclone, Spooky in my embrace.

The shadow baby girl points at the Warrior-Wizard. "Emma." Then Spooky vanishes.

My arms close on empty air.

Spooky appears again. With a giggle, she flies into the mists.

A cry explodes from my throat.

CHAPTER THIRTY-TWO

Charli: Ghoul Battle

I run after the fleeing, giggling, naked Britta, but she angles upward, out of my reach. How in blazes can I keep my baby out of trouble?

Kylie grabs my right hand, and my feet lift off the ground. The Angel can fly faster than my daughter. We'll catch her shortly.

"Ha ha. Did you all miss me?"

"*Rancor*." If I weren't preoccupied by my fleeing kid, I'd give the little guy more of a greeting. Why can't Britta behave herself? She's not even a day old, and I can't keep up with her.

"Can I get an invite to the party, please?" The Woodpecker flies beside us a short distance before falling behind.

"Where's Morrow?" There's a frown in Kylie's voice. "You don't need a party invite as his Familiar."

"He sent me. I'm autonomous in his absence. I'm not in any party until someone invites me." The Woodpecker still struggles to catch us.

Kylie slows, even though it means letting Britta get further away. "Come on, Woodpecker. You're invited to the party. Latch on."

"Ha ha, thanks." Rancor lands on Kylie's right shoulder. "What are we doing? I have something to tell you when you're ready for it."

"Give us a moment, Rancor." I need to have Britta in my grasp first.

An unfamiliar feminine voice hails me over chat. "Hello, Charli. Can you hear me? Hello? Earth to Charli." The chat session is identified as party chat for party TwoWorldOrder. Geez, I've been added to a third party? How did that happen? The speaker's icon is a ghostly feminine face labeled *Mylynna, Mist Succubus*.

I don't have time right now to investigate my membership in this new party. But I respond while we're flying to intercept little miss Cave Goblin. "This is Charli. Who is this?"

"Hi, Charli. You don't know me, but my name is Hera Ford. I'm Mylynna in Khertaan, in party TwoWorldOrder. I have someone here who wants to speak to you."

Mylynna's image is replaced by that of another woman, someone I do recognize, with black-spotted red skin, though her image is also translucent.

"*Slithy?* Where in blazes are you?"

Kylie proves she can sense Britta despite my daughter's attempt to Hide from us. The Angel zigs and zags in sync with the Cave Goblin baby, who doesn't look like a baby, but a naked woman my age... a foot shorter than me, but with the body proportions of an adult.

The Frogkin female in my chat view rolls her eyes. "I could just as easily ask where you are. You look different than I remember. I'm not in Khertaan, but able to access it. I'm in what's best referred to as the Fanciful Pegasus timeline. I'm talking to you as Susie, even though I'm guessing you're seeing my Slithy icon in the chat view. I'm accessing the Khertaan program via a computer at the Fanciful Pegasus facility… are you familiar with the place? It doesn't matter. I've added you to every party in Khertaan. Don't leave any of them. Contact as many as you can and tell them not to remove you. You're the key to everyone in the game earning enough XP to reach level thirty as soon as possible."

Kylie swipes at Britta. "*Gotcha.*" Her hand closes over the green girl's wrist… and passes right through. Britta flickers and her location shifts instantaneously by three feet. Her Displace skill caused Kylie's first attempt at grabbing her to fail.

I make a grab for Britta, too, but she jerks her arm out of the way an instant before I touch her, as though she anticipated my action. She has the Anticipate skill, too, after all. Arrggh.

Slithy continues. "The Fanciful Pegasus timeline is fading from existence. The facility here and everyone in it are fading away. I'm not sure how to stop it, and I don't know whether there's anything you could do to help, either. But if you think of anything….

"Anyway, I'll go to sleep shortly so Slithy can respawn in Khertaan, but there's something I want to do first. I have a map showing the locations of the respawning chambers, and I'm going to see if I can find one of them. *Any* one of them. Finding one might help me understand how to save this timeline. It's got to be worth a try. Are you with Kylie?"

"Yeah… we're kind of busy right now. Can you give us a moment?" I try to snatch Britta again, with no more success than before.

"Sorry if I caught you at a bad time." Slithy's chat avatar frowns.

"I'm sorry, too." I grab at Britta again, and once again fail. It's a good thing I have an extraordinary Temperance, or I'd be losing my shit. "I'd really love to chat with you some more, Slithy, but my child is misbehaving."

"You have a *child*?"

"Long story. Anyway, she's got skills—Displace, Anticipate, Mislead, Hide, Disguise, and Flight Speed—and she's using them

221

all to evade me. We're in Minook... haven't explored the place yet; don't know what dangers are here... and she's zigging and zagging all over the place."

Slithy chuckles. "Many of those are Mentalist skills, like I have. The trick to catching her will be to act unpredictably, with as little preconceived notions as possible. When you're close to her, don't grab at her, but at some empty space near her. You might miss, but there's a better chance of eventually nabbing her that way than if you continually go for the direct approach. Do what you can to prevent her from seeing you coming. What's your child's name?"

"Britta." Following Slithy's suggestion, I use my Hide and Hide Party skills to make myself and Kylie as undetectable as possible. Kylie rushes at my child, and I wildly swipe at empty air. My hand brushes flesh, but I still close my fingers on nothing. "Arrggh. This is useless."

"Britta, huh? Name sounds familiar, but I can't place it. Good luck with catching her. I'm gonna go. Tell Kylie that Slithy says hi and loves her, and fill her in on everything, okay?" Slithy waves in my chat view and then disappears.

"Bye from me, too." Mylynna appears in the chat view long enough to wave goodbye. "I look forward to meeting you."

I would have loved a longer conversation with the Frogkin girl without distractions, but she picked a horrible time to chat. Now that I'm the mother of a carefree, fun-loving kid with no inhibitions but with the skills to continually evade me, when will there ever be a good time for me to do *anything* other than give her my full attention?

"Um, ladies...." Spyder's metallic voice grates on my nerves as it forebodes more news of an inconvenient nature. "A not-so-welcoming party is headed our way."

I've had absolutely no time to take in our new surroundings, and it's all I can do now to pull my gaze away from the capricious Britta.

The cave from which we exited moments ago lies fifty yards behind us. Ten yards below us lies a paved roadway, with lines drawn in faded paint and weeds growing from the cracks. The unused road leads across a stretch of plateau into the heart of a city, with marble buildings reaching more stories high than I care to count. A dozen rows of one-story buildings lie between us and the high-rises.

The nearest one-story structure is crafted of red brick. A metal door hangs open, from which pour a stream of mooks. According to my level 45 Monster Lore skill, they're a variety of Ghouls. Some of them are Ghoul Harpies, winging their way towards us. They're all moving too darn fast.

"*Britta*, you get your ass over here right this minute." The demand comes rolling out of me, backed by the instincts of a protective mother who feels her child is in danger. There is no Motherhood skill in Khertaan, and none of my other skills or my attribute scores means a hill of beans in this matter. "I said, *get over here.*"

I'm bombarded by a cacophony of voices, all of them asking questions—some about me, some about Britta, some about Minook, and a miscellany of others.

I shout back at them. "*Arrggh.* I don't have time for this. I've got endless Ghouls and a stubborn child to deal with."

Scores of people pop into being—on the road and in the air. My skin tingles as the Priests and Priestesses among them call for the blessings of their deities. These are all PC parties that I belong to, respawning at my location just in time to help with the coming encounter.

A barrage of arrows, bolts, darts, shurikens, and daggers erupts from the newcomers, with some missiles finding their targets on the ground and some in the sky. Perhaps twenty mooks are vanquished, half of them being Harpies.

More doors open on other low-standing buildings. Hundreds more enemy Ghouls pour out. From the tops of the high-rises descend other dangers, screeching their anger at us trespassers. A score of Ghoul Pteranodons and a dozen Black Ghoul Dragons dive at us. Holy crap.

Lightning and fireballs streak towards the oncoming hordes. More missiles shoot this way and that without clear organization. Swords, axes, spears, and hammers clash with those mooks not defeated by the volleys of missiles and magic.

It's utter chaos.

"Britta, please come to Mommy."

"Pbbt." She flies to engage one of the Ghoul Harpies.

Kylie shouts. *"Freeze, fiends."*

I dare to hope the Harpy my baby is attacking will be taken out of commission, even if briefly. But the Angel's Hypnotic Voice has no effect on the Ghouls. They all keep moving, unaffected by Kylie's attempt to hypnotize them into inaction. This does not bode well.

My naked baby girl who looks like an adult Cave Goblin woman drives her claws at the Harpy's chest, but doesn't manage a one-hit-kill. Ghouls don't have vitals, and thus the Vitals Strike skill is of no use against them. The Harpy clutches at Britta with her talons, and though it appears she makes contact, her natural weapons swish right through the mirage of my baby girl's Displaced body. I already know how difficult it is to lay a hand on Britta, and that's the only thing that allows me not to lose my freaking mind.

"Stay with her, Kylie. Get us as close as you can."

What does my Monster Lore have to say about Ghouls? I get plenty of info and relay what I learn over all my recently active party chat channels, so all my allies present can hear. "Listen up. Don't bother with mental or emotional attacks against the Ghouls. They do physical and spiritual damage and that's what will harm them. Enchant your weapons or use natural ones. The Harpies have sonic attacks, the Pteranodons breathe acid, and the Dragons breathe poison gas. If you're hit with any acid, you'll keep taking acid damage until the end of the encounter. Same with the poison gas. The acid effect stacks with the poison gas effect. Some mind-based abilities that don't deal damage might affect the Ghouls, but only when directed at individuals. That's all I know, folks. Do your worst."

A chorus of thanks fills my party chat channels, along with some inquiries as to what I'm talking about. The inquiries are from parties who respawned elsewhere, aren't involved in this encounter, and wonder why I've been force-added to their party if only to tell them about Ghouls.

"This is my cue to leave." Rancor leaps off Kylie's shoulder and flies towards the cave behind us. "I can't handle spiritual damage. Sorry, but I need to stay alive and coherent until I can tell you what I've come to tell you."

Kylie darts through space, dragging me along. I equip my Shadow Stone, the cursed object I took from the ashes of the Scarecrow that party MAD killed in the Mystic Hollow Cornfield on day one. I've shaped the Stone before as a dagger. I might go for something longer this time. Why not?

Since Kylie has a grip on my right hand, I equip the cursed magic item in my left. For all those avatars in the game whose primary hand is their right one, trying to use a weapon in their left hand would inflict huge penalties. But that's where my Ambidexterity trait comes in useful. I don't have an off hand or a primary one. I'm equally terrible at wielding a weapon with either hand.

As we draw up beside Britta—or at least where she appears to be—I shape the Shadow Stone into a dark short sword. As a level 18 Shadow Wizard, I have level 26 Shadow Attack and level 12 Critical Hit—Shadow. I've not tried using these skills with my Shadow Stone before, but it makes logical sense they'll work with it. It's because I have the Shadow Stone that I decided on Shadow Wizard as my subclass in the first place.

Though my fear for my baby girl's safety is still a vise on my heart, I no longer try to grab her, knowing how futile it will be and not wanting to waste any actions. She attacks her previous target, and I stab at it, too, going for a combo attack with her. I'm

225

not afraid of accidentally harming my baby, because the System disallows damage to other party members except under special circumstances, such as when explicitly stated in a notification or quest.

A shimmering longsword connects with the Harpy's chest at the same time my short black blade does—Kylie joins in the combo attack. Hovering in place, not trying to defend, the Ghoul Harpy's eyes lock on Kylie's. Though Ghouls are unaffected by the Angel's Hypnotic Voice, they can still fall prey on an individual basis to the directed effect of her Hypnotic Gaze. What a relief.

The Harpy explodes into a spray of gray pixels.

Numerous cries of "O-a-ooh" sound across the battlefield. Fear grinds at my soul, but my SP holds at 100%. Thank the Gods and Goddesses for their blessing bonuses, or I'd have been spiritually ripped to shreds. Kylie has her Spirit Resistance skill to help protect her, and I'm hoping Britta's level two Iron Will sufficiently protects her. Kylie has Party Spirit Resistance that helps us all, too.

If Rancor had stayed with us, he'd have been rendered berserk about now. It was a good call for him to retreat.

At least three people on the ground stumble about in shock. A dozen people wildly flail about, attacking anyone in reach, having been rendered berserk by the zeroing of their spiritual hit points.

"Incoming." Several people shout the warning through their party chats, which of course I hear, being a member of all their parties.

Ghoul Dragons and Ghoul Pteranodons swoop down for strafing attacks, exhaling black clouds and sprays of black liquid.

Missiles and magic pepper the sky. A few Pteranodons and a Dragon pixelize in defeat as their companions fly on.

Area attacks minimize the benefit of skills like Avoidance, Hide, and Displace. As black clouds and sprays gush over me, I'm more concerned for my baby than myself. Kylie raises a glowing shield to block what she can, and it helps her and me. Still, my HP falls to 69% and my SP to 81%. "Britta, *where are you?*"

Kylie squeezes my hand. "I don't see her. But Georgie says all her hit point pools are still full. She escaped taking any damage from the breath attacks somehow. I didn't take damage from them, either. You need to be careful, Charli. You won't last a minute taking damage like that. I don't want you dying on me."

"O-a-ooh," cry the Harpies again. Fear grips me as before, but the blessings upon me continue to ward me against spiritual collapse.

A dozen people on the ground go up in sparks, and a dozen more turn on their comrades, having been rendered berserk by the spiritual damage they took from breath weapons that didn't deal sufficient physical damage to kill them outright.

Britta giggles in the distance. I spot her... she has her feet planted atop the head of one of the Ghoul Dragons, riding it. How did she get up there? Oh... her Teleport Self skill, I'm betting. How often can she use it?

Kylie chases the Dragon carrying Britta, and Harpies chase us. The Dragons and Pteranodons loop upward, preparing for another strafing attack.

Someone on the ground shouts a spell. Magical fire envelops and destroys the Harpies on our tail. Thank you, ally Wizard!

A cone of blue light erupts from Kylie's eyes, striking every thing between her and the ground, but its effect is selective, not harming any of our allies. A quarter of the Ghouls on the ground and a tenth of the Harpies in the air turn on their fellow Ghouls, rendered berserk by the Angel's Spirit Blast attack. This is the kind of battle Kylie the Spirit Warrior Angel is built for. Geez, she could probably take on all the Ghouls here if she weren't hauling me around.

We catch Britta's Dragon when it pauses its upward flight. The Pteranodons and Dragons dive once more in unison. The Dragon we're chasing faces us and opens its mouth to breath.

Britta slides down the Dragon's face to block its mouth with her body.

"Britta, *no*." What does she think she's doing?

The Dragon changes its mind about breathing and… rather than snapping at where my baby girl appears to be… snaps at what I see as empty air. Britta's Displace skill didn't fool the mook. Yellowed fangs chomp into something substantial that goes *crunch*.

Britta shrieks. She still lives, but her left leg is gone from the knee down.

Rage overwhelms me, my extraordinary Temperance attribute be damned.

The Pteranodons and the other Dragons zoom past us as Kylie and I clash with Britta's Dragon, driving our blades into the sucker's chest in a combo attack.

Ignoring us, the Dragon dives, joining its friends in belching noxious gas on our allies below. A brief notification at the bottom of my view reveals it's at 48% HP and 56% SP. Another combo attack from us could destroy it. My anger says to go after it, but my motherly instincts put my anger in check—I need to make sure Britta is okay.

My baby girl meets us halfway. She flings her arms around me, pressing her naked green flesh against me. "Mommy."

"Oh, my dear girl. It's okay. You'll be all right." It's the motherly thing to say, so I'd say it whether or not she had the Regeneration trait. I'm so glad she has the trait, but her tears and the absence of her lower left leg sting me to the core.

"O-a-ooh," cry the Harpies. Any of my allies who don't have significant blessings or spiritual resistance are succumbing to those cries, soon to go berserk if not already.

Kylie heads for the ground as the Pteranodons and Dragons ascend to prepare for the next wave of strafing attacks. The situation isn't good for the PC parties, who have dwindled to less than a quarter of their original numbers, and that's counting those who've gone berserk already.

Over half the Ghouls on the ground have fallen, and they've ceased filing out of buildings. Half of the Ghoul Harpies and Ghoul Pteranodons have been defeated, too. A fireball engulfs the

Eidson & Thicke

wounded Ghoul Dragon, and it explodes in a cloud of black smoke. One down, eleven to go. My Monster Lore offers a bit more info, and I relay it over all my party chats. "Everyone avoid that black smoke. It's poisonous. A Black Ghoul Dragon releases a poisonous black cloud upon its death."

The Angel sets me and Britta on the ground. "Get to safety. I'm taking these things out." She fades out as she shifts to Spirit Form. From twenty feet above the ground, marking her location for an instant, Kylie unleashes her conic Spirit Blast attack once more. Every enemy in her line of sight is caught in the blast.

All the Ghouls on the ground turn to fighting their nearest neighbors, whether they be friends or enemies. But Kylie's Spirit Blast caught enemies in the air, too. Already descending for their strafing attacks, all the Ghoul Pteranodons loose their acid breaths prematurely, burning Harpies, Dragons, and other Pteranodons. The Harpies and Dragons turn on the Pteranodons in defense. Some Wizard is still capable of tossing fireballs, evidenced by a sphere of flame tearing into the midst of the Dragons. Three of the Ghoul Dragons pop out of existence. There's only eight of them left, along with three Ghoul Pteranodons and a dozen Ghoul Harpies. The three Pteranodons attack each other with clumsy beaks, while the Harpies and Dragons pull away to continue the attack on my allies.

"Stay with me, Britta." The cave behind us is closer than any of the buildings, but going back in there could trigger another Mental Dominator Boss, and I don't relish encountering another one of those. My girl and I make a beeline for the nearest building.

Switching to Third Person POV allows me to see where I'm going as well as what's behind me. Only three allies remain visible on the ground and two in the air. There are bound to be some as well outside my viewing area or otherwise hidden from me, like Kylie. No Harpies, Pteranodons, or land-bound Ghouls remain.

229

Seven Dragons ascend after a strafing attack. A cone of blue light catches them as they reach the top. They tear at each other's wings with reptilian fangs and claws.

Entering the shadow of a high-rise, I stop running. Britta wraps her arms around me from behind and watches over my shoulder.

Motion to my left grabs my attention. A PC has popped in, able to respawn at my location since I'm no longer engaged in the encounter. Another PC respawns, and then three more… ten more… twenty more.

A woman steps up next to me. "I wasn't sure we'd win, but it looks like the enemy is killing each other now." Her voice is familiar.

She's green skinned with green eyes and long, curly, red hair. Pointed white horns protrude from her forehead, curving up. I'd guess she's about my age. She's an inch shorter than me and ten to twenty pounds heavier. She offers me a hand to shake. "It's good to meet you in person, Charli. I'm Mylynna. We should talk."

"Ha ha." Rancor joins us. "Only two Dragons left now. It's almost over. I'm glad all these people are present. I've got something they all need to hear."

But further discussions are tabled. We all watch in silence as the last Dragon defeats its last companion. Kylie appears above the surviving Black Ghoul Dragon and tosses a noose of blue energy over its serpentine neck. It immediately ceases flailing wildly about. Kylie has tamed the berserker. Standing on its back, sword in one hand and a rope of blue energy held taut in the other, she rides it like a natural Cowgirl, landing it on the ground, where it settles down to rest its head.

A collective gasp rises around me as everyone gains XP for the encounter, now officially over. A bunch of these people weren't even level ten an hour ago, and now they're all level twenty or more. I call up my character sheet. Earning myself another attribute point, I've gone from level 27 to 28. Only two levels to go.

I hug Britta to my chest and whisper in her ear, telling her to please let me help her assign her newly gained attribute points. First thing I'll do is coax her into raising her Morals score. And I'd really like to find her some clothes.

CHAPTER THIRTY-THREE

Ronnie: Blue-Haired Girl

The bullets have stopped whizzing by. Mel and I stop for a breather.

I keep my head down so no one will recognize me in this part of the city. "We have to go back."

Mel looks at me like I'm crazy. "What in hell for? You'll be shot, and I'm not so certain someone won't shoot me in spite of my mother's edicts."

I turn my bike around. "Lead the way, Mel. No one will shoot you. I saw someone… a girl… blue hair. She was riding after us on a bike. I didn't recognize her at first, but she's the girl Nick was kneeling beside. I thought she was dead, but apparently she isn't. We have to talk to her."

"It's your funeral, but wherever you're going is where I go." Mel reluctantly turns his bike around.

We stay off the sidewalk, sticking to the edge of the road, where we can still skirt around stalled horseless carriages. We don't rush, so as not to draw undue attention. At any time, someone will recognize our bikes, put two and two together, and open fire on us. How could they not?

Yet apparently no one thinks we'd be so stupid as to come back this way after escaping death so narrowly only minutes before.

As we ride, the face of the blue-haired girl grows more distinct in my mind. Nick knelt beside her. Blood pooled under her head and matted her hair. But she wasn't dead. She couldn't have been, not if she's riding a bike in this world. But where did she go? She was right behind us for a while, but then fell behind.

"Is that her?" Mel nods toward someone on the sidewalk. She has blue hair.

"Could be."

Standing next to the girl, a hulk of a man points an over-sized pistol at a nearby doorway. Are they together? If so, maybe it's not such a good idea to approach at the moment. Maybe we should wait and watch to see if they separate, so we can approach her alone.

She runs, but the hulk anticipates it. He snatches her arm and carries her to the door, with her struggling all the way. They're going inside, but she's not going of her own free will.

I ride past Mel and speed up. Pedestrians had already vacated the area to avoid getting involved. Well, I'm getting involved.

The two enter the building... and the man staggers back outside, backwards, buckled at the waist. The girl must have kicked him in the nuts. Good for her. He's not holding his pistol now, either. I stop the bike short of colliding with him, backing it up to avoid him as he continues stumbling backwards.

He slowly shakes his head. "You've got some nerve, girl, threatening me with my own gun." He catches himself and takes a tentative step forward. "Go ahead. Shoot me if you're gonna. Otherwise, give me back my gun, and you can be on your way."

The blue-haired girl steps into the doorway, aiming the pistol at her assailant. Her eyes catch sight of me, and in the moment I have her attention, the hulk rushes her.

I charge on the bike, striking the backs of his legs as he makes a grab for the girl's arm. With a roar of outrage, he loses his grip, falls face-forward against the building, and bounces back.

The girl ducks under his flailing arm and rushes past me, whispering, "Thank you." She's still got the guy's pistol, which practically dwarfs her.

I back up and turn around while the hulk recovers. "*Miss, hop on.*" I drive after her… except I don't, as the rear of my bike comes off the ground.

The hulk holds my rear fender. "I'll teach you to mind your own business, you son of a bitch."

A shot rings out. The hulk drops my bike, which bounces as I pull away from him. He's down, a bullet hole in his forehead, blood pooling on the sidewalk.

People move even further away from us. None of them act shocked by the hulk's death.

The girl lowers the pistol and jumps onto the back of my bike. "Get us out of here, Ronnie."

It floors me that she knows my name, until I recall that my picture and name is on display to everyone in the city.

"Glad to finally meet you, Mel," says the girl as my companion on the other bike pulls up next to us.

"Um…, how do you know my name?"

He's right. Everyone in this world knows Mel as Princess Karen.

"Nick talked about you."

Neither Mel nor I are able to find our voices.

She laughs. "Are we getting out of here or what?"

"How…." Mel stammers. "I'm sorry, but who are you?"

"I'm a friend of your father's. My name is Erica. In another timeline, your mother Jean killed me. She'll want me dead in this timeline too if she learns I'm here. Can we please go somewhere more private to continue this discussion?" She wraps her arms around my waist.

I could pull another bike from inventory for Erica to ride, but I like her where she is. "Lead the way, Mel. You said you might know of a safe place."

"Sure."

CHAPTER THIRTY-FOUR

Erica: Home

This timeline proves to be too different from Mel's original one. The house he has led us to is more mansion than house, with guards stationed at the gates. His eyes apologize before his words do. "I wasn't expecting my home to be heavily guarded."

"It makes sense, though." If I'd known he was taking us to his place, I'd have suggested going elsewhere. In this timeline, he's a Princess, the daughter of this universe's supreme ruler, so of course his home would be heavily guarded. "Let's try my place." I point the way. Mel follows me and Ronnie.

It's nice I can refer to myself by my name in this world without fear of vanishing. As Nick's lady ghost, I showed up either in timelines where I had no existence at all or at points in time where I did have an existence but had yet to be born. If I'd been identified by name in such a situation, the timeline itself would have rejected me, spit me out and not even given me a ghostly presence.

But I exist as flesh and blood in this timeline, even if Nick doesn't. I miss him terribly. Yes, he's so much older than me in the timeline I remember him from the most, but it's not his age I'm in love with. He and I have a spiritual *connection*. It's what draws me as a ghost to him when our physical forms don't share a timeline.

And now that I'm here, I do sense something of Nick in this timeline. Ronnie and Mel both radiate his spirit in small doses. But I sense more than that. Nick lives in the fluffiness of the clouds and the caress of the wind.

I understand what Nick has done. He's the piece of string used as emergency thread to suture a wound that would bleed out if left unattended. Timelines were broken, and he sacrificed himself to mend them. When they've sufficiently healed, he'll be needed no more, and what's left of him will be plucked out and tossed onto the metaphysical trash heap. He'll be gone forever if someone doesn't save him. I'll give it my best shot. The issues for me are knowing *what* to do and *when* to do it. If I do something to bring him back before the timelines are sufficiently healed— whatever that means—then we're back to where we started, with uncountable timelines on the brink of destruction.

This is almost too much to handle.

One thing at a time. I'm with Ronnie and Mel, and we need a safe place to talk. I'm hoping the house I inherited from my parents in one timeline also exists as such in this timeline.

Though the structures are taller on average, the layout of the main roads is surprisingly similar to what I'm familiar with in other timelines I've visited.

Gates bar entry to us. I never lived in a gated community in my original timeline. A security guard peers from the gatehouse, his eyes widening. "Ms. McKenzie? Everyone has been so worried about you. I'll phone your house right away."

"It's not Ms. McKenzie." Mel waves away the thought. "It's Mr. McKenzie, or Mel will do fine."

The guard raises a brow. "I was talking to the young lady, *Ms. McKenzie*."

He's looking at me. I point at myself. "You mean...?"

The guard nods vigorously. "It's been months, Ms. McKenzie. Are you all right?"

Now I wave away the thought. "Yes, I'm fine. Could you open the gate, please? And I'd rather you not phone ahead. I want my arrival to be a surprise." I don't know what's going on here. Maybe we should stake out my house before barging in, because evidently someone is living there other than me.

"Very well." The gate swings open.

We drive through and I continue to give directions.

Why did the guard refer to me as Ms. *McKenzie*? That's Nick's last name. He's not in this timeline. So who is? I mean, in this timeline, Jean wouldn't be a McKenzie, and neither would Mel. I shouldn't be, either. So *why am I?* This is giving me the heebie-jeebies.

Could the guard have mistaken me for someone else?

"Stop here." We're not in front of my house, but down the road a ways. The building looks newer than when I last saw it in another timeline.

The front door opens and out walks the spitting image of Nick at thirty years of age. He stops at the top of the steps and looks around. His gaze lands on us. He studies us for maybe five seconds and then turns around and goes back inside. If he has been missing me, he doesn't act very excited to see me now.

It's not Nick. It looks like him, but it can't be him. I dismount, and the bike I was riding disappears. Ronnie touches Mel's bike, and it vanishes, too. Interesting.

This is my house, so I take the lead. The front door is unlocked.

Nick sits on a familiar couch, watching a familiar television set. He doesn't look at me when he speaks. "You decided to come home." There's no hint of a question in his statement, no curiosity as to where I've been. His reaction is to be expected. This poor excuse for a person is an empty shell with Nick's appearance. Nick's awareness... his soul... doesn't occupy this vessel. This person is an automaton, going through the motions of a life devoid of passion.

"Hello, Nick." I sit beside him. "Didn't you miss me at all?" I've supposedly been gone for months.

He doesn't tear his eyes away from the television screen. "Our marriage is a sham, Erica. Go do whatever you want and leave me out of it. I'm done caring."

Though I know he's not my Nicky Nick, his words crush my insides. We're married in this timeline, something I've often wished for, but the marriage isn't a happy one. It's as though the universe is punishing me, giving me a glimpse of my ideal life, like dangling a carrot before me, but out of reach. I see it but can't have it.

This is Jean's universe, after all. In her universe, I can expect to be tortured. She despises me as much as she despises Nick. Her revenge on us is to let us be together but not enjoy it.

"Dad?" Mel peers at Nick. "Is it really you? You're so young in this timeline."

Nick glances at Mel and then turns back to the TV. "Who are you calling *Dad*? I've got one kid, and it ain't you."

Wait a minute. This Nick is married to me and has a kid? Does that mean the kid is mine? Where is it? Is it a boy or a girl? What's its name? "Where is the kiddo?"

"Like you give a damn." Nick points at a far doorway. "In her room, where else?"

Mel and Ronnie follow me. My heart is breaking at what I'm finding in this timeline—not only am I married to an unloving Nick, but we have a daughter, and I abandoned them both for months. Is this the depth of Jean's revenge on me and Nick? Can things be worse?

"Oh, it's you." A familiar adult male voice greets me as I enter a room with a single bed and a motif of pink flowers. My brother Jake sits on the edge of the bed. "What made you decide to come home?"

On the floor at his feet sits a four-year-old blond girl playing with dolls, her back to me. She looks over her shoulder and jumps up. "Mommy."

With me being nineteen now, I had to have been fifteen when I had this kid. How old was I when I married Nick? Damn.

I hold out my arms to catch the girl in an embrace, but she evades me. Her affection is directed at someone behind me.

"Come here, my little Susie." The adult female voice holds cheer and a semblance of familiarity. A woman of about Nick's age swoops up the girl. Then she sidles up to me. "Did you find the adventure you were after, Erica?" She glances at Ronnie. "Traveling with a wanted criminal, I see. Not staying long, I take it. The police will be interested to know whose company you're keeping."

This woman isn't someone I've had the pleasure of interacting with before, but I know her. Kendra was Nick's wife in one of the timelines, the one in which the two of them developed a program for accessing the game world called Khertaan. I'm really confused now. Why is she in my house?

She kicks at Jake's dangling foot. "We should go, hon."

Wait. So… the woman to whom Nick was happily married in another timeline is married to my brother in this timeline? And the two of them plus their daughter come around to visit? How often? Yet another added torture for Nick, having Kendra in his life but not being with her. Jean knows how to twist the blade.

Jake stands. Behind where he sat lies another child, this one not even a year old. He nods at her. "I finally got her to sleep. She's all yours now."

I grab my brother's arm as he passes me in the doorway. "I never thought you'd make a good father, Jake. I see I was wrong."

He glares at me. "Don't rub it in, sis."

"What did I say?"

"You know I can't have kids, much as I want to."

"But…." What's he saying? "Isn't Susie yours?"

His gaze grows hot. "You know damn well she isn't. But someone has to look after her, and I care about her and her mother more than your pathetic husband ever did." He glances at the child on the bed. "I pity poor Britta, having parents like the two of you."

I'm in too much shock to say more. Jake pushes past me to join Kendra and Susie headed outside.

So... Nick and Kendra... were they married in this timeline? They had a kid—Susie. Then they got a divorce, after which Kendra and Jake married, and Nick and I married. Nick and I had a kid, Britta. After she was born, I ran away, was gone for months, and am just now returning. Why the hell would I run away like that? What kind of person am I in this timeline?

In her universe, Jean has devised hell on earth for Nick and me. Though I love the idea of being married to him, I can't... for his sake... let this timeline become dominant. I'd rather forever be his lady ghost than to see him unhappy like this.

CHAPTER THIRTY-FIVE

Susie: Hera Ford

So, Charli called her kid *Britta*. Where have I heard that name before? Did I have a childhood friend with that name?

While I'm sitting and reflecting, Glynda shows up again, carrying a rolled up piece of paper with the look of a map. She's as insubstantial as the rest of us, which means... I think... that nothing has improved for my future self.

I wheel aside. "What now? Another password to crack?"

She shakes her head, lays her map on the desk, and starts typing. A printer hums nearby and ejects a map similar to hers, a map of the Respawn Chamber Locations, which she grabs up and hands to me. "Your copy." She retrieves the one she brought. "Let's go." She takes off at a jog.

"Sure, yeah." I hop out of my chair and run after her. It's not easy referring to my map while running. We come to an elevator. There's no button to press to open the door.

But there's a small camera lens mounted next to the door, and Glynda puts an eye up to it. A red beam shoots out, striking her pupil. It's a retina scanner. Memories rise in my head of Dad having me look into some similar device when I was much younger. He must have registered my retinal pattern with Fanciful Pegasus. What had he known back then?

Oh, bloody hell. It was Glynda. She time-jumped back and told Dad to do it. I have memories from my early childhood of Glynda hanging around with us. Back then, I didn't know she was future-me. She was just a friend of the family.

The elevator doors open, and we enter. Glynda punches the button for floor sixteen. There are thirty floors all together, so we're going halfway up.

I take a moment to peruse the map. It's the shared floor plan for floors nine through eighteen. There are twenty rooms on each floor, all laid out the same. Each room on the map is marked with ten different names, one name each for that particular room on the ten different floors, for a total of two-hundred contestant names in total. "Are we visiting any particular contestant's room?"

Glynda chuckles in response. "I'll give you one guess…. You're going to like her, I guarantee it."

The elevator doors open on the sixteenth floor.

The hallway we enter isn't ghostly like the room we left. The structure here is opaque and solid. Both Glynda and I have substance, too. We look human again, not like ghosts of ourselves.

I take a deep breath. "How is this possible? Is this area immune to timeline effects?"

Glynda shrugs. "I'm not sure. But even though you're here now, which means I've been here before, it's difficult to remember where I went from here. That's the reason for the maps. Take a look." She holds her map next to mine so I can compare them.

Her map is missing all the names. I hold up mine and stab my finger at a name I recognize—Hera Ford. "That's where we're going, aren't we?"

"Lead the way."

We pass a door labeled Saiko Haru. Glynda chuckles.

"What's so amusing?" I ask.

"I think it's a Japanese name, pronounced *psycho*."

243

"Ha ha."

We hurry through twisting corridors, passing the doors for Saiko Aimi, Khaled Touma, Gloria Littlecat, and Debra Jones. One door is labeled, Processor 1.

"I don't know what it means." Glynda waves me on.

We come at last to the door for Hera Ford. I try the door handle, but it doesn't budge. Glynda frowns. "This is where we part company. Thanks for getting me here. You need to time-jump back now, and have Suze help you come here again. I'm teleporting through this door, and I don't think we both should go in. It might freak Hera out."

I'm sure Glynda is right. With a nod, I do a time-jump, and find myself standing behind my past self, Suze. The room—along with everything and everyone in it, including me and Suze—are as ghostly as I when I left it. My map is rolled up in my hand. I unroll it enough to see the labels on the map have vanished. Though I knew to expect it, it still seems weird.

Seated before the computer keyboard, Suze wheels aside. "What now? Another password to crack?"

I shake my head, lay my map on the desk, and start typing. The printer hums and ejects a map of the Respawn Chamber Locations. I grab it up and hand it to Suze. "Your copy." I retrieve mine from the desk and take off at a jog. "Let's go."

"Sure, yeah." Suze hops out of her chair and runs after me. In short order, we ride the elevator to the sixteenth floor and thanks to Suze's map are on our way to Hera Ford's room, our bodies back to their normal human selves... not ghosts.

Suze takes a deep breath. "How is this possible? Is this area immune to timeline effects?"

I shrug. "I think so. Still not sure." But something doesn't seem the same this time as when I passed through here just moments ago as my past self. I can't recall the route we followed to get to Hera Ford's room. "But even though you're here now, which means I've been here before, it's difficult to remember where I went from here. That's the reason for the maps. Take a look." I hold my map next to hers so we can compare them.

Her map has the labels mine is missing. It's all the same names I saw before, but something is different.

Suze stabs her finger at the map. "That's where we go. I just talked with her."

The name under her fingertip is Hera Ford. But it's at a different location on her map than it was on mine. I swear it is, even though I can't prove it, because all the labels are missing from my map.

A door we pass that I could have sworn bore the name, Saiko Haru, instead reads, Gloria Rubio.

It doesn't make any sense for me to say what Glynda said before about how the name Saiko sounds Japanese and is pronounced like *psycho*.

What the hell is happening? I should be repeating exactly what happened when my past self accompanied my future self, *especially if this area is immune to timeline effects*. That's how time-*jumping* works… it keeps you within the same timeline. The phenomenon that explains divergent shared experiences between my past self and future self is time-*shifting*. *Have I* time-shifted? Do the Fanciful Pegasus facilities exist in multiple timelines? It seems they must….

I don't like this.

We continue following Suze's map, passing doors for Saiko Aimi, Megan Wright, and Christopher Warden. We don't pass a door labeled, Processor 1.

At last we arrive at the door for Hera Ford. Suze tries the door handle, but it doesn't budge. I turn to her with a frown. "This is where we part company. Thanks for getting me here. You need to time-jump back now, and have Suze help you come here again. I'm teleporting through this door, and I don't think we both should go in. It might freak Hera out."

Suze nods and vanishes.

I knock on the door. "Hera? It's me, Susie. I want to come in, if that's okay with you."

There's no reply. I knock and call again… and again. She's not answering.

Doubt clutches my heart, and I teleport to the other side of the door before the doubt becomes dread.

ᛒᚢᚷᛟᚱᛒᚢᚷ

Ambient light illuminates a hallway constructed of wood stretching out before me, with a door in the left wall at the far end. Framed photos of the white woman I know as Hera Ford hang on both walls. She's younger than me by a few years. In one photo, she's at the beach, her long, curly red hair tossed by an ocean breeze. In another one, a close-up, her green eyes sparkle and cherry red lips curve into the sweetest smile. In yet another, she's riding in a jeep over sand dunes—dressed in a yellow tank top, blue jean short shorts, and sandals.

Reaching the far door, I knock at it. "Hera Ford? This is Susie, Slithy's player. Are you there? I'd like to come in."

Someone mumbles from beyond the door.

I knock again. "Hera? I'm Slithy's player—Susie. May I come in?"

"Susie?" The sound is faint. "*Slithy?*" The second time is louder. "I can't open the door. Can you?" The door handle jiggles. "If you can open it, please do."

The handle on this side of the door doesn't work either. "Hera, stand back from the door, please. I'm coming through." I give her a few seconds. "Stand clear. I'm coming through now." I teleport.

Hera stands with her back to the far wall. She shrieks as I appear from nowhere, standing before the door she'd expected to come breaking down. Her shriek turns to laughter. "*How did you do that?*"

I laugh, too. "I have my ways. But I'm really not here to get you out. Quite the contrary, in fact. I'm here so I can respawn, too. I'm glad I caught you before you went to sleep."

"You were just in time. I was about to drift off. Do you not have your own respawning chamber?"

"Not that I know of." I first entered the game from a computer lab with Mom and Dad. I'd expected the lab to be my respawning chamber, but when I died, I'd wound up elsewhere. "There appear to be several respawning chambers in this facility, but none were assigned to me. I don't feel safe going to sleep just anywhere out there. If you don't mind, I'd like to lie next to you on your bed. I've never found lying on a hard floor conducive to falling asleep quickly, and I'd like to get back into the game as soon as possible. So, if you don't mind...."

"Not a problem." Hera blushes. "I'm just glad to have the company of another human being."

On impulse, I open my arms to her, and she falls into my embrace, sobbing on my shoulder.

"Everything will be all right. You and I will see to it, together." I've never met this woman before today, but already we're bonding. I hold her until she calms.

We lie together on her bed, resting on our sides, smiling at each other. We take turns stroking each other's hair. I adore the red color of hers. She seems to appreciate my blondness.

She falls asleep first. Of course, it would be easier for her. She hasn't seen everything I've seen and doesn't realize the fate of the multiverse lies on our shoulders.

I really don't know what I'm doing. I'm winging it here. But I want to see Mom so badly, I can't stand it. At the moment, that's the most compelling reason for me to respawn. If Susie can't be with Kendra, then at least Slithy can be with Kylie. As sleep overtakes me, I mentally picture Mom's Angel avatar and will my Frogkin avatar to join her.

CHAPTER THIRTY-SIX

Slithy: Back in the Game

"You can't join Kylie at the moment, girlie." The voice is that of my personal support AI, Marta the witch. "But you can join Charli. Both of them are in the city of Minook, but your Momma is currently engaged in combat, while Charli isn't. If you join quickly, you could be in time to earn some XP for the battle your Momma is about to win."

Earning some XP sounds good. "Then what are we waiting for? Respawn me at Charli's location."

I'm standing in the shadow of tall buildings, surrounded by other people, intently watching two dark Dragons battling each other in the distance. They're Black Ghoul Dragons, Marta informs me.

Standing right in front of me, her back to me, is a young woman with straight blond hair. Is that Charli? What happened that she's no longer fourteen with pigtails? She's hugging a naked green-skinned woman who appears to be in a desperate emotional state. Is that her daughter?

Mylynna stands next to them and Rancor the Woodpecker circles overhead. My blood races. If Rancor is here, that means Morrow is, too, though he's nowhere in sight.

One of the Dragons erupts into a spray of pixels, and a black cloud billows outward from the spot where it died. The victorious Dragon continues to flail at the air, as though fighting some invisible opponent.

Mom appears above the surviving Dragon and tosses a noose of blue energy over its neck. The beast immediately ceases its frantic activity. Kylie stands on its back, a glowing blue sword in one hand and the free end of the electric blue rope held taut in the other. She rides the Dragon, guiding it with the noose. It lands on the ground and settles down to rest its head.

A collective gasp rises from the crowd.

"*Congratulations,* girlie." Marta sticks her wicked long nose in my face. "You've earned forty-eight million XP. You are now level 23 Mentalist and level 14 Martial Artist. You have three unassigned attribute points and two unassigned trait points."

Wow, I respawned just in time. Ten seconds ago, I was level 15 Mentalist, level 6 Martial Artist. I just gained 8 levels for being at the right place at the right time.

I tap Mylynna on the shoulder. "Hey."

"Slithy! You made it."

"I did. Just in time to earn beaucoup XP, too."

The blond woman in the cowboy hat spins around. She's the same person Susie talked to through Hera Ford's mirror. Clinging to her like a babe in arms and about the same age as her but maybe six inches shorter, is the naked, green-skinned woman, whose facial features remind me of Charli, despite the difference in skin color.

Charli's eyes light with excited recognition. "Slithy, *you're back!* I've missed you so much. A lot has happened since we saw each other." She wags her head and rolls her eyes. "I got older. And pregnant. And gave birth. This is my daughter, Britta. She's younger than she looks." The blond blushes. "I really need to get her some clothes." Then she calls over her shoulder, "Hey, Kylie, *your daughter is here.*"

"Slithy?" Mom calls from her perch atop the back of the subdued Dragon. "Get over here and give your Momma a hug."

I *want* to find out more about what's been happening with Charli, but I *need* a hug from my Momma first. As a Frogkin, I can cover ground a lot faster by jumping than running. Five long leaps, and I'm on the back of the Black Ghoul Dragon with Mom.

We're hugging and crying and just loving being with each other again.

She holds me at arm's length, looking me up and down. "My little girl. I feel so bad I missed your childhood. Maybe when all this is over, we can be a regular family."

I laugh. "I'd like that."

CHAPTER THIRTY-SEVEN

Mithabel: Apology Delayed

The Elf Tank continued to lead the way along the safe path through the shadow of the spire. The three parties—MAD, XStorm, and Quantized—spoke little on local chat. Any conversations happening were on party chat channels other than MAD's, or on private chat channels. Mithabel couldn't imagine what Dylan and Yuni were talking about, and try as she might not to think about it, she could think of nothing else.

Kaleisha danced close to Mithabel. Only a few of the group knew that Kaleisha was Mithabel's personal support AI made tangible, or that the unconscious Siamese Cat she carried was the shape-shifted Megan, whose awareness had hopped to Debra Jones so the woman could exercise the Hide skill to avoid being seen by parties XStorm or Quantized. Nor did most of the group know the true identity of the British butler in black and white attire who traveled with them, never straying too far from Dylan, whom he served as personal support AI, and who, like Kaleisha, had become tangible. If Quantized or XStorm became aware of the existence of secondary avatars or tangible support AIs, there would be too many questions that neither Mithabel nor Dylan wanted to answer. But more than that, they didn't want ChrisCross to create a secondary avatar and bring Christopher Warden's consciousness into Khertaan. Traveling with ChrisCross was torture enough, but something they could tolerate. If Christopher Warden showed up as a secondary avatar, that would spell the end of an already uneasy alliance.

"Congratulations, chief," crooned Kaleisha over the private communications channel between avatar and support AI. "I don't know the source, but you and everyone else here has earned forty-eight million XP. You're still level 27, but you're now 94% of the way to level 28, up from 69%."

"It's got to be Charli gaining XP for us." Mithabel sighed. "I wish we could communicate with her." She tried yet again.

Kaleisha shook her head. "Sorry, chief, but the communication link between Charli and the rest of MAD has been severed. I don't believe it's her doing, but that the System itself has placed the block. I've inquired about the issue many times, and have yet to receive any response on the matter. You might ask someone in the other parties accompanying you to attempt communications with her."

"I can't believe I'm level 28," Rolag said over local chat. "Picked up another attribute point and using it to pump my Brawn. It will go well with several of my Were-Giant skills— Smash, Stomp, and Crunch—which I'm dying to have a reason to try."

Dylan and Amarynth reported reaching level 28 as well. Mithabel had missed out on some of the XP gains the others had received, putting them ahead of her.

It was no consolation that the members of XStorm were still level 27 as well. They were 79% of the way to level 28, except for Yuni, who was a percentage point ahead of her party mates. Everyone in Quantized was overly excited, the unexpected XP gain boosting them from level 20 to 23.

"Does anyone else have an attribute at 19?" FepXveq betrayed a hint of pride. "I have my Favor at 19, and I wondered if anyone else had boosted one of their attributes that high. I tried to take it to 20 with this latest attribute point gain, but it seems the System won't allow it."

"I just raised my Sensing to 19," Amarynth said. "That puts it in the super-human category, the highest possible according to my support AI. I don't see a reason to raise an attribute value higher still, even if you could. The bonuses you earn for high attributes tops out when the attribute reaches 19. It's the bonus that matters, not the raw score."

"I've had 19 in Intuition for a little while," said the Angel Zyekt. "I didn't try raising it to 20, as I didn't see the need, either."

If anyone else had an attribute at 19 or higher, they weren't saying. At a score of 16, Mithabel's highest attribute was Temperance, which she'd boosted the last three times she'd earned attribute points, and intended to continue to boost when she earned more attribute points. She might have done better putting the points to Constitution, but Megan believed there was merit in leaving it where it was. With Yuni taking Mithabel's place as Dylan's confidant and closest friend, the Tank felt continually on the edge of losing control of her emotions. Boosting her Temperance attribute helped her stay in control. She felt the need for it to reach the super-human category if she were to prevent herself from driving Ullullu's Hair, her magical flamberge, through the heart of the War Priestess out of jealousy.

"Hey, Yuni." If Mithabel dragged the War Priestess into a conversation, then fewer words would be exchanged between Yuni and Dylan. "Could I ask you a favor?"

"Of course, Mithabel."

"Could you try contacting our party member, Charli, maybe on private chat?"

Before Yuni could reply, ChrisCross spoke up. "What's up with this Charli character, anyway? I noticed a few minutes ago she was in the XStorm party roster. I was thinking about booting her, since it appears to be a mistake, but you're saying she's in your party, too? How is that possible?"

"She's in our party, too," said Falco. "I was just going to say something about it."

Zyekt patted his Mouse companion, Niav, who once again rode on his shoulder. "I believe you may all wish to leave Charli in your party roster. She's the common thread between our parties, and may be the reason for all of us earning impromptu XP willy nilly, like the forty-eight million everyone earned just now."

"Let me try contacting her as you asked, Mithabel." A faraway look came into Yuni's eyes.

Everyone came to a stop and waited.

"I have her." Yuni still gazed into the distance. Her lips curved up into a smile. "She's so glad to hear that you're asking about her, Mithabel. She tried contacting you as well, but was blocked." Yuni goes silent. She nods at what she's hearing. "She's been added to every party in the game by someone named Slithy."

"I know her," Megan Wright said over party chat. "A Frogkin girl. I traveled with her for a while."

Yuni continued. "Charli says as long as she's in every party, then every party will receive all the XP that any party does. The idea is to get everyone to level thirty as quickly as possible."

"So much for this being a competition." Mithabel rolled her eyes. She'd had her heart set on winning the prize money, even with the world in danger from inter-dimensional invaders. Assuming they dealt with the invaders, that kind of money would go a long way towards helping Megan Wright and Debra Jones make a life together. Though Mithabel seemed to have lost Dylan to Yuni in Khertaan, Debra Jones didn't even know Yuni's player on Earth, and with any luck it would stay that way. Megan Wright and Debra Jones could make a go of it, without external complications.

The War Priestess pointed to the top of the spire. "She's up there, along with Slithy and others. Several parties. They fought an army of Ghouls—including Ghoul Harpies, Pteranodons, and

Dragons. Before that, they fought something called a Mental Dominator in a cave at the top of the spire. It's the Boss monster for the Spire of Desire territory. Outside its cave is the city of Minook, which appears to have been overrun by Ghouls. Charli and everyone else there is preparing to explore the city, now that the Ghouls have been wiped out." Yuni raised an eyebrow. "Charli says there's more she wants to say, but it will be easier to understand if we see it first. She wants us to come to Minook as soon as possible. The other parties up there are exploring the city now. She'll wait on the outskirts for us. She says, please hurry, and wants to point out that, if we die trying to reach Minook, we can respawn to her location."

"Tell her we miss her," Amarynth said, "and can't wait to see her again. And thank her for earning us a ton of XP."

Yuni smiled. "She says she misses you all, too. She can't wait to see you and to see what you think of how she's changed."

"I can't wait to see that, myself," said Mithabel. "Please tell her I'm not mad at her anymore, and I hope she isn't mad at me now, either. Tell her I'm sorry for not recognizing her value to the party and for treating her like a commodity."

The War Priestess shook her head. "I'll leave any apologies for you to give in person, Mithabel."

The Tank closed her eyes and sighed. She started once more along the safe path. The others fell in behind.

They eventually reached the spire, earning a few thousand XP along the way as parties elsewhere took actions that earned XP for everyone.

The safe path led around the spire's base. An hour and several thousand XP later, they found themselves on the west side of the spire, no longer in its shadow. A cave opening lay before them. They entered, to find themselves navigating the way through a complex of expansive, twisting, turning tunnels. They had entered the Spire of Desire, Kaleisha informed Mithabel.

If not for the map, they'd have become lost for eternity, the Tank judged. She solicited Zyekt's help in interpreting the map.

Out of all three parties, he had the highest Understanding, Logic, and Intuition. His Sensing was only average, but Mithabel's high average Sensing and her Alertness trait more than compensated for it.

After a couple of hours traveling up the interior of the Spire of Desire, continually gaining XP because of Charli's connection to all parties, the group entered a large, domed cavern, the far side of which opened onto the city of Minook. Nothing, not even a territorial Boss monster, stopped them from exiting the cavern onto the roadway that lay beyond.

From the shadow of a tall red marble tower to their left, a young woman in a cowboy hat waved to them. It was impossible to see any distinguishing features from this distance, but the hat was a dead giveaway. That had to be Charli.

Amarynth broke into a run, moving faster than a human woman had a right to.

CHAPTER THIRTY-EIGHT

Fauna: City in the Mists

"Spooky?"

Both Emma and I call for the shadow baby girl.

A giggling echoes around us… it's impossible to pinpoint the direction from which it comes. We call for Spooky again, and the giggling grows fainter. It stops abruptly, replaced by Spooky's voice. "Fauna. Emma."

The sound still lacks direction, but an unseen force tugs at me, striving to pull me off the wooden disk into the misty maelstrom.

Emma takes my hand. "Let's not get separated. Whatever we do, we do it together."

I nod, grateful for her foresight. We approach the edge of the disk and pause, exchanging glances.

We don't say anything. There's nothing else to do if we're to find Spooky. Together we jump into the mists.

The storm sweeps us away. The disk is lost to us now. There's no going back. Grayness fills my vision. My only comfort is the touch of Emma's hand in mine. I tighten my grip and try my voice. "How do we swim in this?"

The mists steal my words. Even I have trouble hearing them. Did Emma hear?

Her reply sounds distant, though she's right next to me. "This place is obviously metaphysical in nature. Travel is likely more mental in nature than physical. Picture Spooky and imagine us flying to wherever she is. It's our best chance at finding her. We can keep calling her name, too. Maybe she'll come to us if she can."

Picturing Spooky as a dark figure within the gray expanse, I call her name. Emma's vocal efforts reach me, but they're so faint, how can Spooky have a chance at hearing them, not being with us? But we keep calling her name and I hold her image firmly in my mind. What else is there to do?

Prolonged thunder deafens me. As the rumbling fades, the mists thin and my hooves touch solid ground. I utter a word of thanks to Khenn Arrth for rolling saving rolls for us. I assume the thunder was a product of the dice rolling. Will they be so loud every time?

Hand-in-hand, Emma and I stand on a circle of gray stone. From the circle, a roadway made from the same gray rock leads into a city of dark stone towers taller than I'd ever have imagined. Pedestrians, mounts with riders, and horseless carriages travel the road. The mounts are a varied lot—horses, elephants, large felines and canines, giant snakes and lizards and scorpions, even a few dragons. Among the horseless carriages are some with six wheels, some with four, and a few with only two.

All is eerily silent.

The towers, people, mounts, and carriages don't appear solid. The traffic attempting to enter the circle of gray stone vanishes at its edge.

A glance back proves the misty storm still persists behind us. Do other places like this one exist within the storm? Spooky might be here or she might be elsewhere. She doesn't have someone like Khenn Arrth to throw saving rolls for her. Emma and I found this place because we got lucky—Khenn threw the dice for us, and made our Luck SRs at whatever level he deemed appropriate.

Or maybe we missed our SRs and ended up in a bad place. Only Khenn knows what the dice rolled. For all we know, we could have had really high SRs or automatic failures. Or maybe we needed impossibly high SRs to find Spooky, and we made SRs at some lower level, which put us *somewhere* of interest, but not exactly where Spooky is. Still, she might be close. I dare to hope, and call out her name.

No sound comes from my mouth.

Emma tugs me toward the city. It's either forward or back into the mists. Going backward isn't an option until we've done some exploring here. I'm with her.

I can't even hear the scuffing of her feet or my hooves on the gray stone as we traverse the circle.

We cross the circle's boundary, and a wall of sound slams into us, as though we've just left a cone of silence. Emma and I first turn to each other with knowing glances, and then look over our shoulders. It's as we suspected.

The circle of gray stone is gone and so are the mists. The world turns solid, no longer ghostly. The road we're on stretches behind us into a desert, with some traffic coming toward us and some moving away.

The road through the desert leads straight to a single dark tower. It's too distant to make out any distinguishing features, but I instinctively know it's our destination. That's where we'll find Spooky.

I walk backwards in a tight circle while Emma moves forward, and we turn around as a couple in a slow dance. Carriages rush past us on either side, horns blaring. We pay them no heed, but continue down the middle of the road, its broken white center line between us.

The sky opens like a rent in the fabric of space-time over the distant, dark tower. Emma and I have seen this effect before. Arachnid Behemoths pour through, falling to the ground near the base of the tower. They keep falling through the rift, piling atop each other, until they're stacked half the height of the tower. The rift closes.

The traffic headed toward the tower screeches to a halt as the Behemoths swarm over the tower. They don't appear to be touching the tower itself, held at bay by some invisible dome protecting the structure. Frantic metal legs jab at the invisible dome in unsuccessful attempts to pierce it, to break through.

I squeeze Emma's hand. "That dome protecting the tower…. Spooky is inside it, I just know it. We have to get in there."

Emma's lips draw a grim line across her face. "I can teleport you inside, but it will take me six hours afterward to teleport in there with you."

"Six hours is an awfully long time to be apart."

The Elf Warrior-Wizard grimaces. "I don't think we're getting inside that protective dome any other way than teleporting, and I only have the Auni to send one of us now. It has to be you. When my Auni recharges, I'll come in, too. We just have to hope those Behemoths can't break through that dome before we can get Spooky and get away. For that matter, we can't be sure Spooky is in there. So while you look for her in there, I'll look for her in the city. In six hours, if I haven't found her, I'll teleport into the dome and find you. If I do find her, I'll make sure she's safe and then come for you."

"I'm afraid." There, I said it. I don't want to be alone in this strange world.

Emma stares into my eyes. "Fauna. It's okay to be scared. You're the girl immune to fire but deathly afraid of it. When have any of your friends ever ridiculed you for that? And we never will. Your fear is part of what makes you *you*. But it doesn't define you. It's not all of who you are. You also have a courage inside that can stand up to giant metal spiders four times your height. Hold onto that courage. We'll get through this. Are you ready?"

I can't stop the tears. "I've already lost Ronnie, Greelia, and Spooky. Nick, Charli, and Ulric are gone. I can't bear to lose you, too, Emma. I'm sorry, but I just can't."

She wipes my tears with a finger. "You *can*, Fauna. You *will*, because you always do the right thing. We *have* to do this. If we don't try to find those we've lost, then what? Are we to leave it to random chance for us to meet them again? No, because we're *fighters*, Fauna. We're *adventurers*, and *this* is our adventure. Now, I won't send you into that dome against your will. We both know you'll be going *toward* danger, not *away* from it. But that's what we adventurers do. We go where others don't, whatever their reasons. *Caution* is our watchword, not *safety*. Don't let fear control you, but *do* let it guide you. You can do this. Just say you will...."

I pull her into an embrace. We hold it until I stop shaking. Stepping back, I nod, my cheeks wet. She gives me a faint smile. With a wave of her wand and a few words, my dear friend sends me hurtling through the space between space.

CHAPTER THIRTY-NINE

Charli: Taking a Break

Kylie and Slithy are at such ease being mother and daughter. They respect, admire, and love each other. The proof is in every nuance of posture, every shared glance, every exchange of words, every laugh and every tear. I want that for Britta and me... some day, when she's older.

My daughter is still less than 24 hours old. She already has the mind of a toddler, but not the mind of the adult she appears to be, as her unabashed nakedness proves.

An invitation to chat from Yuni in party XStorm surprises me. I should accept it.

What does everyone think about this naked green woman clinging to me? I shouldn't let myself be worried about it or distracted by it, but I can't help it. Aren't worries and distractions unavoidable consequences of parenthood? At least Britta is calm at the moment. She's not trying to breastfeed, which I'm glad for. Maybe her earlier attempt to take milk from me was simply an instinctive behavior—she *shouldn't* need to eat. None of us avatars have the need for nourishment, whether one be PC or NPC.

But then, Nick is her father, and *he's* not an avatar. *He* needs nourishment—I think. So maybe *she* does, too, but I sincerely hope not, because neither I nor Khertaan can provide her with nourishing food.

I accept Yuni's chat.

She informs me of her progress and says that XStorm, Quantized, and MAD are traveling together, headed for the spire. I tell the Asian War Priestess about my being added to every party, the reason for it, and that Slithy did it. I tell her where I am, who I'm with, and what we've fought recently. I make special mention of the Mental Dominator, the Boss monster for the Spire of Desire. I'm hoping they won't have to fight it to leave its territory. I already helped defeat it, so every party I'm a member of—which is all of them—should get credit for the defeat.

There's more I want to tell her—especially about Britta and about my having an eighteen-year-old persona instead of my original fourteen-year-old one—but I really don't want to field the questions those topics will raise. Explanations will be easier after they see the changes.

Some truths about Britta—the nature of her conception and who her father is—will remain a secret forever, or as long as possible. The longer I delay talking about her, the longer I delay any revelations that could drive a wedge between me and Kylie or me and Slithy. I like both of them and want to stay friends. I don't know how friendly they'll be if they discover Nick is Britta's father.

After urging Yuni to join me in Minook as soon as possible, and to say hi to everyone for me, I bid her farewell.

Yuni has a few parting words for me. "Amarynth says she misses you. *Everyone* in MAD misses you, of course. And everyone in *all three parties* want to thank you for the ton of XP you've earned us."

It's funny to think I've been responsible for earning so many XP for so many people who've scarcely met me—or never have.

"You're welcome. I miss everyone, too. I can't wait to see everyone again, and to see what they think of how I've changed."

We terminate the chat.

My heart weighs heavy for not being by Amarynth's side. She truly cares about me, and it's not just because I was the first NPC swayed by her High Social Status trait. Deep down she knows it wasn't her trait that persuaded me to join MAD back in the beginning. Amarynth and I meshed. I don't have parents. I never did. Many NPCs don't have back stories with enough depth to include any parents. Amarynth was the mother I never had. We had that kind of bond from the moment we met. She's been proud of every milestone I've hit and has always wanted me to feel included—giving me a sense of belonging. Even though I ran off on my own for a while, seeing her face will always feel like returning home. What Kylie and Slithy have—that's Amarynth and me. I'm privileged to have her. Most NPCs in Khertaan don't have such a familial bond and never will.

A number of parties visit me, introducing themselves, expressing their gratitude for the XP gains my presence on their party roster has made possible. All the names and faces fail to stick in my brain. Everyone is heading into the city to explore, hoping to do their part in earning XP for everyone else. They're all keen to help out.

"If you want to help me," I say to every visiting party, "be on the lookout for clothing for my Britta, please." They all pledge to be on the alert.

One young woman stands out—green skin and green eyes; long, curly, red hair; pointed white horns protruding from her forehead and curving up. She's my age, about my height, and a little heftier than me. Her name is Mylynna. She's a Mist Succubus by kindred, with Houri as class and Harper as subclass.

Mylynna says something that makes her stand out even more. "I talked with Slithy before she respawned."

Now there's an interesting story. "Tell me more."

As she fills me in, I access my Monster Lore about Mist Succubi. The prominent detail is her being a demon with a female identity—an Incubus is the corresponding male-identifying demon. But there's more to the monster than a gender identity. A Succubus is a sensual demon, traditionally luring males into compromising situations leading eventually to their own destruction. In Khertaan, a Succubus is still a sensual demon, but she doesn't target only men, and she doesn't care so much about leading her victims to destruction, but only to tempt them into doing her bidding, whatever that might be. A Succubus in Khertaan has the Dark Sight trait and a Passage trait for a specific *element*, like Air, Earth, Light, or Dust. Mylynna's element is Mist, which means that wherever mists are, she can travel very fast through them to any location they reach. She can lead parties through them very quickly, too. That could be interesting if we ever find areas filled with mists, but so far, I've seen none. My Shadow Passage trait seems more useful. In my experience, shadows are more common in Khertaan than mists.

Once she's done telling me about her conversation with Slithy, I ask her about her character class and subclass. She's happy to talk about them. The Houri class works well with her Succubus kindred, in that it focuses on the emotional aspect of the world. I've seen plenty of action regarding the physical, mental, and spiritual realms in Khertaan, but not so much when it comes to the emotional, other than what we inflicted on ourselves. As a level 23 Houri, Mylynna has skills: level 38 Emotional Armor, level 36 Seduce, level 33 Attraction, level 30 Rejuvenate, level 26 Presence, level 22 Debilitate, level 3 Dominance, and level 1 Emote. That last skill is especially interesting. With it she can implant any emotion in her target, provided she wins a contest of wills between them. That's scary.

With her level 14 Harper subclass, Mylynna has even more skills to sway the emotions of her targets. She's got level 20 Play Guitar and a guitar in inventory, level 18 Sing, level 15 Mass Morale Boost, level 12 Mass Charm, level 10 Popularize, and level

8 Compose Songs. The Mass Morale Boost and Mass Charm skills can potentially affect anyone who hears her sing or playing her guitar. Her Popularize skill can temporarily impart High Social Status to a target, and her Compose Songs skill can be used to invent Songs of Power, the effects of which depend on her intentions.

As someone focused on emotions in a world where I've not seen much demonstrated in the way of emotional defenses, Mylynna comes across as a potentially powerful woman.

"I'm not a Priestess," she adds, "but I have healing and morale boosting ability like one."

I squint at her. "How do you heal?"

"My Rejuvenate skill boosts my Rejuvenation power, which can provide healing to the target in any of the realms—physical, mental, spiritual, or emotional. I must embrace my target face-to-face, which can be somewhat inconvenient on the battlefield, but it gets the job done."

"Sounds quite touchy-feely." I wink at the Succubus, which feels surprisingly natural. Is she practicing her seduction on me? "Not that being touchy-feely is a bad thing." I kinda like this woman. It's not only her traits and skills working on me.... That red hair... I love it. And those horns sprouting from her forehead... would that I had some like them.

Mylynna and the rest of TwoWorldOrder take their leave to go exploring in the city. I could have talked with her for longer, but that's okay. Her party wants to do their part in earning XP for everyone.

Kylie contacts me over the TimeTrippers party chat. "We'll be back soon. Slithy and Rancor are coming with me to fly around the city and get a Dragon's-eye view of the place. I've asked Spyder to lie low. You and Britta are welcome to come along if you want."

"I think we'll sit this one out, but thanks."

"Then perhaps Spyder could stay with you, so no one mistakes her for an enemy mook to be killed."

"Sure, no problem."

Kylie's subdued Ghoul Dragon rises into the air with the Angel and her Frogkin daughter on its back. Slithy squats on all fours, with Rancor perched on a shoulder. Kylie stands on the Dragon's spine, a blue rope stretched between her and the base of the Dragon's neck. I watch until the Dragon and its passengers vanish behind a high-rise.

All my party chat channels go crazy with combat plans as Spyder lumbers out of the shadows. I'm quick to inform them all. "The Arachnid Behemoth is with me. *Don't* harm her. She's a member of the TimeTrippers party." Spyder joins me, lowering onto her bulbous abdomen, making herself as small and non-threatening as possible for a two-story-tall metallic spider with sharp, pointy legs.

After all parties have met me and gone to seek their fortunes in the city, I turn my full attention to my daughter. Picking a spot from which I have a good view of the mouth of the cave where I expect Amarynth and company to make their arrival, I sit with my back to a red marble tower and pat the ground. Britta sits beside me, laying her head on my shoulder.

I pat her cheek. "Britta, baby girl, please let Mommy into your head."

"Aagh." Coming from her, that's *yes*.

I make the awareness transfer. "May I see your character sheet, please?"

Since her birth earlier today, Britta has earned three trait points and four attribute points. She already has them all assigned—two trait points to Regeneration, one trait point to Iron Will (ugh, now she'll be more stubborn than ever), two attribute points to Sensing (bringing it up to 12, the high average category), and two attribute points to Agility (bringing it up to 14, the extraordinary category). "Britta, when you earn more attribute points, could you please assign some to Morals? It would make Mommy very happy."

"Pbbt." That means *no*.

She's impossible. It's one thing for a teenager to have this kind of power. For a willful infant to have it—even if she is extremely smart for her age—is insane.

And she's entirely *my* responsibility. Even if Nick were here, I couldn't count on his help with Britta without him admitting to his lovely wife, Kendra, that he'd cheated on her with me.

Although, technically, that wasn't true. In the universe where I conceived, Nick and Kendra weren't married, whereas Nick and I were.

When everything is over—whatever that means and if such a time ever comes—I want to go back to that universe and live happily ever after with Nick and Britta. If life is a story, *that's* my happy ending.

"Mommy."

"Yes, Britta?"

"Spooky."

"Is something scaring you, hon? Where?" It's exciting that she has said a new word, but it's worrisome that it would be *that* word. Being inside her head, I'm looking through her eyes, and the scariest thing I see is my own lap.

The scene changes to that of a vast city, with buildings as tall as those in Minook. But where the buildings of Minook are high-rises constructed from red or white marble, the buildings I'm looking at through Britta's eyes are towers carved from cracked, dark stone. *That* city looks more like one to be haunted by Ghouls. It's as though she's seeing Minook for what it really is—a dark city of ancient granite, not a renaissance city of pristine marble. I agree, this *is* spooky.

The sounds of a busy city—the chatter of pedestrians, the neighs and trumpets and hisses of a vast variety of beasts of burden, the honks of horns and the squeals of tires—are a barrage of noise. A Dragon and its rider flies by overhead, the whoosh of its wings loud in Britta's ears. The Dragon isn't a Ghoul Dragon or a Pseudo Code Dragon, but a thirty-foot-long Red Dragon with crimson scales.

From this newly-gained POV, we fly along a straight road of gray stone, moving deeper into the city with every passing second.

Without warning, traffic stops. Heads turn towards us. The sounds of the city are replaced by gasps and shrieks.

The people aren't looking *at* us. They're looking at something *behind* us.

Our POV spins around.

In the distance, across desert sands, Arachnid Behemoths fall through a rift in the sky, to swarm over a distant tower of dark stone, maybe a half mile or more away. But the Behemoths can't *touch* the tower—an invisible dome protects it, like a force field.

As we watch, the giant metal spiders scramble over the dome, covering it in a layer of bulbous abdomens with pointed metallic legs rising and falling in rhythm like hydraulics. Oblivious to the city, the Behemoths aim to crack the dome like an egg and destroy the tower within.

"Britta, how are you seeing this?"

"Spooky."

"Yes, dear, it *is* spooky. But my question isn't *what*. I'm asking *how*." It's a miracle she can understand me at all, so I don't mean to be harsh. I try to keep the frustration out of my telepathic voice.

"Spooky. Spooky. Spooky."

Traffic previously headed towards the tower backs up or turns around, jamming both lanes with inbound vehicles and mounts. Some pedestrians stand in shock, while others flee, slamming into those not moving. Horses, cats, dogs, and scorpions with riders burst from the street onto the sidewalks in their flight. Elephants trample vehicles in their path. Riders fall from frightened mounts. Anyone in that mess stands a good chance at losing a life, not due to the piercing leg of an Arachnid Behemoth, but due to the weight of the stampede on one's organs.

A single shouted word stands out above the noise of the crowd, a cry yearning for a response. *"Spooky!"*

The voice sounds familiar. Is that Emma?

Britta giggles.

No, that wasn't Britta's giggle. The sound I hear has an echoing quality not present when my baby girl giggles.

Oh, my gosh. "Britta, is *Spooky* the name of your shadow self?"

"Aagh."

"Are you looking through Spooky's eyes now?"

"Aagh."

Oh, geez. "Where is she? Is Emma there?"

"Aagh, Emma."

"Tell Spooky to go to Emma."

Our POV—which I now understand to be the POV of Britta's shadow self, *Spooky*—scans the tumult of the city from the air until settling on an Elf woman near the outskirts, planted in the middle of the road with traffic passing her to either side.

Spooky flies over the heads of the throng. As she nears the Elf woman, I make out Emma's features. Oh, my gosh. I'd never thought to see her or any of the T&T characters again. My baby girl's shadow self calls out. *"Emma."* Her voice is like Britta's, but with that echoing quality.

"Spooky!" Emma beckons for the shadow baby to come down to her. Spooky complies. Emma holds out open arms, and Spooky settles into them, cooing. Experiencing this through Spooky's POV, it's like Emma is cradling me.

"Oh, little girl, you shouldn't have disappeared on us like that. Please don't leave again." Emma turns to face the lone tower and speaks sotto voce. "Fauna, please be safe." Walking against the flow of traffic, Emma strides *away* from the city, *towards* the Behemoth swarm.

Is she out of her mind? "Britta, can you have Spooky tell Emma that we can see and hear her?" I'd really like to know where they are and what's happening there.

Spooky taps Emma with a shadowy finger. "Britta. Charli."

My heart pounds at the sound of my name on the shadow girl's lips. She is, after all, as much my daughter as Britta is. *I have twins*, and only one of them is with me. Oh, gosh, my eyes are tearing up.

Emma glances down at me, or rather, at the shadow girl she cradles. "Yes, Spooky. You know their names. Your sister and your Mommy. What else do you know, little one? If only you had the words to tell me."

Spooky points at her eyes. "Charli." She points at her ears. "Charli."

Emma raises an eyebrow. "What are you trying to tell me, Spooky?"

Thunder booms in the distance, like giant dice tumbling.

"Oh." Emma's eyes spark. "Charli? Can you really see and hear me? Are you communicating through Spooky? If that's true, tell Spooky to say the name of our goat-hoofed friend."

My heart in my throat, I instruct my baby girl, "Britta, tell Spooky to say *Fauna*."

Spooky repeats the female faun's name.

Emma gasps, but doubt furls her brow. "No. That could have been a fluke. If it's really you, Charli, have Spooky say the name of the fellow that Fauna and I were originally traveling with."

That would be the Rogue character Ulric was playing. How is Ulric faring now? "Britta, tell Spooky to say *Ronnie*."

The word coming from Spooky's mouth sounds more like *runny*.

Emma laughs. A tear runs down one cheek, and she wipes it away before it can fall on Spooky. "It really is you, Charli. I can't believe it." She lifts Spooky up, one hand under either armpit, and aims the shadow baby's eyes at the lone tower. "Fauna is in there, under the tower's protective dome. She felt sure Spooky was in there, and I teleported her inside the dome to go searching. I aim to go in there myself to get her out, but it takes six hours for my Auni to recharge. Once I'm in there, I'll need to wait nearly another six hours before I can teleport her back out, and then six hours after that I can teleport myself back out. I don't know what to do with Spooky in the interim. I can't teleport her in with me. If you understood all that, have Spooky tell me so."

I ask Britta to have Spooky say *yes*, but it comes out of Spooky's mouth the same way I'd expect Britta to say it. "Aagh." I hope Emma understands.

With a sigh, the Elf Warrior-Wizard returns Spooky to a cradling position. "I'll take that as a *yes*." Emma wipes away another tear. "Let me tell you a story."

She starts from the moment of Britta's birth, talks about how I collapsed afterward, how she tried to revive me, but I passed, leaving my baby girl behind. Then lightning blasted from a yellow birthmark on the back of Britta's right hand, and my baby girl disappeared too, while leaving her shadow behind—Spooky. Emma and Fauna have been taking care of her since then.

The Elf Warrior-Wizard falls silent, and I'm not sure if she'll continue. I take advantage of the lull to pop back to my own head and see what's happening around me in Minook. A few parties stand in circles, debating their next moves. From what I overhear, most of the parties are searching inside the buildings. Kylie, her subdued Ghoul Dragon, and the rest of TimeTrippers aren't in evidence. They're still off doing their thing, searching the city from Dragon-back.

Nothing needs my attention in Minook, so I jump back into Britta's head and Spooky's POV. Emma is quiet for perhaps a minute more before she continues her tale. Is she crying?

Ulric, she says, showed up for a while, but was swept away into a storm of mists. He's lost. Emma and Fauna teleported to Khenn Arrth the Trollgodfather, who took their character sheets and promised to help them as much as he could—but then he vanished. And *then* Spooky disappeared. Losing Spooky drove them over the edge. They had to recover her, and to do so, they entered the storm in search for the shadow baby. They eventually found their way to the city where they are now.

So now Spooky is with Emma, but Fauna isn't.

Emma goes into how the city itself had seemed ghostly on their arrival, relating how the city became solid for them.

It's all very interesting, and I'm not in the mood to be up and about myself. Emma's voice is soothing in my ears. But nothing is better than sharing these moments with my two babies.

The Elf Warrior-Wizard reaches the end of her story. "I hope you heard me, Charli. If you see Greelia or Ronnie, tell them I said *hello*. I hope they're okay."

"Aagh," says Spooky, echoing my positive sentiment and agreement.

I take another quick peek at Minook. The situation hasn't changed much. How long has Emma been talking? I'm not tracking the time.

Back in Spooky's POV, I find Emma still marching towards the lone tower and a Behemoth army. She faces no traffic now. Everyone who had been traveling towards the tower has returned to the city—not that it is any safer. Though the Behemoths are attacking the tower, the very sight of them is visiting mayhem, pain, and death on city residents.

Britta and I continue watching through Spooky's POV while Emma strides on in silence. The tower proves to be farther than it had first appeared. But the Elf Warrior-Wizard marches resolutely onward. I wish I could tell her my story, but our communication is only one-way until Spooky gains the ability to speak full sentences. That will come soon enough, I'm sure, but at the moment, she can't even say *yes* properly.

More time passes. All is silent except the soft thud of Emma's footfalls on pavement. Every so often I pull my awareness back to my own body to have a look at the happenings in Minook before returning to Spooky's POV.

Paying another visit to my own head, I spot movement at the cave mouth. It seems hours since I talked to Yuni. I hop into my baby girl's head once more. "Britta, hon, tell Spooky bye bye. There's someone here in Minook I want you to meet." I transfer my awareness back to my body.

Britta sits up and looks around. She's no longer in Spooky's POV either.

I jump to my feet. "Please be on your best behavior, child." I wave when I see Amarynth and try calling to her over local chat, since party chat with MAD has been giving me such problems. "Over here."

The Viking Archer breaks into a run, and she can move *fast*.

I wait for her. Britta stands beside me in all her nakedness. No one has brought her any clothes yet.

Upon reaching us, Amarynth throws her arms around me. Despite my eighteen-year-old appearance, she knows who I am.

I laugh and cry as I nestle in her embrace. "I've missed you so much, Milady."

CHAPTER FORTY

Ronnie: Juggling Bikes

"Let's go. This house isn't a safe place for us to talk." I lead the way out of the bedroom and head for the door to the outside. As I near it, I hear voices from beyond, coming closer.

I push a window curtain aside. A weight sinks into my bowels. Seven black horseless carriages are parked in the middle of the road, some larger than the others. Guards with muskets pile out of the larger ones. Some of the guards are already halfway to the house. Others are headed around to the back. "We have company."

Nick calls from the couch, not bothering to get up. "Thanks for bringing trouble into my home, Erica."

I call for an SR on Luck, but the dice don't appear. It's as though what's about to happen is all scripted and nothing I do will cause events to veer from the script. If I want an SR, I'll need to do the rolling myself. "Are there any dice in the house?"

"I don't really know." Erica rummages in a closet.

"We don't have any." Nick seems put out by my asking.

The guards outside are here for me. I unload two bikes, one for Mel and one for Erica, setting them on the floor. "Don't either of you say a thing or come outside until I'm gone." I open the door, despite Erica shouting for me not to. Holding my arms over my head, I step outside. "You got me. I surrender."

Dozens of muskets level at me as I walk out. I don't glance back, but quickly put distance between me and the door, hoping the guards won't be inclined to go inside. One grabs my arms, wrenches them behind my back, and puts manacles on my wrists. "You're under arrest for the kidnapping of Princess Karen. Confess now, if you want. Please."

At my silence, another guard sticks his musket in my face. "Here I was hoping for a reason to shoot you. You can still give me one. *Where's the Princess?*"

As they lead me to one of the black carriages, a couple of guards escort Mel out of the house. This is not how I wanted things to go. They lead him to a different carriage.

The guards don't bother with Erica. She watches from the doorway as my carriage growls and then speeds away.

I'm seated in the back, with two guards up front. They put on safety straps, but don't bother to put them on me. A mirror hangs from the carriage ceiling, and dangling from the mirror are a couple of fuzzy dice. One of the guards sits behind a wheel used to steer the carriage. They aren't carrying muskets, but do have pistols. One of them has his pistol in hand and keeps eying me. I know why. The manacles on my wrists aren't tight. I could slip out easily. That's what he wants, so he can shoot me.

We exit through the community gate and turn left. Looks like all the other black carriages are following us. Heading back to the city, we travel at a good clip along a road with forested land to either side.

I lean forward. "On a scale of one to whatever, with one being very likely, what's the likelihood an accident occurs before this carriage reaches it's destination?"

The guard with the pistol sneers at me. "One. Definitely."

276

"Great." I nod at the fuzzy dice. "Would you mind rolling those for me?"

He hesitates, but then takes them down and hands them across the back of his seat. "You want them rolled, you roll them."

"I would, but my wrists are manacled behind my back."

He swings the dice back and forth on the cord that attaches them. "They're right here. All you gotta do is take 'em."

"Fine." I slip my hands free, grab the dice, and roll them on the seat.

Removing his safety strap, the guard twists in his seat, brings his pistol up, and points it in my face. "We have ourselves an escapee, boys. Reason enough to shoot him, I say."

The dice show a total of seven. With my Luck of 147, I make a level twenty-seven SR with that roll. The guard said I only needed a level one SR, and I made that many times over. I brace myself for the accident about to happen.

A motorcycle speeds by on our left and cuts in front of us. Our carriage swerves hard to the right as the driver yanks on the steering wheel. The other's pistol goes off, and a bullet strikes the driver in the head. The carriage smacks into a tree, bringing it to a quick stop and slamming the pistol-wielding guard against the interior of the carriage. Momentum throws me against the back of his seat.

A door to the carriage swings open. Erica reaches for me.

Grabbing up the fuzzy dice, I roll again. I get an eight. That's good for a level twenty-eight SR. That's for getting out of this jam without anyone else getting hurt. I hope level twenty-eight is high enough. I stash the dice in inventory. Then I take Erica's hand for balance as I disembark.

Several other black carriages squeal to a stop behind us. Musket-wielding guards jump out.

Erica tugs on me. "Hop on." She straddles her bike seat.

I pull another bike out of inventory. "I'm right behind you."

Her eyes widen at my producing yet another bike, but she nods and revs her engine.

We head out, bullets spraying the road behind and around us. It seems a level twenty-eight SR on Luck is good enough to keep us from being struck. The black carriages are slow to chase us, since everyone who piled out must pile back in. We've a good head start on them.

As we near an intersection, Erica motions for us to turn left. I follow her, since this is familiar territory for her. The road bends, with wooded lots to either side, and a quick glance back proves none of the black carriages are in sight. If I can't see them, then they can't see us.

After a few more left turns, we're back to the main road. Not long after that, we come to the same intersection again, but this time we go straight through, and we soon catch sight of a couple of black carriages ahead of us. Only two. The others must have split off at the intersection to look for us.

We're definitely going faster than the carriages, and there's a good chance the carriages in front of us will stay on the main road for a while. I have a plan, but I want to roll an SR for it before attempting to execute it, so I wave Erica over to the side of the road.

Remaining in her seat, Erica looses a heavy sigh. "They're getting away, Ronnie. I bet Mel is in one of those two vehicles. We need to rescue him."

Not wasting any time with explanations, I roll the fuzzy dice. Maybe the cord attaching the two dice will mess with the results, but I don't take time to detach it. "Come on, dice, five or better."

They come up double twos.

"Sorry, Ronnie." Erica revs her engine. "Now let's go."

"Doubles add and roll again." I re-roll the dice, get double threes, and get to roll yet again. After the next roll, I end up making a level thirty SR. I stash the dice. "I have a plan, Erica, and I'm sure it will work. When we catch up to them, hang back, and get ready to stop. If you get a chance to grab Mel, do it, but watch out for flying debris."

She rolls her eyes at me. We speed down the road.

At first it seems we've lost them, but after a couple minutes I spot them. They're still on the main road, as I'd hoped. As we close on them, I wave Erica back, and she slows. I race up beside the closest carriage and catch sight of Mel inside. Perfect.

As I pull up to the lead carriage, a window lowers, and a guard aims his musket through the opening at me. Emboldened by my level thirty SR, I swerve close to the carriage. The musket fires, but the shot misses me.

Being this close to the carriage is risky, and even the best SR won't deliver a person from acts of pure stupidity. Maybe I'm being ignorant, but I need to do *something*, and this is all I could think of. Pulling past the lead carriage, evading a volley of bullets now coming from both vehicles, I pretend I have a ball in my hand and throw it at the windshield. But at the last second, instead of throwing an imaginary ball, I materialize one of the four motorcycles still in my inventory. The bike flies at the carriage.

The driver of the lead vehicle swerves in an attempt to avoid the bike coming at his face. When it appears he might recover without going off the road, I throw another bike at him.

He brings the carriage to a hard stop before running into a tree, as I'd hoped he would. The first bike is caught under the front of the vehicle, while the second one lies crushed in the road.

The rear carriage—the one with Mel inside—passes the stopped carriage and keeps coming. The carriage with the bike under it tries to follow, but they'll need to deal with that bike under them first. Erica passes the stopped carriage, and the guards inside take potshots at her. She keeps riding. I hope she wasn't hit. I don't think she was.

So now I'm out front of the carriage and Erica is behind it. I'd hoped for a chain of events—stopping the lead carriage would lead to both of them stopping—but that's not how it has played. I suspect that last SR I rolled is used up, and I need to roll another one for whatever I do next.

The guards in Mel's carriage are firing their muskets at me. I weave erratically from side to side to make it difficult for them to predict my location at any given moment, and they miss me.

Another shot rings out, followed by a loud, repeated flapping. The rear wheel on the driver's side has lost its shape and is slowing the carriage, but the vehicle keeps going, nonetheless. Another shot rings out, followed by more flapping. The front wheel on the driver's side has fallen victim to another well-placed bullet from the pistol in Erica's grasp.

The carriage veers into the middle of the road and comes to a stop. Guards fire their muskets through open windows. They aren't firing through the back, and that's where Erica puts herself. They still try to hit her as she closes the distance between them, but she's still coming, so I assume they're still missing. The muskets aren't hitting me yet, either, and with the carriage turned at a slight angle on the road, it's easy for them to shoot down the road. Facing them, I stay to my right as far as possible to increase their difficulty in hitting me as I race up to the front of the carriage.

I don't bother to dismount, but stash my bike and tumble across the shoulder of the road, coming to a stop in the grass in front of the carriage. Keeping low to the ground so they can't shoot me from inside the vehicle, I bring the fuzzy dice to hand and toss them on the ground.

I make a level twenty-eight SR on Luck. It's better to be lucky than good, goes the T&T mantra, and my Luck far exceeds any of my other attributes. I'm a Rogue with no weapons or spells, only a few stashed motorcycles, a pair of fuzzy dice, my Luck, and a quick wit. I hope my Luck doesn't run out.

The driver's carriage door opens. I peek under the vehicle. Seizing an opportunity, I draw a motorcycle from inventory and place it on its side under a descending booted foot. The disembarking driver steps on the motorcycle wheel spokes and can't keep his balance. As he tumbles headfirst away from the carriage, I stash the bike.

The barrel of the driver's musket strikes a stone, jarring the weapon loose from his grip. It lands in the grass not far from me. His momentum carries him away from the weapon. I somersault over to it and stash it to inventory with a touch.

Two other guards disembark on the driver's side of the carriage. They train their muskets on me. I sit and hold up my empty hands. They both look ready to pull their triggers, but hesitate, because, well, I'm not offering any resistance, I'm not wielding a weapon, and Mel is a witness, watching from inside the carriage.

A shot rings out, and a body on the other side of the carriage drops. The two armed guards near me turn, taking their attention off me, and I tumble towards the disarmed driver, who has now gained his feet. Rather than try to grapple with him, I tumble past him, getting close to the carriage. Springing to my feet, I hold up my empty hands as a sign of surrender.

Two more shots ring out from the other side of the carriage. As long as shots are firing, Erica is alive. She's occupying half the guards. It's up to me to handle the three on this side of the carriage.

The driver whips around to face me. A grin grows on his face as he notices I'm not holding his weapon. He involuntarily casts a searching gaze for it on the ground around him. When he brings his gaze back to me again, I'm holding his musket, leveled at his chest, my finger on the trigger.

I don't really know how muskets work, especially the ones in this universe. I've noticed the guards have been able to fire without reloading, so these muskets aren't like the gunnes in T&T. There's a trigger and something of a lever running beneath the trigger. Maybe I should have rolled an SR on Intelligence to see if I could figure out how to fire this thing, but I'm guessing just having my finger on the trigger will sufficiently intimidate the guards. I'm also guessing the lever is for prepping the musket to fire again, but I'm hoping it won't come to that.

"Hold your fire, or I'll shoot the driver." I call loud enough for the guards on the other side of the carriage to hear me.

Putting their backs to the carriage, the two armed guards on this side train their muskets on me again.

I glower at the driver. "Tell your friends to drop their weapons, or you're dead."

"You wouldn't kill a cop." The driver steps towards me.

I take a step backward to maintain the distance between us. "Take another step, and you're dead. If your friends don't drop their weapons, you're dead. One…. Two…."

"*Drop your weapons.*" The driver lowers his voice, talking only to me. "You won't get away with this. We caught you once, and we'll catch you again."

Weapons clatter to the ground, the two on this side of the carriage and two more on the other side.

I keep my musket and my gaze on the driver as I call out. "Mel, get out of the carriage."

He exits on the other side through a door already open.

"Come around here, Mel."

He does as I say and collects the two dropped muskets on my side of the carriage.

Erica shouts that she has the two muskets on her side of the carriage, referring to them as *rifles*. Good to know the correct name.

I give Mel a bike and take the two rifles from him, stashing them while I keep my rifle trained on the driver. Erica comes up front with her bike and and the other two rifles, which she hands off to me to stash.

"Erica, you take the lead, please," I say. "You two go ahead. I'm right behind you."

When they've gotten clear of the place, I draw a bike from inventory, hop on, stash the rifle, and drive away as fast as I can. I'm leaving two bikes lying on the road behind me, because I'm not taking the time to collect them, and they're likely mangled beyond use anyway. There's one bike back at Erica's place that I'd intended for Mel to use, but he never had the chance. With the three of us each riding a bike, simple math tells me I have one remaining in inventory. When I first took seven bikes from the Orc Wizards, I never expected to have a use for so many of them.

Erica and Mel go slow enough for me to catch up. Then Erica speeds up. She doesn't slow down again until we reach an intersection where she decides to turn. I hope she's taking us somewhere we can hide out for a while and have a serious discussion about... well... everything.

CHAPTER FORTY-ONE

Erica: Traveler of the Cosmos

Ronnie brushes aside a curtain to peer out a window. "We have company."

Nick doesn't get off the couch. "Thanks for bringing trouble into my home, Erica."

"Hey, it's my home, too." Hell, in my original timeline, this house never belonged to Nick. I inherited it from my parents. I suppose that happened in this timeline, too, but because Nick and I married, alternate-me agreed to put his name on the deed with mine. Before my awareness took over, my alternate self didn't give a shit about anything, including her own welfare or that of her daughter.

Ronnie materializes two motorcycles and sets them on the living room floor. "Don't either of you say a thing or come outside until I'm gone."

I'm aghast at his intended action. "Ronnie, don't you dare open that door."

He ignores me and does what I told him not to. Holding his arms over his head, he steps outside. "You got me. I surrender."

What does he think he's doing? The cops won't be happy only arresting him. They won't leave here without Mel, and there's a large probability Ronnie won't live to see a jail cell.

Mel knows this, too, and he goes to the door despite my protests. He shakes his head at me. "I'm not giving them an excuse to come in and shoot up the place."

Nick's attention is still glued to the TV. "Much appreciated."

Fingering the handle of the pistol stuck in my belt—the pistol I stole from the hulking guy who wanted my sex and got a kick to the nuts instead—I watch from the doorway as the police take both Ronnie and Mel away, in two different black SUVs. For a moment, I'm speechless, in shock. Nothing is going as it should in this timeline.

I slap Nick up-side his head.

He turns on me slowly, not a single emotion registering in his gaze. Then he just as slowly turns his head back to watching the TV.

I turn off the television. Nick doesn't react. He continues sitting there, staring at a blank TV screen. This sorry excuse for a human being is absolutely not the Nick I know. This person is but a shell of human flesh, going through the motions of a life void of passion—or any meaning at all, really.

The baby screams from her bedroom. She's supposedly mine, though I can't recall giving birth to her. If I go to her now, am I tying myself to this timeline? Nick closes his eyes and lies on his side on the couch. The baby screams again.

What the fuck am I supposed to do?

Am I to chase after Ronnie or Mel, or am I to tend to this baby, or am I to throw up my hands and forget it all—take one of those bikes Ronnie left behind and go explore the world on my own, like alternate-me would do. I can understand the temptation to toss aside all responsibilities—to live wild and free.

The baby screams again. She wins out. She's innocent in all this.

Her name is Britta—the same name as Greelia's baby. That can't be a coincidence. Am I connected in some metaphysical way to Greelia? If I am, does that mean I'm also connected to Charli? I saw the two of them trade places—trade universes.

It's a mystery I don't have the time or resources to solve now. Speaking of mysteries....

A cloaked humanoid of masculine build stands behind Britta's bed, lifting my crying baby in his arms. He's *not* human. A forked tongue flicks from his reptilian snout. He rocks Britta, and she quiets.

Have I seen this man before? If so, wouldn't I remember? "Who are you and what do you want?"

His serpentine mouth curls up in an evil grin that matches the evil gaze in his snake eyes. "Hello, Erica. I am Gondra, Traveler of the Cosmos. I'm here to help you save Nick."

My instincts war amongst themselves. I don't trust this reptile man and yet I want to—because if I'm to be stuck in this universe for the rest of my life, I want the man lying on the couch in the living room to be my Nick. "Tell me what I must do, Mr. Gondra."

"*Gondra* will do." His evil grin grows more evil... cunning. "First you must rescue Ronnie and Mel. How you do that I must leave to you. Bring them to meet me under the bridge at Golden Minnow State Park. I'll tell all three of you the plan there. Now, go. Don't worry about Britta here. Once you save Nick, he'll sort out everything else, including whether you continue to exist or Charli exists in your stead."

"What do you mean, *whether I exist or Charli exists*? How am I related to the Cowgirl?"

Gondra's grin flattens out. "Charli is an NPC avatar from a video game universe called Khertaan, an alternate reality to which Nick opened a wormhole. Though you and Charli are two different people, only one of you is needed to fulfill the cosmic role of Nick's young lover. In the end he will be forced to choose one of you if the timelines are to fully merge."

"Can't he simply have two young lovers?" Not that I'd like it, but I wouldn't wish for anyone—not even a competitor for Nick's affections—to be forced out of existence.

"One would think so, but there's no alternate world where that happens, which rules it out as a possibility in the merged timeline. In every timeline where Nick meets Charli, you were never born, but present only as a ghost. It also happens that in timelines where you were born, so was Jean, and she always plays a part in making Nick's life miserable. To be completely frank with you, Nick has been the most happy in timelines where Jean was never born—and neither were you.

"If, with my guidance, you can restore Nick's soul, he will have the power to choose which timeline to make dominant. If he chooses one with you in it, Jean will be in it, too, and Charli won't be. He'll end up miserable for most if not all of his life. If he chooses a timeline in which he knows some happiness with you, it will be short-lived, with Jean killing both you and him.

"It may be possible for Nick to merge elements of different timelines together instead of taking the easier path of making an existing timeline dominant. But even if he does this, he'll be hard pressed to have both you and Charli in his life. There are so many parallels between you and Charli, and his mind will be under so much stress."

I swallow a lump in my throat. "So... assuming I save Nick, and assuming he overpowers Greelia, Jean, and the other fellow—"

"His name is Seth."

"Assuming Nick overpowers the three of them, and it becomes his choice to shape the nature of the merged timeline, he'll basically be forced to choose between Charli and me? But really, whether it's Nick or someone else who chooses the dominant timeline, once it's chosen, Charli and I won't both exist in it."

Gondra nods gravely. "You understand. And now, you best go, if you're to rescue your friends. Remember, under the bridge in Golden Minnow State Park." He lays Britta on the bed. She sleeps. Gondra turns more and more translucent until he's transparent and then gone completely.

Back in the living room, I touch the seat of a bike the way I've seen Ronnie do, and will it to vanish into some *other-place* that I can draw it from at will. Whatever Ronnie does, it doesn't work for me. "See you later, Nick." I roll one of the bikes out the front door. Maybe we'll come back for the other one later.

I don't know which way the SUVs went once they left the community, but I pick a way and go—fast. When I see a line of SUVs ahead of me, I know it's them. I race past them and cut in front of the lead one.

CHAPTER FORTY-TWO

Kylie: Coin

As reflected by my extraordinary Temperance attribute score, I'm good about not crying or showing my emotions, but having my daughter back wrings the tears out of me. My Passion score is even higher than my Temperance, and there's little I'm more passionate about than my child.

Somewhere out there in the multiverse, Kendra lies asleep, her only task to remain unconscious and alive. But me—I'm *so* active and aware, steeped in responsibility. There's a drive within me to conquer, to excel, to exceed all expectations. Morrow isn't here and neither is his player, Nick, which means everything that must happen in Khertaan rests on my shoulders. As the avatar of its co-creator, no one else in the game understands it like I do.

"That may be true," says ODYSSEY, the nanobot collective that has been growing in my mind ever since a few of the synthetic cells transferred from Morrow to me. "But don't make the mistake of thinking that the program Kendra and Nick created controls every aspect of life in Khertaan. They created a means of accessing this world from Earth, and nothing more. It may seem otherwise to the casual observer, but any changes made to the program aren't to modify Khertaan's natural laws, but to reinforce its connection to Earth."

"What am I?" My personal support AI, Georgie the clown, gives me his best sad face. "Am I real?"

ODYSSEY surprises me with his answer. "You're as real as I am."

Oh, my…. "Are you saying Georgie is a collection of nanobots like you, ODYSSEY?"

"What else would he be?"

"But…." Something doesn't fit. "I can see him. I can't see you."

"You don't actually see Georgie, though, do you? You see what he wishes you to see. He overlays an image of a clown on the visual signals received by your eyes and interpreted by your brain. I could generate an image for you to perceive as me if I wanted, but when I tried that with Nick in the beginning, it didn't go over so well. He created additional mental imagery around me in an attempt to be rid of me—shoving me off an imaginary bus, shooting me with an imaginary rifle… you get the idea."

"You're saying he was hallucinating?"

"There are many ways to perceive reality and even more ways to interpret what is perceived. What is imaginary for one is reality for another. So who can say what is hallucination and what is real? One simple test is: *I think, therefore I am*. But such a test can only be administered by the one taking it. Another simple test is *seeing is believing*. Even in this case one administers the test to oneself, but the test for existence extends to others outside the self. Still, this test begs the question, does *perception* imply *existence*?

"More complex tests for existence are but extensions of these two basic tests. In the end, every sentient entity exists in its own reality, a multiverse populated by what it perceives, when and where it perceives it. It's only when the realities of other entities intersect with our own through some form of interaction that we become aware of them and they become real to us for a while.

When they no longer interact with us and no memory of them remains, for all intents and purposes they cease to exist for us.

"Are some interactions more 'real' than others? What defines *interaction*? Is the overlaying of images on your mental canvas any more or less 'real' when the overlaying is done by optic nerves, nanobots, an overactive imagination, or hallucinations induced by any means?

"If you equate perception to reality, then hallucinations are as real as anything else you see, whether the images are delivered by rays of light or nanobot injection. If you do not equate perception to reality, what test for reality remains? *I think, therefore I am*, or the corollary, *if someone or something thinks, then it exists*. You may ask yourself whether the subject in question can think, but how can you be sure of the answer? If it carries out a conversation with you, then it stands to reason it is thinking, but has anyone ever carried out a conversation with an hallucination?"

"Mom?" Slithy's utterance draws me away from my internal dialogue. My entire discussion with ODYSSEY took but a couple seconds. My Frogkin daughter squints at me from where she squats on the Dragon's spine. "Everything all right?"

I wipe away a tear. "I only wish Morrow were with us, too. I miss traveling as a family. Maybe soon he'll return. Your respawn has given me hope."

Her smile is reassuring. "I'm sure he's trying. But let's make him proud and hit level thirty before he gets back." She gives me a mischievous grin. "What level are you now?"

"Twenty-eight."

Her jaw drops. "What? No way."

"I've been busy."

"I'll say. I'm only level twenty-three. How is this Ghoul Dragon we're riding under your control?"

I chuckle. "Well…. My Spirit Noose skill from my Spirit Warrior class couples nicely with my Dominance skill from my Barbarian class. I might still be able to dominate this thing if I weren't using the noose, but I don't think I'll chance it."

"And you also tamed that Behemoth you and Charli have been traveling with?"

I do my best to demonstrate modesty by shrugging. "With help from ODYSSEY."

"Thanks for the shout out," says the nanobot collective in my head.

"Ha ha." Rancor flaps his Woodpecker wings from his perch on Slithy's shoulder. "I hate to interrupt, but I have something important to say. It's a message from Morrow."

I swear my heart skips a beat or three. It's like there's nothing else happening in Khertaan right now. I kneel beside Slithy to look nose-to-beak at Rancor. "And you're only saying something now?"

"Ha ha, you've been busy, and I didn't want to interrupt the family reunion."

My Temperance filter keeps me from grabbing him by his scrawny little neck. I stand, putting him out of my reach. "Tell us the message, Rancor."

"Ha ha, sure. Morrow said everyone in Khertaan needs to focus on Charli. Don't let her slip from your minds. She's the key to saving as many timelines as possible. If she and her history remain intact, all the timelines she has visited will survive the merge."

"What merge?"

"Ha ha, from what I understand, Nick did something to pack together a bunch of broken timelines to save them, but now they're all merging into one. Morrow says that Nick doesn't exist as a player anymore. Morrow is the last 'vestige' of Nick. He's trapped in a nexus holding the broken timelines together temporarily. If he leaves, the nexus fails and a significant portion of the multiverse collapses. Khertaan itself should survive, but the Fanciful Pegasus universe—where Nick and Kendra created the Khertaan program—won't. A bunch of other timelines won't, either."

"I've seen some different timelines." Slithy glances up at me from her crouching position. "In one of them, this cloaked dude named Seth has a Planet Buster spaceship he's used already to destroy Earth and a bunch of other planets. We *don't* want that timeline to become dominant."

I nod in agreement. "How do we get everyone to focus on Charli? An awful lot of parties seemed to show up here, but they've all gone exploring in the city. It will be fun trying to find them all." I'm not looking forward to the tedious task of searching all the buildings in Minook for adventuring parties. There must be an easier way.

Slithy bobs her head. "There's no need to say anything to anyone. Susie added Charli to every PC party in Khertaan, and now she earns them tons of XP. Trust me, everyone is focused on her. I even saw a bunch of avatars lining up to meet her before we headed out on this little aerial survey of the city."

Something glints on the ground far below and I point it out. "Speaking of our aerial survey, that glinting may be something of interest. Who thinks we should check it out?"

Slithy cranes her neck. "I can't see it from here. You've got me curious, so I vote we take a closer look."

I turn my glance on the Woodpecker perched on Slithy's shoulder. "Rancor? What's your vote?"

"Ha ha, I love glittering things. Let's go."

"Very well." I issue the mental command for my subdued Black Ghoul Dragon mount to take us down. It lands in a courtyard containing the source of the glint. Leaving the noose on the subdued Dragon's neck to ensure the creature remains under my control, I dismount. If it weren't undead, my high average Morals would prevent me from dominating it. And though my Conscience is extraordinary, it doesn't make me feel guilty about dominating an undead beast. "Let's go."

The glinting comes from a clear gem embedded in the stone wall above a hanging tapestry. The woven cloth depicts an elderly Orcish woman with long arms. She's shown as seated cross-legged, with one arm outstretched before her, her hand turned palm up. The other arm lies across her lap.

"Ha ha. What's that about?" Rancor launches from his perch.

"Don't go too close without us, Rancor." I itch to activate my Spirit Blade, even though no mooks are evident.

Slithy snaps webbed fingers. "The woman on the tapestry... it's *Ezmerelda*. The woman in the hut in the Mystic Hollow Cornfield. She gave us some magic Rings." She points at my hand. "You reached into the flames to take them."

"I remember." Morrow had tried a few times to take the rings from the fire. After he consistently failed, I reached in for them, not fazed by the heat because of my Pain Tolerant trait. "What are we supposed to do now?"

"I'm not sure." Slithy leaps closer to the tapestry and looks up. "I have the feeling that an attempt to take that crystal would not bode well for us."

"Ha ha." Rancor hovers near Slithy. "It looks like the woman in the tapestry wants us to hand her something."

"It does." I fly over and stand beside my Frogkin daughter. "Should we return the Rings she gave us? Mine is still stashed in inventory. I've not been wearing it."

"Me neither." Slithy holds up her webbed fingers to show they're ring-free.

"Ha ha, me neither." Rancor claws at the air, drawing attention to his ring-free talons.

"You two stay back." I bring Ezmerelda's Ring from my inventory to my hand, gripped between forefinger and thumb, and approach the tapestry. A word is printed on the open palm of the Orc woman's outstretched hand. The word means nothing to me. "Slithy, Rancor, do either of you know the significance of the word *Ogaltha*?"

"Sorry, I don't."

"Ha ha, me neither."

"I don't remember Ezmerelda saying anything about it when we acquired our Rings from her. We were in a bit of a hurry, though, as I recall. We had Arachnid Behemoths on our asses." I hold Ezmerelda's Ring close to the tapestry.

"Wait, Mom." Slithy voices the uncertainty I feel.

I step back. "What do you have in mind, kiddo?"

"Um… I'd like to try something first." Slithy grits her teeth. "I have the Predict skill. I can use it to get a prediction of the future based on a set of proposed actions, but the skill is only at level one, so I can only use it once a day. I also have the Clairvoyance skill. It lets me ask any question, and I'll get a vision about the answer. The skill is at level three, so I can use it three times a day. I'm thinking this might be a good time to make use of one or both of these skills."

"Agreed. So, which skill do you want to try first?"

"Ha ha, I have something, too, that might be relevant here." A Coin appears in the grasp of Rancor's talons. "Morrow gave this to me right before I respawned. He said it's from Ezmerelda."

"That man was holding out on us? Let me see that Coin."

The Woodpecker drops the Coin on my open palm.

On the face of the Coin is an engraved image of what might be an Orc or Goblin. On the back of the Coin is engraved a single word. "*Ogaltha*. I assume this is what the lady of the tapestry wants." I look askance at Slithy. "Do you want to use one of your skills to see what happens if I give it to her?"

My Frogkin daughter shrugs with a grin. "Maybe I'll save them for something else. I vote you go for it and we see what happens."

"Ha ha, me, too."

"Okay, then." I place the coin over the word Ogaltha on the tapestry.

Ezmerelda's three-dimensional form emerges from the tapestry where her two-dimensional image had been. She's levitating three feet off the ground, her legs still crossed, the coin lying on her open palm. "Welcome, Kylie, Slithy, and Rancor. Follow me if you will."

The tapestry dissolves into a spray of pixels, and a dark passageway gapes behind Ezmerelda. She floats backwards into the darkness, while the Coin glints like the crystal embedded in the wall above the passageway. I grab Slithy's hand. "Latch on, Rancor." He perches on my daughter's shoulder, and I fly us into the darkness, following the glint of the Coin.

I'm not sure if we fly down a passageway or in circles in a large room. I keep my eyes glued to the glint of the Coin. It's the only thing I can see. I could likely see something more if I switched to Spirit Form, but then I'd lose my hold on Slithy, and that's out of the question.

How long do we fly? I don't know. Time feels irrelevant. The darkness goes on and on, and none of us bring ourselves to talk. I need to stay focused on the Coin. Slithy and Rancor instinctively understand this. They do nothing that might break my concentration.

CHAPTER FORTY-THREE

Fauna: Kevin and Dr. Splat

The eerie silence raises the hairs on the back of my neck, but if I don't look up, I can pretend there's no army of metal spiders up there—not hundreds of Behemoth legs thrashing and stabbing at the invisible dome of force providing the only layer of protection between me and those horrid death-dealers.

Beneath the dome looms the dark tower I'd seen from the city. Guards stand ready on the battlements, gunnes aimed upward, ready should our attackers eventually break through the defenses of the invisible dome. It's not the degree of reassurance needed to calm a simple faun girl's nerves.

At the base of the tower sit a number of four-wheeled horseless carriages and two-wheeled conveyances. One of the carriages is a tall, boxy contraption with an array of tinted windows ringing the upper half of the carriage. The door to the boxy carriage slides open, and a muscular young black man in tight-fitting clothes steps out, catching my gaze. "Hello. Um… what the… can I help you?"

Another man, this one old and white, steps out of the same horseless carriage. He's wearing a loose white cloak reaching to his calves. "Greetings, young woman. My name is Doctor Splat. My assistant here is Kevin. May I inquire as to who you are and what world you're from?"

I want to turn and run, but if I do, I'll be moving towards the base of the invisible dome and a bunch of unpleasant metallic spider legs jabbing in my direction. "My name is Fauna.75. I'm part goat and part human—a faun, of sorts. You can call me Fauna."

"Uh huh." The elderly man slowly approaches. "I'm from Earth. Kevin is from Destin here. What world are you from?"

"I'm… from T&T. My world doesn't have a name."

The Doctor squints. "T&T? What's that?"

"Tunnels and Troglodytes… a role-playing game." I feel cornered, but he has stopped coming closer, a small comfort.

"Ah." Understanding lights the Doctor's eyes. "Video game or table-top?"

"I don't know what a video game is."

"Table-top, then." The Doctor looks impressed. He raises his gaze to the overhead attackers. "Are you here to fight the inter-dimensional invaders?"

I don't follow his gaze. As long as those things don't come through the dome, I'm good. "No. I'm here to find Spooky, a shadow baby I have reason to believe came here. Have you seen her?"

Kevin's ears perk. "What do you mean, *shadow baby*?"

I don't feel like going into lots of details. "A baby made of shadows. Her name is Spooky. It's imperative I find her."

"This is the first I've heard of a shadow baby." Dr. Splat puts a finger to his chin. "Is she also from your T&T world?"

I shake my head. "She's from Earth."

"You don't say?" Dr. Splat turns to Kevin. "I think we should help Fauna with her search." He looks back to me. "Where did you see Spooky last?"

"In the eye of a storm. She disappeared. We had to leave the eye to go searching for her, and this place is where we ended up."

Kevin narrows his gaze. "You said, *we*. Who else was with you?"

I hope I'm not making myself, Emma, or Spooky vulnerable to exploitation by bad people. I don't trust Dr. Splat, but Kevin seems nice. "My friend Emma is back in the city. She's searching there while I'm searching here."

"I see." Dr. Splat rubs his hands together. "And your friend, Emma—is she from Earth or T&T?"

Am I wasting time talking to these two? If they can help me find Spooky, that would be great, but I don't like how they—especially the Doctor—are prying into private information. "She's from T&T. Can you help me find my baby or not?"

"I understand your impatience with our questions." Dr. Splat holds up both empty hands. "But please answer one more. Are you the baby's mother?"

"I am not, but she was left in my care, and I must find her." I trot aside, meaning to go around the two busybodies and approach the tower.

Dr. Splat turns to the boxy carriage. "Nigel, send out the hawk. Have it look for any shadowy figures around the tower, under the dome."

A metal bird flies out of the carriage and speeds away.

"What is that?" I stop in my tracks.

Kevin nods. "It's a lot faster way to search the grounds for your shadow baby than you can do on foot. Excuse me—on hoof." He grins at his corrected statement as though it were a joke. His grin fades as he realizes I'm not finding it funny. "It's a drone. Shaped like a hawk. It's hooked up to Nigel, the AI in our van. It will zip around the tower in about two minutes and let us know if Spooky is anywhere in sight. Give it a moment."

I want to relax, but I can't. Do I trust that this hawk will make a thorough search, or that it will recognize Spooky if it does spot her? But their drone moves much faster than I can. There's a lot of territory to cover under the dome, it being twice as wide across as it is tall.

If I'm to wait, I need to make some use of the time. It's my turn to pry. I direct my question at the younger man. "Tell me about the world you're from, Kevin. Where is Destin?"

His smile is drenched in smug knowledge. "You're standing on it. This world is Destin."

"Oh. I thought I was still on Earth. How did I get here?" But I already know the answer. "The storm."

"You were *time-wrecked*." Dr. Splat says it more to himself than to me, but then gives me his attention. "It's like being shipwrecked and washing up on shore. But in your case you don't have a ship, and instead of washing up on shore, you washed up on this planet. There's a good chance if your Spooky was caught in the same storm, then she ended up here on Destin, too."

I sigh with relief. "That's the best news I've heard yet." The good doctor is opening up to me, a sign he trusts me. Maybe I can trust him after all. I'll give the drone another minute to report. In the meantime, what else can I find out? "Is Destin a role-playing game world too, like my T&T one?"

Dr. Splat frowns. "Destin is a reflection of Earth, but an imperfect, incomplete one. The surface is mostly desert, with a few key cities and landmarks replicated. Like the tower here."

My gaze climbs the structure. I do my best to ignore the Behemoth army swarming overhead. The dread in my stomach has eased some, but if I drop my emotional guard, I know I'll be sick. "What is this tower a reflection of?"

"On both Destin and Earth, this is the site of the Fanciful Pegasus facilities." Dr. Splat points at a stone engraving attached high to the face of the building. It's the semblance of a horse head and a pair of wings, beneath which is a clock face, its hands on the twelve and the three. Three o'clock.

The doctor continues. "This tower isn't constructed exactly like the building on Earth, but they both serve the same functions. Both have access to Khertaan. The rooms housing the contestants coexist on both worlds, which is why the Behemoths attack the place. They want the contestants dead before their avatars reach level thirty in Khertaan. Whether they kill them here or kill them on Earth hardly matters. Killing them in either place will put an end to their avatars in Khertaan."

I can't leave that thread of information hanging. "What happens when the avatars reach level thirty?"

Kevin smiles and points straight up. "At level thirty, the avatars become like you and me… able to fight those things."

"I'm only level ten." I blurt it out, unable to stop myself. "Why do *they* need to be level thirty?" Neither Kevin nor the doctor answer, so I push. "Well?"

A haunted look fills Dr. Splat's eyes. "It's best you don't know."

"Let me decide that."

"Once I tell you, you can't un-know it."

"*Tell me.*"

"Very well." Dr. Splat closes his eyes. "The Khertaan avatars aren't only needed to fight the invaders currently attacking the timelines. The likes of you and Kevin can fight the Behemoths, the Orc Wizards, and the Mad Cow Ballistas. Seth also has a Planet Buster, a space ship capable of destroying entire planets, as the name suggests. The likes of you and Kevin would be hard pressed to destroy a Planet Buster, but it is possible. It will be easier for the level thirty Khertaan avatars. But that still isn't the big reason why we need them.

"There's another generation of inter-dimensional invaders coming, Seth's Elite… the *Dread Naughts*. His Elite is the ace up Seth's sleeve. No one in the multiverse is currently equipped to combat them. As soon as Seth's avatar in Khertaan reaches level thirty, he'll have the ability to open the portal to their universe. If that happens, and the Khertaan avatars aren't ready, everything as we know it will cease to exist. The Dread Naughts are automatons of destruction. They can't be reasoned with. They don't take direction. Seth himself will be powerless to control them. In the end, the Dread Naughts will even destroy each other. It is said the one who releases the Dread Naughts will be spared, but Seth the Destroyer is sworn to take his own life after all else is vanquished.

"So, you see… we need the Khertaan avatars to reach level thirty as soon as possible. Otherwise, all matter across the multiverse will be reduced to formless energy."

Dr. Splat meets my gaze, and I can see he speaks the truth as he understands it. I turn to Kevin, and the darkness in his eyes tells me he believes what Dr. Splat has said. Both of them have all but accepted the demise of… *everything*.

I'm so small. So insignificant. Finding Spooky hardly matters. She and I will be dead along with everyone else once the Dread Naughts are freed. "Can Seth be stopped from reaching level thirty?"

Kevin wags his head. "I tried. I entered Khertaan, but I couldn't find him. There's someone in there—Megan Wright—who I thought could help me, but we didn't get far. Nigel is monitoring her progress, and when she gets close to where we think Seth is, I plan to go back in again."

There's too much information packed in what Kevin just said to know what's most important. "*You* went into Khertaan?"

"Yeah… well… sort of." He nods at the boxy carriage, what he referred to as a *van*. "Nigel can hook me in." His eyes spark with insight. "*You* could go in, too. If you want. We have plenty of room in the van. Nigel could hook you right up. If you're interested in helping me stop Seth. The more help, the better."

Adventure is what I'm built for. "Of course, I'm interested. But I need to know Spooky is safe. I need to find her first."

The metal hawk returns to the van.

Dr. Splat shakes his head. "I'm sorry. Nigel says the drone has searched everywhere under the dome outside the tower. The only thing it noticed that doesn't belong here is *you*. If Spooky is under the dome, she's inside the tower, and *that* is not likely."

"Unless she teleported in there." After all, teleportation is how I came to be under the dome.

"Perhaps." Dr. Splat shrugs.

"You don't think she did."

He waves at the structure. "You can try teleporting inside."

"I can't. I'd need my friend Emma to help me with that."

Kevin chuckles. "How did you expect to get out of here if you did find your shadow baby?"

"Emma will come for us."

"And when will that be?"

"Less than six hours now."

Kevin beckons. "Come on. Let Nigel get you outfitted. Then I'll go with you to look for Spooky inside the tower. When Spooky is safe and Emma arrives, you can go into Khertaan with me. It's doubtful Seth will reach level thirty before then. He's not likely ahead of the PC avatars, and the highest level any of them has attained so far is twenty-eight. Going from level twenty-eight to level thirty will take more XP than it took them to get to level twenty-eight from level one."

"But they're earning XP at a greater rate now." Dr. Splat's voice quavers. "You've got to be ready to go back in at a moment's notice, Kev." His gaze shifts to me. "But we can still have Nigel outfit you, Fauna. We can get you into the tower. But Kevin needs to stay out here, I'm afraid."

Kevin winces. "Sorry, Fauna. But come on. Let Nigel outfit you."

The van contains two seats up front and two sets of bunk beds in the back. Several devices of strange make, constructed of metal and covered in blinking lights, decorate the heads of the bunk beds from floor to ceiling. Between the driver's seat and the head of one set of bunk beds, the drone sits on a metal shelf below a tinted window.

"Have a lie down up there." Dr. Splat points at the upper bunk bed booth behind the driver's seat.

I climb a ladder at the head of the bed and roll onto the mattress. A metal box attached to the ceiling hangs above me, with small doors that open downward. I suspect the box contains the equipment necessary to outfit me.

"Lie on your back, close your eyes, and relax."

Despite the sinking feeling of vulnerability, I follow the doctor's orders.

"Fauna, your forehead will feel cold. You may also feel some pinching and pressure. That's all expected. It's best if you don't open your eyes during the procedure. Nigel, please outfit our friend Fauna here with all communications modules and the Khertaan adventuring module."

"Procedure commencing." The new voice sounds high pitched and doesn't put emphasis on syllables the way I would.

A squeaking—like hinges in need of oiling—tells me the doors to the overhead box have opened.

A chill spreads from between my shut eyes up the center of my forehead, and from there outward to my temples. There's some pinching and some pressure as I was warned, but nothing really painful. I keep my eyes closed, imagining needles and blades lowering from the overhead box, poised over my face. There's a bit heavier pressure across the whole of my forehead and then it eases as does the cold.

"First phase complete. Second phase ready to proceed."

"You can open your eyes now, Fauna. Remain on the bed and don't move."

That didn't take long and was far less terrifying than I'd imagined. But, what's this about a second phase? I open my eyes and lie still, as Dr. Splat directed.

A metal arm extends from the open metal box above me. Metal fingers hold a tiny glass bulb. "Second phase commencing." A thin red beam emits from the glass bulb, striking my right eye before I can blink. The burst doesn't even last a second, and the arm retracts into the metal box. "Process complete."

I don't understand what just happened to me, but I'm relieved it's over.

"Come on down from the bed, now, Fauna." Dr. Splat offers a helping hand as I make my way down the ladder. I don't need his help, but I take it anyway so as not to be rude.

Another metal arm extends upward from below the shelf holding the drone, a mirror grasped in its metal fingers. I look into the mirror. I'm the epitome of fatigue and worry. My sudden smile brightens my visage and my mood.

If the procedure changed my appearance in the slightest, I wouldn't know it, this being the first time I've ever seen my own face. The procedure left no visible scars or punctures. Whatever has been done to me, it's not obvious. I turn my smile on Dr. Splat. "What now, doc? How do I get inside the tower?"

"Come with me." Kevin stands outside the van's open door, holding out his hand to help me disembark.

These fellows enjoy taking my hand. Do they really think me that dainty? Perhaps it's my natural charm, my Charisma of 19—it's high for a beginning T&T character, and since most boosts in attributes don't typically go to Charisma, 19 is probably fairly decent for an experienced T&T character too. Still, as a Rogue, I should probably think about raising it at some point.

I take Kevin's offered assistance. "Thanks. Lead the way, please." The words are but thoughts, but... they're something more, too.

Kevin hadn't opened his mouth when he offered me his hand. I'd heard his voice in my head and had responded in kind without thinking about it. "So, we're communicating via telepathy?"

"Yep. When you're in the tower, we can stay in contact. If we both allow it, we can see through each other's eyes or hear through each other's ears. The senses of touch, taste, and smell can also be shared if desired."

"That... might prove useful."

"If you'll allow me to see through your eyes, I'll direct you to the tower entrance while I stay with Dr. Splat."

"Sure." I approach the base of the tower. Kevin directs me to veer to the right, and I arrive at a closed door. On the wall next to the door is a small glass lens. Kevin directs me to put my eye close to it and look at it. When I do, red light shoots from it into my eye, and immediately the door slides open with a *swoosh*.

"If you come to any other doors that don't readily open for you," Kevin says, "look for the retinal scan device, like the one you just used. When you look into it, the System will recognize your authority to access the room. You're in the System as having full access throughout the building."

"That's good. Thanks." I enter the darkness beyond the doorway. Overhead lights bloom to life. Kevin tells me they're motion sensitive. The door slides closed behind me.

With Kevin's guidance, I make a systematic sweep of the first floor. None of the rooms are locked or occupied or contain much more than tables and chairs. All the areas are dark before I enter, but overhead lights come on automatically upon my arrival.

Kevin bids me to wait on searching behind three of the doors until last. Two of those doors have panels above them, labeled with the letter *B* and the numbers one to thirty. The left one opens to my retinal scan. There's but a six-foot square closet behind the door. I don't step inside.

There's no retinal scan device to open the right door. Kevin tells me it also conceals a closet similar to the first one, and it's probably safe to ignore it. The closets are called *elevators*, he says. I don't take the time to inquire about their purpose. I can't imagine Spooky would be hiding in one of them. They're too confining for her tastes. Not that I really know her tastes. She is a newborn, after all. But I just don't see her staying put in such a small space.

Behind the final door are stairs leading up and down. Kevin says there's only a basement below the first floor. I descend the stairs to check it out first. The floor is completely dark. Motion sensors—distributed along hallways and stationed in each room—trigger the overhead lights to come on as I approach.

A hallway twenty feet wide runs the length of the basement, with stacks of shelves forming aisles perpendicular to the main hallway. Boxes of supplies, replacement parts, and other equipment rest on the shelves, packed to the ceiling. A wheeled conveyance which Kevin refers to as a forklift sits at the far end of the main hallway, next to a large door. Nothing here looks recently disturbed. I open the door. Beyond it, a ramp leads outside. When I step away, the door slides closed.

Two other doors in the basement lead into elevator rooms, according to Kevin. He says there's little purpose in checking them, but I insist. Upon my performing a retinal scan, the rightmost elevator door slides open, revealing another closet room, as empty as the one on the first floor.

"Might as well go on in," Kevin suggests.

I enter. The door slides shut behind me. Panicked at the thought of being trapped, I sigh in relief as I spot a retinal scan device inside the elevator. I use it and the door slides open again. I rush out.

"Don't be scared," Kevin says. "Go back in. I'll teach you what elevators are for."

Back in the elevator, I remain calm as the door slides shut. I refrain from using the retinal scanner to open the door again. An array of numbered buttons, along with one button labeled *B*, are situated to the right of the door. "Press the button labeled *1*," Kevin directs me.

I do so.

Above the door is a glass panel about six inches square, displaying a red *B*.

The floor and walls of the elevator tremble. My bones vibrate. I'm overcome with a sense of motion, like my stomach wants to be where my heart is. The red *B* over the door is replaced by a red *1*. The trembling stops and the door slides open.

I'd expected to see the basement outside the elevator, but instead I'm back on the first floor. This is amazing. The elevator has powerful transportation magic.

I stay inside the elevator. After the door closes, Kevin directs me to press the button labeled *B*. There's trembling and motion again. The display above the door shows a *B*. I'm not surprised when the elevator doors open to the basement.

It's obvious to me that the elevator will take me to the second floor if I press the 2 button, and I do so without any prompting from Kevin. The trembling and sense of moving lasts twice as long this time. The readout above the door goes from *B* to *1* to *2*. The elevator door slides open and I step into a busy hallway.

People are attired in colorful dresses, black pants and shoes, white tunics and blouses—clothing I'd find too restrictive for adventuring. None of them pay me any mind, sparing me not even a glance as I emerge from the elevator. I'm reminded of ants at work. Each knows its role and performs its duty with single-mindedness. None of them seem concerned about Arachnid Behemoths attacking the protective dome over their heads. Perhaps they aren't even aware of the giant spider army. Have they been informed about the danger they're in?

"They're *androids*," Kevin says in my head. I don't know what that means. Kevin tries to explain it. I'm still not sure I understand, but they evidently aren't alive and so aren't concerned about death from pointed metallic spider legs piercing their chests.

They look alive enough to me. "Something you should know," I say to a passing android. "Arachnid Behemoths are attacking this tower."

He doesn't break stride. "Affirmative." I get the same response from two other androids I try to warn. I guess Kevin is right. These androids don't care about a threat to their continued existence. What must life be like for those who have no compulsion to survive? They exist for as long as they do, and then they are gone, just like any of us, but without the worry factor.

Many of the rooms on the second floor contain desks at which the androids sit, tapping their fingers atop devices located on the desks. Images and text magically appear on glass panes arranged before them.

"Those devices on the desks are called *computers*," Kevin says.

It's difficult looking for Spooky in these rooms, with shadows filling the spaces under the desks. I could easily spend an hour on the second floor alone. It will likely take much longer than six hours to search the entire tower interior. But overall there's too much light in this place for Spooky to feel comfortable here. I don't believe she'd confine herself to hiding under a desk or in a shady nook. She has too much energy to stay still.

As viewed from the city, the dark mood of the tower had given me the sense Spooky might be attracted to it, but being inside has erased that feeling. If she came to the tower, I doubt she stayed.

But I'll do a cursory search of each floor. Until something changes—such as Emma arriving or Kevin saying he's entering Khertaan—what better use of my time is there than to carry on my search? I can't go back to the city to rejoin Emma. I hope she's all right.

The third through eighth floors are as well lit and filled with androids, desks, and computers as the second floor. I reach the landing for the ninth floor, but the elevator door doesn't open when the closet stops trembling. I don't panic.

"Do another retinal scan," Kevin instructs. I comply, and the door opens.

No androids traverse the hallway outside the elevator. A name plate on the first door reads, *Khaled Touma*. I don't see a retinal scanner. There's a door handle, but turning it doesn't open the door. "I thought you said I had full access to the building, Kevin."

"You do, except for the individual contestant rooms. They're all sealed for the safety of the contestants. There's no way your shadow baby could be inside one of those rooms."

"Um... I think she can teleport. I think that's what she did when she initially left us, because she simply vanished. Are the rooms dark inside? Do they have motion sensors?"

"On the other side of that door is a short, lit hallway. It leads to another door beyond which is the contestant's bedroom. The lights in the bedroom are controlled by motion sensors. If Spooky went inside one of those bedrooms, the lights would come on. She'd have to stay still for several minutes to have the lights go off and stay off. Is she the patient type?"

"No. But I'd like to go inside one just to see the situation for myself. Can you let me in?"

Kevin doesn't reply at first. He's probably conferring with Dr. Splat. After a minute, he comes back to me. "Okay, you can go in one of them. The one you're currently at, the one for Khaled Touma, is fine."

A click sounds, and the door unlatches. I swing it open and enter a hallway uniformly lit by an unidentifiable light source.

Photos of a man in his late twenties decorate the walls. His trimmed black hair accents his olive skin. A spark of joy highlights his brown eyes. He's someone who loves his life and the people he's with. Or maybe it's all an act. In one candid shot, I sense the self-doubt in his gaze, failing to strike a desired pose. If I could give him a hug, I would.

At the far end of the hallway of photos stands a door to my left. Kevin remotely opens it for me. I enter as quietly as my goat hooves clopping on the wooden floor allows. Light filters through a curtained window near the ceiling as I enter. Oh, with this kind of light, there are plenty of shadows here.

The main attraction in this room is the bed to my right, against the far wall, located beneath the window. On the bed lies the man from the photos in the hallway. He doesn't stir from his sleep. "You said he's a contestant?"

"He is. In Khertaan, he's known as TehnKhar, an Elitist Priest of War and a Guide. He's a member of party ZAvengers."

"What happens if I wake him?" I'm so tempted.

"*Don't.* That's another reason the contestant rooms are sealed. If one of them is awakened by external means, it could do permanent damage to their brains."

"Even with the light coming through the window, there's enough shadows in this place, Spooky could be hiding here. But the lights were off when I entered. If she were in here, I wouldn't expect her to be still, unless she fell asleep. I don't see her on the bed. But I think I need to check all the contestant rooms. I'll be careful not to wake any of them. I can't say the same thing for Spooky. If she has gone into one of their rooms, she might wake them. For their sakes, I need to check them all."

"That could take a while."

"I've still got time before Emma arrives."

Kevin is silent while he confers again with Dr. Splat. "Okay. You can go into each room. If the light isn't on in the room when you first enter, check the bed to see if Spooky is there. If she's not, then you have to leave immediately."

"And if the light is on in the room when I first enter?"

"That depends on why the light is on. It might be because Spooky is in the room, or it might be because the contestant is currently awake. If the contestant is awake, that could be a problem. But we'll deal with that situation if and when it arises."

"Okay, I agree to your terms." I back out of Khaled Touma's room and quietly close the door. "How many more contestant rooms are there?"

"There are twenty contestant rooms on each floor, for ten floors. That's two hundred contestant rooms."

"Then I better get moving."

ଽଓଷଊଋଌଵଽଓଷ

So many people of diverse backgrounds answered the call to compete in Khertaan. The photos in the hallways outside the bedrooms reflect many facets of their lives before they arrived at the Fanciful Pegasus facilities. "What's the purpose of the photos, Kevin?"

"When they reach level thirty and awaken, the contestants run the risk of losing their identity to their avatars. The photos will remind them of who they are."

It takes a couple of minutes to check each room, and I finish the ninth floor in a little over forty minutes. I move to the tenth floor, where the process goes smoother, and I finish in just under forty minutes. Luckily, none of the contestants on either floor have been awake, and the lights in the rooms have all been off when I entered.

On the eleventh floor, one of the rooms belongs to Megan Wright. That's the person Kevin mentioned earlier. I'm extra careful as I back out of her room and close the door. "What's so special about her?"

"Her mother is from Earth and her father is from Destin. Even before she entered Khertaan, she demonstrated a capability for fighting the inter-dimensional invaders. Inside Khertaan, she's demonstrated an ability to put two sides of her personality to work simultaneously, not only her subconsciousness, which all the contestants are doing, but her conscious mind as well. And we've seen proof she can mentor others to do the same, as she's done for her friend Debra Jones."

I continue checking the contestant bedrooms, finishing floor eleven and then twelve through fourteen, without finding either Spooky or any awake contestants.

One of the rooms on floor fifteen houses a contestant named *Processor 1*. "What kind of name is that?"

"It's an android," Kevin informs me. "We've not given it an official name yet. Its avatar in Khertaan goes by the name FepXveq, short for *Front End Processor X Variation in Estimated Quantities*. We're experimenting to see what happens when a machine brain reaches level thirty."

"I didn't understand half of what you just said, but that's all right."

On floor sixteen, I come to the bedroom of contestant Hera Ford. The light is already on when I enter.

There are two bodies lying on the bed, but neither of them is Spooky. Two women face each other in their sleep, not touching. "What is this about, Kevin?"

"The redhead is Hera Ford. I have no idea who the blond is. She shouldn't be there. But don't wake her. It wouldn't be good for her. I'll see if I can find out anything about her in the System. Even unregistered, if she's sleeping in a contestant's bedroom, she'll have a PC avatar. I believe there were alerts about illegal avatars in the game. She could be one of them…. Hold on a second… Dr. Splat is talking to someone… outside the van. I need to see what's up."

CHAPTER FORTY-FOUR

Megan: Obsidian Guards

Everyone else hurries out of the cave while Mithabel, Debra Jones, Kaleisha, and I hang back in the shadows. When all eyes are occupied elsewhere, we exit the cavern too, Debra Jones flying behind Kaleisha. I'm curled up in my feline form in Kaleisha's arms, but my awareness is in Debra's head, so I'm seeing everything through her eyes. She's still making use of my Hide and Flight Speed skills to keep her existence secret. How much longer can we keep this up? If someone does notice her, what will we say?

The whole idea about keeping both her and me secret from the other parties is to avoid explanations about secondary avatars. Fortunately, I'm able to take a form of a feline, and no one has questioned my presence, especially since I'm lying unconscious in Kaleisha's arms. But we have no way to give Debra an alternate physical appearance. The next best thing is for her not to have any physical appearance at all. But eventually someone will pierce the veil of the Hide skill she's borrowing from me and see her. And when they see her, they'll wonder why they're seeing double, because—except for their attire—Debra and Dylan look exactly the same.

"I'm thinking Dylan and I should travel apart from each other." It's like Debra is speaking in my head, but I'm actually in hers, so it's a matter of perspective. "You and I could go adventuring separately from the others. If someone happens to see us, they'll think they're seeing Mithabel and Dylan. What do you think, Megan?"

"I'm all for it. Let me ping Mithabel about it." I initiate a private chat channel with Mithabel, which hasn't always worked for us, but our foray into the pocket dimension seems to have removed whatever was interfering with our communications. I tell her our idea, and she's fine with it. We don't bother the others in party MAD about it.

In a shady alleyway, I transfer my awareness back to my own body. My Siamese Cat form stretches and yawns in Kaleisha's arms. The Jamaican AI drops me from four feet up, and I instinctively turn in the air so my paws land under me. I rub against Kaleisha's leg. "Thanks for the ride, gorgeous."

"Anytime, chief."

Mithabel and Kaleisha head over to where Dylan and Amarynth are talking with Charli and others.

I look up at Debra, who no longer has my Hide and Flight Speed skills, and thus is no longer hidden or flying. But she has all of Dylan's abilities, which are stacked heavily towards appearance and presence. She's more gorgeous than ever. I meow at her, and she picks me up. I like being carried. She pets my head, and my purring makes me vibrate against her breasts.

She kisses the top of my head. "My sweet little pussy."

"We should form our own party." I've not thought of a name for it yet, but I like the idea of just me and Debra in a party of our own.

"I like that." Debra leans against the alley wall. "We could call ourselves *Beauty and the Beast*." She grins.

"A little on the long side. How about *Beast and Beauty*?"

Debra wrinkles her nose. "Still a bit long, isn't it? How about *Beastly Beauties*?"

"But you're not beastly."

"Oh, I can be, darling."

I chuckle evilly at that, a strange sound to come from a Siamese Cat. "Well, it's settled then. You want to create the party or shall I?"

She shrugs. "I'm not sure how to do it."

"I'm not sure, either. Hey, Kaleisha, can you hear me?" Mithabel's support AI has always been my de facto support AI as well, when I've been able to communicate with her, which has typically always been only possible when I'm able to communicate with Mithabel.

"Yes, I hear you, Megan. What do you need, chief?"

I guess I wasn't totally expecting Kaleisha to appear before me when talking to me, though I'm disappointed she doesn't. "Debra and I want to be in a party named Beastly Beauties. Can you do that for us?"

"The party name can't contain spaces. Is that okay?"

"Fine, no spaces."

"Accessing the System…. It's done. Party BeastlyBeauties has been created, containing you and Charli."

Her statement takes me aback. "Um… why did you add Charli?"

"I didn't. She was automatically added. I don't know why. You could remove her if you want, but I believe if you keep her there, then your party will earn any XP she does, which means any XP earned by party MAD will also be earned by BeastlyBeauties. And vice versa. I see no downside in retaining her, other than she'll be privy to everything said on your party chat channel. If you don't want her to hear what you have to say to each other, there's always private chat, which is what you're doing now anyway."

"Okay, leave her in… for now. Would you please invite Debra to the party?"

"Done… and accepted."

So, Debra and I have our party of two plus one. I don't use party chat, but continue speaking to Debra over the private chat channel we already have set up. "So, where to first?"

She raises her hands, palms up. "Let's check out one of these desolate-looking buildings."

Desolate, indeed. Overgrown with ivy, the building we've chosen is constructed of cracked blocks of gray stone, with weeds growing from the cracks. Suspended from a pole over the entrance is a weathered wooden plaque reading *Fisher's Apothecary*. Hmm. The wooden door is of sturdy make, but the hinges squeal in protest as Debra pushes it open. Dust billows in a cloud as she steps inside. The only light in the place is what little sunlight falls through the open doorway.

My Dark Sight trait kicks in once Debra takes another couple steps into the place. I have a better view from the comfort of her arms than if I were walking on the floor, though of course I could fly if I so desired. I don't desire it at the moment. Riding in her arms is exactly where I want to be.

The interior walls are bare stone, with ancient dirt packed in the cracks. No vegetation grows in here. The room we've entered is ten feet wide by twenty feet deep, with a dusty counter dividing the room into two ten by ten halves. A couple of broken wooden tables lie in pieces to either side of the entrance. Stone shelves loaded with broken vials line the walls behind the counter. A waist-high wooden door hanging only on its top hinge allows access through the counter to the area behind it.

"Let's go through," I suggest to Debra.

"One second." She closes the door behind us and sets me down. Then she pulls an unlit Torch from inventory. "I've been dying to try a spell." She holds the Torch at arm's length and says, "Goddess Scintilla, please bless this Torch to light our way."

"It amuses me to do so," says a disembodied female voice. No flames lick the Torch, but the end of it glows, shedding light enough for us to see the full length of the room.

317

"That's better." Debra doesn't pick me back up. Extending the magical Torch before her, she strides over to the counter and its ruined door. "Come on, little pussy. Let's do some adventuring."

I scoff at the idea of walking behind her, and activate my Flight Speed skill. I'm sure we make a striking pair—a divinely beautiful, barefoot Polynesian Priestess dressed in black velvet slacks and long-sleeved satin top, with a Siamese Cat flying alongside her head.

Shards of broken glass and chunks of clay fill the shelves, covered in dust and cobwebs. In the center of the back wall hangs a faded red curtain. Behind the curtain lies an open doorway, beyond which is an open area stretching beyond the extent of Debra's Torch. In the near distance, wooden crates lie in broken heaps, once upon a time containing vials, some of glass and some of clay, all now broken. The crates appear to have been smashed by something with tremendous force capable of destroying foot-high crates stacked three deep in a single blow.

With broken glass lying about, I don't think going barefoot is a good idea for Debra. "Do you want some shoes?" I produce a pair of high-heeled platform slippers, holding one each with my front paws.

Debra takes them and looks them over. "As long as I don't need to run in them." She slips them on, which instantly adds three inches to her already tall frame, making her appear to be six feet tall. "Thank you."

Passing through the doorway, we see that the storage area extends ten feet to either side of us. The far wall is just over twenty feet away, with a wooden door marking the exit. We spend ten minutes searching for something useful among the ruined crates, finding nothing of interest.

"I still have about twenty minutes left on this Torch," Debra informs me. "What say we try another building?"

Exiting through the back door onto a paved road, we cross to another building, this one looking on the outside much like the apothecary we just left. The sign over the door identifies the place as *Ned's Emporium of Oddities and Othersuch*. The name calls to me. "I hope there's *something* not ruined in here."

We enter a foyer five feet square, with two doors of stout wood, neither of which appears aged or damaged, both standing tall enough to admit someone half again my height. The door to the left bears the label, *Oddities*. The one on the right is labeled *Othersuch*. Both doors bear a solid circle of white paint where a door knob would normally be. I'm guessing touching the white circle will open the door.

My Danger Sense fires. "Traps are present on the doors and mooks lie in wait behind each one. Give me a moment to check the doors."

Debra nods. "Hmm. I didn't know your Danger Sense worked for traps."

"Yeah, the feature kicked in when Mithabel bumped the trait to level 2." Closely scanning the surfaces of the doors in my flying cat form, I apply my level 28 Detect Anomaly skill and my level 1 Alertness trait. Each door frame sports a shallow indentation about eight feet up.

I switch from Siamese Cat to Elf. I'm dressed in my two-piece black Bikini, with nothing on my feet, but as an Anjai I have no issues with going barefoot. I'm also wearing the duplicate of Ezmerelda's Ring and the Bracelet of Action I acquired at Ye Olde Magic Shoppe as part of a trade back in Maron. Because of the quirky nature of the place we're entering, I equip the duplicate Faerie Wing—if by chance we meet the proprietor, Ned, maybe he'll appreciate its oddity. And because my Danger Sense is firing, I equip Ghost Maker, my magical Battle Axe.

"My Danger Sense says there's no Boss behind either door. The mooks behind the Oddities door deal physical damage only. Those behind the Othersuch door deal both physical and emotional damage. Let's go through the Oddities door first. You want to do that blessing thing Dylan always does at the beginning of an encounter?"

With a vigorous nod, Debra raises her hands to the sky. "I call on the power of Scintilla, Goddess of Light, to place her blessing upon us for fighting our enemies."

A disembodied voice replies. "Oh, sweet Daughter, thank you for asking my blessing. Of course I'll help you against your enemies. I suppose you'll be wanting an enchantment for your Shurikens as well as one for the Axe wielded by my other Daughter?"

I brandish Ghost Maker. "My Axe is already magical. Will another enchantment work on it?"

To my surprise, the disembodied voice answers me. "Normally it would not, but an enchantment from me will work, because both you and my Priestess are my Daughters."

I hold Ghost Maker towards Debra. "Light me up, Sister."

The Priestess of Light casts her spell on Ghost Maker and then on her own hands, to confer a magical bonus to any Shurikens she might throw. My Battle Axe and her hands glow with orange light like the Torch Debra still carries.

Kaleisha graciously calculates our total pluses for us. I've got a total of +189 damage on Ghost Maker, with +27 Critical Hit capability. The battle axe doesn't only deal physical damage, but mental, spiritual, and emotional damage, too. I've been aching to use this thing, and I may finally be getting my chance.

With her shurikens, Debra has +139 damage and +14 Critical Hit. She also has skills that allow her to shorten her combat heartbeat duration to seven seconds and make an extra Shuriken attack during that time. That's bad ass.

I'm loaded up on defenses, too. My physical armor rating is at +230, and thanks to my Natural Armor trait, my armor ratings for the mental and emotional realms are at +108, while my armor rating for the spiritual realm is +5 more due to my high average Morals attribute. Debra, on the other hand, has next to nothing in the way of armor, be it physical, mental, spiritual, or emotional.

I'm curious. "Can you enchant your clothing to act as armor, Deb?"

She shakes her head. "I wish. My Light spell only boosts offensive ratings of weapons. My other spells are for healing and exorcising undead."

"Then stay behind me and throw your Shurikens over my shoulder."

"Sounds like a plan."

"Maybe you should stand just outside while I open the door."

"That sounds like a plan, too." Debra skips outside to wait on the sidewalk. She's in a perky mood. We both like that it's just the two of us doing this together. Feeling flush from excitement, I press in the indentation on the Oddities door.

The door doesn't open, but draws a fraction of an inch into the room beyond, revealing tracks running down the length of the door frame. Within the tracks, a guillotine blade rises out of the floor, and continues rising until its top half slides out of sight into a slot in the top of the door frame. The lower half of the blade remains visible, poised within the doorway, ready to drop on anyone or anything passing beneath it. Holy crap, what a way for a business to welcome would-be patrons.

A clicking sounds. I half expect the door to open of its own accord, but it remains closed. What am I supposed to do now? Push the white circle? Right. With that blade hanging up there, ready to drop on a fool. I have no intent of being that fool.

I scrutinize the blade and don't detect any anomalies. It is what it appears to be… or a higher-level illusion than I can penetrate. I press the indentation again. The clicking sounds and the blade lowers in the track—not fast like it's trying to chop off a head, but slow enough for a sloth to get out of the way. When the full length of the blade has lowered below floor level, the door draws in a fraction of an inch, once again concealing the blade tracks.

Okay, I get it. When we first arrived, the damned blade trap wasn't set. My first press of the indentation set it, and my second press unset it again. I push the white circle, and the door slides open to the right. The blade stays put.

The room beyond is thirty feet square, lit by a dark blue ambient light. As I'd feared, the contents of the room lie in ruins. Smashed tables once displayed wares of various natures—mirrors, birdcages, basins, chalices, vases, monocles, spoons, and more, all broken or bent. The exception to the destruction are three tall, blocky, obsidian statues standing with their backs to the walls—one to my left, one straight ahead, and one to my right.

Eight feet tall, they're roughly humanoid in form but put together from oblong blocks of black stone, a massive one for the torso, with groups of smaller ones for the limbs, neck, and head. Their arms end in six-inch cubes—no fingers, just solid fists.

I'm tempted to ask Charli to use her Monster Lore to help us identify what we're up against, but toss away the idea immediately. This adventure is for me and Debra, and we'll keep it that way unless we find ourselves way in over our heads.

The statues haven't moved, but I haven't stepped through the open doorway yet, either. I'm guessing they're guardians for the shop, though in that case they've failed in their duties.

I wave Debra over. "They aren't attacking. You stay here while I go in. If the door closes, you should be fine to open it—just touch the white circle on the door. *Don't* do it if the blade rises from the floor. You good with that?"

"I am if you are."

Glowing Battle Axe at the ready, I step across the threshold.

A section of floor falls out from beneath me. Instinctively, I kick my Flight Speed skill into action, saving myself from plunging into the darkness below.

Plunging isn't the right word. The section of floor only falls a dozen inches, and slowly rises back to place. Intended to titillate, not harm, though someone could easily twist an ankle from the trap. What other examples of Ned's dark humor might I face in his establishment? I keep my Flight Speed skill going and maintain a height of three inches off the floor as I fly forward.

322

At the far end of the room to my right, a curved counter occupies one corner. "Stay put, Deb, but be ready for anything." I fly towards the counter.

Like the statues, the counter is crafted from obsidian. Curiously, there's no space for a proprietor to stand—the 'counter' is a quarter-circle solid block of black stone standing three-and-a-half feet tall. I detect an anomaly—a fine crack running a foot from the edge around the top of the block, outlining a smaller quarter-circle area. Is it a trap door? Looks like it.

"I'm going to try something, Deb, so stay alert." I lay my hand on the trap door and push down. With a creak, the stone gives beneath my hand, dropping an inch before coming to a hard stop, exposing a narrow opening running along the trap door's edge.

"Megan, behind you! The Golems!"

The sound of stone grinding on stone hits my alert ears the same time as Debra's warning. I spin around to see a six-inch cube of obsidian flying at my face. Instinctively, I Dodge....

...but fail. *Oof.* The Stone Golem's blunt hand slams into my shoulder and sends me sailing across the counter... to bash the back of my head against the wall, dropping me on my back atop the trap door. It's not a stunning blow, but the fact I didn't avoid its blow has me on edge. I don't have a Dodge skill, per se, but I shouldn't need it being a level 27 Tank with a +40 Morale modifier from my Priestess. What level is *this* thing?

It could have been a fluke. Sometimes shit happens. There's always a chance for any action to succeed, unless the probability of success is absolutely zero.

"Your HP holds at 100%, chief." Bless Kaleisha for the status report. I feel the hurt, but my immense armor rating absorbed all the damage. That's cool.

I jump to my feet, still atop the counter. Unless the Golem gets multiple attacks per combat heartbeat or has an incredibly short cool down period, it shouldn't get another go at me until I've had my turn at it. I leap off the counter, Ghost Maker raised over my head for a strike. The blade descends....

The damned Golem sidesteps my attack. It's got a Dodge skill of its own. This thing has to be close to my level—a real challenge. All right, then. I can't attempt another Dodge action until my combat heartbeat resets, and I've assumed my enemy doesn't have another attack action to use just yet, but damn if it doesn't throw punches with *both* hands, trying to fist bump itself... with my head in the middle. *Damn.* I Parry one of the hands with Ghost Maker, turning the blunt attack aside, but the other hand plows into my left temple.

Once more I go flying, slamming against the wall to my right, in front of the counter. Does this thing have any other surprises? If not, I might have some for it.

"You're still at full HP, chief."

"Guess I'm not a Tank for nothing." Also being an Anjai with Natural Armor doesn't hurt, either.

The Golem presses me, aiming a punch for my gut. No, it's a Feint, trying to draw me into wasting a defensive action. I don't fall for it, but my only defensive action remaining this combat heartbeat is a Block, which I've only seen Mithabel use in attempting to protect allies. Can it be used to protect one's self? I might find out.

Sure enough, I'm still on cool down, but the Golem comes at me with dual fists *again*, aimed at both my shoulders, going for a combo attack, trying to pin me to the wall, the nasty bastard. I try to Block, imposing the flat of my Battle Axe blade between me and the Golem's left hand.

The Block works.

The Golem's right hand slams into my left shoulder, and I imagine most PCs would be pulverized at this point, but Kaleisha informs me I've yet to take a scratch from the grueling punishment. Music to my ears.

Is this thing done yet? It's combat heartbeat is insanely short—or it has some powerful traits or high-level skills. I'm positive it's not illusionary. With all my skills, I'd have seen through an illusion—unless its *extremely* high level.

My attacker takes a step back. Is it finally waiting for a cool down timer to expire? I still have a Feint action—and what else? I haven't used my Stun, Reflect Any Attack, or Shock Wave skills yet in this combat heartbeat, or any of my Anjai skills.

I Feint an attack. Let's see if this thing has more defensive actions available to it. The Golem moves to Parry my weapon, which fails to have any effect, since I was bluffing.

I go in for a Stun.

What the hell? It's got another Parry action and easily bats Ghost Maker aside.

With my combat heartbeat about to end, it's time to sneak in one of my untested skills—one that not even Mithabel has tried yet, it's so new.

It's time for a Shock Wave.

A shell of force expands outward from me in all directions in three-dimensional space, smacking into my opponent Golem and the two others closing on me. The blast has no visible effect on the building or its ruined contents, but all three Golems stagger under the impact. My alert ears catch a muffled human cry, masculine in tone, coming from beneath the trap door. It's not clear whether it's a simple cry of pain or holds some intended meaning too muffled to be discernible.

In addition to my HP remaining at full, Kaleisha reports the Golems at 98% HP. They don't have MP, SP, or EP ratings, so this will be a purely physical battle. I figure that's all my support AI has to say, but then she adds, "Ned is at 90% HP, 96% MP, and 95% SP and EP."

I had no idea I was fighting the shopkeeper too. "*Ned* is here? As in *the proprietor, Ned*?"

"Yes, he's included in the encounter, chief."

"Holy crap."

The cool down timer for combat heartbeat number one ends— the first ten seconds of the encounter—and heartbeat number two begins—the next ten seconds. Time seems to slow during combat, probably due to the adrenaline rush. Assuming the Golem has the same default combat heartbeat I do, it's about to unleash the same kind of attacks on me as before, but now with one of its friends at its side. This encounter is putting my defensive capabilities to the test. I need to be on the alert for a cooperative combo attack from both Golems using both fists. That could hurt.

They come in first with a cooperative combo of one fist each. I easily Parry one obsidian-block hand and absorb the other's attack with my armor. My back is already to the wall, so the smack sends me nowhere. I do stumble, but use my flying ability to stay upright. Could I have withstood their cooperative combo if I hadn't Parried? It would be interesting to know.

The second Golem comes at me with a punch while the first one holds back. I don't take the bait to waste a defensive action, and as I take the blow to the chin, I release my Shock Wave attack.

The Golems stagger back. I expect but don't hear another muffled male human cry of pain. Kaleisha informs me the Obsidian Guards, as they're technically called, are at 97% HP, while Ned is at 81% HP and around 90% on his metaphysical health ratings. He's gonna die before his Guards do, at this rate.

"Oh, one more thing, chief, Ned is now Stunned."

Oh, wow. In addition to damaging opponents, the Shock Wave has a chance of stunning them, too. Slick.

The Golems rebound, both of them swinging again for another attempted cooperative combo, still only one fist each. I Block one of them and take the other like before.

I suspect a two-pronged, double-fisted cooperative combo is coming, and if it lands, I doubt it will be pretty. I've already had a Dodge attempt fail, so my best bet from the defensive actions remaining to me might be the Feint or Reflect Any Attack.

I go for the Feint, trying to draw the next attack where they think I'm moving rather than where I actually go. They prepare for a cooperative combo—no—they're Feinting also, and I've seen through it. Have they seen through mine?

I lean to one side, chopping at a Golem leg with Ghost Maker. Their punches go wild above me as my blade bites a stone leg.

"Ghost Maker delivered a critical hit, chief, bringing the HP of the first Obsidian Guard to 24%."

Now that's more like it. If my armor can keep absorbing everything they can dish out and I can land a few more hits with Ghost Maker, I can bring these damned Golems down.

My two opponents jump back, moving rather nimbly for stone statues. As I right myself, the third Golem comes at me, driving with both fists. It doesn't appear to be Feinting, and I attempt to Dodge. It works this time. Okay, then. There's always a chance.

The first two Golems hold back while the third one pounds away. Maybe the two have depleted their actions for this combat heartbeat? I've nearly spent all mine, with only the Reflect Any Attack remaining. The third Golem throws a punch right to my face, and I simply take it. To the casual observer, I'm taking a beating, and it has been painful, but nothing my attackers have done so far has caused me the slightest dip in HP. I don't even have a bloody lip to show for it.

I laugh.

"By the Goddess of Light," Debra says from the foyer, still hanging outside the room, "how have you not taken a scratch yet, Tank?"

I laugh again. "You just answered your own question, Priestess. I'm a bad ass Tank, built to take punishment. It helps to have the blessing and enchantments of the Goddess, too. And being an Anjai. And having Natural Armor."

"I'd be paste by now."

"That's why you're not coming in here, darling."

Though Debra isn't in the room, she's playing a part in the encounter. Without her Morale skill and her Light enchantment on Ghost Maker, defeating the Golems would be a much more difficult prospect.

The second combat heartbeat ends without further offensive actions, and the third one begins. With me being against the wall and next to the counter, it's impossible for all three of the Golems to combo me, for which I'm grateful. But two of them are at me, with the more injured one hanging back. No worries, buddy, Ghost Maker can wait for you.

The front two each throw a single punch at me, a cooperative combo, but I'm feeling full of myself, and don't try to avoid their attack. Let's see what they've got.

Their blunt fists connect to either side of my head, like they're trying to smash out my brains. Sure, I feel it, but Kaleisha says I'm still at full HP.

Laughter rolls out of me.

The two of them come at me again, each drawing back both fists. It's time to see what my Reflect Any Attack skill can do. I activate it.

Nothing. The damned Obsidian Guards faked me out with Feints, and I completely fell for it. Now they're coming at me with the real deal, four fists headed for my ribcage.

In a knee-jerk reaction, I reset my combat heartbeat in an instant with my Bracelet of Action, and activate my Reflect Any Attack action again, this time raising Ghost Maker to assist, as though using it to Block.

Both fists of one Obsidian Guard bounce off Ghost Maker. The Golem is jarred and stumbles backward. The blunt fists of the other Golem connect with my torso, knocking the wind from me. I stopped one attacker but not the other. I'd hoped the skill would reflect the combo attack at both attackers, but no such luck.

If I've learned anything about combat in Khertaan, it's that similar actions don't always have similar outcomes from one attempt to the next. The rules are unknown, after all, learned only piecemeal from our support AIs or through experimentation.

Kaleisha reports no damage was sustained by any combatant just now on either side. The reflected damage didn't harm the Obsidian Guard. Feels like a waste to have used the Bracelet of Action, but I learned something. I need to use a weapon or maybe a shield when reflecting an attack. I'm still uncertain about my ability to reflect a combo attack on all those participating in the combo. If I get another chance to try it, I'll go for it.

One of the two Golems jumps back, and the wounded one charges in to take its place, Feinting with a single punch—an action I ignore. Then it throws two fists, and its buddy throws two fists, too, trying yet again for a cooperative combo. I Parry one fist with ease, but the other three strike flesh.

Oof, *that* hurt... a little. I'm bruised. My ears ring. Kaleisha informs me my HP is at 93%. I'd be hurting a good deal more if I hadn't Parried one of those fists. I'm not feeling quite so full of myself anymore. I'm not invincible here. If these stone dudes manage to land a cooperative combo on me with four or more fists, that could have a drastic bad effect on my HP.

Trying to land an attack with Ghost Maker is tricky at best, since these Guards appear to have two Parries per heartbeat. How did they get that ability? I want it, too.

We wait each other out until the end of their combat heartbeat. Because I used the Bracelet of Action earlier, my current heartbeat is still going.

"Megan." It's Mithabel on private chat. "Do you need help?"

Kaleisha pipes in. "Your HP has been restored to full, chief. Dylan healed Mithabel."

That's right, Mithabel and I share a single HP pool. When either of us takes damage, so does the other. Healing either of us heals the other. "Thank Dylan for me, please. If she can keep us healed to full HP, that's all the help I need. I got this."

"Anything able to hurt you must be pretty powerful. Be smart. If you need help, say something before you're too far in."

"You got it, Mithabel."

I'm prepared for the Obsidian Guards to try another combo or Feint. They go for the Feint, but I don't fall for it. Rather, I take the opportunity to hack at the wounded Guard with Ghost Maker. The Guard is occupied with its Feint and has no chance to Parry, Dodge, or Block. The blade digs deep, slicing the leg free of the bulky body. The Golem wobbles on one leg and then topples, evaporating into a whirlwind of black dust before it can strike the floor. *Whoo hoo!* One down, two to go. "Thank you both for your help, Priestess and Goddess."

In the last second of my fourth combat heartbeat, the two remaining Golems go for a double-two-fisted combo. I easily Block one of their four fists. But the other three make their marks on my body, dropping my HP to 94%.

A moment later, Kaleisha says I'm back to full HP. Dylan healed Mithabel, and thus me. I tell Kaleisha to once again convey my thanks to Dylan. I'd be at 87% HP now if not for her.

My cool down timer expires, freeing up my actions and starting my combat heartbeat anew. Based on how they've acted so far, my foes each have at least one more punch they can throw before they're reduced to waiting out their cool down timers. For each Guard, when it first entered the combat, it had thrown five fist attacks, but after its first round that count had fallen to three. They've each thrown two fists during this round, which I hope means they each have only one fist attack left until their next combat heartbeat. If one of them goes for a punch, I'll take its attack and deal one of my own.

But instead of a punch, one of the Golems decides to Feint—which I read correctly—while the other Golem holds back. Too bad for the Feinting Golem. Ghost Maker bites into its midriff, and obsidian chips go flying.

"You've dropped your target to 25% HP, chief."

I'm so happy to have Ghost Maker.

Both Golems throw two fists at me. I'm free to use my Reflect Any Attack skill again, and I'm still hoping to see it do something awesome, so I activate it, swinging Ghost Maker to intercept the blows leveled at me.

My blade repels all four fists of my attackers. Energy waves blow back in their faces. The Guard I'd struck in the midriff a moment earlier turns to black dust and swirls away in a dark cloud. The other Guard staggers back, but its obsidian face is as blank as ever, showing no pain or emotion. Its mission is to fight until all trespassers are dealt with—or to die trying. Its fate is all but decided, unless it has some other trick up its sleeve. Kaleisha tells me its HP stands at 43%. One good hit with Ghost Maker, and this thing is toast.

We wait out the rest of its combat heartbeat. It has used up its offensive actions and needs to wait on the cool down. I've still got a Shock Wave I can do, but the skill doesn't affect the Golem much. Every time I use it, I do more to the hidden Ned, and I'd rather question him than kill him. Once this last Guard is defeated, I'll ask for Ned's surrender, and go from there.

My combat mind isn't as taxed now that I'm only facing one opponent. We trade some unproductive attacks and parries. But it's only a matter of time….

I land a glowing Battle Axe blade attack. End of Obsidian Guard number three. I'm still full on HP and hardly winded. Goddess, do I feel good.

CHAPTER FORTY-FIVE

Charli: Forgiveness

Amarynth holds me at arm's length. "Look at you. Little Charli is all grown up." Her gaze shifts to Britta, and her eyebrows raise. "And who might this be?"

"I's Britta." My naked daughter puts a finger to her lips and acts coy.

Despite the grammar mistake, my little girl just spoke *a complete sentence.*

"Long story, that." I implore the Viking Archer with my eyes. "You wouldn't happen to have some spare clothing in inventory, would you?"

Amarynth shakes her head. "But one of the others might. I brought a large entourage." Her mouth drops open and she equips her crossbow.

I step in front of her weapon before she can fire. "Please don't shoot the friendly spider, Milady." I say it over local chat, so everyone approaching can hear. "She's on our side. Her name is Spyder, and she's a member of party TimeTrippers. I'll be very unhappy if you kill her, not to mention that if she were killed, she'd explode and kill everyone else in the area, too. Please put away your crossbow."

The Viking Archer keeps her eyes trained on the Behemoth, but stashes her weapon. "Yes, I've seen them explode."

Doing her best to stay in the shadows, Spyder doesn't so much as twitch a leg.

Everyone else is on edge as they approach, but I don't need to say anything more—they all keep their weapons stashed, though it's a couple minutes of closely watching Spyder before any of them feel comfortable enough to take their attention away from her.

Mithabel is first to break the silence, addressing me over local chat, the only way she can. "Hey, Charli. You've really grown since I saw you last." She produces a suit of brown Leather Armor and offers it to me. "I'm sorry for holding a grudge against you. Dylan was okay with what you did, and I should have been, too. Please forgive me?"

Unable to speak, I take the suit of Armor and hand it off to Britta. Tears well in my eyes as I nod to Mithabel. I offer her a hug, and she takes it.

Something breaks inside me. The tears won't turn off. But there's more to it than that. A compulsion comes over me, and I ask over party chat, "Will you forgive me, too, Mithabel?"

The Elf Tank draws back, breaking our embrace, but she still clasps my shoulders. Tears streak her cheek, too. *She heard me.* She nods and laughs. "You're back, Charli. You're really back." She's replying over party chat, and *I hear her*. She draws me again into an embrace.

I melt into her. "I've missed you so much, Mithabel. I've missed all of you. Dylan, Rolag, and Amarynth. So much has happened since I left. I can't begin to explain it all."

When our bodies stop trembling, we break the hug, our eyes searching the other's and seeing the truth—that we're okay. *All is forgiven.* And in our forgiveness of one another, we've healed invisible wounds that couldn't be healed by the touch of a

Priestess. A heaviness I'd grown accustomed to carrying dissolves in my gut.

Wearing the suit of Armor Mithabel gifted her, Britta gives Mithabel a brief hug. She taps her belly, her arm, and then her shoulder. "I like."

"You're welcome, dear." The Elf Tank grins wider than I've ever seen her grin. She looks askance at me. "Are you going to introduce the young lady?"

The collective group of adventurers from parties MAD, XStorm, and Quantized stand behind Mithabel, all with inquisitive expressions. I reply on all three party chat channels, grateful that I can speak to MAD on party chat again. "Everyone, this is Britta, my daughter."

I don't know what response I expected, but I didn't expect the response I get—complete silence.

Mithabel is first to break out of her shock. She extends a hand to Britta. "I'm Mithabel, an Elf Tank and Anjai. I'm so glad to meet you."

Britta slides her index finger into the Tank's grip. "Mithabel."

The Tank glances at me, her raised eyebrows telling me I've got more explaining to do.

I offer a weak grin. "Please forgive her manners or the lack thereof. She was just born this morning."

"What?" The outburst comes from a female Centaur. Her equine tail jerks from side to side. She opens her mouth as though about to say something else, but all that comes out is another, "What?"

"There is no mystery here." A short, white male Angel steps towards me and bows. "I am Zyekt, Psyon and Life-Stealer." He straightens and points his chin at the pink Mouse riding his shoulder. "And this is Niav, my Faithful Companion, a Guide and Mentalist. We've heard so much about you, Charli, and are *so* glad to finally meet you. We understand we owe you for a huge chunk of the XP we've gained since joining MAD."

I bow in return, appreciative of the Angel's show of support more than he realizes. "I'm glad to make your acquaintance, Zyekt and Niav." I give a special smile to the Mouse. "It's nice to meet another Guide."

The Angel turns to the group behind him. "Remember that you are in Khertaan. The laws of nature here do not necessarily match the laws of nature of the world your players call home. NPCs do not lie, unless directed to do so by the System. So, if you do not believe Charli when she says Britta is her daughter born only this morning, ask yourself why the System would have her lie to us about it. I can think of no reason."

Oh, I could just hug this man.

"He's right." Dylan steps forward. Did she just drop hands with the Asian woman standing beside her? The Polynesian Priestess beams a smile, her brown skin practically aglow. When last I saw her, Dylan was gaining in self-confidence, but now she exudes it. "Hello, Britta. I'm Dylan." She holds her hand towards my daughter, palm up.

Her eyes gleaming and lips pursed, Britta lays her hand on top of Dylan's. The Priestess places her other hand atop Britta's, and Britta lays her other hand on top of them all. Dylan moves her bottom hand to the top, and Britta follows suit, after which Dylan does it again, and Britta repeats. They keep going, each moving faster and faster, until Britta is laughing so hard, she has to stop. She places a hand over her heart. "Dylan."

The introductions continue with Rolag, finishing out the party MAD intros, and then moves on to the members of XStorm and Quantized, until Britta and I have met them all.

The Asian woman I'd seen holding Dylan's hand is Yuni, a Priestess of War belonging to party XStorm. She carries herself with a confidence rivaling Dylan's. The two have an easy grace about them and the eye appeal to set them apart in any company, even that of Lady Amarynth. The two Priestesses seem almost inseparable. If Mithabel harbors any jealousy towards Yuni for demanding nearly all of Dylan's attention, she hides it well.

Britta is taken with Zip the Cheetah. Ger-Alt, the Goblin Woman who rides Zip as a mount, seems only too happy to dismount and allow a young Cave Goblin woman to take a ride, after asking my permission, which I appreciate. Zip says he doesn't mind. Once on his back, Britta cries for him to go faster and faster, and proves she can hold on with no issues.

My bones grow chill.

CHAPTER FORTY-SIX

Megan: Finding Ned

"Can I come in, now?" Debra leans partly through the entrance.

I shake my head at her as I brush the grime off my Bikini. "Wait a second. Kaleisha, is my current encounter officially over?"

"Not yet, chief, but it can be if you want."

I'm not one to end an encounter without knowing what I'm giving up in doing so. "Give me a minute, Deb." Stashing Ghost Maker, I slap the top of the corner counter and switch to local chat. "Ned, I know you're hiding. Your Golems are all destroyed, so it's just you and me. I'll accept your surrender. *Now*. Otherwise, I'll be forced to Shock Wave you to death, a process that will take a while, but seems to be reaching you, wherever you are. So, what's it going to be? Surrender or a slow death?"

"Meg, look."

Debra's voice alerts me in the same moment I notice the words—not there just a moment ago—five-foot-tall block letters carved from obsidian, standing in the middle of the room.

HELP ME.

What the bloody hell? Is this plea for help a distraction? If so, how does Ned hope I'll react? If his plea is genuine, then how do I help?

"Where are you, Ned?"

Flowing like liquid metal, the letters meld into each other, creating one large oblong of rock, and then separate into different letters.

UNKNOWN.

" Are you under the trap door?" I go over to it.

MAYBE.

"Can you make a sound?" I'd heard him before. Maybe I can find him by following whatever noise he makes.

A masculine grunting sounds from the inch-wide gap around the trap door. "Are you *inside* the counter, Ned?"

The word doesn't change.

This is some sick shit. I mean, I can get in there. But is it a trap? Stashing the Severed Faerie Wing and my Bikini, I climb atop the counter and switch to Siamese Cat form. I'm not small enough to fit through the inch gap. So I use my Compress Body skill. At my current Anjai level, I can uniformly compress my Elf body down to a couple inches thick at the waist, but compressing a smaller Cat body means I can shrink to a quarter-inch tall at the shoulder. I'm less than an inch long, not counting the tail, which adds another half inch to my length.

A miniature feline the size of a game board piece, I fly into the gap, careful not to touch anything. I've got a bad feeling about all this.

Below the trap door, the counter is hollow and dark. My Dark Sight kicks in. The floor below me is about the same level as the floor of the shop.

Ned's continued grunts sound louder now. Set into the wall in the far back corner is a one-inch tall archway beyond which lies a set of miniature stairs. The grunting wafts up the stairway. I had never imagined my Anjai skills would be put to use like this, but it's awesome they are.

Remaining as a tiny flying cat, I touch nothing—not the floor or the walls or the stairs. I focus on my Hide skill, too, just to be extra cautious. With my paws tucked up, I slowly descend for about twenty seconds before the stairs terminate at the entry to a domed space that feels like a spacious room at my current size, but it's only a foot radius. In the center of this dome hovers a four-inch-diameter ball of flame. Relatively small—but it's huge to me. A six-inch-diameter pool of clear liquid lies below the fiery ball. Smoke rises into a shaft situated directly above the fireball. Ned's grunts echo from the shaft.

Concentrating on Alertness and Detect Anomaly, I fly around the room—staying as far as possible from the fireball while not touching the wall—and scan the area for any sign of another exit. Nothing. The only way to Ned is up that shaft.

The heat from the fire is intense. I fly towards the shaft, and the fireball expands, cutting off my approach. I successfully Dodge, but only by going backwards. "What kind of damage would that thing do to me, Kaleisha, if it hit?"

"Sorry, chief, but I don't have that info. I *can* say, this is categorized as a *trap*, and is triggered by your actions. It doesn't have a combat heartbeat and thus no cool down period. So act accordingly."

"Can I Block or Parry it?"

"Accessing System info.... Ah, I have something new. Parry is not useful against an area attack. Block has a chance of working."

"Then let's try the Block." I equip Ghost Maker. Fortunately, compressing my body includes compressing my equipment, or Ghost Maker would be too large to fit in this tiny domed room. Wielding a battle axe with Siamese Cat paws feels odd. I can't grasp the axe handle with fingers, but it stays in my grip when I dig in my claws. I give a practice swing, and the weapon feels like a natural extension of me, like it does when I'm in Elf form wielding it. I can't imagine how I look as a miniature Siamese Cat swinging around a tiny battle axe, but this is slick.

I fly forward. Fire swells towards me. I Block it… or try. The fire flows around my weapon and envelops me. Pain shoots through me and I'm stopped mid-flight, making precious little headway. The fire recedes as quickly as it blossomed. I don't move another inch, and the fireball remains at its original size. Crap.

"Ouch, chief." Kaleisha doesn't have to tell me it hurts, but I do want to know how much. "You're down to 20% HP now. Belay that, Dylan just healed Mithabel. You're both back to full HP."

"Megan." It's Mithabel again. "Tell me where you are. I'm coming to help. You can't keep taking hits like that. It costs Dylan a good deal of Auni to heal that much damage."

"I'm not in combat, Mithabel. It's a fire trap I'm trying to get past, and if you were here, we'd simply take double the damage from it. How much Auni has Dylan used to heal us so far?"

"Nearly a third of her total. Like I said, you can't keep taking this kind of damage."

"Megan." This time, it's Debra talking, who hasn't been privy to the conversation between Mithabel and me. "Dylan is concerned about how much damage you're taking. What's going on down there?"

"It's a fire trap. I just need to get past it. I'll try one more thing. If that doesn't work…."

"I'll let her know. Please be careful."

I also tell Mithabel I'm trying one more thing. "I used the Reflect Any Attack skill against some Golems. It worked some of the time, and when it worked well, it reflected a combo attack from two assailants. I'm going to try it here. Maybe I can destroy the trap by reflecting its flame attack back on it."

"Fine, but if that doesn't work, that's it. Agreed?"

"Sure. Kaleisha, do you have any more info on my Reflect Any Attack skill?"

"Accessing…. Yes, but the info is incomplete. The probability of success is based on your skill level, your Agility bonus, some trait levels, including Alertness and Danger Sense, and the enemy's class level and Power Strike trait level. There is a 5% chance of automatic success and a 5% chance of automatic failure.

"The skill can be used against melee or ranged attacks, including area attacks. You must use a weapon or shield of a type suitable to your class and able to block or deal damage of the type you're trying to reflect. If you were trying to reflect spiritual damage, for instance, you'd need a weapon that can deal spiritual damage or a shield that can block spiritual damage. If you're trying to reflect physical damage, as would be the case here, you could use a weapon that deals physical damage or a shield that can block physical damage. You should be able to use Ghost Maker in your attempt to reflect a physical attack, even one that's fire-based."

"It sounds like I could use Ghost Maker to reflect any kind of attack, then, since it can deal damage in any of the four domains—physical, mental, spiritual, or emotional."

"That's right."

"Thanks for the info, Kaleisha." Brandishing Ghost Maker with my right paw, I fly towards the shaft again. Immediately flames flood my vision. Swinging Ghost Maker, I invoke the Reflect Any Attack skill.

The expanding flames turn back on themselves. Oh, Goddess, *it worked*.

Sadly, the trap isn't destroyed. The four-inch-diameter fireball still hovers in the center of the domed room. I stop flying, knowing that if I continue, the fireball will expand again, but I can't reflect it again until my next combat heartbeat.

Megan is in my head again. "Kaleisha told me the new info about the Reflect skill. It apparently worked for you, to a degree. Will it allow you to move safely past the trap?"

"I don't know what the exact probability of success is. This first time could have been a fluke. And I made very little forward progress. At this rate, I'll have to invoke the skill maybe twenty times or more to reach the shaft. With a five percent chance of automatic failure each time, I'm likely to fail at least once or twice before I'm clear. So…."

"Did you check for secret doors?"

"Of course."

She's silent a moment. "What else is in the room?"

"Nothing. It's domed, with this fireball hovering in the center. The shaft I need to reach is directly above the fireball. When I fly towards the shaft, the fireball expands, and if I don't reflect it, I get burned. You saw how badly."

"There's nothing else in the room?"

I take in the room once more. "Ah, well, yeah. There's a pool of liquid under the fireball."

"Water?"

Oh, duh. "Yeah. I'm an idiot. Thanks, Mithabel."

She laughs. "Glad I could help. Let me know how it goes."

Of course the pool is here for a reason. This whole escapade beneath the trap door is a puzzle created especially for me.

I use my Water Control skill to raise the liquid from the pool and form a fluid shell around the flame. I'd assumed the water would succumb to the flames, but then the pool should have already evaporated. The fire is magical, but so is the water, and I'm betting the water is enchanted at a higher level.

Flying forward, I watch as the flames expand, but are contained by the watery prison. I fly up the shaft without the flames attacking me, and I stash Ghost Maker.

The shaft rises for a foot and then bends to travel horizontally for a good ten feet, after which it bends upward. Light filters in from above. I fly up and poke my tiny feline head out the top.

I'm at one end of a ten-by-twenty-foot room, which to me looks enormous. In the middle of the room, suspended in midair, is a human-sized rift in space framed by black mists. Through the rift I see a masculine figure in a hooded gray cloak standing in a dark void. My Elf eyes can't distinguish anything else within the darkness.

"Ned?"

"You are Megan Wright—in Siamese Cat form, I see. I've waited so long to meet you. Please, come in."

"Deb?" I want to tell my party mate what's happening.

She doesn't reply. Our private chat channel isn't functioning. I try raising her or Charli over party chat. When that fails, I try Mithabel, but that fails, too. I call for *anyone* to answer me on global chat, with no response.

Something heavy bangs far below me, like a boulder falling on a stone floor. The route by which I entered this room has been closed.

"Am I in the *Othersuch* room?"

"Quite astute of you. Yes."

"Then there's an exit door on one of these walls. I just have to find it."

"You make the assumption that the door leading into the room also leads out. It does not. Now that you're here, the only way for you to leave the room is to die or to pass through the portal and join me."

"Kaleisha, can you hear me?"

"Yes, chief."

That's a relief. "Please tell Mithabel to tell Debra Jones to open the Othersuch door and hold it open, but definitely *do not* enter. Can you do that?"

"Certainly, chief."

Moments pass. A door opens and Debra sticks her head in. Her mouth moves, but I hear no words.

"*Don't come in*, Deb." I fly toward her.

The hooded man gestures. An attack is coming of some sort. I equip Ghost Maker but not with the speed necessary to Reflect Any Attack. I should have kept it equipped the whole time. I'm so scared of losing it.

A wave of despair washes over me.

Continuing is of no use. We've lost the battle to save the world. The multiverse is ending, and all who resist will die horrible, agonizingly slow deaths. Better to end one's own life now than to be subjected to the nightmare to come. I try to cut myself with Ghost Maker, but it doesn't work. I stash the weapon and search my inventory for a more suitable one. Every weapon I have is disgusting.

CHAPTER FORTY-SEVEN

Yuni: Delivery

We all watch Britta riding Zip the Cheetah. The young Cave Goblin woman is Charli's daughter, though they both look the same age and they aren't the same kindred. Still, Britta behaves like a child, and her vocabulary is extremely lacking. But most importantly to my believing Charli's claim is that Dylan believes her. My Polynesian Priestess friend is quite taken with the youngster, watching her intently and clapping for her as the Cheetah races around, occasionally making a pretense of trying to unseat his rider.

"Musume." My fat cat AI, Inuki, pops up in my view, waving a paw. "I have high priority information for you."

"Let's hear it."

"The Shadow Marble you carry…. It's time to finish your special quest regarding it."

"What do I do?"

"You must give it to Charli without anyone else seeing you." Inuki grimaces. "There are lots of eyes here, so be careful."

"Will this complete the quest?" My cheeks warm. I haven't forgotten the two-hundred-million XP the quest is worth.

"Yes, that's the info I have. Good luck."

There's no time like the present, especially with everyone watching the Britta and Zip show. My skin itches with nervousness, but I'm a Priestess of War—one of my skills is Courage. I call on it, and a calmness settles on me. I'm also an Anjai, with the Hide skill, which might help in this situation, but I don't use it yet. I sidle up to Charli and initiate a private chat. "I have something for you, and no one else can see me give it to you. It's a special quest I got back in Maron."

Her gaze lingers a moment on her daughter before she turns to me and extends a hand. "Okay. Grab hold."

I do as she bids without question.

We already stand in shadow, but the world grows colder and darker still. What I can see of the blue sky turns gray. "Oh, this is strange." My voice sounds far away.

My surroundings blur as we travel into deeper shadow, Charli dragging me along, but friction-free, my body sliding across the ground like I'm on a sled in snow. We round the corner of a building, out of sight of the others.

Charli releases my hand. "Okay, let's see what you got."

The sky returns to blue. The world grows warmer and the shadows less deep. I suck in a breath and draw the special quest item out of inventory. Cupping it in my hand, I offer it to the Cowgirl. "It's called a Shadow Marble. That's all I know. I don't know what it's for or why I'm to give it to you. Please take it before someone sees. The quest is ruined if anyone sees."

To my relief, she doesn't hesitate, but lifts the Marble from my palm, more eagerly than I'd expected.

Inuki smiles broadly. "Congratulations, musume, you have gained two-hundred-million XP and are now level 28 Priestess, level 19 Anjai. You are 51% of the way to level 29. You are now the top PC avatar in the game."

Emotion swells within me, but I do not cry. Crying is not becoming of a Priestess of War.

"Mithabel!" Dylan's cry over local chat echoes around the corner of the building.

I don't wait for Charli to carry me back through the shadows, but rush out of hiding, searching for the cause for alarm. To Britta's disappointment, the Cheetah comes to a halt. Everyone's attention turns to the Elf Tank. She's on her knees, holding a glowing orange sword with a curvy blade, the tip pointed at her stomach as though she's about to commit harakiri.

"I call upon the Goddess Scintilla, to heal your emotional wounds." A ray of light strikes Dylan's hands where she lays them on the top of Mithabel's head. As the light fades, Dylan stumbles backwards.

Mithabel lowers her weapon, looking up at Dylan standing over her. "Thank you, Dylan."

I reach the the group. "What happened?"

The Tank stands without giving a reply. She looks into Dylan's eyes, but I can see from where I stand that Dylan isn't returning the gaze. The Priestess of Light stares at something none of the rest of us see.

I grab her hand. "Dylan. Say something."

She's not talking. Her eyes aren't focusing.

"It's Megan and Debra." Mithabel glances back towards the cave where we entered Minook. "They're in deep shit trouble. We have to help them."

Her demeanor changes in an instant, from alert and commanding to unfocused and muttering. "It's no use. We've lost." She lifts her weapon again and places it to her throat. Before anyone can stop here, she slides the blade across her neck.

But she can't hurt herself. The System doesn't allow us avatars to commit suicide, thank the Goddess. Nevertheless, some external force is affecting her. She and Dylan both need our help to fight whatever is doing this to them. Swallowing the panic swirling in my brain, I ask Inuki for a status report on my hurting allies.

"All status values are at 100% except EP. Emotional hit points are at 60% for Mithabel and 3% for Dylan."

Three percent? Emotionally speaking, Dylan is practically dead, and Mithabel is suicidal. "What's causing this?"

"Nothing is attacking them, musume. They should not be losing EP like this."

"It's a Shadow Gaunt." Niav's voice squeaks over local chat. "If it reduces them to 0% EP, they'll become Ghouls. You need to heal Dylan, *quickly*."

"I can't heal EP." I don't have the Advanced Healing spell that Dylan has. I shout over local chat. *"Can any one heal emotional damage?"*

"I can." The responding avatar is identified as Mylynna.

"Get over here now."

"I'm coming. But I'm not close. It will take me a minute."

"We don't have a minute." No one else responds. "Where is this Gaunt? We need to kill it." I call for the blessing of Athlea, Goddess of War, upon us all. It's the least I can do, and it may help Mithabel and Dylan resist whatever is attacking them.

Everyone scans the area, but no one sees a hidden enemy.

"Mithabel's EP has fallen to 20%," Inuki tells me. "Dylan holds at 3%."

"Does anyone have a way to boost their protection against emotional damage?" I'm desperate to save them. I look around for Charli. She hasn't joined us. She should have been right behind me. Why isn't she here?

Is all this my fault? Was giving Charli the Shadow Marble the reason for what's happening now? If not, it's pretty damned coincidental. "Charli, *say something*, please."

Screeches echo across the city. Everything goes dark except the orange glow of the curvy blade slashing in futility at Mithabel's throat. The sun goes out as Night descends on Khertaan, bringing an end to the reign of Eternal Daylight.

CHAPTER FORTY-EIGHT

Ronnie: State Park

Mel and I follow Erica along winding roads. We arrive at a public parking lot, and Erica brings her bike to a halt.

Golden Minnow State Park, reads the sign.

"What are we doing here?" I stay seated.

Erica climbs off her bike and briefly studies a painted map of the park before stabbing an index finger at it. "That's the bridge. We need to meet someone under it." She points her chin at a sign with a list of park rules. "No motorcycles allowed on the trails. We're walking the rest of the way."

Mel dismounts. "Who are we meeting?"

I'm glad to have him ask the question, because I'm just as curious. I stash our bikes.

"Someone named Gondra. Don't be alarmed by his appearance. His face is covered with scales, he has a forked tongue, and he wears a cloak, but other than that he seems nice and on our side. He's going to tell me how to save Nick." Erica heads down a trail. "Come on. Keep up."

Mel doesn't move to follow. "You say he wears a cloak?"

I don't move, either. "We saw a couple people wearing cloaks. They weren't nice. One of them, sad to say, was Mel's mom."

Erica stops to face us, her face flushed. "Did the other one have a snake head?"

Mel shrugs. "We couldn't see his face. Our guy wore a hood."

Erica grimaces. "That was probably Seth. Gondra told me his name. Jean, Seth, and a girl named Greelia are battling to dominate a group of timelines we're a part of."

"Greelia?" The name of the Goblin Warrior makes my ears perk. "How is she involved in this?"

"She's a very strong-willed individual. Are you two coming or not?" Erica heads down the trail.

"One moment, Mel." I bring out the fuzzy dice. "I feel the need for some luck." I roll. The total comes up six. "Good enough. Let's go." We hurry to catch up with Erica.

It's not long before a bridge comes into sight. We leave the beaten path to head below. A dry creek bed full of smooth pebbles lies under the bridge. No one waits for us.

Erica calls for Gondra, cupping her hands around her mouth.

A cloaked figure moves within the bridge's shadow. Had he been there all along? His cloak is hooded, but the hood hangs down in the back. His uncovered head is as Erica described, much like the head of a black snake, but human-sized. He carries a long, wizardly staff in one hand, bearing weight on it as he steps forward. "I am here." His voice is raspy and some words not well pronounced, like he's struggling to speak the Common tongue. "I see you brought your friends. Good. We can skip the introductions—you all know my name and I know yours. Is it safe to say we all have a common goal, of saving Nick and helping him to finish the job he started, of fixing the broken timelines in a way that allows us all to continue living our most desirable lives?"

"Yes, that's why we're here." Erica nods and glances askance at Mel and me, knowing she's speaking for all three of us and hoping she hasn't overstepped her bounds.

I don't like being rushed into anything. "You say we can skip the introductions, Mr. Gondra, but I know nothing about you. Mel and I haven't had great luck with people in cloaks of late, so maybe you could tell us about yourself—what you are, where you're from, what's in all this for you, and why we should trust you."

The cloaked Lizardman blinks at me with a translucent eyelid. He has no eyelashes. "That's fair. I'm a Grummozerii from the planet Grummoz. My world was destroyed by Seth and his Planet Buster in my original timeline. I've been doing everything I can to eradicate the Planet Buster before Seth finds a way to shift it across timelines and destroy all alternates of my world. So... I have a stake in all this, and that's why you can trust me."

Mel, Erica, and I exchange glances. Mel nods. "Okay, Mr. Gondra—"

"Please, just call me Gondra."

"Very well, Gondra. Supposing we believe and trust you, what do you want from us?"

"I need you to take me to Greelia."

"How do you know Greelia?" I clench my fists. Not that I intend to punch this guy's ugly snout, unless he intends her harm.

"I know her because I have seen her metaphysical projection upon the metadisc. But I need to be in her physical presence. I've tried and failed. She's protected by forces I'm unfamiliar with. But I believe the three of you working together can take me there."

"And why do you believe that?" I unclench and clench my fists. "I don't even know where she is, and I doubt either of my friends here knows."

Erica looks at her hands and nods. "I do."

Gondra flicks his tongue. "Good. Then it's settled." He steps close to Erica and offers her his left hand. "Let us join in a circle."

I unclench and clench my fists again. "How does going to Greelia help us save Nick?"

Gondra closes his eyes briefly before answering. "You have the right to know. I have already visited your other two T&T friends,

Fauna.75 and Emma. I took some of their life forces, their experience points, just as I have taken some of yours, Ronnie. Only a thousand from each of you—not enough to impact anyone's current level rating. If I do the same with Greelia, I will have life force from each of the main characters from Nick's T&T world. When I combine that with life force from his Khertaan avatar, Morrow, I'll have enough to paint a complete picture of who Nick is. I can use it to *grow* Nick again, much like the ODYSSEY nanobots are able to grow."

"ODYSSEY what?" Am I the only one to whom that statement makes no sense?

"The ODYSSEY nanobots…. Tiny robots that can live in one's brain. They allowed Nick to transfer his awareness between alternate versions of himself across timelines. In many ways, the nanobots are like a virus, but selective. When in proximity of other sentient life, they can elect to send a few of themselves from their current host to a new host. All three of you have them, and they've been growing in your minds for some time now. Mel, you received yours first, being Nick's son. Erica, you received yours next. Ronnie, you received some, too, during the brief time you traveled with Nick. You might not have realized it, but you were relying on the ODYSSEY nanobots to enable some form of existence for yourselves, even if as ghosts—while the timelines have been fluctuating."

I shake my head to clear it. "I have no idea what a robot is."

Gondra grins. "Think of the nanobots as germs. You can't see them, but they're there. Some are beneficial and some make you sick. ODYSSEY nanobots are like beneficial germs living in your brains. You can talk to them if you try."

I've got an Intelligence score of 21, so I'm not stupid, but this is way over my head. "Mel? Erica? Do we buy what this guy is selling? Are you in?"

Neither of them reply. They both have that glazed-over look, like their minds are far away.

Mel's face brightens. "I'm talking to them now."

Erica nods vigorously. "Me, too. I'm talking to mine. It's like telepathy, Ronnie. Just imagine projecting your thoughts to ODYSSEY, and see if he answers."

I'm skeptical, but I turn my thoughts inward and give it a try. "ODYSSEY, are you there?"

"Hello, Ronnie."

"How long have you been in my head?"

"Ever since Ulric played his first T&T game with you as his character. Your being part of Nick's game world gave us access to you. We helped the four of you—Fauna, Emma, Greelia, and yourself—to escape your world and travel to Nick's."

It's as though I'm talking to myself, while the disembodied voice of someone else answers. It's not any stranger than my asking for a saving roll and then two dice appearing from nowhere to make it. So I have talking metal germs in my brain. Welcome to the life of an adventurer.

Gondra's voice cuts through the conversation in my head. "Are you still with us, Ronnie?"

"Me and my nanobots, yes."

"Are there any more questions before we make this attempt at traveling?"

Mel raises his hand. "What exactly are we doing?"

"If we could all form a circle by joining hands, I'll walk you through the steps." Gondra stands between Erica and Mel, with Erica's hand already in his left. "Each of you have a part to play, and it will be easier if I instruct you in turn as we go. The desired end result is that we all end up where Greelia is."

"And what are the possible undesired results?"

Gondra holds his hand out to Mel. "Too many to list, nor can I tell you what the worst possible result might be. If you aren't fully committed to making this work, then any result you can imagine is entirely possible. Everyone must focus on your role with all your willpower. Do that, and we'll succeed."

Facing Gondra, I take Erica's hand in my right and Mel's in my left. Mel and Gondra close the circle.

Gondra turns to Erica. "It is your role to focus on Greelia's location. Your mind will guide us through the Cosmic Mists. Close your eyes." He waits for her to comply. "Picture Greelia as you last saw her. Imagine yourself standing some distance away from her. Hold that image in your mind. Do not let it falter. When I next speak your name, you may open your eyes. Until then, pay no mind to anything further I have to say."

Erica's brow furls. Gondra says nothing to Mel or me until Erica's expression relaxes.

He turns to Mel. "As someone with genes shared with Nick, you're our best bet at interacting with ODYSSEY. Our friend to my left is envisioning where we need to go. You must direct ODYSSEY to take us there. Before you start… know that the ODYSSEY nanobots in all three of your heads can communicate with each other." He flicks his forked tongue in Erica's direction. "The nanobots in her brain will inform the nanobots in your brain of the destination. Your nanobots can inform you, inserting the image from her brain into yours. This will give you a target. You'll focus on that target and direct ODYSSEY to take all four of us there. You must not accept failure. No matter what ODYSSEY claims, do not relent until we achieve success. Do you understand?"

Mel nods. "I'm ready. I can do this."

"Then close your eyes. You know what you must do. When I next speak your name, you may open your eyes. Until then, pay no mind to anything further I have to say."

As with Erica, Gondra says nothing more until Mel enters a relaxed state. "Your turn, Ronnie."

I meet the Lizardman's gaze. How can I possibly play any role in this attempt to journey through what Gondra called the Cosmic Mists? I'm a simple T&T Rogue with no weapons. The only equipment I have are motorcycles and fuzzy dice. I know next to nothing about nanobots, and any traveling between timelines or universes I've done was instigated by someone or something else.

"Yours is the most important role."

He must be lying.

"Our two friends and the collective ODYSSEY nanobots won't succeed unless you give them the boost they need. I've observed you, and I know no one luckier than you. You need to work that luck now."

"You risked everything on my Luck?" I can't believe what I'm hearing.

Gondra nods. "Just concentrate on getting good luck, and get it like you always do."

"But I don't always get good luck. I have failed a time or two. What if I fail this time?"

"Concentrate hard enough not to fail."

I scoff at his ignorance. "It doesn't work like that. It's entirely random. Out of 36 possible combinations of the dice on one roll, four of them are automatic failure—there are two ways of rolling a one-two combination, and two ways of rolling a one-three combination. That's a one in nine chance of automatic failure."

"So the odds are in our favor. Besides which, there's no alternative. Time is wasting. Do it. Please." The Lizardman holds the sibilant of the last word with a hiss.

"There's always an alternative."

"Not for your friends." He hisses the end of his sentence again.

I stare into those reptilian eyes. How can I trust this creature? I don't. Erica and Mel trust him, but he didn't tell them everything, and now their fates rest in my hands. "I'm doing this for them, not for you. I call for an SR on Luck." I'm hoping for two dice to magically appear, like they've done in the past, but they don't show. I'm still in a scripted scene, and the script says I'll fail. If I want a dice roll, I need to use my stashed fuzzy dice, which I really, really don't want to lose.

But I don't see any other way out of this that doesn't spell catastrophe. I will the fuzzy dice out of inventory, the connecting cord between my teeth. Looking down, I open my mouth and let the dice fall.

The first die shows a one. The second die shows a two.

Automatic failure.

What happens next will undoubtedly be worse for me than what was scripted, and I can't bear to drag Mel and Erica down with me. "*Universe*, please don't let my bad luck reflect on those I've tried to help. I freely accept all the bad luck you would have thrown at them due to my bad roll. Help them in their efforts, please, and do with me what you will."

The fuzzy dice vanish. So does the park, Mel, Erica, and Gondra. I'm standing with hands outstretched to either side, but no longer grasping the hands of my friends. Swirling mists envelop me.

The Cosmic Mists fade, and I'm elsewhere.

Tall, stately stone walls surround me. A red carpet lies beneath my feet, a length of it stretching across a tile stone floor and lined with stern female guards armed with rifles and attired in green nurse uniforms. The carpet leads to a golden throne upon which sits a woman adorned in gold jewelry.

Queen Jean.

"Well, well, how nice of the kidnapper to turn himself in. Tell me where you're holding Princess Karen, and I'll consider letting you live another day."

"I don't know any Princess Karen."

"Guards, bring in our most recent guest."

Doors open behind me. Four guards with rifles enter and march along the red carpet towards me, escorting in their midst a man wearing a black bag over his head. The double doors through which they entered are closed and a heavy bar dropped in place to keep them shut. Once the guards come alongside me, they force their prisoner to his knees.

The Queen gestures. "Remove his hood."

The black bag is roughly lifted from the prisoner's head.

It's Nick.

Queen Jean holds up three fingers. A guard aims her rifle at Nick's temple. Jean lowers one of her fingers, her arrogant gaze locked on me. She lowers another finger.

This isn't the real Nick. This is the Nick from this universe, a sorry excuse for a human being. But does he deserve to die this way?

I can't trade Mel for this alternate-Nick. But I can try my best to save this guy. I grab for the guard's rifle.

But she's too alert and too prepared, and sidesteps my lunge, batting me in the back of the head with the butt of her gunne. I go down, planting my face on the carpet. The number -5 floats in front of my eyes. My Constitution is 33, so now I'm down to 28.

A boot jabs my ribs, but not enough to do damage. I roll onto my back. Three rifles point down into my face. One rifle is still aimed at Nick. A deafening shot rings out, and Nick keels over on the carpet beside me, blood pooling under his head, his dead eyes staring at me.

I'm hauled up and forced to kneel. The four guards who had escorted Nick surround me, their rifles trained on me. They don't stand close enough for me to try to nab one of their weapons.

"Bring in our next most recent guest." The Queen's voice doesn't waver. She's calm and in control.

Behind me, the double doors are unbarred and opened again. Four more guards escort in another individual wearing a black bag to hide their identity, but I know who she is. Relatively short, green-skinned, female, wearing the bare essentials—it has to be Greelia.

The bar clangs in place on the double doors again.

The guards force their second prisoner to her knees on the far side of Nick's corpse. At Queen Jean's command, they remove the black hood. As I suspected, it's my former adventuring companion, Greelia, the Goblin Warrior.

"Greelia. How…?" Before I can finish my question, a rifle butt strikes me between my shoulder blades, knocking the wind from me.

Queen Jean holds up three fingers. A guard aims a rifle at Greelia's head. The Goblin Warrior doesn't look at me, but stares at the Queen in silent defiance. Queen Jean lowers one finger.

I don't know what version of Greelia this is, if she's the Greelia that Gondra needs to find or an alternate, but this woman holds her head high, her eyes full of defiance, what I'd expect from the Greelia I know. Whether this woman is my former adventuring companion or an alternate version of her, I can't let them murder her. "Promise me you won't shoot her, and I'll tell you where Mel is."

The Queen's only response is to lower another finger.

"He's at Golden Minnow State Park. Under the bridge."

Jean keeps the last finger pointing up. "*Who* is at Golden Minnow State Park?"

"Mel."

"I didn't ask you about anyone named Mel." Jean bends her finger.

"Princess Karen…. She's at Golden Minnow State Park. Please don't shoot." Sorry, Mel. If there was any other way….

"There, was that so hard?" Queen Jean finishes bending the last finger all the way down.

Another shot sounds, this one louder than before, echoing in the emptiness of my soul. Greelia collapses onto her face next to Nick, her blood mixing with his.

"Thank you for your assistance, Rogue. Take him away. Strip him naked and toss him into a cell. Don't let him get his hands on any dice. I've scripted him a nice, long life in hell."

CHAPTER FORTY-NINE

Erica: Cloaks

Inside, I'm crying. Gondra asked me to envision Greelia, but when I do, I can't help but see Morrow, too, in the nexus occupied by the two of them and Renee. Morrow is all that's left of my Nicky Nick, and I'm going back to him with very little. But I'm going back. I can't wait to see him again, even if I can't allow him to see me.

"You need to focus on Greelia." The nanobot collective integrated in my brain only wants to help me stay on mission.

But ODYSSEY's urging can't make me put Nick out of my mind.

"Lady ghost? Is that you?" Morrow senses me and calls for me, drawing me back to him.

"*Morrow*. Yes, it's me. Mel, Ronnie, and Gondra are with me. May I bring them to you?"

"If they are willing, bring them."

ODYSSEY sounds off in my head in alarm. "Erica, if we're to execute Gondra's plan, you need to focus on Greelia, not Morrow."

"Trust me. What I'm doing is a more reliable way to reach her." I put aside my mental image of Greelia and concentrate solely on Morrow. His energy brushes mine and tugs at my spirit.

He's in a nexus, not a timeline. Can I take my flesh-and-blood self into the nexus? If Morrow and Greelia could do it, why can't I? I will my physical body to accompany my awareness. I won't be lady ghost to him any longer. I'll be Erica. If anything could bring together the fragments of Nick's soul, it would be his soul mate, in the flesh.

This is why I'm crying inside. I terribly miss my Nicky Nick.

I sense his nearness. ODYSSEY speaks to me in rising tones of urgency, but I only hear noise. Mists rise in the darkness behind my eyelids, and through them flashes the green of Morrow's mohawk, a beacon to my lost vessel.

Ronnie's hand slips from mine—a distraction. The mohawk is swallowed in the mists. *Dammit.*

No. I won't be denied a reunion with my Nicky Nick. I squeeze Mel's hand so I don't lose him, too. "Nick, it's me, Erica. I'm coming, my love. *Nick.* Do you hear me? It's Erica. Call to me. Don't lose me. *Nick,* call to me, *dammit.*" I'm beyond desperate. I *must* reunite with him.

His face appears in the mist, but oriented horizontally. There's no sign of his mohawk—rather, his brown hair is cropped short. His eyes are closed. He lies on his side on a tile floor, unmoving except for the expansion and collapse of his chest as he breathes.

I rise out of the floor, lifting Mel and Gondra with me. Ronnie is gone. Mel and I are translucent like ghosts. I'd hoped for a physical form, but we're not in the nexus. Apparently Mel has no physical presence in this timeline either. Gondra appears solid, even though he's rising through the floor with us and holds both our hands. If he'd been holding Ronnie's hand, would the Rogue still be with us? Neither Mel nor I could keep hold of him. Are we to blame for losing Ronnie?

Several ruined television screens line the scorched walls of a room about twice the size of my living room at home. A desk with burn marks sits in a corner, atop which rests a laptop computer, its cover open, the screen dark.

I've never been here, even though Nick clearly has been, and still is, at least some version of him.

"We've failed." Gondra sighs. "Greelia isn't here."

I rush to Nick's side and try to rouse him. "Nicky Nick, are you all right?" My ghostly hand passes through him. He doesn't stir.

Mel gasps. "*This place*. It's real. I've seen it in my dreams. Dad was married to another woman and had a different kid. He was working on a computer program for a video game. His wife helped him." He pulls his hand free of Gondra's and flies towards a wall.

Gondra swings his head in Mel's direction, but speaks to me. "Let's stay with him. Maybe something can come of this visit."

The two of us fly through the wall behind Mel. We're in a hallway. Mel follows it to the end.

Before he can pass through, I call for him to stop. "Is someone in there? If they're awake, you can't let them see you, or you'll be banished from this timeline."

Mel halts, giving me and then Gondra questioning looks. "Seriously?"

Gondra grunts in support of my assertion. "You don't belong in this timeline, Mel. If anyone who does belong here looks at you or otherwise identifies you, such as calling you by the name you're known by in other timelines, this timeline will push you out, and you won't be able to return even as a ghost. But there is a way to fix that. It's how I manage to travel the multiverse without being expelled from countless timelines."

Oh, I need to hear this. "And you're only just mentioning this? Tell us, Gondra. *Right now*."

"It's simple. You need a Cosmic Cloak."

"Oh. Simple. Sure. And where do we find one of these Cosmic Cloaks?" I'm ready to punch him, but I'll kiss him if he comes through on this.

"You can't *find* one, steal one, or borrow one. You have to create yours for yourself. No one can tell you how, either. You make one, or you don't. If you'd felt a deep need for one, your mind would have constructed it already."

"Well, I feel a deep need for one, and have for a long time, but it never occurred to me to create one. So a Cosmic Cloak is what you're wearing, and what Seth and Jean and Greelia are wearing."

"That's right."

I nod at Mel. "We need them, too. With all the traveling across timelines we're doing, we need them. Let's each make one. Are you with me?"

He raises an eyebrow. "Oh, definitely. I don't want to be banished from any timelines." Turning to Gondra, he starts to ask something, but closes his mouth. Gondra already said no one could tell us how to make our Cosmic Cloaks. Mel closes his eyes.

Seems like a good starting point to me, too. I picture myself in the nexus with Morrow, hovering behind him, where he can't see me. Greelia stands off to one side, wearing her dark brown Cosmic Cloak, her attention not on anything within the nexus. I picture the same kind of cloak wrapping my shoulders. But not dark or brown. I need a cloak that reflects my personality.

In my mental movie, Morrow pivots, slowly turning around. In a couple seconds, he'll lay his gaze on me. I'll need to be protected. I need a Cosmic Cloak.

Morrow completes his pivot, but he's looking down, not seeing me yet. "I can't look at you, lady ghost."

"I want you to, Morrow. Look at me and say my name. Please."

He raises his chin, his eyelids still partially lowered, his eyelashes fluttering. Then he lifts his gaze, looking full upon me, seeing me for who I am.

"Erica?"

"It's me." I fly to him, confident, and lay my hand on his cheek. Pastel pink fabric drapes my forearm. I put my hand behind his neck and pull him close, planting my lips on his. "Mmm, my Nicky Nick."

He draws away from me. "I'm not...." His eyes widen. He comes close again, embracing me. Our lips meet once more, and we kiss in earnest.

It doesn't matter that Renee is also present, watching us. Is she jealous? I don't know or care. Morrow and I make love on the floor of the nexus. He screams my name. I'm on top of him, my bright cloak covering us both. He thrusts up into me, repeating my name.

I stroke his cheek. "I love you, Nicky Nick." I wish he wasn't Morrow, but the real Nick.

"I love you, too, Erica. God help me, but I do." His mohawk draws into his head and the color fades. His once-green hair is brown and trim. He *is* my Nicky Nick.

He becomes a shower of sparks in my arms—tiny bits of his soul released from the avatar that had trapped them. I hover over the spot where he'd lain, aching to have him back inside me. Greelia still stands off to the side, motionless as a statue. Renee stares at me, her emotions impossible to read, if indeed she has any. Then she fades out, gradually, until her last vestige is gone.

Next, the entire nexus fades out, including Greelia. I'm back in the hallway with Gondra, a pastel pink cloak covering me. But Mel is gone. "Where's...?"

He appears, wearing a cloak, dark and drab like all the other Cosmic Cloaks I've seen others wear. Am I the only one with any fashion sense?

All three of us are protected now against accidental banishment from the timeline. None of us are translucent— technically, we're no longer ghosts.

"Well, look at you." Mel appraises me. "Couldn't be satisfied with the same old cloak as everyone else?"

"What can I say? I like what I like." I flash him a sugary smile and then cover it with a stretch of pastel pink cloth, peeking over it with all the mischief I can muster.

With a chuckle, Mel takes the door knob in hand.

Gondra clears his throat. "You don't need to open the door. Wearing your Cosmic Cloak, you'll always look solid, but you can take either solid or incorporeal form as you wish. You can pass through the door without opening it. You can walk on the floor if you want, but you can fly, too, like you could as a ghost. Go ahead. Try."

"All right." Mel's feet lift off the ground, and he passes through the door as though it were a fog bank. I wave Gondra through and follow him in.

We enter a large bedroom. On the near edge of a king-size bed lies a woman I recognize—Kendra. Her eyes are closed. She's breathing, asleep.

Mel flies over her. "She's Dad's wife in this timeline. She's gorgeous, super smart, and seems really nice. If I could have chosen who I wanted as my mother, I'd have chosen her over Jean."

Inside, I laugh as the idea strikes me that in some timeline, maybe I could have been Mel's mother. In our current manifestations, Mel is older than me by ten years, maybe more. But in some timeline where I married Nick, Mel might have been born to us. Why not?

My Cosmic Cloak doesn't talk to me like ODYSSEY can, but my perception feels sharper, even extrasensory. I sense a nearby presence, like I'm hearing someone breathing. Mel and Gondra glance around, sensing the same thing. We fly through the bedroom wall in the direction our senses lead us, and enter another bedroom. A young woman lies asleep on the bed.

Seated on the bed next to the woman, and very much awake, is a girl of five or six years. She stares straight at me, and a momentary panic swells in my chest. But I'm not expelled from the timeline. My pink Cosmic Cloak protects me as advertised.

The girl holds a finger to her lips. "Shh. Don't wake her. Don't wake any of them."

I whisper in reply. "We won't be loud. My name is Erica. Who are you?"

"Susie." She points at the sleeping woman. "Her name is Glynda."

"Are you all right?"

"Yes."

"Are you the only one awake in the house?"

She shakes her head. "Super Glynda is awake."

Super Glynda? "Where is she? Can you take us to her?"

An alternate version of the sleeping Glynda appears from nowhere, standing next to Susie. "I'm Super Glynda. Let's talk in the dining room, where we won't disturb anyone. Suze, you come, too, please, and I'll make you a sandwich." She indicates the direction of the dining room with a nod of her head, and then disappears. Susie disappears too. The kid has powers. Okay then.

Mel, Gondra, and I fly through the indicated wall and enter a kitchen. The dining room lies beyond the kitchen counter, and Susie sits at a table large enough for a family of four, where an extra chair has been pulled up to accommodate five.

Super Glynda raids the refrigerator in the kitchen. "Go ahead and have a seat." She comes carrying a loaf of bread, some empty plates, and two plastic containers—one containing ham and the other sliced Swiss cheese. "Who all is hungry?" She sets everything on the table and takes a seat next to Susie. She takes two slices of bread from the loaf. "Sandwich for you coming right up, Suze."

Where do I know this woman from? "You look familiar."

Super Glynda winks at me. "I'm impressed you see the resemblance. I'm Slithy, the one with all the frogs. Technically, Slithy is my Frogkin avatar. Other than her having red and black skin, I'm told we look a lot alike, especially our flowing blond hair." She tosses hers. "You met Slithy amongst the shards of shattered timelines. Slithy urged you to pick a shard before it was too late, and I'm glad to see you did."

Mel grabs a slice of cheese. "Why are you called *Super* Glynda, and are you twins with the sleeping Glynda? The two of you look identical."

Our hostess takes a deep breath. "I'm called Super Glynda because I come from the sleeping Glynda's future. She's the person who initially went to sleep to create Slithy, although the connection between Glynda and Slithy has since time-shifted to another timeline. It's complicated, like everything else dealing with timelines.

"Back to my name.... As a time-traveler who sometimes visits myself, I need a way to refer to my future and past selves. We can't all be called Susie. So, the youngest Susie present becomes Suze. The next older one becomes Glynda, and if there's a third one of us around, which isn't often, she's Super Glynda. I've yet to have more than three of myself present in the same place and time, but I suppose if I do, I'll go with Hyper Glynda."

"Hyper Glynda," echoes little Susie—or, rather, Suze. She reaches for the sandwich the distracted Super Glynda has yet to finish building for her.

Mel snorts. "Why reuse the name *Glynda*? Instead of Super Glynda, you could be Nancy or Pepper or... well... anything other than Suze or Glynda."

"It's not like I ever made a conscious decision about it. It's always been Super Glynda." She shrugs. "Though I do like Pepper. Think I'll use that instead of Hyper Glynda, if I ever need a fourth name. Thanks for the idea. But I'm stuck with Super Glynda for the third name—it's so embedded in the timeline, I couldn't change it if I wanted. Anyway, for those keeping up...., *I'm* Super Glynda, the person who Glynda will eventually become, just as Glynda is the person who Suze eventually becomes. We tend to time-*jump* between different points of time within a single timeline. That's how there can be three versions of me together in one house. Time-*shifting*—that's a different thing, which does happen to me sometimes, but usually not on purpose, like ODYSSEY does for Dad. You all know about ODYSSEY."

We three adults nod. Susie—that is, Suze—continues reaching for a sandwich not yet built.

Mel swipes another slice of cheese, and talks as he chews. "Isn't it a paradox for three of you to be in the same house at the same time? I thought paradoxes were bad for time travelers."

I grab a slice of the cheese, too. And a slice of ham. I don't need any bread. When did I eat last? Do I need to eat when I'm wearing a Cosmic Cloak? As a ghost, I never needed to eat. Gondra isn't partaking and shows no interest in the food.

Super Glynda waves off Mel's concern. "There are *never* any paradoxes. If I tried to create one, I'd fail. My future selves don't attempt any time-jumps my past selves already know weren't made. For instance, Suze here knows that Glynda and I are here today. She grew up knowing it, which is how both Glynda and I know it. So when I felt the need to time-jump here, I already had the knowledge that I'd done it, and that I wouldn't introduce a paradox. In fact, if I chose not to time-jump here the number of times I grew up knowing I did, *that* would be a paradox."

Placing a finished sandwich on a plate, Super Glynda sets it before her younger self, who grabs it up and chows down. Watching her younger self, Super Glynda smiles. "Now, if a *Pepper* were to attempt a time-jump to *this* particular time and place, trying to make *four* of me here simultaneously instead of the three we all know about, things could go one of a few ways. For all we know, maybe there *is* a Pepper here, but we just don't know it, because she's hidden from us, watching us like a peeping Tom."

She casts a searching gaze around the room, chuckling, before continuing. "Or perhaps a Pepper tries to time-jump here, but the time-jump simply doesn't work the way she wants it to. She might go nowhere, or end up at an unintended time or place, or… maybe she goes where and when intended, but is shunted off to a different timeline, effectively performing both a time-jump and a time-shift. I really don't want to end up in another timeline, because I don't know how to time-shift on purpose. I like this timeline, and want to stay in it.

"So, I'm careful. My memory isn't perfect, I admit. Some situations stand out so much, I'll remember them for years, like this meeting. But I typically keep my time-jumps short, so I don't have to bother with a journal or other record.

"And now… get ready, because you're about to be surprised. A touchy-feely moment is upon us, one that my Mom is never to know about. Do you hear that, Suze? Don't ever tell Mom about what happens next."

Little girl Susie lays down her partially-eaten sandwich and puts a hand over her heart. "I promise."

A distant door creaks open. We all leave the table and peer down the hallway in the direction of the ruined computer lab. A hand appears first, holding onto the edge of the door for support. Then a foot appears, and then the head.

Oh, God, *it's Nick*. Not Morrow, but *Nick*, the one who was lying on the floor of the ruined lab just moments ago. He's awake. And this version of him isn't an empty shell. He's not inhabiting the sixty-something body from our shared timeline… looking instead to be thirty-something in this current manifestation… but *it's him*. Before me is the awareness, the spirit, the essence of *my* Nick. His presence draws me like a magnet, wrenching tears from my eyes and pumping adrenaline into my blood.

"*Nicky Nick*." I fly at top speed and throw my arms around him, locking my legs around his. "Oh, God, I've missed you so much." I pepper him with kisses. He returns them, unabashed, even with his daughter duo watching his displays of affection for me. Even if Kendra were awake and watching, he'd not hold back. He pulls me tight against him—utter bliss.

Finally the kissing ends, but I can't leave his arms. No matter what age he manifests, I could stay in his embrace forever, while the multiverse burns around us.

But even the hugging eventually must stop. Releasing him from the grips of my arms and legs, I float before him, my gaze locked with his—while I flounder internally under the weight of my emotion.

How can one man affect me so? I've met many men who've wanted to be with me in one way or another, but I've never wanted to be with any of them the way I do Nick. When I'm not with him, I don't feel whole. There's something about him that goes beyond the physical and fills an inner need for me. I felt it from the sixty-something version of him who came to the department store seeking perfume for his wife. That was a lifetime ago, and yet only yesterday. Or perhaps it was earlier today. Time is irrelevant. Seconds bleed into hours into days into years and centuries, and it doesn't matter how many. Wherever and whenever we both exist, we belong together.

"You saved me, Erica." He brushes a strand of blue hair from my face. "Your love brought me back. I owe you my life."

"How?" I can't formulate a lengthy question. I pull him back into another hug. I can't get enough of his touch, the press of his flesh against mine.

Seems he can't get enough of me either, tightening his hold on me. "Just now. I—that is, Morrow—was in the nexus. You came to him. Do you not remember? You told him to look at you and to say your name. He hesitated, but then he did as you asked. And you didn't fade away. You weren't a ghost. It was you, the real you. The next thing I know, I'm not Morrow anymore, but Nick. *Me.* And all because of you, Erica. Because you love me *that much.* I love you, too. God knows how much I love you."

Deep inside Nick is the same magnetic draw for me that I have for him. He can't deny it and be truthful—and I shouldn't put him in that position, not if I really love him. I keep my voice to a whisper. "I know you're married to Kendra in this timeline and that Susie is your daughter. I don't want to get you in trouble with them. But you and I are soul mates, and we *will* be together— somehow, somewhere, some when. Count on it, mister." I draw away from him and raise my voice. "Sorry to hog you, Nick. I'm just so glad you're alive! Come say hi to everyone."

"Hey, Dad." Mel meets Nick halfway between the computer lab and the dining room. He puts his arms around Nick and holds the hug for a couple minutes. Neither of them say anything until Mel pulls away. "Do you recognize me?"

"Of course, son." Nick's brow furrows. "I don't understand how I can see you and Erica in this timeline. You're ghosts... except... you're not. And you're both wearing cloaks for some reason? Someone explain to me what's happening here...."

Suze jumps up and down at his feet. "Hug me, Daddy."

Nick picks up his little girl to give her a long embrace.

Super Glynda wipes her tears. She's crying as much as I am. Joining Nick and Suze, she throws her arms around them both. After a minute, she laughs and steps back. "I need to be going soon, Dad. Mom's still sleeping and Kylie is still in Khertaan. I'm sleeping in my room, too—you know, my younger self. Slithy is in Khertaan now, but, well... *how* she's there is a long story. Just... don't wake me or Mom. It could be bad for us if you do. We each need to wake on our own terms.

"I can't tell you what needs to be done, Dad. If I tried even making a suggestion, I'd trigger a time-shift to avoid a paradox. I'm glad you're back with us, and I'm thankful to Erica for making it happen. Don't worry. I'll not mention her to Mom." Super Glynda turns to me. "Thank you for bringing my Dad back to life. I hope you find happiness, without taking mine or Mom's."

I give her a weak smile. "Thank you, Super Glynda. Future-future-Susie. Will I ever understand about the frogs?"

She chuckles. "Maybe some day." She turns to Mel. The two of them stare at each other in silence, their lips struggling with words neither of them speaks. They're distant alternates of each other. In their own timelines, each of them is Nick's only child. How must it feel to look into a mirror and see a reflection looking back that doesn't look like you?

Finally, without a word between her and Mel, Super Glynda steps aside to face Gondra. "You know more than you say, Alien, and I understand why. Sometimes you lie, because you can't speak the truth, but the lies you speak lead to the desired outcome as well as the truth could. I can't fault you for that, since I operate the same way sometimes. Take care, Gondra."

The Lizardman flicks his forked tongue. "Good fortune to you, as well, time traveler. But this is not our final goodbye."

"I'll take your word for it." Super Glynda turns to Suze, the youngster still cradled in Nick's arms, and pats the girl on the head. "Bye, bye, little me. Always be brave, and try not to cause our Mommy and Daddy too much grief. Remember, not a word to Mommy about Erica here. The lady in pink will always be our secret. Deal?"

Susie giggles. "Deal, Super Glynda!"

With a salute to Nick, his daughter-from-the-future vanishes, time-jumping to some place and time unknown to those of us she leaves behind.

With Super Glynda gone, all eyes turn expectantly on Nick.

He looks back and forth between us. "What?"

"We've been trying to save you, Dad." Mel rubs his nose. "Gondra here was collecting bits of you from your game characters, and all we had left to do was find Greelia."

"But Erica here found a shortcut." Gondra puts a hand on my shoulder. "I must say, I have greatly underestimated the power of love. But bringing you back to your senses, Nick, is only half the solution to the problem we face. You need to finish what you started and mend the broken timelines."

Mel nods. "Yeah. If you don't do something, Mom will rule everything and force me into a mold I don't fit. I can't be her Princess. I'll die first."

Nick raises his hands as though in surrender. "Let's retire to the living room if we're to discuss the fate of the multiverse. Susie, could you fetch Daddy a bag of chocolates and a soda from the fridge? Are there any sweet buns in the house? I'm feeling the need for an energy boost."

I don't say anything, but if he's looking for an energy boost from sweet buns, I'd be happy to oblige.

CHAPTER FIFTY

Kylie: New Quest

It's been a long day. Not that days really matter, since there aren't any nights in Khertaan. I want to glance just for a moment at the System clock, but I'm afraid to take my eyes off the coin glinting in the darkness.

I'm aching to talk more with Slithy and Rancor about what's happening outside Khertaan, but the surrounding darkness is too oppressive, and the need to stay focused on the coin and to follow it weighs heavier with each passing moment. I'd like to reach out to Charli or Spyder to let them know where we are and ask how things are with them. But… I can't risk the distraction.

The local chat channel is void of even random exchanges. There's not one sound on the special effects channel, and no background music playing. I can't even bring myself to ask Georgie a question, and he doesn't volunteer anything. A sense of isolation nearly overwhelms me, only kept at bay by Slithy's hand gripping mine.

Not even ODYSSEY speaks to me. He can hear my thoughts and knows how I'm feeling, but offers no words of comfort.

We've been traveling through the darkness long enough, if we're traveling in a straight line, we should no longer be within the confines of Minook or the Spire of Desire. Am I flying in a circle? What's the alternative? Could we be traveling in an extra-dimensional space? Could the traveling be only in my mind?

I fly as fast as I can, trying to catch the coin. It speeds up, too, maintaining its distance. I slow, and it slows. So that's the game it's playing. I slow to a stop, and it does likewise.

The glint brightens, shooting blinding rays of light in four directions, like a four-pointed star. Fighting to stay calm, I shield my eyes with my free hand. Eventually my vision adjusts to the brightness.

The coin at the center of the light hovers over Ezmerelda. She levitates three feet above a white marble floor, her legs crossed as though she's sitting on an invisible slab. Using Third Person POV to look around without physically diverting my eyes from her, I see windowless white marble walls curving around us to enclose a circular space. There are no visible doors. The walls rise tall around us, extending into blurry brightness hundreds of feet above.

Slithy still holds onto me, and Rancor still rides her shoulder. All three of us have survived the journey to this place. I squeeze Slithy's hand, and she squeezes back, lending me her serenity. The three of us are about to receive the most important quest in the game, and we all know it.

I switch back to First Person POV and wait for Ezmerelda to speak.

The old woman's limbs are elongated and thin, like she's got no fat or muscle under her grayed skin, only bones. Her feet are bare, her toes elongated and bony, like her fingers. She wears a blue fabric blouse with short sleeves and a blue fabric skirt with a hem reaching just below her knees. A thin brown leather cord hangs around her neck. The cord runs through a hole in the center of an inch-and-a-half-diameter white ball of marble.

Her lips part, revealing that she's not missing a single tooth. Her wise brown eyes see everything, yet are centered on me. She smacks her lips. "The Shadow Gaunt has grown powerful, turning every NPC once living in Minook into Ghouls. He is about to do the same to the latest arrivals to the city. If he brings about the deaths of even a couple high-level PCs—which he is close to doing even as we speak—it will be enough to raise him to level thirty.

"The Shadow Gaunt is the avatar of Seth the Destroyer, of whom you have some knowledge, Frogkin. Once the Shadow Gaunt reaches level thirty, he will be freed from Khertaan to fight by Seth's side. As terrible as the Shadow Gaunt is, he is not the worst of what will be loosed upon the multiverse.

"Once he reaches level thirty, the Shadow Gaunt will be positioned to open a portal to a singular dimensional pocket universe where the Dread Naughts are imprisoned, creatures from the future so devoted to destruction, they seek to destroy the multiverse before they themselves can be created, in an attempt to bring about the Ultimate Paradox. They have already traveled back to our time. All they want now is to be released."

The elderly woman closes her eyes and draws a deep breath. I steel my jaw, wanting to ask questions, but instinctively knowing more information is forthcoming, if I'm patient. Slithy and Rancor also refrain from asking the questions that must be burning inside them.

Ezmerelda exhales and opens her eyes. She points at Slithy. "You are the single best hope to save the multiverse. You must reach level thirty as soon as you can. I will give you a quest. Take with you anyone who will accompany you in fulfilling it. Once the quest is complete, you and all who are with you at the end will receive sufficient XP to reach level thirty. Do not become distracted from your quest, no matter what anyone says."

Slithy bows. "Tell me what I must do."

The old woman reaches up and snatches the coin from where it hangs above her. "Take this." She tosses it at Slithy, but the throw is short.

My Frogkin daughter leaps forward and catches the coin before it hits the floor.

"Bring it to me in Caravel and place it in my hand. Then the quest will be complete." Ezmerelda waves us away. "Now go."

"Thank you, Ezmerelda." Slithy inspects the coin. It still shimmers, but doesn't appear to be the source of the light in the room now.

I don't ask how we're supposed to get out of this place with no doors. I think I know the answer, and even if I'm wrong, I suspect Ezmerelda would lose respect for us if we asked.

Darkness falls upon us, hiding everything except a dim glimmer from the coin in Slithy's hand.

My daughter is the Chosen One. I can't help but feel simultaneously proud and terrified. "Take my hand, Slithy. Rancor, keep your perch on her shoulder. We're getting out of here."

With my daughter's hand in mine, I fly straight up. The light of the coin grows stronger the higher we go, until it illuminates the walls. Up and up we continue until a ceiling looms overhead. Set into one wall, without a landing or any stairs leading to it, is a closed gray metal door. I fly over, and it slides open at our approach. A balcony awaits us just outside.

Beyond the balcony, the sky is dark as night. How is this possible? Khertaan is the land of Eternal Daylight. I fly to the balcony and set down with my daughter.

"What the hell?" Slithy closes her fist on the coin, blocking its light. Utter darkness swallows us.

"Give me a moment. Don't go anywhere." I release my daughter's hand.

"Not likely."

"I'll just be a moment." I switch to Spirit Form.

The world turns to shades of gray around me. We're at the top of one of the marble towers, with other towers all around us, reaching our height. Smaller buildings stand far below. If it weren't for the ubiquitous darkness, I'd have no reason to doubt we're still in Minook. I fly up a little further, so I'm higher than the towers.

To the west stands a single structure, looking to be another tower, not located on the Spire of Desire, but somewhere miles away.

I fly down, switch back to physical form, and take Slithy's hand. "I know the way to Caravel. There's a tower to the west of the spire. That's go to be it."

She still has the coin's light covered in her hands, or perhaps she has stashed the coin in inventory. In any case, we have no light.

She squeezes my hand. "I trust you, Mom. That's where we need to go."

I don't launch to the air yet. "This is your quest. Do you want to recruit anyone else?"

Predatory screeches echo across the dark city, coming from the direction where we left Charli and the others. My skin tingles.

Slithy tightens her grip on my hand. "I have a really bad feeling about this. We need to go while we still can. Who can fly faster, you or the Ghoul Dragon?"

"The Dragon is faster than I am, especially if I can't see where I'm going. If I'm in Spirit Form, I can see, but then I can't take you along." I focus to sense the location of my Spirit Noose and whether it's still holding the undead beast. "The Dragon is waiting for us at the bottom of this tower. It won't take but a minute to go down and fetch it."

"Let's do it."

"Did you stash the coin?"

"I felt it safer to, yes. Do you need its light?"

"Not at the moment. Hold on."

Using the Spirit Noose's location as a guide to where I need to go, I descend, taking Slithy and Rancor with me. When the blue glow of the Spirit Noose comes into sight, the going becomes easier. We set down on the back of the Black Ghoul Dragon. The Spirit Noose sheds enough light for us to position ourselves on the Dragon as we had before. "All right, everyone hold on." Leaving the Noose lying on the Dragon's back, I mentally command the undead creature to rise.

It obeys. I don't need to hold onto the Noose to direct it. Good. Our little band might make it to our destination after all.

Once the Dragon is in the air and circling the tower, I squeeze my daughter's hand. "Slithy, I need to switch to Spirit Form again if I'm to see our destination. Hold onto the Dragon. Please don't fall."

"I promise I won't. Just get us to Caravel as fast as you can."

We head out. I've no idea how long it will take us to reach the distant city. Slithy squats on the Dragon's back, holding its bony spine with webbed fingers.

The clown Georgie, my personal support AI, honks his nose. "*Congratulations*, pumpkin. You've entered a new territory, the desert called the Sands of Time."

Hmm. I suppose that means we'll need to fight another Boss before we can leave the Sands of Time and enter the city of Caravel. Something to look forward to.

We travel in silence until Georgie honks his nose again. "Joy, joy, pumpkin, *congratulations* are again in order. You've just received over a billion XP. You've gone from level twenty-eight to level thirty."

What the hell?

CHAPTER FIFTY-ONE

Fauna: Equipped

I back out of Hera Ford's room, closing the door on the room housing two sleeping bodies. "Kevin, are you still there?"

His telepathic response is immediate. "Hey, Fauna. Can't talk long. Emma and Spooky are here. They're fine, but, listen.... Megan Wright has found Seth's avatar in Khertaan. I need to go help her. Come back to the van. Dr. Splat will fill you in."

"All right, I'm coming."

Back in one of the elevators, I stare at the panel of buttons. Kevin had said ten floors held contestant rooms. They started on floor nine, so that means floor nineteen doesn't have contestant rooms. What's on that floor and the ones above it? I have access to them, and though I've no more need to look for Spooky, I'm way too curious. It's the adventurer in me. I want to go to Khertaan, but how long can it take to peek at another few floors?

I punch the button for floor nineteen. The elevator closet rises past floors seventeen and eighteen, stopping on floor nineteen. The door opens to a dark hallway, and I exit. Motion sensors turn on the hallway lights.

The first door I come to has a retina scanner, and the door opens for me. The room beyond isn't lit overhead, but banks of small lights blink on and off at random intervals, accompanied by a constant soft humming. I'm reminded of the devices decorating the heads of the bunk beds in Dr. Splat and Kevin's van.

As I enter the room, overhead lights activate. The air chills my skin. The blinking and humming continue, oblivious to my presence. There's no one here, and I wouldn't dare touch anything. I leave the room and check another, finding it to also house banks of blinking lights and a constant soft humming.

I skip floors twenty through twenty-four. I do want to get back to the van soon. I'll check floors twenty-five and thirty. I can't leave without checking floor thirty. My curious nature won't let me go back down the elevator without going all the way to the top first.

Floor twenty-five is constructed much like the first floor, with desks and computers. People rush about the place, but they aren't actual people—they're ghosts. I don't bother to exit the elevator, but punch the button for floor thirty.

The elevator closet rises, the numbers steadily increasing until they reach thirty. Then it strikes me… in one way of looking at things, I've reached level thirty. Ha.

The elevator door slides open to darkness. I step out of the elevator, and the lights come on. I'm at one end of a hallway with swirled-white-and-red marble walls and floor, leading straight ahead from the elevator and ending at a polished wooden door with no door handle.

As the elevator closes behind me, I stride forward, my hooves softly scraping the marble floor. At the end of the hall, I gaze into a retina scanner, and the door slides open.

The large room beyond is well lit by overhead illumination. Shadows flit across my vision outside a large plate glass window through which the scrambling, stabbing legs of Arachnid Behemoths loom large, only ten yards away, relentlessly attacking the protective dome separating them from the tower. A fire burns hot inside me at seeing the giant metal spiders so close—and so many of them. I want them all dead—and to be instrumental in their deaths.

A stretch of red carpet leads to a desk of polished wood. Behind the desk, in a matching high-back chair, sits a man attired in smooth, black fabric. He sits straight and tall, his hands clasped on the desk in front of him. A name plate centered before him on the desk reads, *Franklin Freeman*.

He motions to a chair before his desk. "Please, have a seat, Fauna.75."

I don't enter the room. "How do you know my name?"

"You're in the System now. If the System knows you, I know you. So, please, come have a seat and let's talk."

I still don't enter. I don't trust this guy—at all.

"Please, Fauna.75. May I call you Fauna?"

"Yes."

"Come. Sit. I insist."

I wanted adventure. This is it. The thick red carpet silences the clop of my hooves. The offered chair is plush leather. I stand behind it, my hands resting on the back. "What do you want to talk about, Mr. Freeman?"

"I can see you're a cautious sort, but courageous, as well. I wouldn't trust me, either." He winks at me. "I understand you're from a table-top role-playing game world. I find that most interesting. My career has been dedicated to finding a way for game world characters to interact with the worlds I inhabit, and here you are, more than proving the concept. Tell me… who created you?"

"Tell me who created you first."

He smiles. "Fair enough. My parents are Chester and Brenda Freeman. My father was a casualty of war while I was but a boy. My mother is still alive at the age of seventy-eight. She lives in Brighton." He points his thumb at the plate glass window behind him. "You could see the city from here if not for the Arachnid

Behemoths swarming over my force field. Do you know why those Behemoths are here?"

I nod. "To kill the contestants."

He returns the nod. "Exactly. Do you know why they wish to kill the contestants?"

I shake my head.

He grimaces and shakes his head, too. "They want me to fail, Fauna. They want to bring an end to my life's ambition. And they might succeed. My force field generator could fail. No technology is perfect. My developers are becoming ghosts. My androids can't do anything but perform the duties they are programmed to do. I don't dare wake any of the contestants prematurely, and I'm not sure any of them would demonstrate the courage you have. Dr. Splat and Kevin aren't ghosts or androids, but they have their priorities. I need someone to take the fight to the Behemoths, and you're just the woman to do it. What do you say? If I give you the necessary and sufficient equipment, will you kill those damned things out there?"

Laughter rolls from my lungs. "I was born for adventure, Mr. Freeman, and hate those Behemoths as much as you, if not more. I'm in. Where's this equipment you speak of?" Never having possessed weapons or armor, I'm itching all over for some.

He stands. "Right this way." He places his hand under the edge of the desk. A door opens in the wall to my left, and he leads the way into a room stocked with suits of light-colored armor hanging on wall hooks. Taking down a pure white suit, he hands it to me. "This color suits you. The armor is designed to stop bullets and turn blades. It will stop those Behemoth legs from piercing or crushing you, though it won't stop them from knocking you back or pinning you down. You'll need to stay nimble. Go ahead and put it on."

The suit opens both at the waist and over the torso. I slip my hooves into the lower half of the suit. They poke out at the bottom. I slide my arms into the sleeves of the upper half, my hands protruding from the ends. With my limbs in place, the suit closes up of its own accord, sealing at my waist and over my chest. Only my hooves, hands, head, and hair remain exposed.

The suit is comfortable… not hot or bulky. A panel of buttons is embedded in the sleeve on my right forearm. The panel includes a retina scanner.

Mr. Freeman punches some of the buttons on my arm panel, and small lights blink on. "Look into the retina scanner, Fauna." When I do, he punches another few buttons. "This armor is now locked to you and will respond to your eyes—that is, instead of pressing the buttons, you can look at them for the length of time you'd need to press them. It takes months to fully train someone to use this kind of armor most efficiently, but we don't have time for that. You shouldn't need any of its advanced features in fighting the Behemoths. Once they're gone, we can get you some training if you like. For now, try looking at the blue button here." He points.

I focus on the indicated button. It lights up, and my vision blurs briefly. A shiny coating spreads from the control panel across the surface of my armor, until it's all a highly-saturated, stark blue.

"Fantastic." Mr. Freeman gives me thumbs up and ushers me out of the room, talking as we walk. "The key thing to remember… when your armor is in its default state—white, in your case—it provides basic armor protection, and only to the areas of the body it covers. When it's blue like this or some other standout color, it generates an invisible force field that extends additional protection to *all* parts of your body—head, hair, hands, and hooves included."

Pausing at his desk to close one door and open another in the opposite wall, he leads me into a second room, this one stocked with light-colored gunnes of various shapes and sizes. "All the armor and weapons I have stocked on this floor are from video game worlds." He lifts one of the gunnes and weighs it in his hands. "Pulling the trigger and immediately letting go will fire one round. Keeping the trigger depressed will fire continuous rounds until the selected ammo type is exhausted—at which time this ammo indicator light will turn red. It will be green or orange otherwise, with orange indicating the ammo is nearly depleted.

"You can replenish ammo any time after the orange light comes on—just tilt the barrel toward your feet and wait for the ammo indicator light to turn green. Then you can start firing again.

"You can switch ammo types any time the trigger isn't depressed. The buttons on the side panel select the ammo type. When you switch the ammo type, you'll need to load ammo of the new type before you can start firing—a red indicator light will remind you." He puts back the gunne he'd first selected and assesses me before strolling over to a gunne that's half again as long as I am tall. "This one should do you nicely." He hands it to me, hope alight in his eyes.

The barrel is wide enough for me to stick my hand in. I don't do that, of course. "Are Kevin and Dr. Splat equipped with this kind of weaponry?"

"Not currently. I may need to remedy that. I've kept all this equipment secret except from an elite few who've trained with it. Unfortunately, those few aren't responding to my summons. You're the first person to arrive since I put out the call."

I might know what happened to his trainees. "What floor were your trainees on?"

"The one just below me. Twenty-nine. Why do you ask?"

"I didn't stop at floor twenty-nine, but on twenty-five, all the people are ghosts. I didn't get off the elevator there—was afraid whatever affected them might affect me, too. But maybe what happened on twenty-five also happened on twenty-nine. We're lucky it hasn't spread up here. How much training did your elite force already have?"

He grimaces. "Forty hours. But none of them ever had the opportunity to use this equipment against real enemies. You'll be the first to put it to test on the battlefield."

"Lovely." My Strength is 17, which is great for a beginning T&T character, but not enough that I wouldn't tire out real quick from using this weapon. "You have anything lighter?"

He studies other weapons, takes one off its shelf, and hands it to me. "See how this feels."

I raise the weapon to look down the barrel at the sight, and put my finger on the trigger. It feels almost natural. "I like it."

A panel of buttons sits on the right side of the gunne, a retina scanner situated on the edge of the panel nearest my face. "Tell me about the ammo types and which buttons select them." I hold the gunne out before me, the panel facing up.

Mr. Freeman points at one of the buttons. "Okay, so… this red one selects the flame thrower."

I thrust the gunne at him. "I don't want it. Nothing with fire."

He raises an eyebrow. "Okay…." After another minute spent assessing his stock, he brings me a third weapon.

It has a red button on its ammo type selection panel, which gives me pause. But the weapon is light enough. The barrel is still big enough for me to stuff my hand into, but the gunne is only about as long as I am tall.

Mr. Freeman nods his approval. "No flamethrower on this one. It's swapped out for a grenade launcher. The brown button is for copper bullets, which reload the fastest of all your ammo types. Everything else takes at least twice as long. The grenade launcher needs to reload after every grenade it throws, so the indicator light will go straight from green to red. The silver button is to select silver bullets, intended for werewolves and the like. The blue button is for metal blades—swords without hilts. Yellow delivers lightning bolts. Aqua blasts water. Black sprays acid. Green blows poison gas.

"This switch is a three-way to set the ammo power level. The low setting doesn't have as much punch as the other two, but the ammo lasts longer, so if it suffices, leave it there. The high setting has the most punch, but doesn't last as long. Use it only if the low or middle setting isn't having an effect on your target. The middle setting gives you a compromise between the low and high settings when the low setting isn't sufficient and the high setting is overkill."

I point to a switch he hasn't mentioned. "What's this for?"

"That's only useful when you have the metal blades ammo selected. Push it to the right to convert the weapon to a slashing melee weapon, with no reload time required. It's not as easy to handle as a regular sword would be, but if the enemy is five feet away and charging at you, having a melee weapon quickly in hand might save your life. Push the switch back to the left to return to firing metal blade missiles.

"So, what do you think? is this weapon agreeable? If so, we can lock it to you."

"This one is good, yes." I look into the retinal scanner.

Mr. Freeman punches a sequence of buttons, and a red beam of light strikes my eye. "Okay. You're locked in, and you can look at the buttons or switches now instead of pressing them, just like you can do with the armor. With both the armor and the gunne, if the retinal scanner emits a red beam at any time, you'll need to point the beam at your eye to start or continue using the item. It won't work for anyone other than you without the correct button sequence being entered first, and only I know the correct sequence for that."

I nod, and then sigh. "Um... do I need to know anything more about the buttons on the armor?"

He grimaces. "Like I said before, the key thing to remember is that your head, hair, hands, and hooves aren't protected if the armor is white. Otherwise, they are, even though they won't appear to be. So, if your armor is white at any given moment, focus on one of the buttons to turn on additional protection.

"Whatever color of button you press, that's the color the armor will become. Depending on the color you choose, your extended protection will be only against certain types of attacks. Red protects against fire and heat. Brown boosts your protection against blunt force weapons, like explosions, bullets, and clubs.

Silver grants you resistance to magic. Blue helps against sharp and pointed weapons. That's the setting it's on now, to provide the best defense against piercing giant metal spider legs. Yellow protects against electricity. Aqua repels water. Black repels acid. Green repels gases. All fields allow oxygen to filter through to you and retains what oxygen you already have, but if you're surrounded by water or poison gas or the like, you will eventually run out of breathable air...."

"Oh, I don't need to breathe, so no problem." I shrug and smile.

"Oh... okay. Great. Fantastic, really. Well, then.... Aside from the individual settings, you can select button combinations for special effects. It's too much to teach you in ten minutes. I'd like you to get out there asap and start dealing with these monsters."

"Fine." I select copper bullets as my ammo for the gunne and set the ammo power switch to maximum. A sheen washes over the gunne, and it's no longer white, but polished brown. "How do I get outside the dome?"

His gaze narrows. "How did you get inside?"

"I was teleported in."

"Can you teleport out?"

I shake my head. "Someone else did it for me. She's at the van with Dr. Splat and Kevin, but she can't teleport me again until she recharges her Auni, which will be nearly six hours from now."

"This presents a problem." He scratches the top of his head. "I can't get you outside the dome without disrupting the force field, and even a localized weakening of it is risky." He pauses, considering alternatives, and then shakes his head. "We must take the risk."

He points at the control panel for my armor. "When you're at the dome and ready to pass through, enter the sequence *blue, yellow, silver*. A dome of energy will take shape over you. It's not a force field, but quite the opposite—a local force field destabilizer. It will open a hole in the dome that you can pass through. The destabilizer effect doesn't last long—only about three seconds—

and once it's done, you'll need to reselect whatever armor boost you want—blue is my recommendation against the Behemoths, though brown would help more if one smacks you rather than stabs you. And I can't emphasize it enough—if you don't select an armor boost, the suit will still offer you some basic protection, but not for your extremities. Think you can remember all that?"

"Khenn Arrth? May I have a Saving Roll on Intelligence?"

Thunder rumbles in the distance, the sound of rolling dice. I can't see or know the result, but I don't need to. If I got a good roll, then I'll have an easy time remembering what I just learned. Otherwise, if I don't get through the dome, I'll come back here for a follow-up lesson.

Blue, yellow, silver. I got it. "All right, I'm off."

"Who is Khenn Arrth? Is he the one who created you?"

"In a manner of speaking, yes. He's the creator of T&T... sort of."

"I see. Well, off with you. Good luck, Fauna."

"Thanks, Mr. Freeman." I'll take any luck he offers, because as the saying goes on my home world, it's better to be lucky than good. I board the elevator and punch the button for the first floor, my gunne pointed at the ceiling and resting against my armored shoulder.

I am Fauna.75, three-quarter human, one-quarter goat, all Rogue and all woman, standing five-feet-one-inch tall on bare hooves, covered ankles to neck in bright blue armor fit for a knight, carrying a five-foot-long shiny brown gunne loaded for Behemoth. It's time to kick some giant metal spider butt.

CHAPTER FIFTY-TWO

Charli: Shadow Magic

As an NPC, I have some autonomy, but not full free will. The System can compel me to take certain actions, as it compelled me to take the Shadow Marble from Yuni. It's cold stone, polished smooth, and perfectly spherical.

Also as an NPC, I don't have a support AI of which to ask questions or clarification. The System doesn't inform me what I'm to do with this Shadow Marble. That both it and I are associated with shadows can't be coincidence. I also have a cursed Shadow Stone, removed from the ashes of a rare Scarecrow mook killed by party MAD on the first day of the game. I went back later and collected the ashes.

Commotion in the distance vies for my attention, but the System has other ideas for me than to allow me to check on my friends. I sit cross-legged on pavement and set down the Shadow Marble before me. Drawing my Shadow Stone from inventory, I place it next to the Shadow Marble. Then I proceed to sprinkle Scarecrow ashes over both of them.

Is this the process for creating a new spell? I'm a Shadow Wizard and supposedly can create new spells, given the proper components. That's why I'd made a special trip to go back to the scene of the Scarecrow's death and collect those ashes, thinking they might serve as spell components eventually. Now seems to be the time for it, though the process is being forced upon me by the System, rather than it being undertaken of my own free will. Why is the System doing this to me?

Arcane words issue from my mouth, not issued over any normal chat channel, but spoken on a special Shadow channel which until now I'd not known existed. The Shadows reveal their secrets to me, embedding knowledge into my brain, knowledge which moments ago I did not have and might never fully comprehend.

The Shadow Marble and Shadow Stone melt beneath the Scarecrow ashes, their solid substances turning to liquid and running together. I touch the pool of black liquid, and it glides onto my hand, coating my fingers, my palm… my entire right hand up to the wrist. I bring my hands together as though in prayer, and half the liquid flows from my right hand onto my left, until both hands are covered with a thin coating of magical Shadow.

The System reveals to me the identity of what I wear… Shadow Gauntlets. Like the Shadow Stone used to create them, they are cursed—I can never take them off or replace them with another item. The Shadow Stone, Shadow Marble, and the vial of Scarecrow ashes are no more.

Power surges through my hands, not only the ability to inflict physical harm with a strike, but the ability to summon Shadow creatures more powerful than even a level four Summoning spell could have called. In this moment, I have a singular ability greater than that of anyone else in Khertaan, whether PC, NPC, mook, Boss, or deity.

Does that make me the Goddess of Shadows?

Something greater than me but inside me reaches towards the sky with both hands and calls upon a dark, ancient power.

Screeches echo across the city in answer to my call. The summoned dark ones descend upon us, their numbers blocking the sun, bringing Night upon the land of Eternal Daylight.

What have I unleashed? I do not know, for it was not by my will it was done, even though it was wrought by my hands and words. The System wanted this and used me and Yuni to make it happen.

CHAPTER FIFTY-THREE

Yuni: Emergency Update

The screeching of thousands of assailants descending from the sky chill my blood, but they can't deter me. I can't let Dylan become a Ghoul. I have to kill her before she loses her last remaining 3% EP. I hope to save Mithabel from a dreadful fate, too, but Dylan comes first for me, even if she's not a Priestess to my Goddess.

I don't know how much Auni to pour into my Enervation spell. What details I have about it are in terms of points of damage, not percentages of damage, and I don't have the luxury of time to experiment on Dylan to determine how many hit points she has in total. "Inuki, based on all the data you have available, give me your best estimate on the number of Auni I need to put into my Enervation spell to guarantee Dylan dies."

My fat cat support AI meows. "Taking into consideration all applicable bonuses and the rate at which we have seen HP percentages for PCs fall—"

"*Now*, Inuki."

"One hundred should do it."

"Athlea, hear me, and take the life of the one before me." My fingers slide along the brown cheeks of the Priestess of Light. "I'm sorry, Dylan." Of the 166 Auni points I have available, I put 120 into the spell. I trust Inuki. I'm just adding a buffer.

Dylan turns to ashes in my grasp, swept away on the breeze. I killed her. I blink back the tears.

"Give me that, Tank," says Ger-Alt, the female Goblin leader of party Quantized.

"Step away, lady," says my brother.

I turn to see what's happening.

A spark of red light banishes the shadows around me. A flaming missile streaks from my brother's hands, searing me as it passes, but unable to deal damage to a fellow member of XStorm. The face of Ger-Alt lights up as she jumps out of the missile's way. The projectile strikes Mithabel and bursts into flames, covering her body. They dissipate in an instant, and nothing of the Daughter of Orange Metal remains. The Elf Tank is dead.

I bow. "Thank you, brother."

Bradford bows in return. "Anything for you, sister."

"Musume, musume, musume." Inuki is more excited than I've ever seen him. "You've done it. *You stopped the Shadow Gaunt.* It can't turn Dylan and Mithabel into Ghouls. But more than that, you and Bradford gained everyone XP from killing Mithabel and Dylan. Seems there were others killed, too, and you've earned XP for all of them. Three Obsidian Guards and two other PCs, Megan Wright and Debra Jones. So… guess what? You're *level thirty*. Hee hee. So is everyone in XStorm and everyone in MAD… except Mithabel and Dylan. They'll have to respawn first."

All those around me gasp as they receive news of the huge XP gain. From what I hear over local chat, everyone in Minook, whether PC or NPC, has reached at least level 29. Through Charli, everyone has benefited from what Bradford and I did.

But Charli isn't saying anything and hasn't made an appearance since I delivered the Shadow Marble to her. "Brother, can you give me some light?"

"Will this do?" Small flames cover Bradford's body, shedding light in a five-foot radius sphere.

"It will have to. Come with me."

Shrill cries of despair sound from above. Wings rustle in the darkness overhead.

As we hustle towards the corner where I left the Cowgirl, the Cave Goblin woman introduced as Charli's daughter flies up beside us. "Where Mommy?"

"Oh, Britta, we're going to see about her now. You should wait here."

"Pbbt." She stays abreast of us.

I can't make her stay behind, and I can't let her stop me from checking on her mother.

We round the corner. Charli kneels on the pavement, her head raised to the sky, her hands together before her as though she's in prayer. We draw closer, and the light of Bradford's flaming skin reveals black gloves on both of Charli's hands.

She lowers them and looks at me with dead eyes. "I can't control them."

My heart rises in my throat. "Can't control what, Charli?"

"The System forced me to release them. I didn't know what I was doing, and I couldn't stop it."

I kneel beside her. "What did you release, Charli?"

She drops her chin and stares at her gloved hands.

The Mouse Guide, Niav, squeaks over local chat. "Heads up, everyone. Those things flying overhead are Dread Naughts. There are possibly thousands of them up there, and according to my Monster Lore, they're all level thirty. The Shadow Gaunt must have released them."

Charli draws a deep breath and stands. "The Shadow Gaunt didn't do it." She clenches her black-gloved fists. "*And I didn't do it on purpose.* Let's send them all back to the hell they came from."

The System clock flashes in the upper right corner of my view. *12:00 AM, Day 4.*

393

"Emergency System update occurring immediately," Inuki tells me. "The game will resume once the updates are complete."

A ball of white light envelopes me, imploding to nothing. Darkness consumes all.

End Transcription Four

www.ingramcontent.com/pod-product-compliance
Lightning Source LLC
Chambersburg PA
CBHW030914050726
47498CB00003BA/743